ALWAYS E

ALISON ROBERTS

MIDWIFE'S BABY BUMP

BY
SUSANNE HAMPTON

12/5/15

MILLS &
BOON

MIDWIVES ON-CALL

Welcome to Melbourne Victoria Hospital—
and to the exceptional midwives who make up
the Melbourne Maternity Unit!

These midwives in a million work miracles
on a daily basis, delivering tiny bundles of joy
into the arms of their brand-new mums!

Amidst the drama and emotion of babies arriving at
all hours of the day and night, when the shifts are over,
somehow there's still time for some sizzling
out-of-hours romance…

Whilst these caring professionals
might come face-to-face with a whole lot of love
in their line of work, now it's their turn to find
a happy-ever-after of their own!

Midwives On-Call

Midwives, mothers and babies—
lives changing for ever…!

Eight special stories to collect and treasure:

Just One Night? by Carol Marinelli
Meant-To-Be Family by Marion Lennox
Always the Midwife by Alison Roberts
Midwife's Baby Bump by Susanne Hampton
Midwife…to Mum! by Sue MacKay
His Best Friend's Baby by Susan Carlisle
Unlocking Her Surgeon's Heart by Fiona Lowe
Her Playboy's Secret by Tina Beckett

**These titles are also available in eBook format
from www.millsandboon.co.uk**

ALWAYS THE MIDWIFE

BY
ALISON ROBERTS

Published in Great Britain 2015
by Mills & Boon, an imprint of Harlequin (UK) Limited,
Eton House, 18-24 Paradise Road, Richmond, Surrey, TW9 1SR

© 2015 Harlequin Books S.A.

Special thanks and acknowledgement are given to Alison Roberts
for her contribution to the *Midwives On-Call* series

ISBN: 978-0-263-24705-3

Dear Reader,

One of the perks of being a writer is the joy of including things that are special to me in my stories. Or exploring things that have always intrigued or inspired me.

I got to do this a lot in Aiden and Sophia's story for the *Midwives On-Call* continuity, and that made it a real joy to write.

I adore Melbourne. I've spent a lot of time there in the last decade or so, because it's home to some of my very best friends and my daughter has been living there for the last three years. So I got to include places like the Southbank, in the central city, and Queenscliff—which isn't part of the city but is gorgeous, and *so* worth a day trip if you're ever lucky enough to be spending time in Melbourne. I even gave one of my friends (and her dog) a cameo appearance in the Queenscliff chapter! :)

I also got to learn a lot more about Murderball, or wheelchair rugby, and I find that totally inspiring. Throw in some babies, a gorgeous motorbike paramedic for a hero and a 'three dates' rule that's begging to be broken and it's no wonder I had so much fun writing this book.

I hope you have just as much fun reading it.

With love

Alison xxx

Alison Roberts lives in Christchurch, New Zealand, and has written over sixty Mills & Boon® Medical Romances™. As a qualified paramedic she has personal experience of the drama and emotion to be found in the world of medical professionals, and loves to weave stories with this rich background—especially when they can have a happy ending.

When Alison is not writing you'll find her indulging her passion for dancing or spending time with her friends (including Molly the dog) and her daughter Becky, who has grown up to become a brilliant artist. She also loves to travel, hates housework and considers it a triumph when the flowers outnumber the weeds in her garden.

Books by Alison Roberts

A Little Christmas Magic
200 Harley Street: The Proud Italian
From Venice with Love
Always the Hero
NYC Angels: An Explosive Reunion
St Piran's: The Wedding
Maybe This Christmas...?
The Legendary Playboy Surgeon
Falling for Her Impossible Boss
Sydney Harbour Hospital: Zoe's Baby
The Honourable Maverick

Visit the author profile page
at millsandboon.co.uk for more titles

For Annie, Carol and Linda—who will always make Melbourne a very special place to visit for me.

Love you all xxx

CHAPTER ONE

THE BLIP OF the foetal heart monitor had definitely slowed down. Her decision might be a no-brainer but Sophia knew it wasn't going to be popular.

'I'm sorry,' she told her patient, 'but I'm not happy with the way things are going. We need to get you to hospital.'

'No-o-o...' First-time mother Claire Robinson had her heart set on a home birth. 'You said I'm almost fully dilated. It can't be much longer.'

'You're exhausted, sweetheart. Every contraction is harder for you and things are slowing down.' She still had the hand-held Doppler against the distended abdomen of the pregnant woman. 'Can you hear that the baby's heartbeat has slowed down, too? It's a sign that baby is getting distressed.'

'What does that mean?' Claire's husband, Greg, was looking pale and anxious. 'Is the baby in danger? Is *Claire* in danger?'

'No.' Sophia hastened to reassure them both. 'But that's what I want to make sure isn't going to happen. The labour hasn't progressed quite the way we wanted.

and…' How could she tell these parents-to-be, without scaring them, that it was her instinct that something wasn't right that was making the transfer seem urgent? 'Let me make a call and see how far away an ambulance might be.'

The call was answered instantly.

'My name is Sophia Toulson,' Sophia said. 'I'm a midwife with the Melbourne Maternity Unit at the Victoria. I'm at a planned home birth…' She moved away from the young couple, lowering her voice as she gave the address details and then voiced her concerns.

'An ambulance is probably fifteen minutes away,' the dispatcher told her. 'But we do have a SPRINT guy in your locality.'

'SPRINT?'

'Single Paramedic Response and Intervention. An intensive care paramedic on a motorbike.'

'I think we just need the transport,' Sophia said. 'It's not an emergency…' But she could hear the note of doubt in her own voice. An exhausted first-time mother and a stalled labour. The potential for an emergency was there. Was that why alarm bells had started ringing?

'I'll change the plan,' Claire offered desperately, as Sophia ended the call. 'I'll have more pain relief than the gas. You can rupture the membranes. Whatever it takes…' She was sobbing now. 'We don't want to have our baby in a hospital…'

'I know.' Sophia smoothed damp strands of hair back from Claire's face. 'But you know what the really important thing here is?'

She didn't wait for a response. Greg was perched on

the end of the bed, holding Claire in his arms as she lay back against him. She caught his gaze and then Claire's.

'My job is to keep both you and baby safe. At the end of the day, the only thing that matters is that you get to hold your healthy baby in your arms. I promise that where the delivery happens is not going to take away even the tiniest bit of joy that moment's going to give you.'

A joy that Sophia might never be able to experience herself but that didn't mean she couldn't share it happening for others. It was precisely why she'd chosen this profession. Why she loved it so much. And why she was so passionate about doing whatever it took to ensure a happy outcome.

'That's all I want,' Greg said, his voice cracking. 'For you both to be okay. We always said that we'd go to the hospital the minute we were worried about anything.'

'But I'm not worried. I'm just so tired... Oohhh...' Claire's face scrunched into lines of pain.

'Another contraction?' Sophia reached for the Entonox mouthpiece. 'Here you go. Deep breaths...'

The loud rap on the door made her jump. Surely the ambulance hadn't arrived this quickly?

'Shall I go?' Greg asked.

Claire spat out the mouthpiece. '*No*—don't leave me... It's.... *Ahhh*...'

Sophia wasn't going anywhere either. The contraction had produced a rush of fluid. Claire's membranes had finally broken. It was a sign that her labour was progressing again but Sophia wasn't feeling relieved. Quite the opposite.

The fluid soaking into the pad beneath Claire's hips had the stain of meconium that meant the baby could be in trouble. And…

Oh, dear Lord…yes…that was a loop of umbilical cord showing.

'G'day…' The rich, deep voice came from behind her. 'I let myself in. Hope that's okay.'

Sophia looked up. The man was wearing a high-vis heavy-duty jacket. He had a motorbike helmet on his head with the red, white and blue colours of Melbourne's ambulance service and the title 'Paramedic' emblazoned across the front. The chin-guard and visor were flipped up so that she could see his face but she barely registered what he looked like. There was relief to be felt now— that she had professional help in what had just become an obstetric emergency.

'Claire's waters just broke,' she said quietly. 'We've got a cord prolapse.'

'What's that?' Greg was leaning in, trying to see what was happening. 'What's going on? And who are you?'

The paramedic's helmet was off by the time he'd taken two steps closer. 'I'm Aiden Harrison,' he told Greg. 'Here to help.' He was right beside Sophia now. 'Modified Sims position?'

'Knees to chest, I think. Claire? We're going to get you to turn over, I want you on your knees with your bottom up in the air. Greg, can you help?'

'What? *Why?*' Claire was panting, recovering from the contraction. 'I don't want to move.'

'We've got a small problem, guys.' The paramedic had dropped his helmet and leather gloves, along with a rolled-up kit he'd been carrying. He didn't sound stressed. Rather, he made it sound as if whatever the problem was, it was going to be easily remedied. 'Your baby didn't read the rule book and part of the umbilical cord has come out first. We need to take any pressure off it, which is why we're going to let gravity give us a hand. Here…let me help.'

Somehow he managed to make it seem like nothing out of the ordinary to be getting a woman in labour to get into what seemed a very unnatural position, on her knees with her head lowered. Sophia was ready with the Doppler to check the baby's heart rate again.

Aiden listened, his gaze on his watch. 'Ninety-eight,' he said. 'What was the last recorded rate?'

'One-forty.' Sophia ripped open a packet of sterile gloves. In a blink of time, this had become a potential disaster. The baby's oxygen supply was being cut off. 'I'm going to try and ease the pressure.'

'Oh, my God…' Claire wailed. 'What's happening?'

'You're going to feel me inside,' Sophia warned her. 'I'm going to be pushing on baby's head to take the pressure off the cord.'

Greg's face was as white as a sheet. 'How are you going to take her to hospital if she has to stay in that position?' He glanced sideways to where the paramedic had discarded his bike helmet. 'You're not even driving an ambulance, are you?'

'No, mate. I ride a bike. Gets me where I'm needed faster.' Aiden reached for the radio clipped to his shoulder. 'SPRINT One to Base. How far away is our back-up?'

They could all hear the woman's voice on the other end. 'Should be with you in less than ten minutes.'

'Copy that. Make it a code one.' He nodded at Greg. 'Hang in there, mate. We're under control.'

'I'm getting another contraction,' Claire groaned. 'Ohhh… I want to *push*…'

'Don't push,' Sophia warned. 'Not yet.'

She looked up to find Aiden's gaze on her face. A steady gaze but she could see he knew exactly what she was trying to decide and the almost crushing responsibility for making the right choice here.

'The cord's pulsatile,' she told him. 'And Claire's fully dilated.'

Aiden nodded. If they were in hospital right now, an assisted delivery with forceps would be the fastest and safest way to get this baby out. With Sophia using two fingers to push on the baby's head, the cord was being protected and the blood and oxygen supply was still adequate. She knew what she was doing, this midwife. Intelligent-looking woman, in fact, which probably explained the anxiety he could see in her eyes. She had to know exactly how dangerous this situation was for the baby.

Her hand was probably already aching, although Aiden couldn't detect any signs of discomfort. Could she keep this up until they arrived at the hospital? The other option was not to slow down a natural delivery but to try and speed it up. To get the baby out fast enough to avoid potentially devastating complications from lack of oxygen. She was still looking at him and he got the feeling she was following his train of thought.

'She's also exhausted,' she added. 'Labour's been a bit protracted. That was why I called for an ambulance in the first place. I'm not sure...' Sophia bit her lip as her words trailed to an inaudible whisper. She hated feeling indecisive and it rarely happened, but a baby's life was at stake here and there was another option. But if they encouraged Claire to push and she was too tired to be effective, they would have to wait for another contraction and they could end up in a much worse position, with the baby's head cutting off any oxygen supply. The baby could end up with severe brain damage. Or it could die.

The weighing-up process was lightning fast but agonising. Sophia found she was holding the gaze of the paramedic. Light brown eyes, a part of her brain noted. Unusual. It was a calm gaze but it was intelligent. He knew what the issues were. It was also confident. Crinkles appeared near the corners, like a smile that didn't involve a mouth. There was a good chance they could pull this off.

It was Aiden who broke the eye contact. He crouched beside the bed so that he could look up at Claire who had her forehead resting on clenched fists.

'How tired are you, Claire?' he asked.

'She's stuffed, mate.' It was Greg who responded. 'We never thought it was going to be this hard, you know?'

But Aiden didn't seem to be listening. He was holding Claire's frightened gaze now.

'The best thing for your baby is going to be getting born as fast as possible,' he said. 'And we can help but you're going to have to do most of the work. Do you think you could do that?'

'I want to push,' Claire said with a sob. 'But I'm scared.'

'We're here with you. How 'bout we give it our best shot with the next contraction?'

'O-okay. I'll try.'

'Good girl.' He was smiling at Claire now and the mix of approval and confidence in his voice was compelling. Sophia could have felt defensive about having someone else make that decision for her, but instead she was as ready as Claire to put every effort into making this work. She believed it was the right decision. It *would* work.

Who was this knight in shining armour who'd ridden up on a motorbike instead of a horse just as things were turning to custard? This paramedic with his warm brown eyes and streaked, golden-blond hair that made him look like a surfer.

When the next contraction was due a couple of minutes later, they turned Claire onto her back again and Sophia released the pressure holding the baby's head away from the cervix and the cord. The clock was ticking from that moment on and the three of them, Aiden, Sophia and even Greg—who couldn't help but catch the urgency—coached Claire into giving everything she had. And then a bit more.

'You can do it,' Aiden told her firmly. 'Push, push, push. Keep going. *Push.*'

'Crowning,' Sophia confirmed. 'Keep going, Claire.'

'You're doing great,' Aiden continued. 'But don't

stop. We can't wait for another contraction. This is it. *Push…*'

'*Can't…*' The groan was agonised.

'Yes, you can. You *are* doing it. You're awesome… One more push, that's all we need.'

Good grief, this man had the most amazing voice. Sophia could feel her own abdominal muscles clenching. *She* wanted to push—how ridiculous was that?

'Oh, my God…' Greg's voice was choked. 'I can see him, Claire. Our baby.'

Sophia could see him, too. Could touch and help him into the world, but she'd lost track of how many minutes it had taken since the blood and oxygen supply had been cut off by the pressure of the baby's head and body on the prolapsed umbilical cord.

The baby was limp and blue. It looked lifeless.

Her heart sank like a stone. This had been the wrong decision, then, to let imminent labour progress instead of stalling it and trying to get Claire to hospital before she delivered. This was her patient and her responsibility. How could she have allowed this man she'd never even met before to come in and take charge the way he had? It would be unthinkable to lose a baby like this.

But the motorbike-riding paramedic was by her side, with a kit unrolled and resuscitation gear at the ready and she hadn't yet lost faith in the calm confidence he displayed.

A tiny bag mask to deliver oxygen. Fingers that looked so large against a fragile chest delivering compressions that were gentle but effective.

'Come on, little guy. You can do it. You're gonna be fine…'

The words sounded incongruously casual but Sophia could see the intense concentration in the paramedic's eyes. The fierce determination to save a tiny life.

And there was movement. A gasp as lungs expanded for the first time. A warbling cry. Skin colour that was changing from a deathly blue to a much healthier pink. Arms and legs beginning to stir.

'Hey…welcome back, little guy.' Aiden's hands cupped the baby to gently lift and place the newborn boy against his mother's skin. Both Claire and Greg had tears streaming down their faces. There was an over-powering sense of both relief and joy but fear hadn't been banished yet.

Sophia was watching anxiously. With the level of re-suscitation needed, the baby would have still been under intense monitoring in a clinical setting, not being held and touched like this by his parents.

And then Aiden's gaze shifted away from the infant.

'Apgar score nine at five minutes,' he murmured. She could swear there was a ghost of a wink accompa-nying the report. He knew how anxious she was and he wanted her to know that he was still doing his job—that the baby was being carefully monitored. Sure enough, she could see him resting a finger lightly on the baby's upper arm, taking a brachial pulse. She could stop wor-rying and focus on Claire. She could deal with the de-livery of the placenta and check for any tissue damage.

The emergency was over, almost as quickly as it had appeared.

The ambulance would be arriving within minutes and then they'd have the bustle of preparations to transfer the new family to the maternity unit, where Claire and the baby could both be checked by specialists, but this was a gift of time.

Private time in their own home—the place they had wanted to be in to welcome their first baby.

Aiden stepped back. He stripped off the gloves he'd put on to work on the baby and moved to one side of the room, where he propped an elbow on a tall chest of drawers. He was due to go off duty and he had his usual visit to make as soon as he was done but he wasn't going to leave until the back-up arrived and he didn't want to crowd the young parents as they had their first minutes with their newborn.

Besides, he could watch the midwife as she dealt competently with the delivery of the placenta, transferring it to a bowl where she inspected it for any damage that could suggest part of it had been retained. She was tiny, he noticed. Only a bit over five feet tall. Funny that he hadn't noticed how small she was before. Maybe that was because she'd given off the impression of being confident. Good at her job and in control.

She hadn't felt so in control at one point, though, had she? He remembered that almost telepathic communication between them as they'd weighed up the option of whether to try and stall the labour or push it forward.

Her eyes were a rich brown, weren't they? A nice match for her hair, which had an auburn tinge to its dark colour. It was pinned up to her head to keep it out of the way and Aiden found himself wondering how long it would be if it was unpinned. How soft it might feel.

Good grief… Okay, she was pretty cute but there was no need to get carried away.

But then she looked up from her work and her smile told him there was nothing to worry about.

He could feel that smile as much as he could see it. Gorgeous was the only word for it.

Sophia hadn't noticed the paramedic moving to the other side of the room. Had he apparently read the vibes in the room in the same way he'd seemed to ever since he'd walked in the door?

He'd done the perfect thing, anyway, so she followed his example. Any more cleaning up of either mother or baby could wait until the ambulance arrived. This was a time these new parents could never have again and it was precious. She wasn't about to leave the room and Aiden had chosen the spot that was far away enough to be unobtrusive while still being available so it was a no-brainer to move quietly until she was standing beside him.

He acknowledged her arrival with a grin.

'Good job,' he said softly. 'Thanks for inviting me.'

Her breath came out in a huff of laughter. How could anyone make a life-threatening emergency sound like a party? But paramedics were like that, weren't they? They lived for the adrenaline rush and a 'good' job was one that other medical professionals dreaded having to face. She'd met paramedics who came across as cowboys—galloping from one callout to the next and over-eager to show off their skills.

This one rode a motorbike, for heaven's sake. A mechanical horse. And he'd had no hesitation in taking command and encouraging management that had had the very real potential to have ended in disaster.

Except it hadn't, had it? Another glance at the bed was enough to bring a lump to Sophia's throat. The baby lay in Claire's arms, tiny eyes open and staring up at his parents. Greg's fingers were touching the tiny starfish hand of the baby and his head was touching Claire's. They were both looking down, aware of nothing but their newborn infant. They were talking softly, too, counting fingers and toes and doing what all new parents did in the first minutes of sharing the miracle of new life.

They had probably forgotten the presence of their medical team and wouldn't even hear the murmur of other voices but Sophia looked away, unconsciously allowing them a little more privacy.

It was somewhat startling to find that the paramedic was still looking at her.

'Babies are my favourite thing,' he said softly. 'It was a treat.'

For the first time since he'd let himself into the house, she realised how good looking he was. Oh, she'd noticed the brown eyes and the way they crinkled at the corners and the streaky blond hair. She'd been aware of the intelligence and intense concentration his features could advertise. But he was still grinning at her and she was distracted enough from her patient to appreciate the way everything came together. And not just his face. He had a presence that she'd appreciated on a professional level. Now she was getting the full force of it on a very personal level. Was it so overpowering because he was so much bigger than she was?

No…everyone was pretty much taller than her when she could only boast five feet three inches in bare feet and he probably seemed broader because of the jacket he was still wearing but he gave the impression of a large man. A powerful man, yet she'd seen how skilful those hands had been, positioning the baby's head and fitting the mask to the tiny face. How carefully controlled and gentle his movements had been.

It felt like something was melting deep inside her belly.

He wasn't just incredibly good at his job. He'd done it with humour. With an ability to defuse a terrifying situation. With a confidence that had given them all the belief that they could do it and maybe that had been the reason why they had been able to do it.

Her smile felt odd. As if she was offering him something that she had never offered anyone before on such short acquaintance. Something that came straight from her heart.

'It's me who should be thanking you,' she whispered. 'I can't believe I told Dispatch that we only needed transport, not a SPRINT paramedic.'

'I was eavesdropping on the radio traffic. I'd just ordered a coffee not far away.' He grinned. 'Don't suppose it'll still be hot when I go back.'

'I owe you one, then.'

The crinkles appeared around his eyes again. 'Might just hold you to that.'

Were the butterflies dancing in Sophia's stomach

embarrassment? Did he think she was flirting with him? Suggesting a date, even?

If he did, he didn't seem put off. Or any less relaxed.

Maybe the butterflies were there for an entirely different reason. How long had it been since she'd met such an attractive man? One who had impressed her on so many levels?

Not in the last six months, that was for sure. Changing cities and throwing herself into a new job had left no time at all to think about expanding her social life to include men. She was only beginning to gather a new circle of girlfriends.

Not that this one would be interested, anyway. She could hear an echo of his voice. *Babies are my favourite thing...*

She could feel herself becoming tense. Trying to squeeze something tight enough to suffocate those damned butterflies.

Could he sense that, too? A flicker of something she couldn't identify passed across his face.

'Might be hard to call in the debt,' he said. 'When I don't even know your name.'

'Oh...' She hadn't introduced herself, had she? How rude was that? He'd have paperwork to fill in for this job. He would need more details about Claire as well. 'I'm Sophia,' she said. 'Sophia Toulson. I'm a midwife.'

His grin widened as an eyebrow lifted. 'I should hope so.'

The information about their patient she'd been gathering mentally to help him with his report evaporated as Sophia laughed.

Those cute eye wrinkles deepened and his eyes

danced. 'Come out with me,' he said softly. 'Sophia Toulson, midwife extraordinaire. Come out with me tonight. I'll take a beer instead of a coffee as payment of that debt.'

Sophia's smile died on her lips.

She wanted to say yes.

She really, *really* wanted to say yes, but she could feel her head beginning to roll from side to side.

'No… I can't… I…' The words followed her smile into oblivion. How could she possibly even begin to explain why she had to say no?

Not that Aiden seemed offended by the rejection. His shrug was casual. 'No worries. Maybe another night.'

And then there was a loud knock on a door outside the room. 'Ambulance,' the call came, along with the rattle of a stretcher's wheels.

The snatch of time was gone and Sophia realised that it would have been better spent starting the enormous amount of paperwork she needed to do to record everything that had happened during the emergency birth.

And then she caught Aiden's glance and, if the same thought had occurred to him, he didn't care—he was happy having spent that time doing exactly what they had been doing. And, suddenly, so was she.

Inexplicably happy, in fact, given that she'd denied herself the pleasure of spending more time in this man's company.

But he'd asked. And, for a blink of time, she'd considered saying yes.

That feeling of connection hadn't been one-sided and that, in itself, was something to feel happy about.

Wasn't it?

CHAPTER TWO

IT MUST HAVE been enough because that happiness stayed with her for the rest of her shift.

In fact, this was turning out to be the best day yet since Sophia had made such big changes in her life, leaving her home town of Canberra to shift to Melbourne.

Word had spread quickly through the Melbourne Maternity Unit about her successful management of an obstetrical emergency in the community. With its international reputation for excellence, the MMU attracted the best in the field but this case was earning her congratulations from every quarter.

Alessandro Manos, who headed the neonatal intensive care unit, had been the specialist called to check the baby and he'd been thorough.

'There's no sign of any complications from oxygen deprivation,' he told Sophia. 'He's a lucky little boy that you were there to manage the birth.'

She fastened the disposable nappy and reached for the soft sleep suit Claire had given her to bring up to the unit.

'It wasn't just me. I probably would have chosen to

try and delay the birth and get her in here if I hadn't had some expert paramedic assistance. He was…' Oh, yes…there was a definite extra buzz to be found in the satisfaction of a job well done. 'He was really amazing.'

'Who was?' Isla Delamere—Alessi's fiancée—had popped into the NICU. Her look suggested that the only amazing man around there was her husband-to-be.

'The paramedic who helped me through an acute cord prolapse this afternoon.'

'Oh, I heard about that. How's the baby?'

'Perfect.' Was Alessi referring to the baby he'd just checked? His gaze was resting adoringly on his wife as he spoke.

Sophia's smile had a poignant edge. They might have wanted to keep Isla's pregnancy secret for a bit longer but the news had slipped out and there was no way these two could hide how they felt about each other. They were so happy. And why wouldn't they be? They'd found love and were on the way to being a family.

That had been her own dream once.

People probably assumed it still was. That—like most women her age—she was simply waiting to find the right person to make that dream come true. Only her best friend, Emily, knew that there was no man on earth who could put the pieces of her dream back together.

That it had been permanently shattered.

Maybe it was just as well that the baby scrunched up his face and started crying at that moment.

'I'd better take this little guy back to his mum. She'll be missing him and he's hungry.'

'I'll come with you,' Isla said. 'I want to hear more about this paramedic. Was he hot? Single?'

Sophia shook her head as she wrapped the baby in a cotton blanket and picked him up. An image of those unusual brown eyes, somewhere between hazel and chocolate, flashed into her head. She could even see the crinkles in the corners—the smile that had seemed intimate because it was only intended for the person who had the eye contact.

'Hot enough, I guess,' she said lightly. 'But I doubt very much that he's single.' Liar, her mind whispered. He wouldn't have asked you out if he wasn't single. Her voice rose in pitch as it tightened. 'And even if he was, I wouldn't be interested.'

'Why not?' Loved up herself, Isla was keen for everybody to share her happiness. And maybe she'd picked up on the fact that Sophia was being less than truthful. 'Work is where most people find their partners, you know.'

'I'm not looking for a partner.' With the baby, who'd stopped crying for the moment, in her arms, Sophia led the way out of the ICU and headed towards the room where Claire had been taken for assessment. 'And I do go out. I'm going out tomorrow.' This was a good opportunity to change the subject. 'You're coming, aren't you? To the gardens?'

'For Em and Oliver's vow renewal ceremony?' Isla smiled. 'Of course. I wouldn't miss it. I think everybody from the MMU is going. It's the perfect way for everyone to move forward, isn't it?' she sighed, probably unaware of the way her hand touched her own belly so protectively. 'Em's very brave, isn't she?'

'She certainly is.' Sophia's arms tightened a little around the precious bundle she was carrying, jiggling him as he started grizzling again. They'd all known that Emily's foster-daughter would only have a short life but her death had been gutting. Only last week they'd all gathered in the children's section of Melbourne's botanical gardens to attend the memorial service for little Gretta. So many tears had been shed as the CEO of the Victoria Hospital—Charles Delamere—had spoken so beautifully about how Gretta's short life had touched the lives of so many others.

They'd all been clutching pink balloons that had been released into the sky at the end of the ceremony. The balloons had all held little packets of seeds—Kangaroo paws—all different colours. Apparently they had been Gretta's favourite and Emily had a vision of new plants growing all over Melbourne. It had been a beautiful ending to a very touching ceremony.

'The plan is that later anyone who can will head for the Rooftop for a drink.'

'I heard that. Did I tell you that Darcie's bringing Flick?'

'The midwifery student?'

'Yes. She's due to start shadowing you next week. We thought it would be a good way for her to get to know everyone a bit better. You don't think Emily will mind, do you?'

'It's an open invitation. We all know Em and Oliver and everyone's thrilled that they're back together. The sad bit's been dealt with and this is about the future. It should be a good party.'

'How formal is it?'

'Not at all. You can wear whatever you like. But I did talk Em into buying a new dress and getting her hair done so I don't plan to turn up in jeans myself.'

Emily Evans had been the first real friend that Sophia had made after moving to Melbourne. They'd clicked instantly and it had been Emily who had helped Sophia settle into her new job and home so happily. An evening with a few wines a couple of months into their friendship had sealed the bond when they'd realised how much they had in common. Their journeys may have been very different but the result was the same—they would never know the joy of holding their own newborn infants in their arms.

Had it been stupid to pick this career? Leaving Isla behind, Sophia had a few moments alone, holding Claire's baby boy. This was the part of her job she loved best. The weight of the tiny body that fitted so snugly against her chest. The joy in the mother's face as she handed it over. Watching a tiny mouth latch onto a breast for that first feed…

It was always there, though…that empty feeling in her own arms. The ache in the corner of her own heart.

Emily's journey had been slower. The hope had still been there for all those attempts at IVF and it must have turned to such joy when she'd finally carried a pregnancy almost to term. How devastating would it have been to experience the stillbirth of her son?

More devastating than it had been to wake from an

emergency surgery to be told that you'd not only lost your baby but that your uterus had had to be sacrificed to save your life? There would never be a transition period of chasing an IVF dream to lead to acceptance for Sophia. She'd only been twenty-one but her life had changed for ever that day.

But it hadn't been stupid to choose this career. Yes, she could have shut herself away from the emotional fall-out by choosing a nursing career that had nothing to do with babies or children, but that would have only made the ache worse in the long run and at least, this way, she got to share the joy every day of her life pretty much.

Love always came with some fine print about what you were risking but if you never took that risk, you shut yourself off from what life had to offer. Nobody had ever promised that life was easy and she'd seen more than her fair share of heartbreak in this job, but she'd seen far more people reaping the rewards of taking risks.

Look at Em. She'd chosen to love two children who weren't even hers, both with medical conditions. She'd been brave enough to risk the heartbreak she'd known was coming right from the start. Sophia had thought she was being brave, becoming a midwife and working with other people's babies every day, but, compared to Em, she was still hiding from life, wasn't she?

The next half-hour was happy enough to banish any personal reflections as Sophia spent time with Claire and Greg and the baby who now had a name—Isaac.

The first breastfeed was no drama and she left the happy parents preparing to go back home for their first night as a family.

Weaving through the busy, inner-city streets to get back to her small, terraced cottage when she finally signed off duty wasn't enough of a distraction, however. The ache was a little heavier today. Not just the empty ache of not having a baby to hold. There was the ache of not having a hand to hold. Having someone in her life who was her special person.

It wasn't that she wasn't making new friends here. Good friends. It was because she was essentially alone. She had no family nearby. Her best friend was back with her husband. Sophia had no one who was always available to share the highs and lows of life. And a best friend could never take the place of a life partner, anyway. She had no one to cuddle up to at night.

How stupid had she been, turning down that offer of a date with Aiden Harrison?

Why couldn't she be a bit braver?

If only she could turn the clock back to that moment. She could see those dancing eyes so clearly. A mix of attraction and humour and…confidence that she would say yes?

He hadn't been upset by her stuttering refusal, though, had he?

Maybe, by now, he was feeling relieved.

Oh, for heaven's sake. Sophia gave herself a mental shake. She needed to get over herself or she wouldn't be contributing anything positive at tomorrow's celebration. Maybe she needed to take a leaf out of Emily's book and convince herself that the risk of loving was always worthwhile.

Maybe she could even go down that track herself one day and think about fostering kids.

'It's only me.' Aiden let himself into the big house in Brunswick—his usual stop on his way home. 'Where is everyone? Nate?'

A dark head popped out from behind a nearby door. 'We'll be out in a sec, Aiden. The other boys are in the lounge.'

The lounge was a large room and, like all the other rooms in this converted house, it had polished wooden floors. Unlike most lounges, it had very little furniture, however, because the residents didn't need sofas or armchairs. The four young men who lived here were all quadriplegics who needed a high level of domestic and personal assistance. The youngest lad, Steve, was only eighteen. Nathan, at twenty-four, was the oldest.

Not that his younger brother intended to live here for long. This was a halfway step—a move towards the kind of independence he really wanted. At some point they were going to have to talk about it and maybe tonight would be a good time. While he hadn't said anything yet, Aiden was worried about the idea of Nate living independently. He himself had a demanding job and he wouldn't be able to drop everything and go and help his brother if something happened. At least here there were always carers on hand and it was a lot better than the residential home he'd been in for the last few years.

Or was the anxiety about the future more like a form of guilt? That he hadn't been able to care for his brother himself when the accident had happened because he'd only been a kid himself?

That it was his fault that the accident had happened in the first place?

That, if Nathan was capable of living in a normal house, he'd want it to be with *him* and then he'd have to take full responsibility. Oh, he'd have a carer to come in a couple of times a day to help with the transfers from bed to wheelchair and for the personal type care of showering and toileting, but what about the rest of the day? What would happen if Nate fell out of his chair or something and *he* was in the middle of a job like that obstetric emergency today?

He wanted his brother somewhere he was protected and surely this was as good as it got? This was like a regular blokes' flat, with a sports programme playing on its huge-screen television and guys sitting around, yelling approval at the goal that had just been scored.

And then he saw what they were watching. Murderball. The loud, fast and incredibly aggressive form of wheelchair rugby that Nate was currently passionate about. Two of the other guys in the house were part of a local team and Nate was desperate to make the grade. Physically, he certainly qualified.

Many people thought that quadriplegics—or tetraplegics—were always totally paralysed from the neck down but the repercussions of a cervical injury or illness were as individual as the people who suffered them and they were graded according to whether the impairment was complete or incomplete and by how much sensory and motor function remained.

With the C6 spinal injury Nate had received at the age of ten, he had little movement or sensation in his lower body. Thankfully, the injury had been incomplete so he still had a good range of movement in his upper body and better hand function than many. If he got his strength up, he'd probably be lethal on a Murderball court.

'Hey, Aiden. Wassup?'

'All good, Steve. How 'bout you?'

'This is our game from last week. Wanna watch?'

'Sure. Not for long, though. I promised Nate I'd take him out for a beer tonight.'

The young woman who'd greeted him came into the lounge. With her short, spiky black hair and facial piercings, Samantha was unlike any of the carers he'd come across in the years of Nate's care so far.

'He's out of the bathroom, Aiden. You can help him finish getting dressed if you want.'

Nathan's face lit up as Aiden went into his room.

'Hey, bro…' The hand held up for a fist bump took away any awkwardness of the height difference between the brothers and Nate's lack of hand strength. 'What do you call a quadriplegic on your doorstep?'

Aiden rolled his eyes. 'I thought you'd given up on the quadriplegic jokes.'

'Matt.' Nathan snorted with laughter and then pushed on one wheel of his chair to turn it towards a chest of drawers. 'What do you reckon? Leather jacket or the denim one?'

'Either's good. We're going to a garden bar but it's not cold out. Want a hand?'

'Nah…I'm good.'

Rather than watch Nate's struggle to put the jacket on unaided, Aiden looked around his brother's room. The poster collection was growing. Action shots of Murderball games, with wheelchairs crashing into each other and flipping sideways and the occupants only staying with them because they were strapped in.

He waved a hand at the posters. 'You could get really injured doing that stuff, you know.'

'Nah.' Nathan had one sleeve of his jacket on but it was taking a few attempts to get his other hand into a sleeve hole. 'A cracked rib or a squashed finger, maybe. Wouldn't be calling you out with any lights or sirens. Hey…any good jobs today?'

'Yeah… Last call was the best. This midwife was calling for transport to take a home birth in to the maternity unit in the Victoria because it had been going on too long. I overheard the call and decided to poke my nose in just because it was handy and things were quiet. Thought I'd just be waving the flag but the minute I walk in, the woman has a contraction and, *boof!* Umbilical cord prolapse and it's turned into an emergency.'

'Wow. What did you do?'

Aiden settled himself onto the end of Nathan's bed. This would need a few minutes because Nate always wanted a blow-by-blow account of every interesting job. If he'd been able-bodied, he would have been a paramedic himself, no question about it. You'd think he'd only be reminded of what he'd never be able to do by hearing about it but he never seemed to get enough of hearing about Aiden's professional exploits.

Or anything else about his big brother's life, come to that. He particularly loved to hear about the women he met and those he chose to date. What they looked like, where they'd gone on their dates and whether they'd stayed the night. He'd been careful how much he'd said about the midwife on today's job because Nate would have picked up on that pretty fast and, for some reason, Aiden hadn't wanted to answer the inevitable questions about how cute she was or whether she was single and, if so, why hadn't he asked her out yet?

Nate was so sure that someone was going to come along one day who would make him break his three-dates rule. Aiden was just as sure it would never happen.

If he couldn't take responsibility for his own brother's well-being, why the hell would he make himself responsible for anyone else? He didn't even own a dog, for heaven's sake, and he'd chosen a medical career where he generally never had to see his patients more than once.

Aiden Harrison was only too well aware of his limitations when it came to relationships and he'd found the perfect balance. Life was good. And it would continue to be good as long as Nathan didn't insist on putting himself at risk. Yes…tonight was the night for having a serious talk about the future.

'Let's go.' He matched the invitation with movement, standing up and opening the extra-wide door so that Nathan could manoeuvre his wheelchair into the hallway.

'Is it okay if Sam comes too?'

'Huh?'

'Samantha. You know…my carer? I asked her if she'd

like to come out and have a beer with us and she was keen. There's plenty of staff on tonight so it's no problem.'

'I…ah…' Was he going to be playing gooseberry while his brother was having a *date*?

Surely not.

But *why* not? He knew better than anyone that a disability didn't change who you were and his brother was an awesome guy. Why wouldn't a girl be smart enough to realise that? He had to admit it was a disturbing thought, though. What if Nathan fell in love and got his heart broken? Maybe a man-to-man talk about how well the three-dates rule worked needed to take priority over the talk about how risky independent living could be.

Not that either of those talks was going to happen tonight.

'Sure,' he heard himself saying, as though it was no big deal. 'There's plenty of room in the van. Maybe one of the other guys would like to come too.'

'Nope.' Nathan scooted through the door ahead of him. 'I only invited Sam.'

They were in a very different part of the botanical gardens this time. The guests crowded around the couple who were standing beneath the wrought-iron archway on the steps to the Temple of the Winds. The greenery of overhanging trees shaded them from the hot sun of a stunning autumn afternoon and once again Charles Delamere was in place as the master of ceremonies

'Ten years ago,' he told them, 'Emily and Oliver made their wedding vows. Circumstances, grief, life drove them apart but when the time was right fate brought them together again. They've decided to renew their vows, and they've also decided that here, in the gardens that are—and have been—loved by the whole family, is the place they'd like to do it.'

Emily and Oliver exchanged a look that was tender enough to bring a lump to Sophia's throat. She glanced over at Toby, Em's foster son, who was being held by Em's mother, Adrianna. This was a real family affair.

There had been so many tears at Gretta's farewell in the children's playground and there were probably just as many as the couple exchanged heartfelt vows, declaring their love and promising their commitment, but there was real joy this time. An affirmation that the risk of truly loving was worthwhile.

It was contagious, that hope. Maybe there was someone out there for her, Sophia thought. Someone who could see past the fact that she could never give him children of his own. Maybe she could find what Emily and Oliver had. How good would that be?

Something would have to change, though, if she was going to become as brave as Emily. Not that she knew quite what that something was but she was definitely going to give it some serious thought.

And, in the meantime, she could celebrate her friend's happiness. The Rooftop Bar was a good place to be on a sunny Saturday afternoon. Adrianna took little Toby home after a short time but told Oliver and Emily to stay and celebrate with all their friends. She would sort the final packing that was needed before they all went on their family honeymoon to the Great Barrier Reef the next day.

As often happened, the men gravitated together at one point and Sophia found herself sitting with a group of the women she knew best around a deliciously shaded table. Right beside Emily, she impulsively gave her friend another hug.

'I'm just so happy for you, Em. For you and Oliver. You so deserve every bit of this happiness.'

'It'll be your turn next.' Emily's smile was radiant. 'I'm sure of it.'

Isla overheard the comment. She was smiling as she refilled Sophia's glass with champagne. 'Good timing that she's met that hot paramedic, then, isn't it?'

'What?' Emily's jaw dropped. 'How come I haven't heard about this? Who is he?'

'Nobody,' Sophia muttered. 'Just a guy that turned up for that cord prolapse job yesterday.'

'And he's gorgeous,' Isla added. 'Soph said so.'

'I said he was good at his job, that's all.'

'She couldn't stop talking about him.' Darcie Green had joined them. 'I can vouch for that.'

Emily's sideways glance was significant. 'Just remember what I told you,' she said, raising her glass. 'You don't have to marry the guy. Just get out there and have some fun.'

'Why shouldn't she marry the guy?' Isla asked, between sips of her tall glass of soda water. 'Have you got something against marriage, Soph?'

'Not at all. I'm thrilled for Oliver and Em. And for you and Alessi. And...' Sophia glanced around the table, trying to distract the focus of attention. 'And what's

going on with you and Lucas, Darcie? I'm sure I wasn't
the only one to notice the sparks flying at the ball.'

Lucas was the super-hot senior midwife at the MMU
and, while the husbands of the women about to give birth
were less than impressed with his popularity, there was
no shortage of expectant mums keen to become his patients. No shortage of women in Melbourne just as keen
to fill another potential role in his life either.

Darcie was an English obstetrician, on secondment
to the MMR. She was dedicated to her job and professional enough to have made several people sharpen up
at work. Lucas didn't seem to be in that number, however, and the antagonism between them had been noted
on the grapevine, but the obvious sparks at the ball had
not come across as being between two people who didn't
like each other. Not at all.

Not that Darcie was about to admit anything. She
shrugged. 'We all had a good time at the ball,' she said,
carefully avoiding eye contact with any of the other
women. 'But if there was anything serious going on,
I'd say it was between Flick, here, and Tristan.'

There was a murmur of agreement amongst the
women and more than one knowing smile accompany-
ing the nods.

'I'm sure I wasn't the only one to see you two leaving together,' Darcie continued lightly. 'Just what time
did you get home, young woman?'

Felicia Lawrence, the student midwife, turned bright
red. For an awful moment, Sophia was sure she was
about to burst into tears.

Whatever had happened that night was really none of their business. Sophia needed to give her an escape route.

'So you two aren't dating or anything interesting like that, then?'

Flick shook her head with more emphasis than was needed. 'I'm not remotely interested in dating,' she claimed. 'My career's the only important thing in my life right now. Like Sophia.'

'I didn't say I wasn't *interested* in dating.' Sophia eyed her glass of champagne suspiciously. Had she had too much? 'I just…haven't met anybody. It takes time, you know—when you move to a new city.'

'But you've met the hot paramedic now.' Darcie was smiling. 'What was his name? Andy?'

'Aiden.' It seemed to be Sophia's turn to blush now. She could feel the warmth in her cheeks as she said his name aloud. 'Aiden Harrison.'

'Is he single? Did he ask for your number?'

'No.' She bit her lip. 'He did ask me for a date, though.'

'And you said *no*? What were you thinking?'

Darcie and Flick seemed very relieved to have the spotlight turned onto someone else's love life and, for Flick's sake, Sophia was happy enough to take centre stage.

'I'm not sure,' she admitted. 'Maybe I thought he was just being nice. I'd said I owed him a coffee because he'd had to abandon one to come to the job. He said he'd take a beer instead. It seemed—I don't know—a bit of a joke, maybe?'

'Nonsense,' the women chorused. She was gorgeous,

they assured her. Intelligent. Fun. Any guy would have to be crazy not to be genuinely interested.

Emily caught her glance in a private moment. She was the only one who might understand that moment of panic. That dip into a whirl of thoughts that had been spinning for so many years now. The issue of meeting someone you really liked and then agonising over when to tell them. On the first date? Did you say something like, 'Yeah, I'd love to go out with you but you should know that if you want to have kids some time in the future then I'm not the woman for you'? Or did you wait until things got serious and then field the repercussions of someone feeling a bit cheated? Deceived, even.

Yes. Emily's glance was sympathetic. But there was something else there, too. Encouragement?

'What does it matter if it did start out as a bit of a joke?' she said. 'Isn't the whole idea to have fun? To let your hair down a bit and enjoy the best of what life has to offer that doesn't have anything to do with work? It doesn't ever have to be anything serious.'

You don't have to marry the guy. Was that code for 'You don't have to even tell him'?

'How many guys do we know who have no intention of getting serious?' she added. 'They're just out to have fun. We could learn something from those guys.'

'Like Alessi.' Darcie nodded. 'Oops…sorry, Isla, but he was a terrible flirt and nobody lasted more than one night. Until you, of course…'

'Not a good example,' Emily chided. 'But you're right. Soph could use a bit of that attitude and just get out there and enjoy herself with some attractive male company.'

Sophia found herself nodding. And hadn't she just made a silent vow that very afternoon that something needed to change in her life? Maybe she wouldn't have to give too much thought to what that something was.

'Maybe I will,' she said aloud. 'Not that there's anyone around who's offering the company.'

'The hot paramedic did. You're probably putting anyone off asking by sending out *I'm not available* vibes. Change your attitude and they'll be around in droves. You might even meet *him* again.'

Sophia laughed. 'I don't think so.' But she reached for her glass of champagne, feeling lighter in spirit than she had for a long time. 'But, hey...I'll give it a go. The next time I get asked out—especially if it's the hot paramedic—I'll say yes.'

'Promise?' Emily raised her glass to clink it against Sophie's. The other women followed her example and the glasses met in a circle over the centre of the table.

'I promise,' Sophie said.

CHAPTER THREE

HE HAD THE best job in the world, no doubt about it.

Aiden was rolling slowly, the red and blue lights on his handlebars flashing as he eased through the crowds on Southbank. The wide, paved area on the south side of the Yarra River offered spectacular views of the river and city from cafés, restaurants and upmarket hotels.

The gorgeous autumn afternoon had tourists and locals enjoying the exercise, food and entertainment. A juggler had attracted a good crowd and so had an old aboriginal man playing a didgeridoo. Aiden could hear the hollow, haunting notes of the music over the bike's engine. He angled his path to avoid smudging the work of a street artist who was working with chalk and then he could see his destination. Another huddle of people, but they weren't there for entertainment. He'd been called to a woman who'd collapsed on one of the riverside benches beneath the trees.

'I've put her in the recovery position,' a man told Aiden as soon as he'd propped the bike up on its stand. 'I did a first-aid course last year.'

'Good work.' He flipped up the chinguard of his helmet. 'Did anyone see what happened?'

'She was walking around, looking weird,' someone else offered. 'Like she was drunk. And then she sat down and just toppled sideways.'

Aiden had reached the unconscious woman. He stripped off his gloves, tilted her head to make sure her airway was open and then felt for a pulse in her neck. It was there. Rapid and faint enough to suggest low blood pressure. Her skin felt cool and clammy. He shook her shoulder.

'Hello? Can you hear me? Open your eyes, love.'

No response. Aiden looked up. 'Does anyone know this woman? Was she with someone?'

There was a general sound of denial and shaking of heads. Aiden checked for a MedicAlert bracelet or necklace as he ran through the possible causes of unconsciousness in his head. He couldn't smell any alcohol and there was no sign of any head trauma. The woman was young, probably in her early thirties. This could be due to epilepsy or drugs or diabetes. At least he could eliminate one of the possible causes easily. Unrolling a kit, he took a small lancet, pricked the woman's finger and eased the drop of blood onto a testing strip for a glucometer. He also reached for his radio to give Dispatch an update. Whatever was going on, here, this young woman would need transport to hospital.

The glucometer beeped and it was a relief to see that the reading was low. Hypoglycaemia certainly fitted with the limited information he'd been given of her appearing drunk and then collapsing. It also fitted the physical signs of the clammy skin, rapid heart rate and a low blood pressure. Back-up was on the way but it would take time to get a stretcher through the crowds from the nearest point an ambulance could park and Aiden had everything he needed to start treatment.

IV access was the first priority and there were plenty of willing hands to hold up the bag with the glucose infusion. He got the small cardiac monitor out of one of the panniers on the back of his bike as well. It had only been a few days ago that he'd read an interesting article suggesting that sudden death in young diabetics could be due to cardiac problems from electrolyte disturbances.

The glucose infusion was working its magic well before he started attaching electrodes. The young woman opened her eyes, blinked a couple of times and then groaned.

'Oh, no…it happened again, didn't it?'

'I'm Aiden, a paramedic. What's your name, love?'

'Hayley. I…' She looked up at the crowd of onlookers. 'Oh…God…this is so embarrassing.'

'You're diabetic?'

'Yeah…I knew I needed to eat. That's why I came along here. I was heading for the food court in Southgate. It came on so suddenly…'

Aiden could see an ambulance crew manoeuvring a stretcher through the crowd. More people were stopping to stare, wondering what was going on. No wonder the poor girl was embarrassed. The sooner they got her into the privacy of the back of an ambulance, the better.

Checking her blood-glucose levels again could wait until then as well. Aiden kick-started his bike and followed the crew, until he could park beside the ambulance. He needed to fill in his paperwork and he had a feeling that Hayley was not going to be keen to be taken to hospital.

'I don't need to go,' she insisted a few minutes later. 'I feel fine now.'

'When was the last time you had a hypo?'

'A couple of weeks ago,' she admitted reluctantly. 'But before that, it hadn't happened for ages. Over a year.'

'That means your control is becoming more challenging. You need a reassessment.'

'I'll go to my doctor. Soon.'

'It could happen again today.'

'I'll eat. I'll go and get a sandwich right now.'

It took time to persuade Hayley that it would be a good idea to go the emergency department at the Victoria but none of the paramedics were happy to let her go when she didn't have someone with her to monitor her condition. And Aiden had something else that was bothering him.

'Have you thought of wearing a MedicAlert bracelet?'

Hayley made a face. 'It's bad enough having to live with something like this, without advertising it. And have you any idea how much harder it makes it to find a job? People look at you like you've got a disability or something.'

Her words stayed with Aiden as he watched the ambulance take his patient away. He stayed where he was, astride his bike, watching the mill of the people he could still see on Southbank. This wasn't a bad place to park up until he got another call. Central city and covering a patch well away from the nearest ambulance station. A young man in a wheelchair went past amongst the crowd.

There was a disability that couldn't be disguised. And he knew what it was like to attract the intrusive attention of people who felt they had the right to ask personal questions. They'd often been directed at him over the years—as if Nathan's brain didn't work any better than his legs did.

'Why's he in a wheelchair, then?'

'Oh, the poor boy. Can he feed himself?'

'How does he go to the toilet?'

The guilt was always there, welded onto his soul, and the curiosity of strangers turned the screws painfully for Aiden, but Nathan had developed a resilience in his teenage years that had astounded him. He could deal with any situation now with a humour that often shocked the nosy people. Like those awful jokes he kept adding to.

'What do you call a quadriplegic under your car? Jack.'

Despite himself, Aiden found his lips quirking. What did it matter what other people thought? Nathan had it sorted. He was happy. In fact, he was happier than he'd ever been right now. The way he'd been looking at Sam the other night… Was something going on already and, if so, how badly could that end? He needed to have a serious talk with his younger brother. Try and get him prepared for something that would hurt more than public scrutiny or pity.

His radio crackled into life.

'Code One,' Dispatch told him, giving him an address

not far away. 'Twenty-four-year-old female with severe abdominal pain.'

'Copy that.' Aiden tilted the bike off its stand and kicked it into life. He activated the lights and then the siren. Traffic was building up but he'd be able to weave through it fast. He loved a code one response and the freedom it allowed. With a bike, he got way more freedom than an ambulance to break a speed limit or use the tramlines. He just had to be a bit more careful. Hitting tram lines at the wrong angle and the ambulance would have to stop for him instead of getting to the job.

It took less than four minutes to arrive on scene. Another thirty seconds and he was in the room with the young woman who was bent over a chair and groaning loudly.

'It's the fish I had last night. Ohhh.... It *really* hurts and I've been sick.'

Aiden blinked. Dispatch hadn't bothered mentioning that his patient was pregnant.

'How far along are you?'

'Thirty-seven weeks.'

'And how far apart are the pains you're getting?'

'I dunno. It's happening every five or ten minutes, I guess. But I'm not in labour. It's that fish... I knew I shouldn't be eating prawns.'

It took very little time to convince his patient that this was, indeed, labour.

'I'm not going to hospital. I'm having a home birth. Can you call my midwife?'

'Sure. What's her name?'

'Sophia Toulson. Her card's on the fridge.'

The phone in his hand seconds later, Aiden found himself smiling again. It was surprising how strong the hope was that Sophia would be available and able to get here fast.

For his patient's benefit, of course…

Flick was excited. This was the first home birth she had been to since starting to shadow Sophia.

'But what if something goes wrong? Like a post-partum haemorrhage or something?'

'We call for back-up. The Melbourne ambulance service is fabulous. And we're not far from the hospital. In most cases, if there's going to be trouble, we get enough warning.'

'You didn't the other day, with that cord prolapse, did you?'

'No.'

And her pager hadn't warned her that the paramedic on scene had been riding a motorbike. She could see it parked outside Gemma's house.

'Nice bike,' Flick murmured.

'Mmm.'

Those butterflies were dancing in her stomach again. How many SPRINT paramedics rode bikes in the city? It didn't mean that she was about to have another en-counter with the man her friends were all now referring to as 'the hot paramedic'.

Except it appeared that she was.

'Hey…' Aiden Harrison was grinning. 'We've got to stop meeting like this. Rumours will start.'

Flick gave a huff of laughter and Sophia gave her

a warning glance before letting her gaze shift back to Aiden, her lips curling into a smile.

'You did say that babies were your favourite thing but you don't have to take over my job, you know.' She moved past him. 'Why didn't you call me when the pains started, Gemma?'

'I didn't think it was labour. I thought I had some dodgy prawns last night because I started getting cramps just after I'd eaten. They went away for a while this morning and then one was so painful I screamed and my neighbour called the ambulance.'

'Contractions are four to five minutes apart,' Aiden told her. 'Lasting about ninety seconds. Vital signs all good. Gemma's been happy to keep walking around.'

'Let's get you on your bed for a minute,' Sophia said. 'I want to check how baby's doing and what stage of dilatation you're at. This is Flick, by the way. Our student midwife. Are you happy to have her assisting? It's very valuable experience for her if she can be hands-on.'

Gemma nodded as she let Sophia guide her towards the bedroom.

'I can stay until I get another call,' Aiden said. 'Unless I'm in the way.'

It was entirely unprofessional to get distracted by noticing how much she didn't want him to disappear. Even worse to take another look at him and find it so hard to look away. Those eyes were just as warm and interesting as she'd remembered, and that smile made it impossible not to smile back.

Oh…help. How long had they been staring at each

other? Long enough for Flick and Gemma to exchange a surprised glance and then a complicit grin.

'It's fine by me if you stay,' Gemma said. *You know you want to*, her tone suggested. 'My mum's on her way but I told her not to hurry. This is going to take ages, isn't it?'

'Let's find out. Flick, get some gloves on and you can examine Gemma and find out what her stage of dilatation is.'

Keeping her voice low, it was possible to use this opportunity as a teaching and practical experience session for Flick.

'Tell me how you'll make the assessment.'

'At two centimetres I'll be able to fit one finger loosely through the cervix but not two fingers. Two fingers will be loose at four centimetres. There's two centimetres of cervix palpable on both sides at six centimetres, one at eight and there's only an anterior lip or a bit left laterally at nine centimetres.'

'And what are you feeling?'

'Nothing.' Flick's eyes widened. 'I can't feel any cervix at all. Am I doing something wrong?'

Sophia smiled as she double-checked Flick's findings, shaking her head at her student, who had been correct in her evaluation. 'You're fully dilated, Gemma,' she told their patient. 'Let's check the baby's position and then get set up. What do you need to do now, Flick?'

'The four Leopold's manoeuvres. First one checks the upper abdomen to make sure it's the baby's buttocks and not the head and then the umbilical area to locate the baby's back and—'

'Can I go to the bathroom first?' Gemma pleaded. 'I really need to go.'

Aiden helped Flick set up for the birth while Sophia stayed close to Gemma. They spread waterproof sheets over the bed and one of the armchairs in the living room and gathered some clean towels. Flick opened a kit and checked the resuscitation gear they carried in case it would be needed.

Aiden found himself glancing frequently at the door, waiting for the reappearance of Sophia and Gemma.

The attraction he'd felt the first time he'd met the cute little midwife had come back with a vengeance. Those lovely brown eyes were so warm and that smile made him feel like he'd just done something outstanding. Something that deserved approval because he'd some-how made the world a better place.

Heck…all he'd done was crack a fairly weak joke. Imagine how Sophia would look at him if he really did something to be proud of.

He wasn't going to let his opportunity slip past. He might have made a note of the number he'd used to call her but that was just her pager service. He was going to ask for her personal number as soon as he got the chance—as long as he didn't get called away first. Who knew how long this labour might take? Gemma was tak-ing long enough just to go to the loo.

And she was being noisy about it, too. They heard a cry of pain. And then another.

And then Sophia's calm voice. 'Could you bring a couple of towels, please, Flick? Lean on me, Gemma…

Yes, that's your baby's head you can feel. Deep breath and give me one good push…'

The wail of a healthy newborn could be heard a moment later and Aiden moved to peer in the bathroom door at the crowded scene. Gemma was still sitting on the toilet and Sophia was guiding her hands to help her hold the slippery baby against her skin. Gemma was sobbing and Sophia looked…as if she was blinking back tears?

'She's gorgeous, Gemma. A dear wee girl… Flick, have you got the clamps and scissors? Gemma, would you like to cut the cord?'

'No…' Gemma shook her head.

Somehow, Aiden had moved further into the small space without noticing and he was now blocking Flick's access to the toilet. Some signal passed between Sophia and her student and Aiden found himself holding the clamps in his gloved hands. He attached one a few inches away from the baby and then another to leave an isolated area to cut. He'd done this before and knew to expect how tough it was to cut through the umbilical cord.

He already felt involved in this birthing scene but then Sophia smiled at him again.

'Can we give baby to Aiden for just a minute, Gemma? I'd like to get you cleaned up and comfortable in bed to wait for the placenta.'

Flick gave him a clean towel and Aiden carefully took charge of the tiny infant, with Sophia's assistance. This was the closest he'd been to her and he could smell the fragrance of her hair. Almost feel the warmth of her skin through the gloves as their hands brushed. And then he looked at the tiny scrunched-up face of the baby and got completely distracted.

The miracle of birth never failed to amaze him but he never wanted the responsibility of one of these himself. The enormity of bringing a new person into the world and trying to keep them safe for ever was overwhelming. As he backed away, carrying the precious burden in his arms, he looked up to find Sophia watching him.

He couldn't read the expression in her face but it struck him as poignant and something inside his chest squeezed hard. But then it was gone. She smiled and turned back to her patient.

'Put your arm around my shoulders and we'll take this slowly. You might find your legs are pretty shaky.'

The five-minute Apgar score was a perfect ten and Aiden returned the pink, vigorously crying infant to his mother. There was no reason for him to stay on the job any longer and watch as Sophia guided Flick to help the baby latch onto Gemma's nipple and begin its first breastfeed.

And then Sophia supervised Flick in attending to the delivery of the placenta and checking it for any damage, and it really was time for him to leave. He stripped off his gloves and picked up his helmet and kit.

Flick was giving Gemma a wash with a hot, soapy cloth and Sophia was putting the placenta into a bag. This was it—the best opportunity he was going to get. He stepped closer.

'I know you were busy last time I asked,' he said

casually. 'But are you doing anything special after work today?'

Wide, surprised brown eyes met his gaze. 'Not really,' she said, 'but I won't finish for a while. We usually spend a few hours with a new mother and make sure she's happy before we go.'

'Maybe we could meet up later, then?'

Gemma looked up from watching her baby suckle. 'Are you asking Sophia for a date?' She grinned.

Flick was staring at Sophia and seemed to be stifling laughter. What was going on here?

Sophia tied the bag and stripped off her gloves. Her cheeks had a rosy glow and she seemed to be carefully avoiding meeting his gaze. 'It's not about a date,' she said. 'I happen to owe Aiden a coffee, that's all.'

She made it sound like that was the only reason he might be interested in taking her out. Aiden couldn't let that pass.

'Yeah…' he said slowly. 'I'm asking for a date. Would you like to come out with me this evening, Sophia?'

'Um… I…' Sophia bit her lip. 'Maybe you can call me later. We're both at work and this isn't, you know, very professional.'

'I don't mind,' Gemma said.

'And I'm not going to tell anybody,' Flick added. She looked as if she was trying not to smile. 'Was that a *yes* I heard there, Soph?'

There was definitely an undercurrent here that Aiden had no way of interpreting but right then Sophia met his gaze again and he didn't care about anything other than hearing her say that word.

'Okay. Yes.' He could see her chest rise as she took a deep breath. 'I'd love to go on a date with you, Aiden.'

'Cool. I'll pick you up about seven? Where do you live?'

'How 'bout I meet you somewhere? A nice bar, maybe?'

So she didn't want him to know where she lived? No problem. When you had a three-dates rule, it was probably better not to intrude too far on anyone's personal space. Aiden named a trendy bar that he knew wasn't too far from the Victoria, guessing that Sophia probably lived reasonably close to where she worked.

'I know it.' She nodded. 'I'll meet you there at seven.'

At six-thirty p.m. Sophia was staring at the pile of clothes on her bed.

It might be a cliché but she really *didn't* have anything to wear. Nothing that would project the image she wanted anyway, which was one of a confident young woman who wasn't the least bit desperate. Who was happy to go out and have a bit of fun but wasn't looking for anything remotely serious.

Something frilly? She didn't possess frills. Something low-cut that would show a bit of cleavage? No. That might send entirely the wrong message about the kind of fun she was after.

What *was* she after? And why was she feeling so ridiculously nervous?

'Oh, for heaven's sake.' Wearing only her jeans and bra, Sophia went to rummage in her handbag for her phone. She would text Aiden and tell him she couldn't make it after all. One of her patients had gone into early labour? Yeah…perfect excuse.

And she wasn't really breaking her promise, was she? She had said yes. She just wasn't going to follow through and actually *go* on the date.

A small problem became apparent the moment she picked up her phone. She didn't have Aiden's phone number, did she?

She had absolutely no way of contacting him unless she fronted up at the bar in…oh, help…twenty minutes.

But there was a message on *her* phone. For a hopeful heartbeat Sophia thought that Aiden might have sent her a message to cancel the date.

No such luck. He didn't have her number either, did he?

The message was from Emily. 'I hear you said yes,' it said. 'You go, girl. And have fun.'

So Flick had spread the word. Her friends would demand details and she was a hopeless liar. Her voice always got sort of tight and high. She'd never be able to make something up and sound convincing.

Gritting her teeth, Sophia marched back into her bedroom. She jammed her feet into knee-high boots, threw on a camisole top and covered it with a velvet jacket. Pulling the band from her hair, she raked her fingers through the shoulder-length waves and spent no more than thirty seconds in front of the mirror, putting on a slick of lipstick.

Then she grabbed her bag and slammed the door of the cottage behind her. She had less than ten minutes to get to the bar but having to rush was probably a good thing. It would give her less time for her stupid nerves to grow wings.

There was no sign of Sophia.

Aiden ordered a beer and stayed at the bar, an elbow propped and his posture relaxed enough to suggest he was thoroughly enjoying his view of the women coming in through the doors. Enjoying the appreciative looks he got in return even more.

Normally, he would be doing exactly that.

So why did he feel…good grief…*nervous*?

A little out of control even?

Maybe it was because he was meeting Sophia here, instead of having picked her up first. What if she didn't show up?

Hey…no problem. There were plenty of very attractive women who seemed to be here unaccompanied by any male friends.

But he hadn't come here to randomly score. He'd come here because he really wanted to spend some time with Sophia.

And maybe the strength of that want was why he was feeling a bit weird. Why this was assuming an importance that it wasn't allowed to have.

No problem. Aiden took another fortifying swallow of his beer. This was only a number-one date. No big deal. If it continued to feel weird, he could just pull the plug and there wouldn't be a number two.

Suddenly, he saw her. Looking small and a little bit lost as she stood near the door and scanned the crowded bar. And then she spotted him and smiled.

The noise of the people around him and the background music seemed to fade away.

The people themselves seemed to fade away. Until there was only himself.

And Sophia.

How weird was *that*?

CHAPTER FOUR

HE WAS THERE.

He must have spotted her the moment she walked through the door because he was already looking straight at her when Sophia turned her head. She'd been worried she might not even recognise him out of uniform but even in a crowd of people there was no mistaking Aiden Harrison.

Her relieved smile faded as she threaded her way to the bar, however. He hadn't smiled back. He'd looked a bit stunned even… Had he been surprised that she'd actually turned up? Or maybe he was disappointed that she had. There was no shortage of opportunities in a place like this. She could feel the gaze of other girls on her as she made her way towards the gorgeous guy standing alone at the bar. Envious glances.

'Hi…' He was smiling now. 'Can I get you something to drink?'

'A white wine would be lovely, thank you.'

'Do you want to have it here or find a table out in the garden? They have live music here tonight so there won't be any room to move in here soon.'

So she'd end up dancing or squashed against him at the bar? Sophia sucked in a breath. 'The garden sounds great.'

There were rustic tables and wrought-iron chairs, flickering candles and the greenery of a rampant grapevine on an overhead pergola. The last unoccupied table they found in a corner with only two chairs was romantic enough to make Sophia hesitate. This was supposed to be fun. Nothing serious.

Aiden put their drinks down on the table. 'Don't know about you,' he said, 'but I'm *starving*. Fancy some nachos or a big bowl of fries?'

That was the right note to hit. They were here for a drink and something to eat and it just happened to be with company. They'd be able to hear the music out here without being deafened. A fun night out.

'Sure. Nachos are my absolute favourite.'

'Mine, too.'

They grinned at each other. They were on the same page and suddenly everything seemed easy. Over the cheese and bean-laden tortilla chips, the conversation was just as relaxed.

'It must be a great job, being a SPRINT paramedic.'

'Best job in the world. I love having no idea of what's coming next or where I'm going.'

'I love being out of the hospital environment most of the time, too. You get to connect a lot more with patients when you're in their own home. Even more when they've had a home delivery. I feel like part of the family sometimes.'

But Aiden shook his head at that. 'It's the opposite

that appeals to me. I get to ride in, do the exciting stuff and then hand the responsibility on to someone else.'

'Don't you ever follow your patients up and see what happened?'

'I'll talk to the crew that transports them. Or, if I've travelled in with them, I might hang around in the emergency department and see how it's handled from there. Some of the docs are great. If I'm ending a shift, they let me go into Theatre or talk over the results of a CT scan or something. If I can learn something that's going to help me manage better next time, I'm in.'

'You should poke your nose into the MMU some time. You're a bit of a hero up there after that cord prolapse job the other day.'

Aiden shook off the compliment. 'We were lucky.' He raised his eyebrows. 'How's that baby doing? Do you know?'

Sophia laughed. 'Of course I know. I'm still doing daily visits. His name is Isaac and he's doing extremely well. Claire and Greg are over the moon.'

'Good to know. Did he get a thorough neurological check?'

It was Sophia's turn to raise her eyebrows. 'Are you kidding? We've got the best doctors there are. He passed every test with flying colours. He might turn out to be a brain surgeon himself one day. Or the prime minister or something. You'll see him on television and think about what might have happened if you hadn't been there the day he was born.'

'I might have a bit of trouble recognising him.' But Aiden was smiling and Sophia felt...relieved? He did have a connection with his patients that wasn't purely technical. Maybe he didn't want to revel in that connection like she did but it was there—whether he wanted it to be or not.

And the idea of him being a maverick medic who rode around the city saving lives and touching those lives only briefly added to his attraction, didn't it? Gave him a kind of superhero edge?

Oh, yeah…the attraction was growing for sure and it didn't seem to be one-sided. Eye contact was becoming more frequent and held for a heartbeat longer. Their fingers brushed as they shared the platter of food. The butterflies in Sophia's gut danced up a storm as she wondered if he would kiss her at the end of this date.

But then what?

She could hear an echo of Em's voice in the back of her mind. *You don't have to marry the guy. You don't even have to tell him anything. Just have fun…*

Maybe the connection was even stronger than it felt. She could see a flicker in Aiden's eyes that had nothing to do with the candles around them.

'I should warn you,' he said, 'that I'm not looking for anything serious.'

Good grief…was that shaft of sensation disappointment? Or shame even? Was there something about her that wasn't attractive enough to warrant any kind of emotional investment?

His smile suggested otherwise. So did the way his hand covered hers, touching her skin with the lightness of a feather—the fingers moving just enough to sound a deliciously seductive note.

'It's not that you're not absolutely gorgeous,' he murmured. 'But I have rules. One rule, anyway.'

'Oh?' This was confusing. His words were warning her off but his eyes and his touch were inviting her closer. Much closer.

'A three-dates rule.'

'A...*what*?'

'Three dates. I've discovered that's the perfect number.'

'Perfect for what?'

'To get to know someone. To have fun but not to let anything get out of hand. You know...to get...*serious*.'

He made the word sound like some kind of notifiable disease. Sophia's head was spinning. Wasn't this exactly what she was looking for? Fun with a gorgeous guy but within limits. Limits that would mean there was no need to tell him anything about herself that could impinge on the fun. She could pretend there was nothing wrong with her. That she was as desirable as any other young woman who was out there dating. That it was only because of 'the rule' that it wouldn't go any further.

'I love it,' she whispered with a smile.

'Really?' Aiden's eyebrows shot up. His fingers tightened over her hand.

'Really.' Sophia nodded. 'I'm not looking for anything serious either. Three dates sounds like exactly the rule that's been missing from *my* life.'

'Wow...' Aiden's gaze was frankly admiring. 'You're even more amazing than I thought.' He stood up, still holding Sophia's hand, so that she was drawn to her feet as well. 'You do realise that means we'll have to make the most of each and every date, don't you?'

The butterflies had congregated into a cluster that throbbed somewhere deep in Sophia's belly like a drumbeat. She couldn't look away from Aiden's gaze, even when he dropped her hand and raised his to touch her face. A finger on her temple that traced a gentle line around her eye, across her cheek and down to the corner of her mouth. Her lips parted in astonishment at the wave of sensation the touch was creating and it was then that Aiden dipped his head and kissed her.

Right there—in a noisy, crowded garden of a trendy bar. Their corner was secluded enough but it was a long way from being private. Not that the kiss got out of hand or anything. The control of those soft, questioning lips on hers suggested that Aiden was a very experienced kisser. The teasing touch of his tongue hinted at where this kiss could go at any moment. Oh, yeah…it ended far sooner than Sophia would have chosen.

What now?

Would Aiden take her home to his place? Should she suggest that he came to hers?

On a *first* date?

The idea was shocking. Okay, she was doing this to have fun but jumping into bed with someone this fast made it feel wrong. But they only had three dates to play with, didn't they? Did 'making the most of them' imply that they shouldn't waste any time?

But Aiden was smiling again and Sophia had the feeling that he knew the argument she was having with herself.

'Let's plan date number two,' he said. 'And give ourselves something to look forward to.'

'So…how was it, then?'

'What?'

'Date *numero uno* with the cute midwife?'

Aiden shrugged as he looked away from his brother to stare over the veranda railings into the garden of the old house. He upended his bottle to catch a mouthful of his beer. 'Not bad.'

'Score?'

Aiden frowned. Nate loved to hear about his love life as much as his job and he'd always been happy to share the details. He couldn't remember who had come up with the scoring system but it had become a tradition. This was the first time it had occurred to Aiden how degrading it would seem if the women he dated ever knew about it.

Not that he would ever tell them, of course.

But he'd never told any women about the three-dates rule until now, had he? It was a secret, known only to himself and Nate. The astonishment factor of actually sharing the secret with a woman he was on a date with was only surpassed by the totally unexpected way Sophia had embraced the idea.

What was with that? Was there something about him that didn't make him attractive longer term?

The thought shouldn't be disturbing but it was. So was the niggle of doubt that he'd come right out and put a limit on how much time he was going to have with the gorgeous Sophia. How the stupidity of that move had been plaguing him ever since he'd left her at the end of their date with no more than another kiss.

She was…

'That good, huh?' He could hear the grin in Nate's voice. 'Off the scale, was she?'

Aiden merely grunted.

She was perfect, that's what she was. Absolutely gorgeous. Smart. So easy to talk to. And that all too brief taste of her lips…

Man… The way she'd felt in his arms. The way she'd responded to his kisses. He had a fair idea of exactly where their second date was going to end up and he couldn't wait. How, in fact, would he be able to enjoy the day on the beach they now had planned for when their next days off coincided? He would be hanging out to get her somewhere a lot more private. Somewhere they could *really* get to know each other.

But that would mean there was only one date left. And then what?

This had never bothered him before. He'd never even thought ahead like this before.

'Could be the one, then.' Nate was nodding. 'A four-dates woman.'

'No way.'

'Why not?'

'Because I'm not getting into anything serious, that's why.'

'Why not?'

This was getting annoying. Aiden had stopped by after work for his usual visit. He just wanted a quiet beer with his brother, not some kind of interrogation.

'You know why. I'm not interested in getting married or having kids.'

'Doesn't mean you can't have a long-term relationship. Not every woman out there is hanging out to walk down the aisle in a meringue dress or stockpile nappies.'

'They all get to that point at some stage. I know that from painful experience. And the longer it goes on for, the harder it is when you break it off. I'm not going to be responsible for someone else's happiness.'

'Why not?' There was an edge to Nate's voice he hadn't heard before. 'Because you feel you have to be responsible for mine?'

'Whoa…where did that come from?' Aiden glanced over his shoulder as he broke the moment of startled silence. Wasn't it about time for the boys to all roll their chairs into the dining room for their evening meal? Where was everybody else, anyway? In the lounge, watching reruns of Murderball games? If he stepped away from the corner he could probably see through the window and, if there was a game on, he could distract Nate. He had a feeling that he wasn't going to like whatever Nathan was about to unbottle.

'You do, though, don't you?' Nathan swivelled his wheelchair with practised ease and trapped Aiden so that it would look like a deliberate evasion if he tried to step past him. 'You feel responsible for what happened to me and so you think you have to *be* responsible for me for the rest of your life.'

Of course he felt responsible for what had happened. It had been his fault.

Nate was staring at him. He shook his head. 'It wasn't your fault.'

Aiden stared back at him. 'You were too young to remember what it was like. If I hadn't lost my rag and yelled back at Dad, he'd never have come after me. He'd never have knocked you down the stairs and broken your neck.'

The horror of that day as a sixteen-year-old whose life had changed for ever in a heartbeat had never gone. Crouched over the crumpled form of his ten-year-old brother at the bottom of the stairs, his hands had been shaking as he'd tried to hold his phone still enough to call for an ambulance. To stop Nathan moving, even as they'd both heard the dreadful sound of the gunshot that had come from an upstairs room.

Maybe the worst horror had been the relief of knowing that he didn't have to protect Nathan from their father's tyranny any more—the twisted bitterness that had come from blaming an innocent baby for his wife's death.

He'd held Nathan's head still, knowing that moving him could make it worse. And he'd talked to him as he'd crouched there, waiting for help to arrive.

'*I'm here*,' he'd said, over and over again. '*I'll look after you. I'll always look after you.*'

'I remember a lot more than you give me credit for. And you know what? I've had enough of this.'

Nate sounded angry. His clever, brave, determined kid brother was letting his irrepressible good humour go for once. He was angry with him.

Finally. There was a relief to be found in that. He

deserved the anger. He could handle it. He was the one who could still walk. The one who had a job he loved. Who could get out there and kiss gorgeous women. Nate was allowed to be angry about what had happened in his life. The opportunities he would never have.

'It was Dad who pushed me down the stairs. Not you. It's ancient history. Get over it, Aiden. *I* have.'

'How can you say that?' Aiden was shocked. 'You have to live with that accident for the rest of your life. It should never have happened.'

'Oh, get off the guilt train,' Nate snapped. 'Yeah…I have to live with it for the rest of my life. *Me.* And you don't get to feel so guilty about it that you stuff up your own life. I'm not having that put on me, thanks.'

'I'm not—'

'Yeah, you are. You baby me. You're always here, checking up on me. Trying to make life better for me, but guess what? I like my life. I don't need this.'

Aiden stared at his brother. He'd thought he could handle the anger but that was when he'd thought it was going to be about the accident that had wrecked a young life—not about him honouring a vow to look after the only person who'd ever been so important to him.

This hurt, dammit. Enough to make him feel angry right back at Nate.

'I've only ever done what I could to help. You were ten years old.'

'And you're still treating me like I'm ten years old. I'm twenty-four, man. I'm grown up. I've got a *girlfriend.*'

How on earth had this all come out after sharing the news that he'd gone on a date with the cute midwife?

'And there's no way I'm going to play by your stupid three-dates rule.'

So that was it.

'You do know it's stupid, don't you?'

'Works for me.' Aiden's voice was tight. At least, it had.

'I'm going to live by myself one of these days,' Nate continued fiercely. 'I'm going to try out for the Murder-ball team and if I get in I'll give it everything I've got. I'm going to make the best of my life. I don't want to end up like you.'

'What's that supposed to mean?'

'Shut off. Scared of losing control.'

'People get hurt if you lose control.' Surely Nate knew that better than anyone after what had happened.

'So? That's life.' Nate shook his head. 'Get over it and start having some fun. Like me.' The crooked smile was a plea for understanding. Forgiveness, too, maybe, for saying some hard stuff?

The lump in his throat made it hard to suck in a breath. Okay, he was hurt but, man, his little brother had courage, didn't he? He was so proud of him.

A window got pushed up along the veranda and a dark, spiky head emerged. 'You coming in for dinner, Nate?'

'Sure.'

'You want to stay, Aiden? There's plenty.'

'Nah…I'm good.' He needed some time to think about what had just happened. That his brother had grown up and just let him know in no uncertain terms? Or that he thought he had, anyway. He still needed his big brother, even if he didn't think he did. More than ever, in fact, as he strived for independence. Did he think he could do that without a lot of help? Even if he wasn't welcome, there was no way Aiden could back away from his responsibilities here. He might just have to be a bit cleverer in how he looked after Nate.

'Hey…' Nathan stopped the movement of his chair. He looked back at his brother. He looked a lot younger all of a sudden. Worried. Aiden could see him swallow hard. 'We okay?'

If he'd needed any evidence that his brother still needed him, it was right there in how vulnerable Nate looked right now. Aiden didn't hesitate. 'Sure.'

But it was an awkward moment that could go either way.

Aiden did his best to smile. 'You were right, man. She was off the scale.'

Nate's grin tugged at his heart. 'So she gets a second date, at least?'

'Already sorted. We're going to the beach.'

'Maybe me and Sam can come, too.'

Aiden snorted. 'No way. I only invited Sophia.'

CHAPTER FIVE

MELBOURNE IS FAMED for the ability to produce four seasons in one day with its fickle weather. It was also capable of pulling something astonishing out of its meteorological hat—like a blazingly hot day in April when it could just as easily have been more like winter than summer.

How lucky was it that it was like this for date number two when they had agreed that the beach was a good place to go? Sophia stood on the pavement outside the picket fence of her cottage at the appointed time. She was wearing her bikini as underwear beneath her jeans and shirt and she carried a beach towel in her bag—just in case it was warm enough to swim. The thick jacket she had on over her shirt earned her a few curious looks from passers-by but she was just following the instructions that had come with the plan.

Had her choice regarding the mode of transport been a mistake?

'The van's old and clunky,' Aiden had told her as he walked her home from the bar and they'd planned this date. 'But it does have walls. If you're brave, you can come on the back of my bike.'

'You get to use your work bike at home?'

'No. I've got one of my own. A Ducati. A red one.'

'Red, huh? What colour is the van?'

'White. Boring, boring white.' He wanted her to choose the bike. She wanted to see the approval in his eyes when she made the right choice.

'Then it's no contest, is it? I pick red.'

But her stomach did an odd little flip as she saw the sun glinting on the red metal of the huge bike as it rolled to a halt in front of her.

Or was it Aiden's grin as he lifted the visor of his helmet that was doing it?

He unclipped a second helmet and held it out to her. 'Are you ready?'

Sophia had to suck in a big breath. *Was* she ready? This was about way more than a long bike ride, wasn't it?

Those unusual light brown eyes were doing that dancing thing again. A look that implied mischief. *Fun...*

She reached for the helmet as she nodded and returned the grin. 'I'm ready.'

It was a long ride. Leaving the outskirts of Melbourne behind, they took to the open road, heading south. They bypassed the large town of Geelong and sped towards the point where the harbour met the open sea—the quaint seaside village of Queenscliff.

'It's gorgeous,' Sophia exclaimed as they parked the bike and took off on foot to explore. 'Look at the turrets on that house!'

'We're lucky it's not a weekend. With weather like this, it gets really crowded.'

'You've been here before?'

'It's a great destination when I want to get out on the road and blow a few cobwebs away.'

'It certainly does that.' Sophia made a face as she threaded her fingers into the end of her hair where the waves brushed her shoulders. 'I should have tied this up. I might never get the knots out. I didn't even think to bring a brush. It probably looks like a rat's nest.'

Aiden stopped walking. They were outside the door of a bakery and a woman came out, laden with paper bags. She had to walk around them but Aiden didn't seem to notice because he was only looking at Sophia. He caught her hand and pulled her fingers out of her hair. Then he flattened her hand gently against her head with his still on top of it.

'Forget about it,' he told her. 'You look gorgeous.'

And then he bent his head and kissed her. Right there on the footpath, half blocking the door to the bakery.

Sophia had relived the softness of that first kiss in a bar a hundred times by now. Had conjured up the tingle of anticipation and the curl of desire so many times that she'd been sure she had magnified it out of all connection with reality.

Turned out she hadn't.

This was even better. It still had the restraint that being in a public place required but there was a new depth to it. A familiarity. The knowledge that they both wanted this and it was going to go somewhere else. Very soon.

'*Excuse* me.' The voice sounded annoyed. Breaking apart, they could see why. A young woman with a twin pushchair had no chance of getting past them to the door.

Aiden smiled at the mother as he murmured an apology. He held the door open for her but it was obvious she had already forgiven him.

'No worries,' she said, smiling up at him. 'You have a great day.'

'Oh…' Aiden's glance went over the top of her head, straight to Sophia's. 'I already am.'

The woman turned her head and her smile widened. Her gaze told Sophia exactly how lucky she was. Then she winked and disappeared into the shop. The smell of something hot and delicious wafted out as the door swung shut.

'Hungry?'

'Starving.' Sophia took a step towards the door but Aiden shook his head.

'Bit crowded in there. I've got a better idea.'

He took her across the road to the fish-and-chip shop. A short time later, they were walking down the hill and away from the shops. Aiden held the big white paper parcel in one hand and Sophia's hand in the other. He led her across the railway lines and onto a track that took them to a grassy spot with a view through the trees to the water. The meal was still hot and absolutely delicious. A woman walked past on the track with a dog and then a whole family with a toddler in a pushchair and a small child on a bike, but nobody came to share their patch of grass or even looked their way. It felt as if they were almost invisible.

'This is perfect.' Sophia licked salt off her fingers as she looked away from the pelicans and swans gliding peacefully on water still enough to mimic glass.

'Mmm. I find it pays to put some effort into planning date number two.' Aiden turned away from the view with a smile.

'One of the rules? I'll—um—have to remember that.'

Not that she was likely to remember anything other than the look in Aiden's eyes that she could already recognise as the intention to kiss her. She barely even noticed the colourful cloud of parakeets landing on the fig tree that was shading them as Aiden leaned towards her.

The cloak of invisibility was still around them but Sophia would have forgotten about the rest of the world anyway as soon as Aiden's lips touched hers. Or maybe it was the moment she felt things change as the intensity kicked up several notches. Aiden's hand cradled her head as he pushed her back to lie on the grass. Their tongues danced, the pang of lingering salt a delicious foil to the sweetness of escalating desire. She felt the touch of Aiden's fingers beneath the hem of her shirt, a trail of fire on the delicate skin of her belly, and the heat when it reached her breast was enough to make her gasp into his mouth.

He pulled away with a groan.

'You make me forget where I am,' he murmured.

'You're on date number two,' Sophia whispered back. 'I think it's okay to get distracted. Isn't it?' she added, feeling her eyes widen.

'Yes, but there's a time and place for everything. And

this probably isn't the place for what I'm thinking about right now.'

Sophia's inward breath was audibly ragged as she sat up. She'd been thinking along similar lines and she certainly hadn't wanted him to stop. Anybody could have seen them. Like that woman with her dog, who was coming down the track towards them again, presumably on the homeward stretch of their walk. The dog—a very cute miniature schnauzer—ran towards them and the woman called it back with an apologetic smile.

'I doubt there's enough time anyway.' There was a wicked edge to Aiden's smile as the woman disappeared along the track. 'It'll get cold around here when the sun goes down.'

He wanted a whole night with her? The thought made Sophia's toes curl. But this was a daytime date.

Oh, help… What if there was a rule about not going any further until date number three? What if this three-dates business was just a build-up for a one-night stand?

Hard not to believe that it would be worth waiting for, if that was the case.

'We have options,' Aiden added. 'You get to choose.'

'Oh?' Maybe one of those options included going somewhere really private. Sophia grinned. 'Fire away. I like choosing.'

'Option one: we could take the ferry over to Sorrento to get dessert. There's a shop there that has the best vanilla slices in the world and we might get to see some dolphins on the way.'

Sophia nodded thoughtfully. He really had planned

this date carefully. Or—the thought sent a chill down her spine—was this a standard number-two date?

'Option two is a swim. The water is probably arctic but it's warm enough to dry off on the beach and, by then, it'll be about time to head home.'

Home? To his place? After getting almost naked and lying in the sun for a while? It wasn't hard to make a choice.

'It would be a shame to come to the seaside and not have a swim.'

'I knew you were brave.' The kiss was swift but sweet. 'Let's go.'

The walk made the day seem even warmer and by the time they went down the sandy stairs to the endless white beach with a misty lighthouse far away, they were more than ready to pull off their clothes and brave the curl of the surf. The beach was a popular place to be but most people were sunbathing. Some sat in beach chairs, reading, and others were having picnics or playing ball games. There were children paddling and building sand-castles but there were very few people swimming.

And no wonder. The first splash of water was cold enough to make Sophia shriek but Aiden simply laughed and dived through the next wave. She jumped up and down as she went further out, getting more of her body wet each time, and suddenly it wasn't so bad. And then Aiden surfaced right beside her and his smile made her aware of the silky caress of the sea water over her entire body.

'This is gorgeous,' she called over the sound of the waves. 'I love it.'

'I knew you would,' he called back. 'You're my kind of girl.'

They couldn't stay in the water for long and they were both shivering as they towelled themselves dry but then they lay on their towels on the soft sand and there was enough warmth in the sun for the chill to ebb slowly away.

For the longest time, they lay there, absorbing the warmth. Side by side on their backs, saying nothing. And then Sophia felt the brush of Aiden's fingers and his hand curl itself around hers.

'I really like you, Sophia.'

'I really like you, too, Aiden.' Sophia's eyes were still closed and her smile grew slowly. She couldn't remember the last time she'd felt this happy. Even the noises around them—the roll of the waves and the shouting of children enjoying themselves—only added to this feeling of contentment. 'I think this has been the best second date I've ever been on.'

Aiden tightened his grip on Sophia's hand. This was by far the best second date he'd ever been on as well. The only thing wrong with it was that it would have to end soon. They were almost dry and they needed to get dressed again because the heat of the day would start dropping rapidly before long. They had a long ride to get back to the city as well and by then it would be evening. They both had an early start for work tomorrow but did that really mean that it had to be over? Sophia believed that he'd planned this whole date after they'd agreed to go to a beach. She didn't need to know that he'd kept his options open and hadn't planned it to continue on into the evening, did she?

'It's not over yet.'

He heard the words come out of his mouth and they felt…right. Of course it couldn't be over yet.

'Oh? What else is in the plan?'

He could hear the smile in Sophia's voice. And something more. A willingness to go along with whatever he wanted?

He wanted to take Sophia home. To his bed. Okay, they both needed to get to work early but there were a lot of hours between now and then. Why shouldn't they make the most of every single one of them?

'Well, I was thinking…' Aiden propped himself up on one elbow. Maybe he didn't need to say anything here. He could just kiss her again. And then he could look into her eyes and he'd know whether she was happy with the new plan.

He let his mouth hover over hers for a deliciously long moment. Feeling the tingle of their lips not quite touching. Knowing just how much better it was going to get in a nanosecond.

And then he heard it. Faintly at first but getting steadily louder.

Sophia's lips moved under his. Tickling. 'What *is* that?'

'My phone.' He didn't want to answer it. Dammit… all he wanted to do was kiss Sophia but her lips were moving again. Smiling?

'It's a *siren*?'

'Yeah, I know. Cheesy. My kid brother chose it for me.'

And it could be that kid brother who was calling right now. Highly likely to be, seeing as they hadn't spoken yet today. In fact, they hadn't spoken very often for a few days now. Ever since that tense conversation about Aiden smothering Nate because of his misplaced guilt.

He still wanted to kiss Sophia more than answer it but something else was making his skin prickle and he recognised that sensation.

Guilt. He barely knew this woman and suddenly she was more important than his brother? What was he thinking?

'I'd better get that. Sorry.'

'No problem.'

A soft breeze had sprung up, making it colder. Or maybe he just had more skin exposed as he sat up and rummaged in his coat pocket for his phone. Sure enough, the caller ID said 'Nate'. Aiden swiped the screen.

'Hey… What's up?'

'Guess.'

'I can't. You'll have to tell me.'

'I went for the team trials today.'

'Yeah? How'd that go?'

'I got in, man. I'm in the team.'

'That's…fantastic.' The smile that pulled at his lips was genuine. 'Great news. I reckon it calls for a celebration.'

'Too right. We're having a few beers back at our place. Thought you might want to drop by.'

He was listening to Nate but he was looking at Sophia. She still lay on her back, shading her eyes from the sun with her arm. Her hair was still damp and looked almost black where it lay against the pale skin of her shoulders. He couldn't help his gaze travelling further. Over the rest of that gorgeous, soft-looking skin and the perfect proportions of her small, slim body.

He'd never wanted anybody this much.

He'd have to take a rain-check on that celebratory beer with Nate because otherwise he wouldn't get to take Sophia home and make love to her properly.

Slowly…

Or maybe not so slowly the first time…

His throat suddenly felt dry.

'You still there, man? Where *are* you, anyway?'

Impressions flashed through Aiden's brain with the speed of light. That note in Nate's voice when he'd made that suggestion so casually that he 'might' want to drop by.

Things hadn't been quite right between them since that conversation the other day. And if he didn't join in the celebration of Nate making the Murderball team, it could be interpreted as not being supportive of his brother as he achieved one of his long-held ambitions and that could push them further apart. What then? Would Nate choose not to even tell him when he was moving out of the house to try living independently?

His brother was trying out his wings and surely that meant that now—more than ever—he needed support. Aiden had to be there for him one hundred per cent.

How could he even entertain the idea of letting a woman get between them? It wasn't as if she'd still be in his life in a week or two from now but Nate would be. He would always be in his life and he'd always take priority.

'I'm still here,' he said. 'Bad line. I'm out of the city but I'll be back soon.'

'No worries. You went for a ride? You on a date or something?'

'Yeah…Queenscliff.'

'Oh…of course. This is your number two with Sophia. Hey…hope I'm not interrupting anything.' His laugh made a lie of his words but didn't quite ring true for some reason.

'Not at all. Just went for swim, would you believe?'

'Well, don't hurry back, man. Enjoy yourself. Catch you soon.'

The beeping signalled that Nate had hung up. The note of disappointment in his words was still there, though. And the odd edge to the laughter as he'd tried to make light of things.

Aiden dragged his eyes away from Sophia. Closed them, in fact.

'Not a problem,' he heard himself saying into the silence of a dead line. At least he could sound reluctant now. As though there was something he really had to do even though he didn't want to. 'I'll get there as soon as I can.'

Sophia was already pulling her clothes on by the time he shoved his phone back into his pocket.

'Sorry about that.'

'It's not a problem.' He could hear the note of determined cheerfulness in her voice as she echoed his own words. 'We've had a lovely day. If there's somewhere else you need to be now, it's okay. I understand.'

She might understand but he could see the disappointment in her eyes and he felt like a jerk. He could say it wasn't that important and the only place he needed to be for now was with her.

But Nate was disappointed too. He'd have that in the back of his mind all evening if he stayed with Sophia.

The feeling of being torn was unpleasant. The desire to tell Sophia he only wanted to be with her was strong enough to ring warning bells.

It wasn't supposed to feel like this. It was supposed to be fun.

For both of them.

And it wasn't any more, was it? How could being between a rock and a hard place ever be considered fun?

He pulled his clothes on, feeling the added unpleasantness of the sand in his shoes. He watched Sophia roll up her damp towel and shove it in her beach bag.

'You dry enough? It'll be cold on the bike, otherwise.'

'I'm fine. I've got my coat.'

The coat wasn't enough to make her feel fine.

Not at all.

Maybe it would have helped if they'd been able to talk but there was no way they could do that on a bike. Sophia held onto Aiden's waist and kept her face hidden against his back. Damp tendrils of hair still flicked her face and her skin was cold enough to make them sting.

How had that happened?

One minute she'd been feeling more blissful than she could remember ever feeling and then it had all gone wrong, the atmosphere lost thanks to the intrusion of a phone call. He'd just been about to kiss her. To tell her the plans that meant the date wasn't over yet.

Why hadn't he just ignored the call? Why did he have a stupid siren call tone that made it impossible for anyone to ignore? Just as impossible as it was not to think it was probably another woman who'd been calling him. Was he already lining up the next contender in his three-dates game?

What was so fantastic about the news he'd received? Was whoever she was available? *Tonight?*

It wasn't fair. Their first date hadn't really counted and date number two had just been sabotaged.

So much for getting out there and having some fun. This wasn't fun at all any more.

Did she even want a third—and last—date?

There was plenty of time on that long, cold ride to turn that question over in her head. As she made her stiff limbs co-operate in climbing off the big, red bike in front of her house and her fingers work well enough to undo her helmet and hand it back, Sophia was sure that this was goodbye and she had decided that she was quite happy about that.

She was, in fact, more angry than disappointed now.

But then Aiden caught her gaze and held it.

'I'm really sorry about this,' he said. 'If I could get out of it, I would.'

There was something in his gaze that told her he was being absolutely sincere. That he wanted to be with her—maybe even more than she'd wanted him to be. And that it *was* something really important that was dragging him away.

She wanted to tell him that it didn't matter. That they still had one date left so everything would be okay. That it was no big deal.

But the words wouldn't come out. She managed half a smile. A shrug that said, Yeah, it sucks but that's life, isn't it?

And then she turned away and went into her house without a backward glance, leaning her forehead against the closed door until she heard the sound of a motorbike's engine being gunned and then fading into silence.

'What are you doing here?'

Aiden held up the six-pack of beer. 'I heard there was a bit of a celebration going on.'

Nate had been the one who'd come to open the door when Aiden had rung the bell. The wide hallway of the old house was empty behind him.

'You ditched your date to come *here*?'

Aiden's shrug said that it was no big deal but Nate shook his head and his huff of sound was disgusted. 'Man, you're an idiot. How d'you think that made Sophia feel?'

The cardboard handle of the beer pack was cutting into Aiden's hand. He had been an idiot. He'd made Sophia feel bad only to find he wasn't welcome here.

Something was going wrong in his life right now. The wheels were still turning but it felt like they weren't quite on the tracks and he couldn't, for the life of him, figure out why. He looked away from Nate.

'I thought this was more important.' He cleared his throat. 'And...I wanted to...I dunno...put things right,

I guess. Wouldn't want you to think I don't support you in whatever you want to do.'

Nate gave an audible snort this time. 'It's only selection. Miss my first game next week and you'll definitely be in trouble.'

The lightness in his tone didn't match the expression on his face when Aiden turned back. Nate understood what he'd been too clumsy to articulate well and held up his hand, the fingers curled into a fist. 'There's nothing to put right, man. We're brothers. Family.'

Aiden bumped the fist with his own. Nate shook his head but he was grinning as he swivelled the chair on the polished floor. 'Seeing as you're here, you might as well come in for a beer. Hey, what do you call a quadriplegic in a pile of leaves?'

There was relief to be found as he followed Nate towards the lounge. Enough to stop the automatic protest at a joke that would seem so distasteful to people outside this community.

'I dunno. What?'

'Russell.'

There was even more relief in the shared laughter but it still wasn't quite enough to put the wheels completely back on track. Nate had said there was nothing to put right but that wasn't entirely true, was it?

Things had gone unexpectedly wrong with someone else as well. A woman he'd had no desire at all to hurt. Quite the opposite, in fact.

How on earth was he going to put that right?

CHAPTER SIX

'YOU OKAY?'

'A bit nervous, I think. I watched a Caesarean before but I've never been actually involved.'

'I won't ask you to do anything you're not ready to cope with, don't worry.'

Flick nodded, pulling her theatre cap over her dark blonde hair. She looked a bit pale, Sophia thought, which was probably nerves on top of the weariness of a long day.

She was feeling weary herself. It didn't help that she'd been feeling as flat as a pancake ever since that date with Aiden had ended on such an unsatisfactory note.

She hadn't heard from him since and the mix of disappointment and—it had to be admitted—frustration had made her wonder if the downside of dating outweighed any of the potential benefits.

She'd brushed off Flick's friendly query about how the date had gone and she'd tried really hard to focus on her work and let the satisfaction her job always gave her chase the blues away, but that hadn't worked very well today either. Not when they were now in a situation none of them had expected—or wanted—to be in.

They should be heading home by now, after the home birth of their patient Kim's second baby, but things hadn't gone according to plan and, after transferring Kim to the MMU hours ago, a Caesarean section had been deemed the best option for an exhausted mother and a now distressed baby.

Kim and her husband, Peter, were in the theatre's anteroom under the care of an anaesthetist as she received an epidural.

'Put some theatre booties on over your shoes.' Sophia pulled the disposable covers from the dispenser on the wall of the changing room. 'And here's a mask.'

'Do we have to scrub in as well?'

'No. We don't go anywhere near the operating site. Our role is to support Kim in getting the best birth experience she can under the circumstances.'

'Like making sure she gets the skin-to-skin contact?'

'Exactly. But only if the baby's well enough, of course. We have to be prepared, though. What's the most important thing to make sure we've sorted?'

'That her gown can be moved without disturbing the theatre drapes?'

'Good.' Sophia smiled at her student. 'Now, let's get moving. We've got a few things to organise. I'm going to liaise with the ward and check that a midwife is available to take transfer of care in the recovery room and I want you to ring the lab and order a bucket of iced water.'

'For the cord blood gas samples?'

'You're onto it. We've also got to check that both the

transport cot and the resuscitation cot are turned on and I want to make sure you know where all the equipment is. Follow me.'

There was a hum of activity in Theatre as the staff prepared for the surgery.

'We'll move the resuscitation cot over to here,' Sophia decided.

'Why?'

'Hopefully, it's not going to be needed, but if it is, we want a line of direct vision for both the parents so they can maintain visual contact with their baby at all times.'

Kim was wheeled in moments later. Lights were shifted and positioned and monitoring equipment attached. An ECG trace blipped into action on an overhead screen and numbers flashed and changed as they displayed heart rate, blood pressure and blood oxygen levels. Sophia showed Peter where he was allowed to stand, checked the function of the foetal monitor and then smiled at Kim.

'All good?'

'I'm scared.'

'I know.' Sophia squeezed her patient's hand, careful not to dislodge the IV line. 'You've got a fantastic team who are here to look after you and you'll be amazed how fast it goes.'

'I'm not sure any more…about…you know…'

'Watching baby come out?' Sophia glanced at the drape screen the theatre nurses were putting up at chest level. The plan had been to lower the screen after the incision to the uterus had been made but another glance showed how pale Peter was looking. A definite contender for fainting.

'You don't have to see that bit,' she told Kim. 'We can still put baby straight onto your chest.' Her gaze caught Flick's. 'Let's put a chair in for Peter. That way he can hold Kim's hand and he doesn't have to see anything he doesn't want to either.'

The surgeon and her registrar came into Theatre and, for a while at least, Sophia could totally forget about her personal life as she got caught up in one of the more dramatic ways to bring a new life into the world.

She made sure Flick could stand close enough to see what was happening as the surgeon and her registrar stood on either side of Kim's swollen abdomen. The only sounds were the beeping of the monitors and the calm requests for instruments as the initial incision was made and then the tissues quickly dissected with gloved fingers in use more often than a scalpel or scissors.

Sophia was sure that Flick was holding her breath—as she always did—when the careful incision into the uterus was made and they could see the dark whorls of wet hair on the baby's head. Forceps were fitted to lift the head far enough for the surgeon to be able to hold it with her hands and then the baby was eased out, pausing long enough for the registrar to suction the infant's airways.

The baby's eyes were open and an arm waving slowly. Sophia breathed a sigh of relief. It started crying as its legs were lifted clear of the uterus and she heard a gasp that was more like a strangled sob of relief from both Peter and Kim. Flick was focused on the registrar clamping and cutting the cord but then her gaze caught Sophia's and she gave a quick nod. She took the baby from the registrar as Flick helped a nurse to move the screen and she could place the newborn on her mother's chest.

The longest part of the surgery came now, with the precise task of repairing all the layers of tissue, but, with the screen back in place, Kim was unaware of what was happening and time ceased to matter as she and Peter touched and marvelled at their new baby.

'Did you note the time and sex of the baby?'

Flick nodded. 'I've got the labels ready for the cord blood gas samples.'

'Good. Now, double-check this with me. We have to make sure that the details on the maternal and neonatal wrist labels match.'

Thirty minutes later, Kim was ready to be transferred to a ward bed and taken into Recovery. The paediatrician had checked their daughter and she was wrapped and warm. Sophia put the small bundle into Peter's arms to be carried into Recovery. The transfer of care to the ward midwife would happen there but Sophia wasn't ready to leave yet. This was her favourite time after the tension of a Caesarean, to help with the first breastfeed and watch the bonding happening between the baby and her parents. Kim's mother was waiting nearby, too, with their three-year-old son, who would be able to come and meet his new sister before they got transferred to the ward.

'That was amazing,' Flick said quietly, when they were finally heading home. 'But I am *so* tired.' She stepped into the lift and leaned against the wall.

'Me too. This is when you really feel it, when the excitement's all over.' Sophia pushed the button to take them to the ground floor. It wasn't just physical weariness either. With the prospect of heading home alone as soon as she stepped out of the Victoria's front doors, she knew that she would end up feeling flatter than ever. 'The café will still be open. Let's go and get a coffee.'

Flick groaned. 'Oh, no…not coffee. Even the thought of it makes me feel ill.'

'Really?' Sophia's head swivelled to take a closer look at her student. 'That's not like you.' She noted the pale skin and dark circles under Flick's eyes. Something clicked into place. 'Wait…you're not pregnant, are you?'

'I think it's just something I ate.'

The lift stopped with a jerk as she spoke and then the doors slid open but was that enough to explain the way Flick was avoiding her gaze?

'I've got to go. See you tomorrow, Soph.'

'Hang on…' She'd put her foot in it, even making the suggestion, hadn't she? It certainly hadn't been her intention to upset her student. 'Hey…I'm sorry, Flick. I didn't—'

Flick raised her hand, without turning. 'It's okay. I'm fine. Really.'

'Sophia?'

The voice from behind made her spin round without thinking. It was so unexpected. So…welcome?

'Aiden… What are you doing here?'

No. It wasn't welcome. She didn't want to talk to him right now. She needed to talk to Flick. Or maybe Flick needed to talk to *her*. Turning her head again, just as quickly, she could see Flick disappearing towards the front doors. She could hardly run away from Aiden.

She didn't want to talk to him. He'd interrupted a conversation she'd been having with her student and she was on the brink of excusing herself and running away.

He didn't want that to happen. Catching sight of her as she'd stepped out of the lift had been like a slap in the face. Enough to bring back the guilt he'd been wrestling with ever since he'd cut their date short to go and see Nathan.

He'd picked up the phone half a dozen times since then, with the intention of trying to contact Sophia, but something had always got in the way. A call to a job made it easy to hang up but it was never enough of an excuse. He'd been…scared? Well, nervous anyway. He hadn't been able to come up with any plausible plan to put things right so he'd known he could well make things worse. And he hadn't wanted to face the potential rejection.

But actually seeing her instead of a faceless phone call brought back all the reasons why he wanted to put things right.

She looked tired. The way she stared after her student had a worried edge to it. And he could sense that her mood was different. More serious. Sad, even? Oh, help…was he flattering himself or could that have something to do with him?

Despite all of that—or maybe because of it—she was still the most gorgeous woman he'd ever met. He wanted to put his arms around her and hold her close. Kiss whatever it was better. But he could only say something and hope that she might choose to stay in his company for just a little longer. Long enough for him to think of something. Some way to put things right.

'I came in to check up on a patient from today,' he heard himself saying. 'Cyclist that got clipped by a tram. I was worried about her.'

'Oh…' A rush of mixed emotions washed through Sophia. The attraction that came from imagining him on the job, weaving through heavy traffic with the lights and siren going on that huge bike. Admiration that came from knowing how calmly he would have taken charge of the emergency. Warmth that came from knowing that he did care about his patients.

And there was more threaded through those feelings. She couldn't pretend that the personal attraction had been quashed by the disappointment of that last date. Maybe the strongest memory right now was the sincerity she'd seen in his eyes when he'd left her on the footpath. She'd been too angry to believe that he wouldn't have been abandoning her unless it had been for something too important to ignore, but that anger had faded into the flatness of the last few days.

She wanted to believe it now.

She wanted…

'Would you like to grab a coffee or something?' Aiden seemed to be watching her carefully, as though he was aware of the struggle she was having, trying to capture a thought that would determine her response to this unexpected meeting.

'I…um…' There was no point looking towards the

main entrance but she turned her head again anyway, despite knowing that Flick was long gone.

'Do you need to catch up with her?'

'No.' Sophia pushed her concern about her student to one side. She would see her soon enough and, if that startling suspicion had any grounds, it would only become more apparent with the passing of time. She sucked in a breath and looked back at Aiden.

'I was planning to get a coffee,' she admitted. 'It's been a long day. We had a case that got complicated and we had to bring her in for a Caesarean. And...' Something she couldn't identify was melting away deep inside her. 'I believe I still owe you a coffee?'

Aiden's smile lit up his face and she saw a flash of what looked like relief in his eyes.

'I believe you do.'

The tension eased as they began walking towards the cafeteria together but now Sophia was aware of how she must look. Her hair had been squashed beneath a cap for too long and she had crumpled scrubs on under her jacket. Any make-up she'd started the day with must have worn off long ago and she was probably tired enough to look years older.

Except that—oddly—she didn't feel that tired any more. And a sideways glance showed that Aiden's uniform was pretty crumpled as well. His boots looked scuffed and he had a big scratch on one hand.

For both of them, their appearance was nothing more than evidence of what they did for a living. A badge of honour even?

Aiden held the door of the cafeteria open for Sophia.

The relief he'd felt when she'd agreed to have a coffee with him should have been a warning but he was going to ignore it. So what if it felt like a major victory? That the wheels were back on exactly the right tracks? It shouldn't feel this good, of course. Not when all he might be winning was the chance for a third—and final—date.

But he was feeling better than he had for days so why shouldn't he make the most of it? Sophia looked happier too. She was smiling as they headed for the machine that provided coffee that was dreadful but free. She put a polystyrene cup under the dispenser.

'What can I get you?' she asked. 'Cappuccino? A latte?'

'I think a long black might be the safest choice.'

'Done.' With the button pushed the machine whirred into life. 'And I think I might push the boat out and have a hot chocolate.'

There would be a rush before too long, when staff on an early dinner break came in, but, for now, the cafeteria was almost completely deserted. They found a table in the corner and sat down. Sophia was at right angles to Aiden. Their knees bumped under the table and the eye contact they made was instantaneous. And intense enough to make her heart skip a beat.

'This doesn't count as a date,' she murmured.

'Of course not.' Aiden nodded, his face serious. 'It wasn't planned so how could it be?'

'Mmm.'

'And besides...we never got to finish date number two, did we?'

'Ah...' The tension was back again. They had to both

be thinking of that moment. Not that any words had been spoken but Sophia could actually feel the impression of that half-smile she'd summoned. The dismissive way she'd shrugged and turned away. 'No…' She had to drop her gaze. 'It didn't feel finished.'

'We should do something about that, then.'

It took courage to meet his gaze. 'Yes. I think maybe we should.'

The intensity humming between them bore no relation to the casual words from Aiden.

'I've got a thing I have to go to tomorrow night. Would you like to come with me?'

'What sort of a thing?'

Not that it mattered. She would have agreed to go anywhere with him.

Or maybe it did matter. A flicker of something in Aiden's face made Sophia realise that, whatever it was, it was important to him. That he was inviting her into a part of his life that might not be something he shared with just anyone. That he was taking a risk?

'A surprise,' he said, after that tiny hesitation. 'If I tell you what it is, that would make it more like a new date and it's not. It's—'

'A half-date?' Sophia suggested.

'Just a thing. Let's not try and define it.'

'Okay.'

'So you'll come?'

'Sure. How could I resist? I've never been to a "thing" before. I'm intrigued.'

'Don't get too excited. It's a bit…different.'

'I'm even more intrigued now. Give me a clue?'

'Uh-uh.' Aiden shook his head but he was smiling. 'I'll pick you up at seven-thirty.'

'Dress code?'

'Definitely casual. And warm.' Aiden took a sip of his coffee and made a face. 'This is awful. I don't even think it deserves to be called coffee.'

A bubble of happiness made Sophia giggle. 'Guess I still owe you one, then.'

Aiden's nod was thoughtful. 'I'll put this in the category of medication. Something to wake me up after a tough day.'

'So what happened? How badly injured was your cyclist?'

'Multi-trauma. She's up in Intensive Care now but I wanted to see what had been found. The head injury made her combative so it was hard to assess her.'

Sophia nodded. She had plenty of questions and was genuinely interested in the responses as Aiden told her more about the case, but there was an undercurrent that made it all so much more enjoyable.

She was going to see him again tomorrow night.

They were going to a *thing*…

Parking outside a suburban gymnasium was a surprise. So the 'thing' was a sporting event of some kind? This was weird but Sophia was prepared to keep an open mind, especially when Aiden took her hand to lead her inside.

And there was another surprise. The seats were crowded and the atmosphere loud and vibrant but the last thing she'd expected to see were the teams on the basketball-style court. They were all young men and they were all in wheelchairs.

'What is this?'

'Murderball.' Aiden waved to a girl with spiky black hair and facial piercings who was in the first row of seats. 'Wheelchair rugby.' He led her towards some empty seats in the third row. 'It's my brother's first game.'

Wow. No wonder she'd got the impression that this was a private part of Aiden's life.

'Your brother is paraplegic?'

'Tetraplegic. You have to have disability in all four limbs to qualify to play.'

'But...' Sophia stared at the activity below as she took her seat. The team members were rolling across the floor with some doing fast spins, looking like they were warming up. They were definitely using their hands and arms.

'There's a scale,' Aiden told her. 'The level of disability is graded from zero point five, which is the greatest restriction, to three point five. If you were able-bodied you'd score five and if you were totally paralysed you'd be a zero. There are four on the court at any one time and they have to have a total score between them of no more than eight points.'

The teams were lining up, face to face in the centre of the court, and then they peeled off, high-fiving each other.

'Which one is your brother?'

'Number three for the Melbourne Mobsters. The red and black team. He's not going to be on in the first quarter. He may not get on at all but I hope he does. This is his first game.'

'Oh…' That made it even more of a big deal to be here. No wonder Aiden was looking tense, with his jaw knotted and his focus intently on the court. Sophia slipped her hand over his to give it a squeeze and found it caught and gripped hard.

'What's his name?' Sophia grinned. 'Just so I can yell when he scores a goal.'

'Nathan. Nate.'

A whistle blew and the referee threw a ball high in the air and then it was all on. A player for the Canberra Cowboys put the ball on his lap and sped away from the others to cross the goal line between cones. A cheer erupted from the crowd but it was nothing on the noise level when one of the local boys scored less than a minute later.

The game was fast and furious and Sophia was hooked well before the first quarter ended. She gasped at the first collision she saw between three players going for the ball that made the chairs tip and her jaw dropped when one player fell backwards with a crash, but the game carried on with a supporter rushing onto the court to right the upturned chair, and within seconds the fall was forgotten.

A hooter sounded to signal the rolling rotation of the players but Nathan wasn't one of the new team members. Sophia tried to figure out the rules but the game was so fast, she was having trouble. This was like a mix of basketball, rugby and bumper cars.

'Why do they bounce the ball sometimes?'

'You have to either bounce it or pass it to someone else within ten seconds.'

'What happened there?'

'Penalty awarded for a foul. That cowboy hit a mobster's chair behind the main axle, which makes it spin out of control.'

Scores jumped quickly but stayed close. The noise level steadily increased until Sophia had to shout to be heard as the final quarter began.

'That's Nathan. He's *on*.'

She'd barely known this game existed before coming here tonight, but suddenly it felt personal. Nathan looked a lot younger than Aiden and he looked a bit nervous. Sophia felt nervous herself. The chairs were clearly designed to cope with the impacts with their metal bumpers and spoke guards. And the players wore gloves and elbow protection but surely there was a huge potential for injury down there?

Aiden obviously thought so too, given the way he winced visibly the first time Nathan's chair got hit. But, moments later, a wide overhead pass from the other side of the court saw Nathan catch the ball and dump it on his lap. He spun his chair on the spot and took off, his arms almost a blur as he powered towards the goal line. Three other chairs converged on his path but he saw them as he looked up to bounce the ball off to one side. With another lightning-fast spin, he changed direction and had a clear line to speed towards the cones.

The cheer was the loudest yet. Maybe because she and Aiden were both on their feet, yelling at the tops of their voices. She saw the girl in the front row, who'd waved at Aiden when they arrived, leaping about and waving two huge pompoms in the red and black team colours.

The Melbourne Mobsters lost by two points but it didn't seem to matter. The crowd was happy to cheer any of the players who came close enough to the spectators to receive a high five or a kiss from a girlfriend. Still holding Sophia's hand, Aiden pulled her towards the front row as a chair rolled directly towards them. Nathan got a kiss from the girl with the spiky black hair and then a fist bump and a one-armed hug from his brother.

'You made it. Didn't see you up there, bro.'

'Wouldn't have missed it for the world. You rocked it, man.'

Sophia nodded her agreement, unable to wipe the grin off her face. 'Most exciting game I've ever watched,' she said. 'Of anything.'

Nathan Harrison's eyes were the same unusual shade of brown as Aiden's and they had the same ability to focus with instant intensity. The slow grin was eerily familiar as well.

'You have to be Sophia,' he said.

She nodded again but didn't miss the glance that flicked between the brothers. Or the disconcerting way Nathan was shaking his head as he looked back, still grinning.

He must have seen her confusion. 'Sorry. It's just that it's the first time I've met one of Aiden's girlfriends. He doesn't usually give me the honour.'

Because a three-dates rule didn't allow for inclusion in a private part of his life? She hadn't imagined that hesitation in inviting her, had she? Or underplayed the significance? But she had no idea whether it meant anything. Or whether she even wanted it to mean anything.

The moment could have been incredibly awkward but it was the girl beside Nathan who saved it.

'There's a first time for everything,' she declared. 'Otherwise nothing would ever change.' She grinned at Sophia. 'I'm Sam,' she said. 'And I'm delighted to meet you—which is what Nate's really trying to say.'

'I knew that.' It was impossible to miss the significance in the glance Sam shared with Nathan. Their love for each other was blindingly obvious.

So was the bond between the brothers. Aiden declined the invitation to join the team and supporters at a local bar, saying he had a horribly early start the next day, but she could hear the fierce pride in his voice when they took their leave.

'You did good, man. Can't wait for the next game.'

Aiden could feel the remnants of a ridiculously proud smile he'd been suppressing as he started up the old van he'd used to collect Sophia that evening. He could also feel the way she was looking at him. The intensity was almost palpable.

'Aiden?'

'Yeah?'

'That call you got at the beach the other day.'

'Yeah?' Oh, help. He'd hoped that had been forgotten by now. That he'd put things right. It had needed something special and inviting her into a part of his life he'd never shared with a woman had seemed like the way to go, but maybe he'd been wrong.

Maybe he was still in the dog box.

'Was it a call from Nathan?'

'Um…yeah…' He turned his head, the query of why she was asking on the tip of his tongue but the word never escaped.

He didn't need to ask why.

She understood.

She might not have any idea why the bond was so strong between him and Nathan but she knew it was there and how important it was.

Weirdly, he could feel something inside his chest crack and something warm seeped out.

Something really nice.

He did have a really early start tomorrow but that hadn't been the real reason for declining the after-game social occasion with the team. He'd known he wanted to take Sophia home and be alone with her.

And the desire to do that had just leapt right off the scale.

CHAPTER SEVEN

THIS WAS THE way the last date should have ended.

Once again, Sophia was pressed against her front door the moment it shut behind her but she wasn't standing there with her head bowed, listening to the sound of a fading engine.

This time, it was her back against the door. And her arms, as she lifted them in a helpless gesture, unable to think of anything else to do with them as she met the intensity of the kiss she was receiving.

Who knew that you could actually *taste* desire? Was it her own or Aiden's or the chemical reaction of mixing them that made this so incredibly delicious?

For the longest time, that was enough. The silky glide of tongue against tongue. The endless variations of pressure in lips that was a conversation all by itself. But then Aiden's hands left her neck, where they'd been cradling her head, and they trailed down to cup her breasts. His lips left hers to touch the soft skin below her ear where she could feel her own pulse pounding and suddenly it wasn't enough.

Not nearly enough.

And she knew what to do with her arms, now, too. She could wrap them around his neck and run her fingers through the softness of that closely cropped hair. Press her lips against that vulnerable spot on his temple.

She couldn't say who started moving first. If it hadn't been her, Aiden didn't seem to have any problem finding her bedroom, but it was a tiny house. The interruption of removing clothes felt like a nuisance and Sophia hastily stripped off her sweater at the same time Aiden peeled off his leather jacket. They both kicked off their shoes but then they looked at each other and abandoned undressing to kiss again.

And time seemed to stop. Taking their clothes off was no longer a nuisance. It was a game to be savoured. A slow reveal of buttons coming undone and zips being separated. Exposed skin that needed exploring. Touching and kissing with murmurs of appreciation and the odd whimper of escalating desire.

Too soon—and not nearly soon enough—they were in her bed and now there were no limits on the touching. No stopping the roller-coaster of sensation that was pushing them towards ecstasy. The interruption of Aiden leaning over the side of the bed to find his discarded jeans and fish in the pocket for a foil packet was unbearable.

There's no need, Sophia wanted to say. *Don't stop.*

But, of course, she didn't say it. And it wasn't entirely true, anyway. Okay, there was no way she could get pregnant but there were other reasons to use protection...

And maybe that was why she found the interruption unbearable. She didn't want to have to think about anything like that—even for the few seconds it took.

Easy to forget about it again, though. To cry out with the pleasure of feeling him inside her and then to simply surrender to the mounting tension that was taking them both to that place like no other. Where the world could stop turning for as long as it took.

It took quite a while for either of them to get their breath back as they lay there, their limbs entangled and the only sound their rapid panting.

'Oh, my God,' Sophia whispered, when words were finally available. 'How did you *do* that?'

'I was going to ask you the same thing.' There was a smile in Aiden's voice as he eased himself free. He didn't let go of Sophia, though, and she found herself rolling onto to her side, with her head cradled against his chest. 'You're amazing. You do know that, don't you?'

She could feel the edge of his nipple against her lips as she smiled. 'I do now. You're pretty amazing yourself.'

He pressed his lips to the top of her head. 'Maybe it was the combination.'

'Mmm.' Post-coital drowsiness was enveloping Sophia. She could feel herself relaxing into sleep and the thought that she would wake in Aiden's arms was blissful.

But he moved, just a little. 'I should go,' he murmured. 'I wasn't kidding about the early start.'

'You don't have to.'

The soft sound was regretful. 'But I know exactly what would happen if I stayed and I only had one condom in my pocket.'

The temptation to say something was even stronger this time. 'You don't need to worry about me getting pregnant.'

He moved enough to break the contact between their bodies. 'Don't take it personally but I've never relied on anyone else for contraception and I'm not about to break that rule.'

'Oh...' Sophia could feel the chill of exposed skin. And then she felt the dip of her mattress as Aiden sat up and swung his legs over the side of the bed.

He turned then but it was too dark to read his expression. 'I'm never going to have kids,' he said quietly. 'I had to be a father to Nate when he was growing up and that was enough. More than enough.'

There was a world of pain behind those words. But there was also a warning note. He'd shared more than his body with her tonight. He'd shared a lot of his personal life but there were limits. This wasn't something he was ready to talk about.

He leaned towards her and gave her a swift kiss. 'I do have to go.'

'Okay.'

Sophia listened to the sounds of him getting dressed again. She sat up, pulling the duvet around her like a shawl.

'It was the best half-date I've ever been on,' she told him. 'Thank you.'

The glimmer of his smile gave her the impression she'd said exactly the right thing. Not pushing him to talk any more about his 'rules' or the reason they were so iron-clad.

He came close and this time the kiss lingered.

'Just as well it was a half-date,' he said. 'That means we still have one left.'

One.

Sophia's heart sank.

'Would it count as a date if we didn't go anywhere? Like—if you came round for dinner one night or something?'

Something like a chuckle rumbled in Aiden's chest. 'I don't reckon it would. Do you?'

'No.' Sophia injected complete authority into her voice. 'I'm quite sure it wouldn't. Give me your phone number and I'll text you when I've had time to go shopping.'

Finding time to go grocery shopping wasn't so hard because there were supermarkets that regularly stayed open until at least midnight.

Finding time to cook something as amazing as Sophia wanted it to be was another matter. With what felt like a blinding flash of inspiration, a couple of days later she remembered the slow cooker tucked away at the back of one of her kitchen cupboards. Perfect. Getting up a little earlier to get ready for work, she had time to sear meat and brown the vegetables and then all she had to do was push the button and let the cooker work its magic while she worked with Flick for another busy day of home visits.

The concern about her student was still there but had been pushed into the background. Flick had dismissed her reaction to coffee after that Caesarean case as being due to a bit of a tummy bug and Sophia had been embarrassed that she'd blurted out the first suspicion that had sprung to mind—that Flick might be pregnant. The fact that she'd been pale and quiet for a few days after that fitted with her having been off colour and if she still seemed on the quiet side now, that could well be due to the extra studying she was doing. Flick seemed determined to learn everything about her chosen career and today was a great one for introducing her to things she hadn't done before.

It was good for her to have her teaching to distract her, as well. If she hadn't had Flick in the car with her as she negotiated the heavy traffic in places, she might have been tempted to wonder about how that meal was progressing as it simmered gently.

Or notice the desire that was simmering a little less gently deep in her belly. Would they go to bed again? Or maybe the real question was when and not if. Before or after dinner?

The car jerked a little with the firm pressure of her foot on the accelerator. 'What do you think is the most important thing about the postnatal care we give for up to six weeks after birth?'

'Support,' Flick answered promptly. 'Help with things like breastfeeding and bathing baby and how to cope with fatigue.'

'And?'

'Monitoring the health of both the baby and the mother. Especially after a Caesarean in case of infection. And making sure they don't think that breastfeeding is a reliable form of contraception.'

Hmm. Expanding on that topic was not going to help her stay focused. 'Good. What else do we do?'

'Watch out for signs of postnatal depression?'

They discussed the kind of signs that could be important as Sophia drove them to their first visit of the day but their first mother—Judith—seemed to be coping extremely well, having had a home birth two days ago.

'I'm lucky I've got Mum staying. I'm getting plenty of sleep between feeds.'

'Looks like baby's getting plenty of sleep, too.' Sophia smiled at the tiny, perfect face peeping from the folds of blanket in Judith's arms.

'I've been a bit worried about today's visit, though. I'm not sure I want her to have the test.' Judith's voice wobbled. 'It's going to hurt her, isn't it?'

'They usually cry,' Sophia said gently. 'But I think it's more about having their foot held still than any pain. It's a tiny prick. And the crying helps. It makes the blood come out faster so the test is over quickly.'

'It's important, Jude.' Their patient's mother was sitting nearby. She looked over at Sophia. 'There's all sorts of diseases it can test for, aren't there? Treatable things?'

'Absolutely. More than twenty different disorders, in fact.'

'Like what?'

'Maybe Flick can tell you about some of them.' Sophia smiled encouragingly at her student.

'There's hypothyroidism,' Flick said. 'And cystic fibrosis. And the enzyme disorders that prevent the normal use of milk.'

'And amino acid disorders,' Sophia added. 'Things

that can lead to something like brain damage if they're not picked up but which can be easily treated by following a special diet.'

'But she's not going to need a special diet for ages. I'm breastfeeding. Can't we put the test off until then?'

'It needs to be done as soon as possible after baby is forty-eight hours old.' Sophia checked her watch. 'And that's right about now.'

'I'll hold her, if you like,' Judith's mother offered. 'Why don't you go and have a quick shower or something?'

'No.' Judith closed her eyes. 'If it has to be done, I want to be the one holding her. Let's just get it over with.'

Flick stored the card with its four blood spots in Judith's file. 'I'd better remember to take that to the lab later,' she told Sophia as they drove to their next appointment. She shook her head. 'Poor Judith. I think she cried more than the baby did. Imagine how hard the six-week vaccinations are going to be for her.'

'Remind me to give her some pamphlets about that on our next visit. And we'll talk to her about how important it is.'

They had a hearing screening test to do on a final visit to a six-week-old baby later that morning and a lesson in hand-expressing breast milk for a young mother in the afternoon.

'I want my partner to share the night feeds,' she told them. 'And he really wants to, don't you, John?'

The young father nodded. The look and smile he gave his partner was exactly what Sophia would want for herself. Overflowing with love and a determination to provide support—even if it meant sacrificing sleep. Unaccountably, an image of Aiden filled her mind. How ridiculous was that? He was so against the idea of ever having a baby that he wouldn't trust anyone else to deal with contraception.

'But I really hate the thought of using one of those breast pumps,' the mother continued. 'It's so…mechanical.'

'Hand expression isn't hard. We'll show you how to do it.'

Flick took notes as Sophia provided the instruction. By the end of the day she'd also had plenty of practice taking blood pressures and temperatures on mothers, weighing babies and filling in report forms.

'You're getting very competent,' Sophia told her. 'You'll be doing all this on your own in no time.'

'Thanks. I'm loving it.' Flick opened her mouth as though about to say something else but then she merely smiled. 'See you tomorrow, Soph. Have a good night.'

Sophia smiled back. 'I intend to. You have one too.'

'Oh, man…that has to be the most amazing thing I've ever smelt.'

As an icebreaker, on opening the door to her dinner guest, this was enough to make Sophia smile and stop wondering about what was going to happen before or after they ate.

'Let's hope it tastes as good as it smells.' At least that was something she was pretty sure she didn't need to worry about. She'd been pretty impressed herself to come home to the aroma of those slow-cooked lamb shanks with red wine and mushrooms. The potatoes were cooking now and all she needed to do was mash them and dinner would be ready.

They had time to relax and, seeing as Aiden was holding out a bottle of very nice wine, it would have been rude not to taste it.

'Come in. I've got the fire going. It's pretty cold out there tonight, isn't it?'

'Sure is.' Aiden went straight to the flames of the small gas fire and stood with his back to it, his hand fanned out to catch the heat. He looked around. 'This is really nice.' His grin grew. 'Can't say I really noticed the other night.'

That grin—along with a ghost of a wink—chased away any lingering awkwardness over this date that wasn't a date. Suddenly, Sophia felt completely comfortable in his company. No, it was more than that. Being with him in this small, book-filled room with the smell of hot food and the sound of rain on the roof felt...well, it felt like *home*.

'It is nice, isn't it? Most of this stuff isn't mine, though. I'm house-sitting for a nurse at the Victoria who's gone overseas for a year. Sad to say, the year's half-over now. I'll have to start thinking about finding a place of my own before too long.'

'Where were you before this?' Aiden took the corkscrew Sophia handed him and dealt expertly with opening the wine while she took a couple of steps back into the kitchen to fetch glasses.

'Canberra. It's where I grew up.'

'You've got family there?' Aiden poured the wine.

'Just my parents. Dad's a pharmacist and Mum's a teacher.' Sophia sat down on the sofa and it felt good when Aiden came to sit beside her. 'How 'bout you?'

'No folks. There's just me and Nate. Mum died due to complications with his birth.'

'Oh…that's awful. Do you remember her?'

'Yeah…' For a second, Sophia could see the pain of that loss in his eyes but then his gaze slid sideways, as though he knew he might be revealing too much. 'Not as well as I'd like to, though. I was only six when she died.' He took a huge swallow of his wine.

Sophia's heart ached for the little boy who'd lost his mother. She'd never lost one of her maternity patients but she knew it still happened in rare cases and she could imagine how terrible it would be for the whole family.

'That smell is driving me mad.' Aiden's tone had a forced cheerfulness to it. An attempt to dispel any negative vibe? 'I didn't get time for lunch today.'

'Oh…' Maybe she couldn't do anything to comfort that little boy of years gone by but she could certainly fix this. 'Let's eat. Why don't you choose some music to put on while I mash the potatoes?'

His choice was surprising. 'You went for vinyl?'

'Retro, huh? The girl who owns this place is really into the old stuff.'

Sophia laughed. 'It's more like she's never thrown anything out. Dot's in her early sixties. At least you chose one of my favourites. I adore Cat Stevens.'

'Me, too.' Aiden took the plate from her hands but held her gaze. 'And how did you know that lamb shanks are my all-time favourite food?'

The warmth in that gaze made the pleasure of approval all the more intense and Sophia had to break the eye contact. 'Lucky guess. Or maybe we just have a lot in common.'

The food tasted just as good as it had smelled. The flames on the fake logs of the gas fire danced merrily and the music was the perfect background. All that was missing, Sophia decided, was candlelight.

Except wouldn't that make it too romantic to be a non-date? And what could she talk about that wouldn't take them into ground that might be deemed too personal and put it into the same category?

'You must have had a busy day, if you didn't get time for lunch.'

'Sure did. Two cardiac arrests, one straight after the other, would you believe?'

'Did you get them back?'

'Transported the first one with a viable rhythm but I think the downtime had been too long. The second guy woke up after the third shock and wanted to know what all the fuss was about.'

'No, really?'

'Yeah…' Aiden refilled their glasses and then raised his in a toast. 'Doesn't happen very often but when it does, it makes it all worthwhile. Even missing lunch.' He picked up his fork again. 'Did I tell you how amazing this is? I can't even mash potatoes without leaving lumps in.'

Sophia smiled. 'Tell me about the save. How old was he? Was there bystander CPR happening when you got there?'

Aiden told her about the successful case in so much detail she felt like she'd been standing there, watching the drama.

'You're really good at that.'

'What?'

'Telling a story. You could write a book about your job and people would want to read it.'

Aiden shook his head. 'I've just had practice, that's all. Nathan is a frustrated paramedic, I think. He always wants every gory detail about everything and doesn't let me get away with leaving stuff out. It's become a habit.'

Sophia forgot about any boundaries she might have been watching so that they could keep this time light. And fun. There was such a strong undercurrent to Aiden's words. It had the strength of showing the bond between the brothers in that Aiden was so used to sharing every detail of his life with Nathan, but it had rocks and rapids in it, too. Did Nathan resent that Aiden was out in the world, doing such an exciting and physical job, while he was trapped in a wheelchair? Did Aiden feel guilty about it?

'How did it happen?' she heard herself asking quietly. 'How did Nate become a quadriplegic?'

Aiden stopped chewing his mouthful of food and swallowed. Carefully. He reached for his glass of wine but didn't look at Sophia.

'He got pushed down a set of stairs.' His voice was flat.

'Oh, my God…' If she'd still had any appetite, it evaporated at that moment. 'How old was he?'

'Ten.'

A ten-year-old boy who'd probably loved to ride his bike and play soccer or rugby. A boy who'd already had it tough by having to grow up without his mother.

An echo of those sombre words Aiden had spoken the other night slipped into her head.

I had to be a father to Nate when he was growing up and that was enough. More than enough.

Had he been referring to the growing up before that dreadful accident or the trauma of readjustment that would have come afterwards?

She had so many questions she wanted to ask but didn't dare push further into such personal territory. The silence grew. Aiden was staring at his wineglass.

'Must have been drinking on such an empty stomach that did it,' he mused. 'I never talk about this.'

Then he looked up and caught Sophia's gaze. 'Or maybe it's because I'm with you.'

Something inside her melted into a liquid warmth. Some of it reached her eyes and she knew she'd have to blink a lot to make sure it didn't escape and roll down her cheeks. Her voice came out as a whisper.

'You can tell me anything. Or not. You're safe, either way.' She tried to smile but it didn't quite work.

Aiden wasn't smiling either. He felt like he was drowning in that moisture he could see collecting in Sophia's eyes. The *caring* behind them hit him like an emotional brick and tugged at something long forgotten. Poignant.

Did it remind him of the way his mother had looked at him, maybe?

'It was my father who pushed him down the stairs,' he found himself telling her. 'And it was my fault.'

The shock on her face was all too easy to read and Aiden cringed inwardly. He shouldn't have told her. She would think less of him. As little as he thought of himself?

But then her face changed. She looked like she was backing away even though she didn't move a single muscle.

'I don't believe that,' she said. 'Not one bit.'

How could she say that with such conviction? She barely knew him and she knew nothing of what had happened. A flash of anger made it easy to unchain words.

'My father was an alcoholic. He resented having to raise kids on his own and he blamed Nathan for causing Mum's death. He was a bully and he got really nasty when he was drinking, which was pretty much every day.'

The horror of that childhood was written all over Sophia's face. He could see it that way himself now, with the benefit of hindsight but, at the time, it had just been how things were.

'I knew how to handle him. I learned how to keep Nate safe. But that day? I was sixteen and I'd had enough. Instead of trying to defuse him, I flipped the coin. I started yelling at him and telling him just what a miserable bastard he was. I knew I had to get out of the house before I attacked him physically and I'd almost made it to the front door.' He had to stop for a second. To swallow past the constriction in his throat. 'He came after me but Nate was trying to follow me, too, and he was at the top of the stairs. Dad pushed him to get past and he fell.'

'You *saw* it happen?' Sophia's words were raw. Had she even thought before she reached out and covered his hand with her own? The warmth and pressure of that human contact almost undid Aiden but he couldn't pull his hand away. Instead, he turned it over and threaded his fingers through hers to lock them together.

'That wasn't the worst of it. I didn't know how badly hurt Nate was but I knew not to let him move before the ambulance could get there. So I held his head and kept him still and told him that everything would be okay. And then...and then...'

He could feel the tension in her hand. The terrible anticipation.

'And then we heard it. I didn't even know he had a gun in the house. Just as well, maybe, given how much I hated him that day. But I never had to think about killing him again. He did it himself.'

He choked on those last words. He'd never told anybody this story. Ever. Something was breaking inside his chest. Making him shake. Forcing a kind of horrible, dry sobbing sound to come out of his throat. He had his eyes screwed tightly shut so he didn't see Sophia standing up but he felt the tug on his hand and it was easy to comply with the silent instruction because he had no idea of what to do. How to deal with this awful emotional tidal wave.

How did Sophia know what to do?

She was tiny but he could feel an enormous strength

in the way she wrapped her arms around him and held him so tightly. He had no idea how long they stood there like that but it was long enough for the wave to recede. And now it felt like a huge expanse of sand that had been washed clean.

Deserted. And amazingly peaceful.

He loosened the grip of his arms around Sophia. How had she managed to keep breathing for so long?

'Sorry. I shouldn't have dumped all that on you.'

'I'm glad you did.' She moved a little in his arms so that she could look up at him. 'And, Aiden?'

'Yeah?'

'I was right.'

'What about?'

'It wasn't your fault. Not one bit of it.'

The anger was gone but he could still feel disappointed. Sophia was taking Nathan's side. Was there nobody out there who could understand? See the truth the way he saw it? He stepped back. Could he make some excuse and simply leave?

No. One look at Sophia and he was caught.

'I know why you think that,' she said. 'And when you love someone, it's easy to find a way to take the blame when something bad happens to them, but this wasn't your fault. It was your father's fault.'

'I *provoked* him.'

'And how many times did you *not* provoke him? You'd been living with that for ten years. You'd found every way under the sun to keep your little brother safe. Confronting your father and escaping would have been the only way to make sure of that in the long run and I think you'd finally got old enough to know that, even if it was subconscious. Okay, it went horribly wrong but it was a brave thing to do. How old were you?'

'Sixteen.' Aiden could barely get the word out. He was trying to process what she was saying. Was there any truth in it?

He'd been *brave*?

No way…

'There you go.' Sophia's smile was heartbreakingly tender. 'Just a kid yourself.' She raised her eyebrows. 'Was that when you decided you wanted to be a paramedic?'

'Yeah… They were amazing. I think they looked after me just as much as they looked after Nate. It's something I have in the back of my mind with every job I go to. It's not just the person who's sick or hurt that's your patient. The people who love them are too.'

'And that's part of what makes you so good at your job. No wonder Nate wants to hear your stories.'

That was how this had all started, wasn't it. Aiden jerked his gaze to the table. To the half-eaten meals of that delicious food Sophia had prepared.

'I'm sorry,' he said again. 'I kind of ruined dinner, didn't I?'

'It was my fault,' Sophia said. 'I asked the questions that got you started.'

'I didn't have to tell you. I chose to. Because I wanted to.'

The look he was receiving could only have come from a woman.

'Mmm…okay. I accept that it wasn't my fault.'

In the heartbeat of silence that followed, Aiden made the connection. And found himself smiling, albeit reluctantly.

'How 'bout I zap those plates in the microwave? You still hungry?'

He couldn't look away from her eyes. He was drowning again but this time it came with a lick of fire that would evaporate any moisture.

'Oh, yeah…I'm hungry.'

He caught her hand as she turned towards the table.

'But not for food.'

She gave a tiny gasp as he pulled her into his arms and bent his head to taste her lips. And then she melted against him and he knew, with absolute certainty, that things were going to be all right. He didn't have to leave. Didn't want to.

Things were going to be better than all right, in fact.

Life itself seemed to have just become that much better.

CHAPTER EIGHT

THIS WAS NOTHING like last time.

Oh, the desire was the same. That being carried away on a wave of physical sensation that led to ultimate satisfaction, but there was something very different about the way Sophia could feel herself responding.

This physical nakedness had come in the wake of emotional nakedness on Aiden's part. He'd opened his heart to her and made himself vulnerable and it made her want to protect him, even as her own heart broke to think of what his childhood had been like. Weird how it could break but swell at the same time as she saw the depth of the love he had for his brother.

No wonder he shied away from any other responsibilities in his life—like a relationship that lasted more than three dates. Or having a child of his own.

And the guilt he'd carried with him ever since that accident. Was it more than not wanting extra responsibilities? Was he preventing anyone else getting too close as a kind of penance?

She'd told him he was safe to tell her anything and he had. Way more than she'd expected.

He deserved the same kind of honesty from her. To know that he was safe from more than any emotional repercussions of being close, but something stopped her saying anything when he tore open the foil packet of the condom.

It would spoil the moment, she told herself. Bring the rush of escalating desire to a grinding halt and maybe it was more than simply desire for Aiden at the moment. Maybe he needed the intimacy as a kind of reassurance. A reminder that he deserved the good things in life because of who he was.

The good things in life.

Like being loved…

No. Sophia had to shut down the realisation because it was blinding. And terrifying. Far easier to stop thinking and simply feel. To give herself up to the touch of Aiden's hands and mouth. To give in to her own need to feel the closest physical touch possible from another being.

It came back, though, in those quiet minutes of lying there entangled in each other's arms, as heart and breathing rates gradually settled back to normal.

No. This was nothing like last time. Because this had been more than sex. More than having fun. On her part, it had been making love.

Aiden had opened his heart to her and she had fallen into it. Fallen in love with him.

This wasn't supposed to have happened. How could it, when you knew right from the start that it was only going to last for three dates?

* * *

He'd fallen asleep.

He hadn't meant to. He never stayed a whole night because it was one of the rules. He'd learned long ago that it added a depth that made things more difficult when it was time to move on because it gave the impression that he might be happy to stay longer. That it was about more than a bit of fun.

He'd taken the fun element out of the evening himself, though, hadn't he? Spilling his guts like that about Nate. About his father.

Good grief…he'd never told a woman any of that stuff.

But she'd told him it was safe and nobody had ever said that to him before.

And he'd *felt* safe.

He'd even felt…absolved from the guilt for just a heartbeat. The way she'd twisted the idea of being at fault and tipped it towards being someone else's choice.

There was a truth in that. Maybe he'd be able to catch that feeling of absolution again one day. It had been too huge not to push away at the time, though. To shut off everything except the need to take Sophia to bed. To try and thank her for what she'd given him? It wasn't surprising he'd fallen asleep after the roller-coaster of emotions that had been stirred up and then released. Physical release had been the last push into a totally new feeling of being at peace.

Safe.

Such a roller-coaster. Like that extraordinary sensation he'd had when she'd told him he'd been brave.

Brave?

She admired him? Remembering it now gave him that same weird feeling of being…what…special? But she didn't know the truth of it, did she? How scared he'd been so often. The way he'd taken Nathan under his bed sometimes and held the toddler close until he'd known that his father had been drunk enough to be no threat for the rest of the night. How he'd stolen money from their dad's wallet so he could buy a toy for Nate's birthday. How often he'd wagged school or lied about being sick so that he could make sure the housekeeper was taking proper care of his brother.

She wouldn't think he was brave if she'd known the awful relief he'd felt when it had become clear after the accident that Nathan would have to be cared for by people far more qualified than he was. That all he needed to do was visit him every day. That he was free to follow the dream that had been born on that dreadful night and become a paramedic so he could help others.

He'd created exactly the life he'd dreamed of but he had hurt other people along the way, he knew that. Some women in the past had been angry. Had accused him of using them. Others had been upset and the tears had been harder to handle than angry words.

How would Sophia react when they'd had their third—and last—date?

The last thing he wanted was to make her cry.

Even thinking about it made him hold her a little tighter as she lay in his arms, with her head tucked against his chest. The movement made her stir and make a tiny sound, almost like a cat purring.

He loved that sound.

'Mmm.' This was more like a word and it was followed by a slow, deep indrawn breath that was painted into sensation by the small hand that moved across his chest.

'You're still here,' Sophia whispered. 'That's nice.'

'Mmm.' He had to agree. It *was* nice.

'What time is it?'

'I don't know. Close to dawn, I think. The birds are getting noisy.'

'We don't have to get up yet, though.' Her hand was moving again. The soft touch reached his abdomen and Aiden could feel his body coming a lot more awake.

'We don't.' Okay, maybe this wasn't the best idea but how could he resist? 'Just as well I came prepared this time.' His jeans weren't far away. There was another foil packet in the back pocket.

He couldn't miss the way Sophia stilled in his arms, though. The way the fuzzy sense of sleepy peacefulness took on a spiky edge.

'What?' The word was no more than a puzzled murmur. Had he done the wrong thing in being prepared for more than once?

'I...' The hesitation lasted long enough for Sophia to take another deep breath. He could feel the press of her breast against his hand swell and then recede. 'I meant what I said the other night. You don't need it.'

Whoa... This was a step into totally forbidden territory. He didn't care what precautions any woman took. He had to know he was taking responsibility for contraception himself.

The desire for sex was ebbing fast. He needed to escape. Carefully, he started pulling his arm away from where it encircled Sophia but he had no idea what he could say. How he could stop this becoming an unpleasant conversation for both of them.

But he didn't have to find anything to say because Sophia spoke first.

'I can't get pregnant, Aiden. I had a hysterectomy nearly ten years ago.'

'What? *Why?*' Oh, God…had she had cancer? The idea that she'd had to face something so terrible at such a young age was unbearable. Instead of taking his arm away, Aiden found himself pushing it further around her. Pulling her closer, as if he could protect her from something.

'It was an accidental pregnancy.' Her voice was quiet. Matter-of-fact. 'It was ectopic but I ignored the early warning signs. It went on too long and then ruptured really badly. They had to perform a hysterectomy to control the bleeding.'

Aiden swore softly, his eyes tightly shut. He could imagine all too easily the emergency that rupture would have caused. The urgent, major surgery that would have been necessary to save her life. But…

'But why did you ignore the signs?'

It seemed a long time before she spoke again and when she did, her voice was so quiet he barely heard it.

'I wanted the baby,' she said.

That took a few moments to process. 'How old were you?'

'Twenty-one. I was a student midwife. I'd always

loved babies. Maybe because I was an only child and I was so envious when my best friend got a baby sister. My parents both worked full time and it felt like we were…I don't know…less of a family, I guess.'

'But you said the pregnancy was accidental.'

'Of course it was. I wasn't stupid. I was only twenty-one and it wasn't as if the relationship was going anywhere. We were both young. Just out to have a bit of fun.'

Like he was with the women in his life? Aiden had to swallow a nasty pang of guilt. Those women had had every right to be angry or upset, hadn't they? He *had* been using them.

'So he wasn't keen on the idea of being a father?'

'He did his best to be supportive but we both knew it couldn't have worked. I actually went down the track of having a termination but when I went to ring up to make an appointment, I couldn't do it. I realised then that I wanted that baby. I…I already loved it.' There was a wobble in her voice. 'So I ignored the abdominal pain that came and went. I told myself that a bit of bleeding could be perfectly normal in the early stages of some pregnancies. That things would settle down once I got to the end of the first trimester and I'd go and get checked out and have a scan after that. When it was less likely that anyone would try and talk me into getting rid of it.'

'And then it ruptured.'

'I was about fourteen weeks by then. I guess it was lucky it happened while I was at work. I might have bled out pretty fast if I'd been anywhere else.'

'I'm glad you were at work, then. Lucky for me, too.'

A tiny sound that could have been an embryonic sob

came from Sophia but then they were both silent for a long time.

'I'm sorry,' Aiden said, finally, into the light of a new day that was filtering through the gap in the curtains. 'You lost something huge and it must have been devastating.' Not only had she lost the baby she'd already loved but she'd lost the chance of ever having another one.

'Yeah…it was tough but that's just the way it is. I'm not going to let it define me. I'm going to make the best of my life. This isn't a practice run, you know? It's the only life we get.'

She reminded him of Nathan. Totally different things to deal with, of course. Or were they so different? Nathan lived with the loss of mobility. He'd had to come to terms with a different perception of his body and where he was going in life.

Sophia lived with the loss of a dream. Wouldn't being unable to ever be a mother involve the same sort of process in coming to terms with that different perception and direction?

The similarity was there. Perhaps the greatest similarity was in the positive attitude to making the best of his life.

He was so proud of his brother's attitude. He loved him to the point where it made his chest ache.

And right now he was feeling a very similar pride in Sophia.

A similar kind of love?

Oh, man…that was a scary thought. He'd never actually fallen in love with a woman. He'd known to get out as soon as there were any warning signs. Had he ignored them for some reason this time?

He tried to search his memory.

Had it been the first time he'd seen her smile? Or when he'd heard her laugh—way back, when they'd first met and she'd introduced herself as being a midwife and he'd joked that he hoped *she* was, given the emergency cord prolapse she'd just dealt with.

No. That had simply been attraction. No danger signs that could have been spotted there.

What about that first date, though? When he'd seen her at the door of that crowded bar? The way the noise of the people and music had just faded away until it had felt like he and Sophia were the only people on the planet?

Yeah…maybe that should have rung an alarm bell, given that it had never happened before.

And she'd loved his three-dates rule. Maybe that was the problem. She'd made him feel safe.

Or maybe it was the way she'd made him feel safe last night. Safe enough to tell her anything.

He couldn't tell her what he was feeling right now. No way.

She'd said that a three-dates rule was exactly what was missing from *her* life. She didn't want the complications of a long-term relationship. She couldn't have a family so maybe it simply wasn't a part of her life plan now.

She wouldn't want to know how he was feeling. It might make her feel bad when she walked away from him to get on with the life that wasn't a practice run.

He didn't want her to feel bad.

He'd make her feel good instead.

Her lips were easy to find. Soft and deliciously responsive. They still had time, didn't they?

This would be a first for him. Sex without protection, but Sophia had shown him something that made her vulnerable and she deserved at least the reassurance of trust.

And…man, it made things feel different.

Nothing like the last time.

Nothing like any time. Ever.

The text message on Aiden's phone came when he was on the point of leaving her house to go to work.

The atmosphere was a little odd. Sophia thought it was because they'd come out to find the remnants of last night's dinner still on the table and it had been a shock. So much had happened since they'd been sitting there.

So much had changed between them?

Yes. The atmosphere was strange. As if they both realised how huge that change had been and it was making them both nervous.

So much for having fun. A limited amount of time to enjoy each other's company. Some 'no-strings' sex.

'I could help clean up,' Aiden offered.

'No. I've got more time than you. I don't start till eight. You've only got ten minutes if you want to get to the station in time to start at seven.'

'Okay. But next time I'm doing the dishes.'

Next time?

Was that going to be date number three or would it still be a non-date if they didn't go out anywhere? Sophia found herself smiling. On the point of clarifying the 'rules' again when the text message bleeped.

That was even more of a shock than the messy table had been. Not that there was someone else who wanted to make contact so early in the day but the way it made Sophia feel.

Jealous?

'It's only Nate,' Aiden said after a glance at his phone. 'I'll call him when I get to work.'

He kissed her goodbye and once again Sophia found herself listening to the sound of his bike roaring away.

No. That feeling hadn't been jealousy. It was deeper than that. She'd known it was probably his brother rather than another woman who was texting him and that made her remember that he had another part of his life that was more important than any woman could ever be to him.

Another part of his life that would swallow him without a ripple when she was no longer a consideration.

Oh, help... If she could feel this bleak before it had even ended, how bad was it going to be when they said goodbye at the end of date number three?

But did it have to end?

Aiden didn't want to have kids.

She *couldn't* have any.

She'd avoided serious relationships because she had less to offer than most women but Aiden didn't want what she didn't have to offer anyway.

Didn't that make them perfect for each other?

The thought came with a leap of something that felt like hope and Sophia found herself holding it as she took plates to the kitchen sink, scraped off the abandoned food and rinsed them clean.

Who would have thought that she might find a man who could not only accept that she couldn't have a baby but would welcome it?

Except that something didn't feel right about this picture. The pieces didn't quite fit. Or maybe there were some missing that were leaving a hole she couldn't identify.

A wipe down of the table obliterated any reminder of last night's meal and Sophia collected her bag and coat to set off on her walk to the Victoria.

She couldn't shake the feeling that something was wrong, however.

That she was too far along a track for turning around to be possible. That she might be heading for some kind of crash and there was nothing at all she could do to prevent it.

CHAPTER NINE

WHAT WAS A girl to do when she couldn't figure out what it was that was bothering her?

Talk about it, of course. To someone she knew she could trust. Someone who knew more about her than anyone and loved her enough to want to help her figure it out.

Her mum?

Sadly, for Sophia, that couldn't be her first port of call. The love was there but the depth of understanding wasn't. Even after all these years, the relief her mother hadn't been able to hide when she'd lost her baby was hurtful.

'It would have ruined your life, being a single mother,' she'd said. 'Your career would have gone out the window and there aren't many men who really want to take on raising someone else's child.'

But she'd loved that baby. That potential little person to love and be loved by. Her career had seemed far less important in comparison.

'There are worse things than not having children.' Had her mother really thought she was offering comfort? 'You're about to be qualified to do the job you've always wanted to do. Focus on that. It'll make you happy.'

Had it been her mother's job that had made *her* happy? Had it been a mistake to have a child at all? One that would have ruined her life if she'd become pregnant accidentally before she had established her career or found a husband?

If it had been a mistake, her parents hid it well and had done the best job they could in raising their child, but that childhood had been a lonely one. There had clearly never been the possibility of siblings and with both her parents working full time, even a family dog had been ruled out as company.

Which was why it had been such a joy to spend time at home with her best friend, Emily, ever since she'd first arrived in Melbourne. To soak in the chaos of an extended family that included an adorably woolly, brown dog by the name of Fuzzy.

With her next day off coinciding with one of Em's, it was a no-brainer to invite herself for a visit and a chance to talk to the person most likely to be able to identify what it was that was bothering her so much.

They were in the garden of Emily and Oliver's house. Well, the house actually belonged to Em's mother, Adrianna, but it was the family home for them all now. And the family was growing, despite the sadness of losing Emily's foster-daughter, Gretta, a few weeks ago.

'How's it working out, having Ruby here with you?'

'Couldn't be better.' Emily lifted two-year-old Toby from his tricycle and took him to sit under the tree. 'I wish she'd rest a bit more, though. Look—she's over there, pruning roses. It's not that long since the in utero surgery on her baby.'

As if sensing she was being discussed, the waif-like teenager looked across the garden and waved at the two women.

'Am I doing it right?' she called. 'I've never tried this before.'

'You're doing a great job,' Emily called back. 'But you don't have to.'

The shy grin in response came with a shrug that was pure teenager.

'She feels like she has to help out,' Emily told Sophia, 'because we're not charging her any rent for the bungalow. And Mum wouldn't let her help with any housework this afternoon. Said it could wait till tomorrow because she felt like putting her feet up and reading her book. I'd rather Ruby was reading a book, too. She could be doing a bit of study or something so that she feels ready to go back to school after the baby comes.'

'I'm sure she will, when she gets used to being here. It must be a big thing, feeling like she's part of a family.'

Emily's smile was that of a contented woman as she nodded, watching Toby doing his stiff-legged crawl towards Sophia.

'Huge,' she agreed quietly.

Toby stopped and held up his arms. Sophia gladly gathered him onto her lap and let the toddler bury his head against her shoulder as he settled in for a cuddle. The faded blue kangaroo toy in his other hand felt a bit damp against the back of her neck.

'That's Kanga, isn't it? Gretta's toy?'

'Mmm.' Emily's smile grew misty. 'He's barely let it go since we lost her. I don't think he understands that she died but he's missing her.'

Toby's curls were springy and too irresistible not to stroke. An African child, Toby had been brought to Australia so that he could receive treatment for his spinal deformity and the scarring on his face from infection.

'How's it going with the adoption process?'

Emily groaned. 'The paperwork is endless. Ollie's confident that we'll get there, though. He says not getting there simply isn't an option.'

Her smile was proud now. Full of love for the man she 'remarried' so recently.

For a long moment, Sophia focused on the gorgeous cuddle she was receiving. Then her gaze drifted over Toby's head to where Ruby was eyeing up another rose bush, rubbing her back as she straightened.

'Do you remember when Ruby was waking up after the operation on the baby?'

'Of course.'

'What we were talking about?'

'Josh?'

'Mmm.' Josh. The baby Emily had lost at twenty-eight weeks—about the stage that Ruby was in her pregnancy now. The one successful round of all the IVF Emily and Oliver had gone through. 'After that. About why you and Oliver had split up.'

'Because he couldn't face adopting a baby?'

'He'd been adopted himself, hadn't he? And it hadn't been happy?'

'Mmm.'

'But he really wants to adopt Toby now, doesn't he?'

'Even more than I do, I think. Although that's not really possible. Hey, Toby…it's about my turn for a cuddle, isn't it?'

Obligingly, Toby crawled off Sophia's lap and threw himself at Emily with a joyful crow.

'Mumma!'

Even more obligingly, Fuzzy slithered closer and put his head on Sophia's lap so that she still had a head to stroke.

'You wanted kids so much,' she said quietly. 'You weren't going to let infertility stop you. And look what you've got now. A whole family, including a husband who adores you.'

'I'm the luckiest woman in the world,' Emily agreed.

'But you did it anyway, even without Oliver, and you were still happy, weren't you?'

'Ye-es…' Emily peered around Toby's head to give her friend a searching look. 'Where's this coming from, Soph? Is something bothering you?'

Sophia nodded. 'I'm not sure what it is. But I remember being at your vow renewal ceremony and thinking how brave you were. And that I needed to get braver too. Make changes in my life so that I could find something as good as what you've found. I even thought I could maybe try fostering or adopting kids one day, too.'

'You have made changes.' Emily's smile was encouraging. 'It's going well with that gorgeous boyfriend of yours, isn't it?'

'It's almost over,' Sophia told her. 'He has a three-dates rule.'

'A *what*?'

'He only ever goes out on three dates with a woman. That way you can have fun but it doesn't get heavy, you know?'

'No.' Emily shook her head. 'You've been out on more than three dates, haven't you?'

'Hmm. The rules got bent a bit. One of them was finishing off a date that got interrupted. And one wasn't really a date because he came to my place and we didn't go out anywhere.'

Emily laughed. 'Sounds like the rule isn't a real rule at all. I wouldn't worry about it.' She frowned. 'In fact, I don't like it. Sounds like an easy escape route for a commitment-phobe to me.'

'Yeah…well, I told him I liked the rule a lot, the first time we went out. That I was only after a bit of fun, too. Nothing serious.'

'Ohh…' Emily gave her another searching look. 'You've fallen for him, haven't you?'

'Yeah…' The word was a sigh. 'The weird thing is that, on paper, we're perfect for each other. I can't have kids and he doesn't want any.'

'Really? Why not?'

Sophia closed her eyes for a long moment, drawn back instantly to that night when Aiden had bared his soul to her and told her things he'd never told anyone. He'd trusted her.

And, yes, Emily knew all about her own story but that was hers to tell. She couldn't share Aiden's. Couldn't break that trust. But there were parts that weren't as private as an abusive childhood with an alcoholic father. Or the guilt of feeling responsible for a dreadful accident.

'He's got a brother. Nathan. He's a quadriplegic. Aiden's more than a big brother to him. He's like a parent, too, I guess. A whole family. I think he's got an unwritten rule about not letting anything interfere with that responsibility.'

'Wow…' Emily was silent for a minute. 'Does he feel the same way about you?'

'I don't know. I think he's let me into his life more than he ever has with any other woman. I've met Nathan. We went to a Murderball game.'

'Is that the wheelchair rugby?'

'Yes. It's really exciting to watch. And Nathan's cool. I really like him. He lives in sheltered accommodation but he seems to have his life pretty well sorted. He's got a girlfriend who has more facial piercings than I've ever seen and they clearly adore each other.'

Sophia was rubbing Fuzzy's head and pulling gently on his ears. She bent her own head, horrified that she could feel tears gathering. It was great to be talking to Emily but she didn't want to spoil a lovely afternoon by falling to pieces. What was wrong with her?

'Oh, hon…' Emily's voice was full of sympathy. 'You've got it bad, haven't you?'

The nod dislodged a tear. She swiped it away.

'I don't know what I'm so upset about. I knew it was never supposed to last more than three dates and the next one has got to count for number three. We can't keep bending his silly rule for ever.'

'That's not the real problem, though, is it?'

Sophia swallowed. 'Isn't it?'

Emily shook her head. She tickled Toby, making him chortle, and then pulled him closer for another hug. 'I think it goes deeper than that.'

'In what way?'

'You're not really perfect for each other. Paper doesn't count.' Emily's gaze was serious now. 'Aiden doesn't want kids. And maybe he has good reason for that. But you do want them, even if you've tried to convince yourself you didn't for all these years. You probably want that as much as I did. You want a real family and you know it's quite possible to have that, even if you can't give birth to your own babies. Look at me.'

'I know.' Sophia drew in a long, slow breath as she found herself nodding slowly.

Yes. That was it, in a nutshell. What had been niggling away in the back of her mind. Aiden didn't want children. And she did. It could never work.

End of story?

Maybe not.

'But Oliver didn't want to adopt children either and look at him, now—leading the crusade to let you keep Toby in the country.'

'He didn't want to adopt,' Emily agreed, 'but he always wanted to be a father. It's a bit different.' It was her turn to sigh. 'Life's an unfair business sometimes, isn't it?'

Toby had crawled off Emily's lap now and was heading towards Ruby. Fuzzy abandoned Sophia and went after Toby like a sheepdog looking after his charge. Ruby grinned as she saw them coming. She bent to pick Toby up but then froze. Something about her posture made both Emily and Sophia share an alarmed glance.

'Ruby?' Emily was on her feet in a flash. 'What's wrong?'

It was too quiet today.

So much easier to silence an annoyingly persistent voice in the back of your head if you could keep busy. Even better if you had a real challenge to rise to.

What Aiden needed was something dramatic. A cardiac arrest, maybe—one that led to a successful outcome, of course. Or some trauma. A crush injury perhaps, that would need careful management, especially if whatever was doing the crushing was still in place. A prang would do. A mess of two or three vehicles with an unknown number of potential injuries and the chaos of disrupted traffic and impatient onlookers creating difficulty for any emergency personnel to get to the scene. He'd get there first and get to do the scene management and triage, which was always a challenge of unknown quantity.

But no. What he had was an elderly homeless guy in central Melbourne suffering from double pneumonia. He was sitting just under a bridge beside the popular walking track that led to Southbank. Apparently, he'd been sitting there for the last three days so people had eventually noticed that he had barely moved. Finally, a concerned pedestrian had called the police. The police had called the ambulance service for a medical assessment. They knew this man and knew he didn't talk much. Asking questions wasn't going to solve anything.

'His name's Bruce,' they told Aiden. 'But that's all we know about him, other than that he's been living on the streets for years. Him and his dog.'

The dog looked as old and thin and unkempt as his owner and seemed happy to sit just as immobile, with his head on Bruce's lap. It seemed to know that Aiden was trying to help but growled ominously if any of the police came too close.

After an initial assessment, Aiden had called for transport so now he was just keeping Bruce company. He had his patient on oxygen and a foil survival blanket was wrapped around his shoulders. He'd taken a baseline set of vital signs. Blood pressure was too low, temperature too high. The respiration rate was way too high and blood-oxygen level way too low. Even with the mask on and oxygen coming from the small cylinder he carried on the bike, there had been little improvement over the last ten minutes. Bruce's lips were still blue and he could almost hear the crackle in his lungs without using a stethoscope.

Where on earth was the back-up for transport? Had they been diverted to exactly the kind of drama he was desperate for himself? Something that would stop the argument in his head that was gaining momentum— on both sides.

He couldn't even talk to the two police officers who had moved a safe distance away from the dog and seemed to see something on the river that was interesting enough to keep them chatting.

He only had Bruce, who didn't talk. And a sad-looking dog who was going to look even sadder when they had to take his master away in the ambulance. The police had called a pet shelter that was sending a rescue crew to help. Aiden doubted that these two would ever be reunited and that sucked.

'I'm sorry about this,' he told Bruce quietly, crouching beside him and checking that the oxygen saturation probe was still covering a finger. 'But we have to take you somewhere you can be warm and comfortable so the antibiotics have a chance to work.'

He took Bruce's heart and respiration rate again, just for something to do, but it felt wrong to be so silent. The noise of the city was a distant hum. The sound of voices and laughter came occasionally as a pair of joggers or cyclists went past on the track but the snippets of normality vanished as quickly as they came. He had to talk to Bruce even if the old man couldn't respond or possibly didn't even understand. But what could he talk about? He'd only had one thing on his mind for the last couple of days.

'I'd like to go out tonight,' he found himself telling Bruce. Still quietly enough for nobody but the dog to overhear. 'But, at the same time, I don't want to because if I do, it's going to be the last date I have with this girl and that would be a real shame because she's…well… she's perfect, that's what she is.'

The perfect woman for him, at any rate.

He never wanted to have children.

Sophia couldn't ever have children.

And hadn't that vow to never take on the responsibility of a family of his own been the whole basis of the three-dates rule? To get out before he fell in love? Before she fell in love with him and wanted more—like living together or getting married? Before her biological clock started ticking more and more loudly and the desire to have a baby became the priority?

But he'd never been on this side of the equation. Never been the one who didn't want things to end.

Sophia had welcomed the rule. She didn't want anything long term either. And why would she? She wasn't planning on having a family any more than he was so she wouldn't see herself in the role of a mother. Or a wife.

Someone was going to get hurt and Aiden had the horrible feeling it was going to be him.

Could they stay friends, perhaps, after their official dating period was over?

Friends with benefits even?

No. As if that could work.

As if it could ever be enough.

'I didn't get out in time.' The words came out like a sigh of defeat and triggered a move to check his watch. Where on earth was that back-up? He could hear a siren in the distance but that wouldn't be the crew coming to transport his patient because the job wouldn't have been assigned the urgency of needing lights and sirens. It would be well down the list and probably getting bumped repeatedly as calls came in for more serious incidents.

A glance towards the police officers showed them to be in deep conversation now. Maybe they were enjoying the enforced break from their duties. Life still flowed along the track beside them. A young mother was jogging as she pushed a twin stroller that had a toddler on one side and a baby cocoon strapped on the other. Behind her, an older couple walked hand in hand, and as Aiden watched they turned to each other and shared a smile. In his peripheral vision he saw Bruce move, too. A tiny movement of just his hand as it rested on the dog's head. One finger moving to gently rub a floppy ear.

Something inside Aiden twisted painfully. That dog was probably the only living thing that Bruce had a relationship with. Responsibility for. And, any moment now, someone was going to turn up with a van to take the dog away.

'They'll take good care of him,' Aiden said. 'There are families out there who love to foster dogs.'

Was it his imagination or was Bruce's level of consciousness slipping further? He put his hand on the old man's wrist to feel for a pulse. The dog nudged his hand with a cold nose and that twisting sensation in his gut intensified.

It wasn't just about whether or not you could have kids, was it? Responsibility came with any relationship if you wanted to do the best you could and Aiden had never taken anything on without making sure he did his absolute best.

He was the best paramedic he could be.

The best brother.

When you loved somebody enough, their happiness became as important as your own. More important, maybe. Nathan's happiness had always been more important than his own. Right now, it felt like Sophia's happiness was important, too.

He wanted her to be happy.

He wanted to be the one to *make* her happy.

But if he was really honest, he wanted to be happy himself and that was why this was so damned hard.

Sophia didn't want more than three dates so he couldn't throw the rule book away. And that meant that if he wanted to see her again, it would be for the last time.

And *that* meant he would never see her again.

Did that mean he *didn't* want the date even more than he did want it?

Two men were coming along the track now, carrying a wire crate between them. They wore overalls with the logo of the animal rescue service. Not far behind them, an ambulance crew was wheeling a stretcher. The police officers noted the arrival of assistance and started to move closer in case they were needed.

The wait was over.

The speed with which things were sorted seemed almost indecent after the long wait. Surprisingly, the dog didn't protest at being bundled into the crate and Bruce seemed equally defeated—barely conscious as he was lifted to the stretcher and covered with warm blankets. After handing over his paperwork to the ambulance crew, the last thing Aiden needed to do was change the oxygen supply and take his own small cylinder back to the bike.

'All the best, Bruce,' he said. 'I'll keep an eye out for you next time I'm down this way.'

The old man's eyes opened slowly. His lips moved. Aiden lifted the mask.

'Ask her,' Bruce mumbled. 'Tell her...'

Oh, man... It was a cringe-worthy moment to realise

that he'd been heard and understood when he'd been sharing something so decidedly unprofessional. Aiden didn't want to have to think about it and, lucky for him, he didn't have to. He'd barely got his helmet back on his head when a priority call came through to an address in Brunswick.

'Premature labour,' he was told. 'Approximately twenty-eight weeks gestation. Mother seventeen years old. Nearest ambulance is at least ten minutes away.'

Aiden kicked his bike into life and flicked on the beacons. Anticipation was tinged with relief. This was exactly what he needed.

Drama. A life—other than his own—that was hanging in the balance.

'The ambulance is on its way.'

'How long?' Sophia was kneeling behind Ruby, holding the girl in her arms to support her.

'I don't *want* an ambulance,' Ruby sobbed. 'I just want this to *stop*. It *hurts*…'

'I know, sweetheart.' Sophia tightened her hug. 'But sometimes it's baby who decides when things are going to happen.' She turned to catch Emily's gaze and mouthed her question again silently.

Emily held up the fingers of both hands and her look said it all. Ten minutes could well be too long. She tilted her head towards the house with her eyebrows raised but Sophia had to shake her head. They'd already tried to get Ruby inside but she'd been almost hysterical as the first pain had hit and her waters had broken. She'd frozen and then collapsed onto the ground when Emily and Sophia had taken her arms to help her walk.

Emily's mother, Adrianna, came rushing out of the house with an armload of blankets. 'I'll keep Toby in with me,' she said. 'Where on earth is that ambulance? We called them ages ago.'

'It was only a few minutes, Mum,' Emily said. 'And I can hear a siren.'

'Oh…thank goodness.' Adrianna tucked a blanket around Ruby's shoulders. 'You'll be okay now, love. You'll be safely in hospital in no time.'

'I won't,' Ruby sobbed. 'It's too early. I didn't think I wanted this baby but I do…I want it *so* much…'

'I know.' Sophia kept hugging her. She knew how it felt to be faced with the fear of losing an unborn baby you'd already fallen in love with. She also knew that Ruby's fears were justified. This was far too early—especially if this baby was going to arrive before they had the benefit of all the resuscitation gear that the MMU would have on hand. Emily was looking desperately worried and that was enough to pull Sophia even further from the calm, professional space she was trying to hang onto.

And that siren sounded…different?

It wasn't really a surprise to see the big bike pulling in to the side of the road and a helmeted figure opening panniers to grab equipment.

What was surprising was the way her fear seemed to evaporate the moment she saw that it was Aiden who had responded to the call.

'The ambulance isn't far away,' he told Ruby, as he crouched beside her. 'I'm just the advance party.' He looked up to include all of them. 'Tell me what's happening. How far apart are the contractions?'

Emily filled him in on the sudden start of Ruby's labour. She also told him that the baby had had in utero surgery a few weeks ago to correct spina bifida and that Ruby had been kept on complete bed rest until they had been confident she wouldn't go into labour. By the time she finished speaking, the ambulance had arrived.

'We'll get you into the ambulance,' Aiden said. 'But we'll need to check where we're at before we roll.'

'I'm coming too,' Emily said.

There would be no room in the ambulance for Sophia to go as well but she went as far as the ambulance and waited while Aiden and Emily examined Ruby. Everything seemed under control but suddenly Ruby cried out as another contraction hit and then nothing was under control. Within seconds Aiden was holding a tiny scrap of a baby in his hands.

'Soph? Open that kit for me and get the ziplock bag.'

Her hands were shaking as she complied. She knew to wrap preterm infants in bubble wrap but a plastic bag? The baby wasn't making any sound and this was not looking good.

But Aiden seemed to know exactly what he was doing. He cut and clamped the cord and then put the baby into the bag leaving the head outside.

'Dry the head for me,' he told Emily. 'And cover it with a corner of the blanket. Soph—can you bring that airway kit a bit closer, please?'

One of the ambulance crew got there first and Sophia edged further away. The back of the ambulance was crowded now and all Emily could do was hold Ruby's hand and try to reassure her as she watched what was happening with the baby.

Sophia stood pressed against the open back door of the ambulance. She couldn't look away from that fierce concentration on Aiden's face. He was invested in this job a thousand per cent, determined to succeed, and she loved him for that.

And she felt so proud of him. That he knew exactly what to do and that he was doing it with such confidence and skill.

His hands moved so fast. They looked huge against the tiny pieces of equipment, like the smallest ever size of a laryngoscope blade and breathing tube. The ventilation bag was also tiny and he was squeezing it so gently to deliver such small puffs of oxygen.

'Hook up the monitor,' he told one of the crew. 'I need continuous monitoring of end tidal CO_2.'

The baby still wasn't moving but Aiden wasn't starting any chest compressions. His gaze was flicking between the baby and the monitor.

'Heart rate's over sixty,' he said. 'Let's roll. I want to get this little girl into NICU asap.'

Sophia had to step back so that the doors could be slammed shut. Within seconds, the ambulance took off, with its beacons flashing and the siren on. It looked like any other ambulance by the time it got to the end of the street but Sophia knew what was happening inside and she shut her eyes for a moment, sending out a fervent wish that they were going to be successful in saving that tiny life.

Then she opened her eyes and found herself staring at Aiden's bike.

He'd have to come back for that, wouldn't he?

Adrianna would be only too happy if Sophia hung around until Emily got back so that she could hear a first-hand account of how things had gone during transport and what was happening with the baby. It was quite reasonable to also assume that Aiden would come back with her so that he could collect his bike and get back on the road. Sophia picked up his helmet.

For a moment she held it in her arms, close to her chest. It felt like a connection to the man who'd been wearing it a short time ago. It also felt like an insurance policy. He'd have to come in to find it before he could go anywhere else. Like the way her fear had receded when Aiden had arrived at a potentially tragic scene, the knowledge that she would be able to see him again before long made everything feel a bit different.

Better?

Oh, yes… A great deal better.

But would he ask her out on another date when they actually had a chance to talk?

Their last ever date?

Her breath came out in a long, heartfelt sigh.

Maybe she didn't feel better after all.

CHAPTER TEN

MINUTES TURNED INTO hours but still Aiden hadn't come back for his bike.

Sophia helped Adrianna peel a mountain of vegetables that went into the oven to roast, along with a huge leg of lamb.

'Oliver won't be far behind Em and I'm sure they're both starving. Maybe that nice young paramedic will be able to stay and have some dinner as well.'

This household was like that. A real family home where all comers were made to feel welcome.

'Wasn't he marvellous?' Adrianna added. 'It was such a relief when he arrived and even from here I could see how good he was with Ruby. A very impressive young man.'

'Mmm.' Sophia hadn't dared meet the gaze of the older woman. 'He is.'

When the front door finally opened, it was Emily's voice that could be heard.

'We're home. Sorry we were so long.'

Her tone was upbeat enough to suggest that the news was going to be good.

Adrianna came rushing from the kitchen and Sophia dropped the book she'd been reading to Toby as they cuddled on the couch.

It wasn't just Emily. Aiden was right behind her and Oliver was only a step behind them.

'Ollie gave us both a ride back,' Emily said. 'Aiden was going to get an ambulance to drop him back but when he heard that Ollie had a sixty-four Morgan sports car, he couldn't resist the invitation.'

'How did you all fit in?' Adrianna was wiping her hands on her apron.

'Bit of a squeeze,' Emily admitted, 'but we coped.' Her grin in Sophia's direction was accompanied by a ghost of a wink that suggested she hadn't minded the squeeze at all.

'I'm glad.' Adrianna smiled at Aiden. 'I hope you won't resist an invitation to stay for dinner either. I've made enough to feed an army and I want to thank you for helping our Ruby.'

'How *is* Ruby?' Sophia steadied Toby as he tried to stand up on the couch beside her, holding his arms out to his parents.

'Mumma,' he demanded.

Emily scooped him into her arms. 'Ruby's fine. No complications. She's in NICU. We couldn't persuade her to come home and get some sleep. She won't take her eyes off her daughter.'

Sophia couldn't let her breath out. She'd been too scared to ask. Her gaze shifted to Oliver. As the surgeon who'd been in charge of the in utero surgery on Ruby's baby he would be well up to date on what was happening now and he would be able to tell her. But her gaze kept travelling and only stopped when it caught Aiden's. He was smiling.

'She's doing amazingly well,' he said quietly. 'I had the privilege of being allowed to get involved while they got her settled and stable.'

'Of course you did,' Emily said. 'It was you who saved the baby in the first place.' She stepped closer to Sophia. 'You should have heard what they said about Aiden's management. He's brilliant.'

'I knew that.' It felt like her heart was in danger of bursting with pride and an odd lump in her throat made her words a little hoarse. Sophia looked back at Aiden but he seemed to be avoiding her gaze now.

'I learned a lot,' he said. 'It's not often we get to follow on with our patient's treatment like that. Luckily I've got a boss who knows how valuable it is, so I got covered for the rest of my shift.'

'You're off duty?' Adrianna beamed. 'So you can stay for dinner?'

'Well…'

'How 'bout a beer?' Oliver had taken Toby from Emily's arms to get a cuddle but now he put the small boy onto the floor. 'I think we all deserve a bit of wind-down time.'

Toby was doing his stiff-legged crawl towards his new, favourite toy.

'So that's where my helmet got to.'

'I was just looking after it,' Sophia said. 'I knew you'd come back.'

'Of course.' His gaze caught hers. And held. Sophia

could feel Emily and Oliver watching them. She knew they were both smiling and she could feel the colour creeping into her cheeks.

'For the bike,' she added.

A soft chuckle came from Adrianna, who disappeared back into the kitchen.

Aiden cleared his throat. 'I'd better ring HQ and let them know I'll be a bit late dropping it back.'

'And I'll find us a beer. A wine for you, Soph?'

'Thanks, Oliver. I'd love one.'

'Me, too,' Emily said. 'Toby, what are you doing?'

It was Aiden's turn to chuckle. 'I think he fancies riding a bike. Do you want to try that on, Toby?'

The helmet was far too big but Toby whooped with happiness when Aiden held it over his head.

'Where's my phone? I've got to get a picture of this.' Emily was laughing as she went to find it. 'Ollie, come and see. This is priceless.'

It *was* priceless. Aiden sat on the floor with Toby on his lap, wearing the helmet. All you could see was the white grin on the small, dark face. And the smile on the face of the man protecting the toddler's head from too much weight from the enormous helmet.

Something huge caught in Sophia's chest and squeezed so tightly it was hard to breathe.

Maybe it was the way Aiden was holding Toby so protectively. Or that look on his face that revealed that he was enjoying this as much as anybody else.

Or maybe it was just part of the puzzle. Another piece was that expression she'd seen when he'd been working with such determination to save Ruby's baby. How gently he'd done what had needed to be done.

And what about the first time she'd ever met this man? When he'd been holding Claire's baby boy after that emergency delivery. What had he said? Oh, yes...

'Babies are my favourite thing. It was a treat.'

Right now, toddlers seemed to be his favourite thing.

There was no question that he was more than capable of caring for and loving children. Look at the love he had for his younger brother and the way he still took responsibility for Nathan. So much so that he wasn't going to allow anything—or anyone—else to interfere with continuing to make Nathan his priority.

That was why he'd come up with that stupid three dates rule in the first place, wasn't it?

But he'd make such an amazing father.

Did he have any idea how good he would be? Was it really that he never wanted to have his own child or was he denying himself the opportunity to experience the kind of joy it could bring? Did he realise that he was shutting himself away from the chance of having a real family for himself? From having people who could support him instead of it always being the other way around?

It was actually painful to swallow the lump in her throat but Sophia managed. She even kept her tone light.

'I'll go and see if Adrianna needs some help in the kitchen.'

The kid was adorable.

The fun of the helmet wore off but Aiden apparently

had plenty of other attractions. Like the penlight torch clipped to his pocket. He showed Toby how to turn it on and it was dark enough now for the beam to show up and dance along the wall. The dog, Fuzzy, seemed to find this as good a game as Toby did. He bounced from one spot to the next, wagging his tail and barking to announce that he'd found where the light had escaped to, and this never failed to make Toby giggle with delight.

The beer hit the spot and he got the chance to talk about the in utero surgery that that tiny baby had had prior to her birth, while Emily and Sophia took Toby away for his bath. Fascinating stuff and yet his interest seemed to evaporate when the women returned. It was Sophia who was carrying Toby in his fluffy sleep suit, a bedraggled-looking toy kangaroo dangling from one hand. Sophia's cheeks were pink and her hair was a tousled mop of damp curls. And there was something about her expression that made Aiden catch his breath.

Something so tender it actually gave him a lump in his throat. When he saw the way she pressed a kiss onto Toby's head before she handed him to Oliver for a goodnight cuddle, he had to turn away.

How sad was it that she would never be able to have children of her own?

To be a mother?

She'd be...amazing.

It was easy to push that disturbing sense of regret on Sophia's behalf away during the course of the delicious dinner Adrianna served up in the kitchen. There was great conversation and plenty of laughter, a dog sitting under the table in the hope of something falling his way, and an atmosphere of…what was it?

Something Aiden had never really experienced before.

Family, he realised as he reluctantly made his farewells immediately after the meal. He had to get the bike back to HQ and he'd promised Nate he'd drop in this evening so he couldn't stay any longer.

He wanted to, though.

He'd grown up in a house devoid of the kind of warmth this house was full of, and he'd pretty much lived alone ever since then. Nathan's sheltered accommodation had something of this warmth but it was very different. This was a real home—with parents and a child and a dog and even a grandma thrown in for good measure.

A real home. A real family.

Sophia looked different here. She came with him when he went to find his helmet and torch in the lounge and then saw him to the front door. Her hair was still extra-curly and there was a sparkle in her eyes that made her look extra-happy. Totally irresistible. There was nobody to witness their kiss and it was so good it would have been rude not to have another one.

She didn't just look different here. She *felt* different. Softer. More confident?

As if she was in a place where she felt completely at home?

He was even more reluctant to leave now.

'I have to go,' he murmured against her ear as he held her close. 'Nate asked me to drop in on my way home and he'll be wondering why I'm so late.'

Sophia melted out of his arms like a deflating balloon. 'Of course.'

'See you soon?'

She nodded but some of that sparkle had gone. It looked like she was holding herself very still. Holding her breath even?

'This wasn't a date.' Oh, help…why had he said that? Why bring up the fact that they only had one official date left?

Sophia didn't say anything. She smiled but she was turning away at the same time and Aiden was left with the feeling that he'd killed the sparkle completely. Pretty much like he had when he'd ruined their second date by cutting it short to go and visit his brother.

But that was precisely why he *had* to go, wasn't it?

And why he couldn't let how he felt about Sophia go any further.

It was his problem to deal with. His heart that was going to bleed when this was over.

Gunning the powerful engine of his bike gave him a momentary reprieve from the downward spiral of his mood.

He'd survive.

He'd always survived. He'd learned that long ago. Just like he'd learned how to hide how he felt so that nobody knew.

Nate knew.

He took one look at Aiden's face and his eyes narrowed. 'Man—what's up with you? Bad day?'

'No. Great day. Delivered a premmie baby. Twenty-eight-weeker. Not only that, she'd had in-utero surgery to correct spina bifida a few weeks ago, which is probably why the labour came on so early. I got to hang around in NICU while they stabilised her. You wouldn't believe some of the high-tech gear they've got in there.'

But, for once, Nathan didn't want to hear every detail of the interesting job.

'I've got something to tell you,' he said.

His tone suggested that he didn't think it would be something Aiden wanted to hear. Sudden fear made Aiden sink onto the edge of his brother's bed. What had happened? Was there something wrong that he hadn't been told about? Had Nathan's condition worsened in some way? Had he injured himself playing that fierce wheelchair rugby? Was he *sick*?

'What's the matter?' The query came out more tersely than he'd intended. 'You're not sick, are you? I hope it's not another UTI. Have you been—?'

'For God's sake,' Nathan interrupted. 'Will you stop fussing like some mother hen? No. I'm not sick. It's Sam.'

'Sam's sick?'

'*No.*' Nathan gave an exasperated huff of sound. 'She's not sick. She's pregnant.'

The silence fell like a brick.

Nathan shook his head. 'Don't even think about asking that one. Yeah…it's mine.'

Aiden was still too stunned to say anything. This was the last thing he'd expected to hear. Astonishment warred with something else that was even less pleasant. Fear for the challenges Nate was going to have to face? Or was it more than that? Jealousy, maybe, that there were going to be people in his brother's life who would be more important than he was? Sam. A *baby*...

'You're going to be an uncle,' Nathan told him. 'How cool is that?'

It was Aiden's turn to shake his head. 'How did that happen?'

Nathan laughed. 'You mean you don't know?' He tipped his chair, balancing on the back of the wheels. 'And you with all that medical training. Bro...'

A flash of anger surfaced. 'Cut it out, Nate. This is serious. It's not your physical capabilities I'm questioning. It's your level of intelligence in not using any kind of protection. Have you even thought about what happens next?'

The chair came down with a thump. 'What happens next is that I'm going to marry Sam. We've already applied to get a house of our own. We're going to make this work and we're very, very happy about it.' He had an odd expression on his face. 'It'd be nice if you could manage to be happy about it, too.'

'I...' Again, words failed Aiden. It felt like he was being pushed out of Nathan's life. As if the whole foundation of his own life was crumbling.

'It'll work,' Nathan said fiercely. 'I'm going to make sure it works. I can be a good dad, I know I can. And a good husband. I'm going to have a real family, Aiden, and...and I can't wait.'

You've got a family, Aiden wanted to say. *You've got me.*

But he couldn't utter the words. He knew exactly what Nathan was talking about. He'd just spent the evening with a real family, hadn't he? Did he not want that for his brother if it was possible? That kind of security?

That kind of love?

Nathan was watching him.

'It doesn't mean that I don't still need you in my life, you know.'

'I know.' The words were strangled.

But he wasn't enough. He got that but it still hurt.

'You can't make me feel guilty about this.' Nathan's words were raw. 'I know how much you've given up for me. You've felt responsible ever since the accident happened. You decided then and there you were going to be a paramedic, didn't you?'

'I guess…'

'Because you felt guilty about what happened. How many times do you have to be told, bro?' Nathan's glare was fierce. 'It. Was. Not. Your. Fault.'

'Okay…' Aiden held up his hands in a gesture of surrender. Or maybe a signal to stop. He knew that. Sophia had told him the same thing and he had—on some level—accepted it. Now Nathan was making it crystal clear that he had no choice but to let it go. To believe what everybody told him.

Sophia had done more than try to absolve his guilt. She'd thought he'd been *brave…*

'You don't get to feel guilty about me any more,'

Nathan continued. 'And that means I don't get to feel guilty about you either. Is it a deal?'

'Of course you don't get to feel guilty about me. Why would you?'

'Ooh, let me think…' Nathan shook his head. 'Maybe because you also decided you weren't going to let anything get in the way of looking after me. Anything like a pet. Or a partner. Or—heaven forbid—*kids*…'

Surely it hadn't been that obvious? It wasn't as if Aiden had even articulated what lay beneath the decisions about how he lived his life. The boundaries had simply evolved. And strengthened.

Okay, maybe he had articulated the three-dates rule. It had become a joke that was part of the bond between the brothers. He just hadn't expected Nathan to see through it with such clarity. To come to *disapprove* of it with such vehemence…

Was it because he'd fallen in love himself and was determined to make it the best relationship possible? Hurtful words spoken weeks ago drifted into his mind.

Being told that Nathan didn't want to end up like him. Shut off. Scared of losing control.

As if he was reading Aiden's mind, Nathan spoke again. The anger had gone from his voice. It was quiet now. Serious.

'We only get one life, mate, and if we don't make the best of it, we've only got ourselves to blame. You can't keep me safe because I don't want to *be* that kind of safe any more. I want to live. *Really* live. And that's what you should be doing, too.'

He reminded Aiden of Sophia saying that life wasn't

a practice run. Had he missed something along the way? Had he done the wrong thing in trying to be the best brother he could be?

'I wouldn't be where I am if it hadn't been for you,' Nathan said quietly. 'I'll love you for ever for that.'

Aiden tried to swallow the lump in his throat but it wasn't budging.

'You could have that too, you know. You and Sophia. You're perfect for each other.'

'She doesn't want that. She…she can't have kids. Doesn't want a family.'

Except that didn't really ring true, did it? Not after the way she'd looked when she'd been holding a sleepy Toby. How happy she'd been in that family kitchen.

'And you don't want kids. You've always said that being a dad to me was more than enough.'

Aiden swallowed. He had said that. He'd meant it, too. Hadn't he?

'So it's my turn to find out what it's like. You get to be the favourite uncle. Maybe Sophia would like to be an auntie. Hey, can I tell Sam it's okay to come in now? That you're not going to rain on our parade?'

'Sure.'

But Nathan hesitated at the door. 'You've got one date left with Sophia, haven't you?'

Aiden shrugged. What difference did it make?

'Make it count,' Nathan said. 'Tell her that you love her, man. It might change your life.' He grinned and his face lit up with joy. 'It changed mine.'

There were congratulations to be given after that. And plans. Not that Aiden got to say much. Nathan and

Sam seemed to have everything going just the way they wanted it to and they had the support of everybody in the house.

It was impossible not to get captured by the love these two young people had for each other. The hope that shone in their eyes as they looked at each other and shared the plans for their future.

Impossible not to come away without the realisation that he wanted that for himself, too.

That it was something worth fighting for.

It was late but maybe it wasn't *too* late.

The phone rang and rang. Any second now, and it would go to voice-mail and Aiden had no idea what he would say. Somehow he had to tell Sophia how he felt about her but you couldn't do that in a voice-mail, could you?

But then the ringing stopped and he heard Sophia's soft voice.

'Hey, Aiden…what's up?'

'Ah…' He couldn't do it over the phone either. He couldn't tell Sophia how much he loved her when he couldn't see her face. Couldn't touch her. He cleared his throat. 'I just wanted to…to…ask you out.'

'On a date?'

Oh, God…was that reluctance he could hear in her voice? A hint of fear even?

'Yeah…'

He heard what sounded like a slow, indrawn breath. 'Okay. When?'

'Um…I'm not sure. I'll text you.'

'Needs planning, huh?'

'Yeah…' He found a smile. 'The best dates always do.'

'Especially number three?' There was a catch in Sophia's voice. 'Saving the best for last?'

'Something like that. I'll text you as soon as I've got it sorted.'

It wasn't until after he'd put the phone down and started browsing his computer for ideas worthy of the perfect date that it clicked.

That reluctance.

Making it clear that this was date number three and therefore the final one.

Maybe Sophia didn't *want* it to be the final date any more than he did.

He turned back to his browsing with renewed enthusiasm.

Hope even?

The trill of her phone announcing a text came at a truly ungodly hour but Sophia woke instantly and completely as she reached to grab her mobile.

Not that she was expecting any of her women to be going into labour, but a phone call at this time of night could only signal an emergency.

Except it wasn't one of her mums-to-be.

It was an invitation for a date. If she was up for it, a taxi would be arriving to collect her in twenty minutes.

What kind of date started at four a.m.?

Certainly not a kind that Sophia had ever experienced. But, then, she'd never gone on a date knowing that it would be the last either. And she'd certainly never gone on a date with a man she was so totally and hope-lessly in love with.

Her fingers were shaking as she entered her response.

Bring it on.

CHAPTER ELEVEN

WITHOUT THE LIGHTS of the city, the night became an inky blackness surrounding the car.

Where on earth was she being taken?

Sophia had rugged up, knowing there could well be a hint of frost with the approaching dawn, but in the heat of the taxi, being wrapped in her puffer jacket and woolly accessories had her feeling drowsy.

Maybe this was all a dream?

Pulling off one woollen glove, she checked her phone. Yes. There were the text messages sent and received so recently. The last one had sent her digging through a drawer to find items of clothing that wouldn't normally make an appearance for a month or two yet.

Dress for something cold! Aiden had instructed.

Real doubt might have surfaced surrounding this date at that point but Aiden had sent another message.

Trust me.

So here she was. Speeding off in the night to an unknown destination. In a car being driven by a total stranger.

Her mother would be horrified. Sophia could almost hear an echo of her voice.

'How could you be so *reckless*, Sophia?'

A smile tilted her lips as she silently answered that voice.

Because it was Aiden who asked me, Mum. That's how.

Maybe she dozed for a while, lulled by the warmth and the rumble of the car's engine, overlaid with some easy listening music on the radio. Any minute now and she'd be hearing a track from Cat Stevens. Not that she needed the cue to think back to that evening with Aiden. To the shock of hearing about his appalling childhood. To the way his vulnerability had stolen her heart. To the understanding she had gained about why he had chosen the career he had and why he felt he had to shut anything out of his life that could get in the way of his devotion to his younger brother.

She loved him enough to know that she would never do that.

Enough to have this final date and let him go?

Yes.

But she was going to make the most of every minute of it. Especially when it had obviously been planned with great care. Like date number two. He'd taken her a long way out of the city that time, too. Was she being taken back there, perhaps? Were they going to watch the sunrise from a lighthouse overlooking one of those gorgeous beaches?

'Where *are* we going?'

'We're here, love.' The taxi driver was slowing his

vehicle, as if he was looking for a signpost. 'In the heart of the Yarra Valley.'

Nowhere near Queenscliff, then. This was pretty much the opposite direction out of Melbourne. Sophia hadn't been in this area yet but she knew it was famous for food and wine and stunning scenery.

A long way to go for a date for breakfast, though.

And the driver wasn't heading for the winery the sign had advertised. He was turning onto a side road that appeared to lead to nothing more than a big paddock beside a small lake.

Well…there was something more. A couple of trucks parked near a group of people. And a motorbike.

And someone breaking away from the group to come and meet her taxi.

Aiden had a big, puffy jacket on, too. And woolly gloves. And a beanie that covered his head and ears, but Sophia would have recognised that smile anywhere.

Her heart recognised it as well. She could feel its joyous squeeze.

'Have you guessed?' His smile widened. 'Have you ever done this before?'

Shaking her head, Sophia took hold of his hand. They were both wearing gloves but she could still feel the warmth and strength of his grip. He led her towards the huddle of people. What looked like a small house made of wicker turned out to be the bottom of a huge basket. On the other side, an enormous puddle of fabric lay on the ground.

A balloon.

This was date number three? A ride in a hot-air

balloon? How scary was this? Sophia's grip on Aiden's hand tightened. In response, he put his arm around her shoulders and pulled her firmly against his side.

You're safe, the gesture told her. *I won't let anything bad happen to you.*

Torchlight showed that the balloon had a background colour of deep gold. Big fans were positioned on either side of the basket and, as Sophia and Aiden watched, people held up the base of the fabric and air began to fill the balloon. And then, with a roar that made Sophia gasp in alarm, a huge flame emerged from the burner as someone turned it on and the air began to heat. Slowly, majestically, the balloon began to rise, tipping the basket into an upright position.

There were openings in the side of the basket and the pilot showed Aiden how to use them as footholds to climb in. Standing inside, he waited only until Sophia had her foot in the first rung and then his hands came under her arms and he lifted her as easily as if she weighed no more than a child.

And there they were, standing inside this huge basket with only the pilot for company.

'This is Jim,' Aiden told her. 'You're in safe hands.'

Sophia shook the pilot's hand. Then she looked at the ground crew, who seemed to be packing up. This was puzzling. She'd seen pictures of balloon rides like this and people were usually crammed into these baskets like human sardines.

'Haven't you got any more passengers?' she asked.

'Not today.' Jim grinned at Aiden. 'This man saved my kid's life a while back. I owed him a favour.'

Another blast of the burner punctuated his sentence and they were lifting off the ground. Aiden led her to the opposite side of the basket and pointed. Far in the distance, over the top of the Dandenong Ranges, the sun was starting to appear—a blindingly brilliant sliver of light that painted the bottoms of nearby clouds deep shades of orange and pink.

Despite the layers of clothing, it was freezing. Sophia was more than happy to be tucked against Aiden's side and each blast of the burner surrounded them with a welcome wave of warmth. It illuminated the balloon, too, and Sophia gasped with delight the first time she looked up. The dark gold of the fabric she'd seen on the ground was now a glowing, rich hue and there were patterns on it. Aboriginal designs of lizards and kangaroos and birds, and there were hand- and footprints and chains of coloured shapes filling other gaps.

'It's gorgeous.' She raised her voice to be heard over the roar of the burner but then it stopped and Aiden's response fell into complete silence.

'So are you,' he said. 'I love you, Sophia.'

Hearing Aiden say those words was like an emotional version of a burner being turned on inside her heart, lighting it up and making it glow.

The silence around them was astonishing. Somewhere down below a rooster was crowing to announce the approaching dawn but Sophia only had to whisper to be heard.

'I love you, too.'

Saying the words out loud was like a seal. The truth was out there now and it would never change. Dawn might be breaking around them to reveal stunning scenery but there was nothing she wanted to see more than what she was seeing in Aiden's eyes right now.

But it was heart-breaking, too. They loved each other but this was the last time they would be together like this. On a date.

The prickle of imminent tears made her wrench her gaze free of Aiden's. She was not going to cry in front of him. Or ruin this spectacular date he had organised. She blinked hard. Gulped in a breath of the icy air. Tried to find something to focus on. There were ponds of ground fog on the patchwork of fields and vineyards below and away in the distance she could see other balloons rising over the misty landscape. One was coloured like a rainbow. She concentrated on that, waiting for its burner to make it glow again, but it wasn't enough. She could feel a tear escape and trickle down the side of her nose.

'Oh, hon...'

Her view of the rainbow balloon vanished as Aiden gathered her into his arms. And when she raised her head all she could see was that look of love in his face. That vanished, too, as his face lowered and he kissed her.

Slowly. So tenderly her heart broke all over again.

A long blast of the burner made them finally break that kiss. Maybe the reminder that they weren't quite alone made them both look out to take in the magic of where they were, floating in the clear air of what was going to be a perfect day. There seemed to Sophia to be nothing more to say but Aiden obviously didn't think so.

'Do you remember our first date?'

'Of course. You kissed me in that garden bar.'

'Do you remember me telling you about my three-dates rule?'

Sophia nodded. How could she have forgotten? She had embraced the idea so enthusiastically. Had she really said that it was exactly the rule that was missing from her own life?

'There's something else you should know about that rule,' Aiden said softly.

'Oh?'

'Mmm.'

Aiden was staring intently at something on the ground. That flock of sheep perhaps?

'It's a load of bull.'

Sophia's jaw dropped. A loud bleating sound came from one of the sheep far below and it sounded like laughter.

'Is it…?' she managed.

Aiden straightened and met her gaze. 'It is if you find the person you want to spend the rest of your life with.' He caught her hands and gripped them tightly. 'I don't want to go on any more dates with you, Soph. I want…I want us just to be together. For ever. I want to marry you.'

'Oh…'

This was the last thing Sophia had expected to happen on this—the final—date. Had she really thought her heart had been breaking earlier? It had only been a crack. This was what it felt like to really break. To shatter into a million little pieces.

'I love you,' she whispered. 'Please, know that.' She had to close her eyes. 'But I could never marry you.'

* * *

Oh…*God*…

How devastating was this?

Aiden had planned this date knowing that his future was on the line here. That the stupid three-dates rule he'd not only invented but had given to Sophia meant that this was his last chance.

And he'd blown it.

The silence around them was deafening. Excruciating. Had Jim heard him putting his heart on the line and being turned down?

His dating rule wasn't the only stupid idea he'd ever had either. He'd chosen what seemed to be the most romantic place in the world to propose but he hadn't given any thought to failure. To being trapped in a floating box in the sky with nowhere to go. Nowhere to hide.

He would just have to grit his teeth and ride it out. To look as if he wasn't dying inside. Surely there was something out there he could focus on. Those other balloons, maybe, dotted in the sky at various levels. Yeah…there was one that had rainbow stripes. Pretty.

'It's not about the three-dates rule,' Sophia said quietly. 'It's about why you made it. About the responsibility you feel for Nate and…and how you feel about having a family.'

'I—' He had to tell her that his brother's world had changed. That his level of responsibility had been downgraded, but she didn't let him continue.

'I understand,' she told him. 'Honestly, I do. And I know that me not being able to have my own babies should make us perfect for each other but…'

He could see the way she took a deep breath. Could see the soft light that came into her eyes. 'But I *want* a family,' she said. 'And there are lots of ways of doing that without giving birth yourself.'

Aiden hadn't expected that. How arrogant had he been, assuming that Sophia had embraced the idea of limited relationships because she had no reason to want something long term when she couldn't have her own children? He had no idea what he could say to that but he didn't need to say anything yet.

Sophia's smile was poignant. 'You should know,' she said. 'Nathan is your brother, not your son, but you pretty much raised him. I love that you love him so much and it says a lot about what an amazing person you are that you've kept up that caring for him.' She scrubbed at her face with her glove as if she was wiping away a tear. Sure enough, her next words sounded choked. 'And I know it was tough. I understand why you wouldn't want to do it again.'

'I've just never considered it as an option,' Aiden put in. He needed a minute to get his head around this. Was this why Sophia couldn't marry him? Because he'd said he never wanted kids?

'I look at Emily,' Sophia said, 'and I know that that's what I want. A family. And I know it can be easier to adopt kids that aren't quite perfect and I'd be okay with that. But you've already spent your life caring for someone who needed extra help.'

'So doesn't that make me an expert?'

That surprised her into silence and it gave Aiden a moment to clear his head. To let the pieces fall into place.

Maybe it was the mention of Emily that did it. The memory of what it had been like in the Evanses' house that night. The way Sophia had looked when she'd been cuddling Toby in his fluffy sleepsuit. The laughter and warmth in that kitchen. The dog under the table.

Family.

He wanted that too, dammit.

The burst of the burner was the longest yet and it ignited something inside Aiden. Determination?

Jim's voice added a sense of urgency.

'Sorry, guys, but we're on the way down now. You'll see our chase vehicles parked up near that lake.'

Aiden didn't even look.

'The "not wanting kids" was just another stupid rule,' he told Sophia. 'Like the three-dates one. I convinced myself that's what worked because I didn't think I had the option of anything else. I felt guilty about Nate and I stuck to the promise I'd made when the accident happened. That I would look after him for ever.'

'Of course you did. Your loyalty is up there with all the other amazing things I love about you.'

'I was wrong,' Aiden insisted. 'Not about being loyal. About believing it was my fault. Nate told me but it wasn't until *you* told me that I started believing it. And now I really do. Nate and I made a deal. I'd stop feeling guilty about him and he wouldn't have to feel guilty about me.'

'He feels guilty about you?'

'He thinks I'm throwing away my own life because I think I need to look after him. He's made it very clear he's going to live his own life. He's getting married. Sam's going to have his baby.'

'Really?' Sophia sounded delighted. 'You're going to be an uncle? That's perfect for you.'

'No it's not,' Aiden growled. 'It's not enough.' He shook his head to emphasise his words. 'Yeah, I convinced myself that I didn't want anything that got in the way of putting Nate first but I did that for too long and it's a good thing that I'm not allowed to do it any more. And it means that for the first time in my life I'm going to be able to choose what *I* want. Just for myself.'

They were getting close to landing now. He could see the shadow of their balloon and its basket clearly outlined on the ground below. There was a truck parked that would carry the balloon back to its base. A car with support crew to help pack up.

Sophia wasn't looking at their shadow getting larger as the land rose to meet them. She was staring at him.

'What *do* you want?' she asked softly.

There was no hesitation on his part. 'You. Us. A family. A dog even.'

There were tears in Sophia's eyes but she was smiling. Laughing, in fact.

The bump of the basket touching the ground knocked them both off balance. A perfect excuse to take the woman he loved in his arms. To kiss her with all the joy of knowing there was hope that nothing was left to get in the way of them being together.

'That's it, folks.' Jim's voice came over what sounded like applause from the ground crew surrounding them. 'The ride's over.'

But it wasn't. Aiden couldn't keep a grin off his face as he helped Sophia from the basket and then pulled her close for another kiss.

The real ride was only just beginning.

'What happens now?' Sophia asked when he finally let her go.

The basket was on the back of the truck now and people were squashing air out of the balloon so it could be rolled up and put in its bag.

'A champagne breakfast,' he told her.

Her smile lit up the world. 'Is that a date?'

He grinned. 'Only if we have a new rule.'

'What's that? A thirty-dates rule?'

'I'm thinking more like a three-hundred-dates rule. And if that runs out, we'll make a new rule.'

Laughing, with their arms around each other, they made their way to the car that would take them to the vineyard restaurant.

'Or maybe we should make a rule about never having another date,' Aiden suggested.

'No.' Sophia tugged him to a halt and peered up at him, her bottom lip caught between her teeth as if she was trying not to smile. 'It's good that you've had so much practice because there's one date that's going to need quite a bit of planning.'

'What's that?'

'Our wedding?' Yes. The smile escaped.

Aiden's smile was coming but not quite yet. After a kiss, maybe. When that tight feeling in his chest of too much joy to handle had had a chance to subside a little.

It might need to be a long kiss, he realised as his lips captured hers.

Just as well Sophia didn't seem to mind.

* * * * *

MIDWIFE'S
BABY BUMP

BY
SUSANNE HAMPTON

Published in Great Britain 2015
by Mills & Boon, an imprint of Harlequin (UK) Limited,
Eton House, 18-24 Paradise Road, Richmond, Surrey, TW9 1SR

© 2015 Harlequin Books S.A.

Special thanks and acknowledgement are given to Susanne Hampton for her contribution to the *Midwives On-Call* series

ISBN: 978-0-263-24705-3

Printed and bound in Spain
by CPI, Barcelona

Dear Reader,

Writing this book came with challenges, as I had never been a part of a continuity and the idea of writing Felicia and Tristan's love story within a much larger story was daunting. But it was equally exciting. It provided the opportunity for my hero and heroine to interact with characters who had already overcome obstacles to love and to introduce characters who would quite soon have their love story unfold.

Tristan Hamilton doesn't see long-term love in his future. He has devoted his career to improving the quality of life of his tiny patients as he doesn't want them to have the kind of sterile childhood he endured. Felicia Lawrence is a midwife in training who wants love, marriage and the whole white picket fence—because she never enjoyed anything close to that growing up. Flick never met her father, and she's determined to provide her future children with a wonderful, loving home, but she won't settle down with just anyone. She's waiting for that one special man.

One unexpected night of passion sees Tristan and Flick's lives steered by fate in a very different direction, and they have more than just themselves to consider. They have to take a leap of faith, learn to trust and open their hearts to a life they never planned.

I hope you enjoy their journey, filled with joy and setbacks, happiness and disappointment, and the discovery that true love is worth the risk.

Susanne Hampton

Married to the man she met at eighteen, **Susanne Hampton** is the mother of two adult daughters— one a musician and the other an artist. The family also extends to a slightly irritable Maltese shih-tzu, a neurotic poodle, three elderly ducks and four hens that only very occasionally bother to lay eggs. Susanne loves everything romantic and pretty, so her home is brimming with romance novels, movies and shoes.

With an interest in all things medical, her career has been in the dental field and the medical world in different roles, and now Susanne has taken that love into writing Mills & Boon® Medical Romance™.

Books by Susanne Hampton

Falling for Dr December
Back in Her Husband's Arms
Unlocking the Doctor's Heart

**Visit the author profile page
at millsandboon.co.uk for more titles**

Thank you to Sarah and Kate,
two young women who dedicate their lives to
helping others and still find time to offer me nursing
and midwifery advice for my books.

I have a deep admiration for the women and men
who choose careers in the field of medicine and
the valuable ancillary services. They willingly and
selflessly provide care for those who cannot care for
themselves and emotional support for their families.

We would be lost without you.

PROLOGUE

IT ALL BEGAN just before lunch on the beach at Port Melbourne. Felicia Lawrence, or Flick as her family and friends knew her, squinted against the midday sun's brilliant glare. Her sunglasses, she quickly realised, were still sitting on the kitchen bench.

As her feet sank into the soft warm sand, she decided not to walk back across the beachside road, up the stairs and unlock her second-floor apartment again. The sun's heat felt so glorious on her bare shoulders and she felt sure if she headed inside she would find chores to do or even some study and she wanted the day to be different. She wanted to step away from her routine. Normally she was up early for her daily walk and back in the shower before six, well before work, but not this day. She was attending the Victoria Hospital ball and it was the first big gala event she had attended so Flick wanted everything about the day to be special.

She was a midwife in training, and it was her final-year placement at the Melbourne Maternity Unit within the large teaching hospital. Another midwife, Sophia, had encouraged her to attend the glitzy social function and she'd agreed. Since they were both single, they would be each other's plus one.

Flick had slept in a little longer, enjoyed a light brunch and headed out about an hour before lunch. Wearing denim shorts and a bikini top, she walked down to the foreshore, tiptoeing over the expanse of broken seashells on her way to the shallows. She was making her way along the pristine sand when she heard her mobile phone ring. Caller ID showed it was her younger half-sister.

'Hi, Megan.'

'Hi, Flick, hope you're doing absolutely nothing, just like I told you last night. No housework, no study, zilch. For once in your life make the day about you, Felicia Lawrence.'

'As instructed.' She laughed. 'I'm walking along the sand and getting my feet wet.'

'Speaking of getting your feet wet, what about looking for a boyfriend while you're out tonight? It's been for ever since you actually dated.'

Flick rolled her eyes. 'Sophia and I are going as each other's date. We just want to dress up in something other than scrubs and have some fun.'

'I guess it's a start.' Megan's voice sounded a little deflated. 'At least you're getting out, which is a damn sight better than your usual non-existent social life.'

Flick stopped walking as she reached the water's edge and let her toes sink into the wet sand. The tepid water rushed up to her ankles.

'I'm studying and doing my final placement. I don't think now's exactly the right time to think about my social life.'

'I'm just saying if you find a handsome prince at the ball tonight, for God's sake, Flick, don't do your usual midnight cold-feet bolt! Just let it happen. You might surprise yourself.'

'I'm not looking for anyone.'

'I know, you've never been looking. You've had a sum total of two boyfriends, which isn't surprising since you were working two jobs to save enough money for both of us to have the chance to study. You've built your life around taking care of everyone else. Look at yourself, Flick, even your career is delivering other women's babies. Plus you have that ridiculously minute herb garden, your latest time-wasting mechanism and another way to fill your life and avoid a relationship. You don't have to hide from men or procrastinate about accepting a date. There are some nice guys in the world, it's just that our mother never brought that type home...or married one. And just because both of your boyfriends weren't *the one*, so you told me, doesn't mean *the one* isn't out there somewhere.'

Flick listened to the sisterly lecture, knowing there were more than a few half-truths. Her two boyfriends had been nice, perhaps too nice, she'd realised not long into each relationship. She had chosen both men because they'd been nothing like the type her mother would date. They'd been sensible, and stable with nice office jobs, hadn't drunk more than light ale, and that had only been on weekends, they'd been averse to gambling and had seemed to share her dream of marriage and children.

They'd both ticked all the boxes but it hadn't taken long to discover that being the opposite of her mother's type didn't guarantee love or anything close to it. There had been no spark, no chemistry, no fireworks. Something had been missing and Flick had known it wouldn't be fair to string either one along. So they'd parted as friends since there had been no passion to incite a deeper reaction, and she'd found out that both had since married. They had offered a picket-fence ending, but Flick needed more. She wanted to raise her children in a happy family but she knew she needed to fall completely and hopelessly in love with the father of her children. She wanted to be swept off her feet by desire and spend her life with the man of her dreams. But she soon realised it was just that. A dream.

'Let's face it, we both had a pretty crappy childhood,' Megan interrupted Flick's thoughts. 'I can't remember one Christmas without our mother disappearing after a takeaway lunch to meet another potential boyfriend. And let's not forget the presents she never bothered to wrap because she spent every spare minute updating her online dating profile. And then we were blamed each time a man left her. It was as if having children was a burden, preventing her from finding true love.'

'True love isn't often found in the front bar of the local hotel…'

'No, but apparently both of our fathers were.'

They shook their heads in unison, neither knowing the other had done the same. There were no fond memories of their childhood, neither had met their father but at least they had each other.

'I know you brought me up and as my big sister you

don't usually take my advice, plus I'm like a million years younger than you...'

'Not quite a million,' Flick cut in, laughing at her half-sister's teasing as she stepped from the watery pool her feet had made and continued on her walk. 'Try four!'

'Anyway, take my little, but ever so much more worldly, sister advice and just let your stunning blonde hair down. Have just one night of fun and don't over think it. You have been so ridiculously responsible your entire life and you need to walk a little on the wild side, even if it's just for one night. And don't spare our mother a second thought. Believe me, she's not thinking about us right now.'

'What makes you say that?'

'Apart from the obvious, Flick, which is the fact she never has thought about us so nothing has essentially changed and never will in our lifetimes.' She paused to draw breath after her rant. 'She took off for Bali yesterday so if the boyfriend is spending money then we won't hear a peep from her. So follow my amazingly insightful advice and please make tomorrow all about you!'

'Maybe I will. Thanks, Megan.'

'You're welcome, big sis. Make me proud. Live a little, take a risk or two...but just don't post *anything* on any social media. Whatever happens tomorrow is like they say about Vegas, it stays there...so it needs to be your secret.'

Encouraged further by Megan's advice, Flick decided she had started the right way to make it her day. To take life with both hands for once and actually have fun. The warm breeze was blowing in from the ocean and she felt good about everything. The fact she had not finished the housework and slept in showed she could step out of her comfort zone, if only for one day. She playfully kicked some of the salty water up with her foot. Then she made a mental note. If she was going to live on the wild side for a day then she needed to paint her toenails bright red to match her mood. She smiled as she thought about the nail polish that Megan had given to her for her last birthday and which lay unused in the bathroom cabinet. She would vamp it up, just tonight.

There were joggers and people being walked by their dogs; others reading books or magazines under the shelter of oversized beach umbrellas; small children building sandcastles and squealing as they ran into the shallow waves to collect water for the moats; and a few very tanned older men in swimsuits so brief and inappropriate that it made Flick shudder a little and look away quickly. *Gold Lycra, really?*

She grimaced at the thought her mother had more than likely dated one of them. Then she mentally reprimanded herself for thinking about her mother again. The woman had singlehandedly deterred Flick from dating for fun after watching her many poor choices come and leave their home on a dating conveyer belt. Flick had weighed up men as potential husbands from the get-go. She was looking for the family she had never had and it coloured her choices. Megan was right. She needed to leave the drama behind. The ball was going to be about having fun and not thinking about anything too serious. And that was what she intended to do.

In general everyone on the beach appeared to be doing the same. They were relaxed and a few gave a casual greeting or comment about the weather as she walked past. Her pace had picked up during the stroll and was now brisk. Nothing really distracted her until she had almost reached home again. That's when a striking figure on the beach demanded her attention. Suddenly she was mesmerised and couldn't look away.

A very masculine, very toned body stripped bare to the waist was jogging towards her. Flick was tempted to shield her eyes with her hand to get a better view, but she refrained. She controlled her curiosity and continued at her brisk pace along the shallows, pulling her gaze down to the crystal blue water. The midday sun was directly above her in the sky but her body was feeling hotter from something other than that. Her heart picked up speed at the sight from the corner of her eye that she could see approaching. Even averted and with the sun's glare, she could make out a very tanned, very taut…and suddenly very familiar man.

He was almost upon her when she looked up and realised it was the elusive and ridiculously handsome Dr Tristan Hamilton, a neonatal cardiothoracic surgeon at the Victoria Hospital. She averted her eyes again quickly. He was appealing enough in his scrubs but now, in little more than low-slung board shorts, he was mind-numbingly gorgeous. Her cheeks, she felt certain, would be pink with thoughts he was stirring. She was just grateful he had no idea who she was and he would just jog by her, completely unaware of how his body was arousing her imagination. Immediately she knew Megan was right—she needed to get out more. Her reaction was embarrassing even her.

'Felicia?'

She froze. Her cheek colour gained momentum. He had not only recognised her, he knew her name. Flick had had no idea he'd even realised they worked at the same hospital let alone knew her by name. She had only been there on clinical placement for a few weeks.

'Dr Hamilton,' she said, attempting to sound casually surprised.

He drew to a halt beside her, his sun-kissed skin aglow with the perspiration from his morning run. 'Please, call me Tristan. There's not a patient in sight so we can throw hospital formalities out the window. I suspect you're younger than me by a *few* years, but the whole doctor thing makes me feel about a hundred. So, please, stick with Tristan.' His deep voice was raspy and breathless from the run.

Flick tried to laugh but all the while her mind was spinning and her body reacting in a way she had never experienced before. 'Sure,' she finally responded a little nervously, still not entirely sure about anything. 'Tristan,' she said, emphasising his name. 'So you like jogging.'

She had no idea why she'd asked such a silly question. It was ridiculous and stupid in equal amounts. Of course he liked jogging and with the sweat that he had built up, he had been running for a while. She clearly liked making a fool of herself. She was grateful that he grinned and nodded and she didn't have to address the way her body and mind were reacting.

With his rapid breathing settling by the minute, he took a sip from his metal water bottle and looked out across the crystal-clear water. 'Beautiful part of the world, isn't it?'

Flick was still a little surprised by his relaxed demeanour and the fact he didn't look at her strangely after her awkward attempt at conversation. She had thought he would be a little rigid and uptight. It seemed to go with the specialist territory but he was not even close to some of the stiff, pompous specialists she had met during her other placements. Age didn't seem to discriminate when it came to the formalities that some of them demanded. He was so different from what she'd imagined and it was unexpected. She was not normally social inept but he was upsetting her usual calm by being so unpretentious and friendly.

At the hospital, he had never acknowledged her with more than a nod. She didn't think he had really noticed her, although she had more than noticed him. She spent a great deal of time out in the community during her placement, but when she was at the hospital she always seemed to catch sight of him as she moved about the maternity unit and the wider hospital. Her heart, for some silly reason, would always skip a beat when their paths crossed but reason told her to stay away. He wouldn't be the marrying kind. More than likely, although there were no rumours to confirm her suspicions, she reckoned him the bachelor type with a little black book bursting with names. She wasn't about to be listed with a hundred others under 'L'.

'It's wonderful,' she managed, still trying to control

her racing pulse and not appear as nervous as she had become with him so close. She hadn't been jogging but her heartbeat was completely out of rhythm. Logic and caring about his address book were suddenly swept away in the summer breeze.

'I love coming down here when there's no one around. It's so quiet some mornings, all you can hear are the waves crashing on the shore and the occasional seagull cry,' he said, with the appreciation of simple pleasure dressing his face. 'It's good for the soul to have time to just be grateful to be alive.'

Flick noticed a far-away look in his eyes. It was as if he was truly thankful. It wasn't a catch phrase or throw-away line. She didn't offer a reply as it was a statement more than a question. She imagined, as a surgeon, he would have lost patients and that would give him a deep appreciation of life. Being a student midwife certainly had done that for her.

'Do you live around here or drive down from another part of town, like me?'

Flick pointed in the direction of a whitewashed apartment building with a blue-tiled roof. It stood out like a sore thumb amongst the stunning modern high-rise glass architecture that claimed most of the prestigious beach road. The building was about forty years old with a Greek island feel to it, which wasn't surprising as her landlords spent half the year on the island of Mykonos and returned to Australia only for the summer months.

'I live up there in one of the flats on the second floor. It overlooks the beach and I love waking up and looking out across the ocean.' She wasn't sure why she needed to give him that much detail. It had just come tumbling out.

'Sweet,' he replied. 'Prime real estate. Although I wouldn't have been able to run to it when I was studying....they must pay student midwives well.'

He even knew her profession. She had imagined that if he'd even noticed her he would have no idea that she was a midwife, let alone on placement.

'It's not as much as I imagine the modern places around here would normally cost. They'd definitely be out of my league. My apartment is quite antiquated and tiny but I like it and I just go without other things to live here. It's a small sacrifice. I drive a twenty-year-old car but wake up to million-dollar views.' Suddenly her nerves were abating and she felt comfortable talking to him. She noticed him smile, the most gorgeous smile, and then he removed his sunglasses and she noticed his dark, charcoal eyes with thick black lashes were smiling back at her too.

'Wise choice, Felicia. A car for a location like this, it's a great compromise. Who wouldn't want to live here and wake up to the ocean view every morning?'

Flick was taken aback again. His comment resonated with someone very down to earth. He just happened to also be extremely handsome. She couldn't help but notice a scar that ran down his chest, ending just above his belly button. Her eyes were drawn to it but she looked away quickly. It was faded and she imagined it was from an operation performed years before but it was significant in size. The fact that he didn't hide it, she assumed, meant that the scar was perhaps by now only on the outside but she wasn't about to test that hypothesis by making mention of it.

'Looks like the hospital has given us both the day off…or are you playing hooky?'

Flick laughed, a little awkwardly. 'No, not playing hooky, I'm on an RDO.'

Tristan fell silent for a moment, as if he was taking a moment to really think about his words before he spoke. Flick wasn't sure if the lull in conversation was her cue to leave so she smiled and turned to walk up the sand towards her apartment before it became uncomfortable.

'Don't go,' he called to her. 'I was wondering if you would like to join me for a coffee or juice. There's a café just up the road and they have the best coffee and smoothies.'

Flick turned back when she noticed that his voice seemed a little unsure. She was surprised by both the invitation and the tone. Before today, the man asking her to share a coffee had never even spoken to her. He had acknowledged her with little more than a nod in the corridor and now he wanted them to spend additional time together. She didn't want to refuse but she also didn't want to sit in the café in her shorts and bikini top and bare feet. She was happy to be on the beach dressed that way but would feel self-conscious in a restaurant filled with the lunch crowd while she was so scantily clad and shoeless.

'I make a pretty good coffee too, I'm not even close to barista standard, but I can promise it won't be instant either,' she called back to him. 'Would you like to come up to my place and I can make us both a cup.'

'I don't want to impose…or cut short your walk.'

'You wouldn't be doing either,' she reassured him, feeling a warmth rush over her. She wanted to be near him. 'I was heading back anyway and I don't have any plans for the next hour or so and I'd feel more comfortable at home dressed like this.'

'I suppose my gear's not really befitting a restaurant,' he remarked, looking down at his shorts and sports shoes as he caught up to her. 'Although you look sensational, so there wouldn't be any complaints from patrons or management if you waltzed in dressed like that.'

Flick smiled nervously. 'Follow me,' she said, half-wondering why she had suggested they head to her place. She barely knew Tristan but something about him made her feel safe. It was crazy, she knew, but her intuition was pushing her in a direction that reason would never normally have chosen. 'And by the way,' she said, 'if we're ditching protocol, my friends call me Flick.'

They talked for more than an hour, sitting on the narrow balcony of Flick's apartment. She wasn't fussed that she hadn't finished cleaning. She was too relaxed to care. More than once, she joked it was more like a wide ledge than an actual balcony. The weather-beaten outdoor furniture had seen better days, but it served its purpose and allowed them to enjoy both their coffee and an uninterrupted view of the beach. Sharing the tiny, sunny space was a three-tiered planter box filled with herbs that Flick used for cooking. Basil, she told him, was her go-to herb that turned average into sensational. And oregano was her landlord's favourite, so she would give him a small bunch every Friday morning when she paid the rent.

'I can see you have a love of cooking and walks on the beach, but what is it that you love about being a midwife?'

Flick didn't have to think about her reply. 'Everything. It's a privilege to travel the journey with a woman to the birth of her baby and then a little beyond that and see how the new family member is adapting to life. And how quickly everyone falls in love with the little person.'

Tristan noticed her face become animated as she spoke. Her love of her work was palpable.

'Do you prefer attending home or hospital births?'

Again her answer was spontaneous. No debate needed. 'Home births. I love working in MMU, but for me being out in the community and assisting with home births, that's what makes it all worthwhile. It's all about continuity of care,' she said. 'The mother feels safe that she knows us, and we're like part of the family from around sixteen weeks into her pregnancy until six weeks after the birth. It's an amazing time and I feel so blessed to be a part of such a beautiful experience.'

Tristan watched her face continue to light up as she spoke. It was definitely her calling and she'd needed no prompting as to why she'd chosen that career. They continued to chat about the hospital, their careers and the gala ball that they discovered they were both attending that night. Tristan became aware of how much of Flick's time he had taken up and reluctantly he knew he had to leave. He didn't want to outstay his welcome and he suspected she would want to get ready for the evening's event.

'Can I drive you to the gala tonight?' he asked as he stood. 'I could swing by and pick you up if you haven't arranged transport.'

Tristan seldom went out socially and even less often accepted an invitation to a woman's apartment so the day was by no means a regular in any way for him. He had met a gorgeous young woman on the beach, who he knew a little about from the hospital, he had accepted her suggestion of coffee at her apartment and now he wanted to take her out. He wasn't sure what was happening. Logic reminded him that it wasn't a date, she already had a ticket and he was merely offering to be a friendly chauffeur, but his heart was warming in a way that he hadn't expected.

He'd already known before they'd shared a chat over coffee that Flick was naturally gorgeous and now he added fun, intelligent and passionate about her career as a midwife. The hour had passed like a few minutes, and he didn't want their time together to end. He wanted more. He felt as if he had just touched the tip of a beautiful iceberg and although he had always kept his personal life very separate from the hospital, he suddenly wanted to throw that rule away and to know everything he could about her.

And his libido had also joined the debate.

'That's very kind of you but I've made plans with my friend Sophia, she's a caseload midwife, and I'm shadowing her during my placement. I couldn't let her down, she's hired a limousine to take us there.'

'I completely understand. My car, nice as it is, couldn't compete with a limousine.'

Flick's lips curved to a smile. 'That's not the way I meant it to sound.'

Tristan returned a friendly smile but his body was imagining what it would be like to kiss her. It took all of his self-control not to pull her to him and feel the softness of her mouth on his. He had no doubt her kiss would be as sweet as she was, but he sensed there would also be passion in her lips…and her body.

Reaching for the chilled water on the table beside him, he gulped the entire glass in the hope of bringing himself to his senses. He watched her walk barefoot inside her apartment and put her glass and cup in the sink. She was so naturally sexy, just watching her silhouette made him want to feel her body against his, and thinking that way was out of character for him.

Swallowing hard, he followed her lead and placed his glass in the sink on the way to the front door. He was fascinated by her. He had never felt this way in such a short amount of time. The midwife dressed like a beach bunny had definitely crept under his skin.

He walked down the outside steps that led to the road below, leaving Flick at the top of the steps, but he couldn't resist turning back for a second. 'Maybe I'll convince you to dance with me before the night is over.'

Flick smiled back at him in silence. She knew it wouldn't take much convincing.

Flick stepped from the limousine and onto the red carpet, wearing a strapless floor-length gown of midnight

blue satin with a crystal-beaded bodice. The price tag
had made her gasp, but she had decided that the dress she
wore to her first ball would be one she would remember
for ever, so she bought it anyway. Her hair was down
and in loose curls that skimmed her bare shoulders. She
wore kitten-heel slingbacks and small crystal stud ear-
rings, and carried an evening purse that she had bought
to match her dress. If she had already blown her budget,
she decided she may as well have the accessories. She
was generally careful with her money, something she
had learnt to do during her studies, so she could afford
to splurge once in a while.

'Ooh, red carpet, very nice,' Sophia said, as she too
stepped out of the limousine, wearing a long cream silk
gown that also skimmed her shoulders and was a stark
contrast against the rich mahogany curls of her hair.
Very high-heeled gold shoes were only just visible at the
hemline. She was quite petite, almost six inches shorter
than Flick, so had decided to teeter all night in the name
of fashion, and a little bit of vanity.

Sophia walked alongside Flick, smiling as they entered the ballroom that was abuzz with the noise of the
guests' chatter and a live jazz band.

'Let's see what tonight brings, then, shall we?' Sophia
said as she linked her arm through Flick's.

They were seated at a round table of eight with a vascular
surgeon and his wife, two single nurses and two medical students, who were also single and more than a little
smitten with the attractive nurses. Unfortunately they
were only first-year students and not exactly husband

material in the young nurses' eyes, so their advances were politely ignored.

The table decorations were simple but effective: huge square-cut crystal vases on each table filled with twelve long-stemmed white roses tied with a large cream organza bow. The tablecloths were black, as were the napkins. It was without doubt the most elegant affair that Flick had attended and she was very happy she had worn a dress befitting the event.

A delicious salmon entrée was followed by a main course of lamb in red-wine jus. When the plates from the second course were being collected, Flick tried not to appear obvious as she looked around the room for Tristan. She had not seen him when she'd arrived for pre-dinner drinks, neither could she find him in the sea of elegantly clad guests when everyone was seated. Her heart sank a little and she surmised that it was more than likely he had been called to an emergency at the hospital. She was surprised when a wave of disappointment washed over her and threatened to dampen the entire evening.

He was all she'd been able to think of while she'd showered, dressed and applied her make-up and during the limousine drive to the ball. While being attracted to him was a little exciting, the thought of acting on it scared her to the core. But something was still drawing her to him despite being scared. It was an odd feeling, one she had definitely never experienced before.

Flick suddenly felt fabric brush across her back and assumed it was the waiter bringing more wine.

'No, thank, you. One glass is enough for me,' she said, placing her hand over the rim of the glass.

'I'll remember that, Flick. Now you've cleared it up, I won't randomly pour wine into your glass each time I pass by you.'

Flick recognised Tristan's voice from the time they had spent together that afternoon and she turned to find him smiling down at her, all six feet two of him dressed in black. While in his scrubs at work he was undeniably attractive and the near-naked, swimsuit look that morning had been amazing, her breath was stolen when she saw him in his black tuxedo. The crisp white shirt exaggerated his tan further and his jaw was freshly shaven. She even noticed the platinum and black cufflinks and his highly polished patent-leather shoes. He was a vision of a male model, only better. And the scent of his cologne made her very aware of just how close he was to her.

'I hope you're enjoying the evening.'

'Very much,' she replied, still absorbing just how handsome and how close he was to her. 'And you, are you having a nice time?'

He nodded his response, acknowledged the others at the table and then walked away without saying anything more. Flick looked ravishing and it validated his earlier decision to arrive late to the event. When he'd left her apartment that afternoon he'd known that his attraction to her was undeniably strong. And nothing good would come of it. But while he didn't want to become involved, he couldn't stay away. As he had sat on his bed, looking at his tuxedo hanging on the door, he'd told himself firmly to step back. Let Flick meet another man that night. There would be a number of eligible doctors who could give her what he couldn't.

But then, looking at his watch and knowing the evening would be over soon, his feet hit the floor and he grabbed his suit. There was no turning back.

Flick was surprised and a little disappointed when Tristan left so quickly but imagined there were a lot of VIPs he needed to rub shoulders with at an event of this scale.

She noticed his table wasn't far from the podium at the front of the ballroom.

'Flick?' Sophia leant in and whispered, with one eyebrow raised as she studied her friend's face.

Flick smiled back nervously.

'When did the most eligible but elusive cardiothoracic surgeon at the Victoria start calling you Flick and not Felicia or Midwife Lawrence?'

'This morning, at the beach,' Flick answered quickly, then, changing the subject, she reached for the menu. 'I wonder what's for the main course?'

'We just finished main course,' Sophia said, as she gently eased the glossy menu from Flick's fingers and dropped her voice again. 'At the beach this morning? You didn't mention anything on the drive here tonight. What exactly happened? You're not getting out of this one that easily, Flick. I confide in you and you keep your rendezvous with Dr Oh-My-God Gorgeous to yourself.'

Flick turned to Sophia and in an equally quiet voice responded, 'I was walking on the beach, he was jogging, we started talking and he had coffee with me on my balcony. End of story.'

'Excuse me…end of story? I don't think so. I think it's just the beginning. I saw the look in his eyes. It's so obvious he has the biggest crush on you. So you, my single, gorgeous friend, are going over to his table right now to pick up where you left off this morning.'

'I can't leave you alone,' she argued, as she shifted uncomfortably in her seat.

'Flick, I know a zillion people in the room. So you're not leaving me alone.'

'But Oliver Evans has just sat down with him. I'm not about to interrupt their discussion. It's probably something quite important and of a serious medical nature.'

'And that is exactly why you are going over to rescue Tristan from a long-winded medical discussion at a social event. He can chat about all things medical tomorrow. Tonight he should be having fun and so should you. How often do we get to let our hair down and enjoy ourselves?'

'I'm not sure, Sophia.'

Looking straight into her friend's eyes, Sophia smiled. 'Believe me, he needs saving. You're the only one who can do it! Stop hiding away, Flick. You have to grab life with both hands.'

Sophia's words struck a chord, and reminded her of her sister's phone call that morning, but it was the feeling stirring inside her that made Flick rise from her chair. 'I hope I don't regret this.'

Sophia rested back in her chair and took a sip of her wine as she watched Flick make her way to Tristan's table. 'I've got a feeling you won't regret anything about tonight, Flick Lawrence,' she muttered.

* * *

Tristan's face lit up as Flick approached and his elated expression wasn't lost on Oliver.

'I think I'm needed back at my table,' Oliver said as he stood to leave. 'I'll catch you in your office tomorrow, Tristan. Enjoy your evening.' He smiled at Flick before he walked away.

'I hope I didn't scare Dr Evans away.'

'Flick, this is a compliment and I hope you take it that way. You couldn't scare a mouse, let alone Oliver Evans. He wouldn't run from a stunning woman. He's being polite in leaving and I will thank him for it tomorrow.'

Flick blushed as Tristan pulled out a chair for her next to him.

As they chatted over the fine wine and the key lime dessert that arrived a short time later, she found she had his complete attention and he had hers. Then later, as she rested back against his strong hand in the curve of her spine as he guided her effortlessly around the dance floor, she felt there was definitely more than just a professional connection between them. There was chemistry and sparks. Everything that had been missing with the men who had held her before was obvious in Tristan's touch. He was bringing her body alive with little effort.

'Would you allow me to drive you home tonight?' he whispered, as she rested her head on his shoulder during a slow number. 'Or do you have a limousine booked?'

Flick had seen Sophia leave the ball half an hour before. Her friend had waved and sneaked out early, and Flick felt so deliciously comfortable she didn't lift her head as she spoke. 'There's no limousine. I would love you to take me home.'

'It was a wonderful night,' Flick said casually as she waited with Tristan for the valet to bring his car.

'Yes, it was so much more than I had expected.' His voice didn't give away too much, neither did his eyes, as the car arrived and he opened her door and waited for her to climb in. After she lifted the hem of her dress inside, he closed it again and went to the driver's side. He tipped the valet and took off into the night with her.

She considered his handsome profile for a moment and was curious if the entire evening had been an improvement on what he had envisaged or if it was spending time with her that had lifted the night. She wasn't sure why she hoped it was their time together as she barely knew the man driving her home but there was something special about him.

Flick smiled and looked from the passenger window at the people walking along the still busy Melbourne city street to their cars. Many had obviously attended the same grand event that they had just left. The men were all in tuxedos while the women wore varied styles. Some had chosen floor-length gowns while a number of the younger female guests had chosen stunning cocktail dresses that skimmed their knees. All of them looked gorgeous with their sparkling jewellery and beautifully styled hair. Flick loved the glamorous feeling of the evening.

She felt a little like Cinderella but she hadn't run anywhere at midnight; instead she was being driven home by a gorgeous and intriguing surgeon. She was glad the darkness of the car masked the colour that rushed to her cheeks.

'I'm very glad you came over to my table.'

'It was Sophia's idea. She said you two looked much too serious and were probably discussing the latest in vitro surgical procedure and, although that in itself is incredibly important, she thought tonight should be about fun. I honestly didn't want to interrupt.'

'So it wasn't your idea?' he asked, keeping his eyes on the road. 'Now I get the picture. Sophia forced you to sit with me?'

'Gosh, it did sound that way, didn't it?' She laughed. 'It's as if I'm making Sophia take responsibility for my actions and I'm not. I did want to spend some time with you.' Flick suddenly felt comfortable enough to be honest. It may have been fate or an accident that had brought them together that morning, but that evening, she had admitted, was of her doing.

'Whatever the catalyst, I'm glad you did.' His voice was deep and husky and eyes left the road and lingered on Flick long enough to make her heart skip a beat. 'And thank you for inviting me up for coffee on your balcony.'

'You mean my slightly shabby herb-filled *ledge*!'

Tristan smiled at her. He doubted that she realised how beautiful she really was and how captivating he found her. 'Let's agree it might be *small* but in terms of view it's a perfectly positioned balcony.'

Flick smiled nervously. She had never felt drawn to a man so quickly. The chemistry was both unexpected and undeniable and made her pulse quicken and her stomach fill with butterflies. He had always been aloof when she had passed him in the hospital corridors. There was no doubting how attractive he was but he'd seemed distant. Flick hadn't taken it personally as she'd surmised a role such as a neonatal cardiothoracic surgeon would be high pressured and he probably didn't even see the medical staff around him at times, let alone a student midwife on placement, who randomly popped into the hospital between home visits.

She'd try not to think about him after he left her sight when she returned to MMU but she knew the nurses and midwives all spoke about him. Many had crushes from a distance but none appeared to have had first-hand experience. She admired him for keeping his personal and professional life discreet and separate.

But as she sat beside him in the privacy of his car, she didn't want to think about the hospital, the midwives, or whether he had a little black book. Instead, she channelled Megan's words. Tonight would be hers. It was time she took a risk.

Tristan's gaze was very intense, his mouth only inches from hers when he said goodnight to her. The chemistry between them was electric and couldn't be ignored. The gentleman in him had insisted on parking his car and taking the stairs with her to her door. Then the gentleman was no longer when, without warning, and without resistance, he took possession of her lips and then her willing body. When Flick fumbled with the keys, Tristan took control and opened the door, scooped her up in his powerful arms and then kicked the door closed with his foot. With his mouth still hungering for hers, he carried her through her streetlamp-lit apartment to her bedroom.

With desire steering every move of his skilful hands, he unzipped her dress and threw it to the floor. His kisses trailed from her mouth down her bare neck as he laid her on the bed. Standing before her, he removed his jacket and tie, unbuttoned his shirt, all the while admiring the beautiful, nearly naked woman now reaching for him. His tanned torso was bare and Flick's fingers needed no encouragement to explore his warm, firm skin as together they removed the rest of his clothes and then her strapless black lingerie.

Tristan was in no hurry as he gently lay down with her in the softness of her bed. His hands took their time slowly roaming her eager body, bringing her to a peak then letting her desire settle for the shortest time before teasing her back to the brink. Flick had never been so ready and so sure of anything when he finally took her and they became one for the first time that night.

The morning light slipped through the gap in the curtains and found Flick lying naked in her bed with Tristan asleep beside her. She was happier than she could ever remember. But also unsettled when she realised the enormity and repercussions of what she had done. She had slept with Tristan on the first night. It had been amazing and he was a wonderful lover in every way.

The feeling of his skilful hands caressing her body had filled her senses and fought with her doubts that it was too soon. They should have waited, her practical side told her. Her mind was spinning as she slipped from the warmth of her bed and into the shower. She needed space. Room to gather her thoughts without the scent of Tristan lying beside her and making her have crazy, romantic thoughts about the way he had made love to her. The way no man had ever done before.

The warm water felt good as it washed over her body and she tried to make sense of what had seemed natural only hours before. Rushing in so impulsively was nothing that Flick ever did but when he'd kissed her at the door she'd been unable to resist him. She just needed a few moments alone to sort out how she felt about the night…and the man still lying in her bed.

Tristan woke and reached out for Flick but he was alone. He could hear the water running in the bathroom. He wondered if it was his cue to leave; to disappear without any uncomfortable goodbye. It wasn't how he wanted their time together to end and it seemed out of character for Flick. Even though they had spent less than twenty-four hours together, he felt that he knew her enough to say that taking a man home on the first night was not something she did often.

He lifted his hands behind his head and lay in the warmth of her sheets, thinking back over the night. It had been amazing and he wished it could be the beginning of something deeper between them but he couldn't do that to her. He would end it as quickly as it had begun, just the way he always did. But this time it felt different.

As he slowly lifted his head from her pillow and climbed from the bed, he felt a sudden ache inside for what he was ending so abruptly. He paused and looked back at the crumpled bed where Flick had been lying and he felt a strange feeling of regret. This was nothing like other mornings when he left a woman's bed. This time he was fighting the urge to stay and if she walked out of the bathroom, with or without her towel and smiled her gorgeous warm smile, he knew he would not leave. This time he wanted to stay.

But she didn't come out. The shower was not running but she was still behind the door. He wasn't sure if she really did want him to go. Perhaps he didn't know her the way he thought.

And perhaps it was for the best.

He wasn't looking for long term. He was fooling himself to think he could make it more than what it was. It wouldn't be fair to Flick to let her think he intended pursuing a relationship, and marriage would never be on the table. Tristan had good reason for not considering himself husband material but he wasn't about to share that with a woman after only one night, no matter how amazing the night had been and how he thought he felt about her. His reasons were solid and not negotiable.

Her diplomatic disappearance under the shower made Tristan think that she didn't want an awkward morning-after goodbye. But knowing she was within arm's reach behind a thin wooden door tugged at a place deep inside Tristan. It was a feeling he'd never experienced before. He looked around her apartment, knowing he would never be there again. Yesterday had been different. His visit had been casual but now they had crossed the line there was no way he would ever return.

One night would be all they would share. One breath-

taking night, his body reminded him as he stepped over
the sea of clothes that lay strewn over the wooden floor.
Her expensive dress entwined with his tuxedo just as
their bodies had all night. Collecting his belongings,
Tristan dressed quickly. He picked up his keys and after
slipping them in his trouser pocket, along with his mobile phone, he left. The bathroom door opened just as
he quietly closed the front door and made his way down
the steps to his car.

Pausing for a moment to look back up at Flick's apartment, Tristan breathed a heartfelt sigh. He wished that
life could be different and he could have stayed in the
softness of her bed, wrap his arms around her naked
body and persuade her to see if what they had could be
more than just one night.

But one night was all he could offer.

And it appeared it was all she wanted.

Flick stepped out of the bathroom. Finally her heart had
won over her head in the steam-filled room. Maybe,
just maybe they could make something more from their
crazy, wonderful night. Perhaps she could learn to trust
him and let him into her life despite the way they'd
rushed into sleeping together. She was willing to try
and she wanted to tell him just that as she slipped back
into his arms. Her freshly scrubbed face was lit with the
promise of what they might share.

Her stomach sank as she looked at the bed. It was
empty. She looked around the room. Tristan's clothes,
his keys, all sign of him had gone. He had left, with-

out any goodbye; he had just climbed from her bed and walked out of her apartment.

His action spoke louder than any words ever could. There was no tomorrow to plan—nothing more to talk about. Clearly for him it had just been for one night.

CHAPTER ONE

TRISTAN SIPPED HIS coffee as he looked from the window of his third floor office at the Victoria. He had returned from early morning rounds and had an hour before his surgical schedule began.

His mind wandered for a moment back to Flick, just as it had every day for the previous three months. He had hoped that as time passed so would his feelings, but they hadn't. Ninety-one days and nights had not erased or even paled what they'd shared that one night together. She was different from any woman he had ever met. She was sweet and funny and desirable. Everything he could want in a woman and then some. But he couldn't be with her, not even for one more night. He was scared that if he caved in to his feelings then he would never want to leave.

Sometimes thoughts of her came to him when he lay down in bed at night, exhausted from a long day's surgery. Lying on his back on the cool cotton sheets, his arms above his head as he stared into the darkness and thought back to that night. The hum of the ceiling fan gently moved the heavy night air but it didn't shift his thoughts. Nor his regrets. His mind was consumed with the memory of the hunger and desire they'd had for each other. And he pictured Flick's beautiful smile. A smile that had lit up the ballroom on that night as they'd sat talking for hours, the sparkle in her eyes as he'd held her in his arms on the dance floor, and the passion that they'd shared in her bed all haunted him before he finally succumbed to sleep. And even in his dreams she would appear some nights.

Dreams that felt so real he could touch the softness of her skin. And taste the sweetness of her mouth.

But Tristan knew that it had had to end before it had begun. He couldn't pursue a relationship. Flick deserved better. Although they didn't speak of her future goals and dreams outside her career, her profession made him feel sure one day she would want a family, and a family was the one thing he couldn't give her.

He looked over at the family photo on his desk. His medical graduation. It had been a day with more meaning to him and his mother and father than to many other graduates. It had been the first step on his journey to becoming a neonatal cardiothoracic surgeon. A journey he had chosen at sixteen when he'd received his heart transplant after spending years wrapped in cotton wool as his name had moved slowly up a waiting list. His mother was beaming in the photograph and his father wore a strained smile. His mother was thrilled that Tristan was alive to live his dream, his father worn down by years of worry.

More study had been ahead but Tristan had never doubted his path and finally he'd qualified. He'd become a heart surgeon who was also a heart transplant recipient and he'd wanted to specialise in neonatal heart surgery.

Tristan was determined to surgically alter the course of seriously ill newborn babies' lives. Giving them a chance for a regular childhood, something he'd never enjoyed. It was his contact with children with whom he felt a bond and it satisfied his paternal longings. He had decided early in his studies that he would never have a child to call his own. With his medical history and the dire genetic inheritance for any future children, it wasn't worth the risk.

His thoughts returned to Flick. He had to be cruel to be kind. One day she would meet a man who could provide her with everything she wanted and deserved, and Tristan did not want to stand in the way of her happiness. She might hate him now but keeping his distance would allow her to meet the right man. Someone who could give her a perfect life. But at least he would always have that one night they'd shared. A night he never wanted to forget.

The beeping of his pager brought Tristan back to reality. He looked down at the details then put a call through to the emergency department.

'Tristan Hamilton. I received your page.'

'Dr Hamilton, transferring you now to the A and E surgical resident,' the young female voice replied, before putting him on hold for a moment.

'Tristan, it's Dylan Spencer. A patient presented in Cas ten minutes ago in first-stage labour, gestational age approximately thirty-seven weeks. On examination she revealed that she's been monitored for the congenital heart disease of her unborn son—transposition of the great arteries. I didn't want to let labour progress without your advice.'

'Any other history?' Tristan asked, concern colouring his voice. 'Who provided the antenatal care?'

'Her husband says they were notified of TGA at the twenty-week scan and his wife has been under the care of Dr Hopkins, the neonatal cardiologist at Sydney Eastern Memorial.'

'What are they doing in Melbourne?'

'Family gathering. Drove down for her aunt's birthday or something like that.'

Tristan shook his head but did not voice his opinion. Transposition of the great arteries was a life-threatening condition for the baby and travelling so close to term was, in his mind, not the most sensible decision or one that he imagined would have been condoned by their specialist. The patient was fortunate labour had not begun on the journey.

'I'll put a call through to Nate Hopkins, but in the meantime please call OR and have them contact the obstetric resident, prep for an emergency C-section and then prepare the adjacent Theatre for a neonate balloon atrial septostomy. You're right, we can't allow labour to progress without intervention. The infant may not survive the birth canal.'

Tristan had just ended his call to the Sydney neonatal cardiologist when the scrub nurse arrived at his office door with A and E medical records in hand.

'Dr Hamilton, here's the notes for the emergency delivery.'

Tristan was already on his feet and heading towards the door, where he took possession of the medical records and slipped his own notes from the phone call inside.

'They estimate from the previous ultrasound the baby may be close to six pounds,' she informed him as they made their way towards the lifts.

'How's the mother?'

'She's holding up well. The epidural was administered but she's still somewhere between shock and denial that she's about to have her baby. Sophia, a community midwife from MMU, is in there with her, along with her student placement, Flick. They're providing some emotional support while the obstetrician prepares for the C-section.'

Tristan flinched a little when she mentioned Flick. Just the mention of her name brought his still raw feelings rushing to the surface again. He had to pretend their night together hadn't happened until one day he could forget it actually had. He would never allow himself to fall in love. Not with Flick or any other woman. Up until now that hadn't been difficult but something about her had got under his skin and was causing him to lose sleep.

The lift doors opened and they both stepped inside.

'As you instructed, the radiographer and paediatric anaesthetist are scrubbing in in the adjacent Theatre now in preparation for the atrial septostomy.'

They entered the empty lift and headed down to

Theatre quickly and in silence as Tristan read the examination observations on the way.

The Theatre nurse met them as the lift doors opened and walked them to the scrub room. 'Dr Hamilton, the father is waiting to speak with you but I explained that would be after the delivery when you have assessed their son and can provide a more accurate prognosis.' Her voice was calm yet firm, her years of experience evident. 'Both parents are aware that major surgery will be needed in the next few days for their son. The paediatric resident discussed the need for the immediate atrial septostomy with Mr Roberts, the child's father, and obtained signed permission. And by the way, we have a medical student in Theatre to observe today.'

Tristan nodded as he scrubbed and gowned and entered the operating Theatre. Everything had been prepared for the emergency procedure on the newborn infant. The slightly nervous but very eager-looking medical student had also scrubbed in and was waiting in the Theatre, his expression close to that of a deer in headlights.

'Tristan Hamilton, neonatal cardiothoracic surgeon,' Tristan introduced himself as he checked the sterile surgical tray. He knew that everything would be in order as the Theatre team was second to none in detail and process, but it had been a ritual since medical school and one he never omitted.

'Jon Clarke, third-year med student. I've heard so much about you and hope to specialise in paediatric cardiology but I'm keeping my options open.'

'Welcome aboard, Jon,' Tristan replied, keeping an

eye on the doors to the Theatre and the impending arrival of the newborn patient. 'In a few minutes we will have a neonate, approximately thirty-seven weeks with a transposition of the great arteries. As I'm sure you are aware, the natural history of untreated transposition of the great vessels in the neonate was quite poor but has improved dramatically. Surgical correction has been possible for over fifty years now with an arterial switch procedure that's considerably lowered mortality rates.

'I'll be scheduling that surgery within the next two days but we need earlier intervention to ensure immediate survival so shortly I'll undertake a nonsurgical procedure to create an arterial septal defect, using a balloon catheter. Essentially we will open a small hole in the heart to allow the blue and red blood to mix and provide sufficient oxygen to the newborn.'

'How did you diagnose the condition so quickly?' Jon asked with interest.

'The mother has been under the care of Dr Nate Hopkins in Sydney. He'd planned the C-section for next week but they travelled here yesterday for some family function and labour ensued. The condition was detected at the twenty-week scan. Thank God she didn't go into labour somewhere along the Hume Highway or we might not have had the same prognosis for mother or child.'

Just then the swing doors opened and the tiny child was wheeled in on open bed. Tristan looked up to see Flick standing in scrubs beside the infant. He caught her glance and held it. He couldn't ignore the look of pain and disappointment in her beautiful blue eyes. But there was no anger. That seemed worse to him. He fought the strongest urge to throw his gloves, gown and surgical cap to the floor and pull her into his arms. But he reminded himself sternly that it was not himself that he was protecting. It was her.

'The vernix has been wiped clear from his abdomen and suction of mouth and nasal cavity done,' Flick said, as she handed over the care of the baby, wrapped loosely in green sterile sheeting, to the Theatre nurse, then left without looking back.

Tristan hated that it was over between them and that one night would be all they ever shared, but there was no other way, he reminded himself as he refocused on the tiny child who now needed him. An infant who would be facing a childhood much like his own if this surgery was not successful.

The radiographer continued the Theatre tutorial for the student. 'I'm providing the two-dimensional trans-thoracic echocardiography. Essentially this is live imaging of the child's heart to allow Dr Hamilton to monitor the catheter's positioning during the procedure.'

'The procedure can also be of potential benefit in patients with other severe congenital heart defects. I can explain them later if you'd like,' Tristan added, as he watched the Theatre nurse unwrap the sterile covers and wash the baby's abdomen with antiseptic solution.

'Today I'll be using the umbilical vein as an access. This simplifies this procedure dramatically. It can be performed at the bedside in the neonatal intensive care unit but as the infant was down here I chose to do this immediately before the transfer to NICU. I also prefer sedation to general anaesthesia if possible.'

Jon stepped a little closer. 'If the condition hadn't been identified at twenty weeks, due to poor antenatal monitoring, how would you diagnose the condition after birth before it was too late to reverse the condition for the newborn?'

'The symptoms would be detected by the neonatologist or the nursing team. The child would present as unusually quiet, he or she wouldn't wake, and they would have a low pulse ox test. All the indicators of a congenital heart condition, so I would be called to consult immediately.'

'Ready to go,' the radiographer announced.

'I'm set too,' said the paediatric anaesthetist.

Tristan nodded and began the intricate procedure, talking the medical student through each step. 'We're now in the right atrium, as you can see on the echocardiography. I will now thread the catheter into the foreman ovale, the naturally existing hole between the atria that normally closes shortly after birth.' Tristan watched the screen to ensure the catheter was positioned correctly.

'Now I will inflate the balloon with three to four mils of dilute radiopaque solution to enlarge the foramen ovale enough that it will no longer become sealed. This allows more oxygenated blood to enter the right side of the heart where it can be pumped to the rest of the body. To ensure that there is flow, I am now locking the balloon. I will now carefully but sharply withdraw into the right atrium to create a permanent flow.'

Tristan continued his explanation of the procedure

and repeated the manoeuvre three times before he then deflated the catheter and removed it completely.

'We can monitor the effectiveness directly via the echocardiography,' he said, pointing to the monitors. 'But it's clear there's been a sharp rise in systemic arterial saturation so we've been successful. This little chap will be good to go until we can schedule his major operation in the next two days.'

Tristan and the medical student stepped away as the nursing team prepared the baby to be transferred to Neonatal Intensive Care. He was pleased that the stunned-deer expression had slowly disappeared from the young man's face and he appeared more at ease. After agreeing that Jon could scrub in on the arterial switch repair surgery, he invited the student to accompany him to visit with the parents once the mother had been released from Recovery and returned to the maternity unit ward. It was equally important to Tristan that the bedside manner of medical students was developed at the same time as their technical skills.

Tristan then headed to Neonatal ICU to brief the nursing team before he went back to his office to finalise some paperwork and grab some lunch. He had an afternoon of hospital rounds and consults, so he needed to eat something substantial.

Flick paced the corridor outside Tristan's office nervously. She had taken a break after she'd visited a new mother in MMU with Sophia. Flick loved shadowing Sophia and was learning so much about the spectrum of roles within midwifery but that day she felt removed from what was happening. She hadn't liked the feeling of not being in the moment during the birth. It was what she loved more than anything but that day her mind and her heart were weighed down by what she needed to say to Tristan.

This was her career and she would not allow Tristan to take that away from her. She would get through her personal issues because she loved what she did. She loved it all—the antenatal care, the birth and the post-natal assistance. She wanted to be a community midwife and spend more time in the field in the future.

But first she had to speak with Tristan. She had made her decision after two weeks of deliberation. She couldn't delay it any longer.

Finally, after taking a deep breath, she knocked on his door.

'Come in,' Tristan called, trying to swallow a mouthful of his sandwich as he checked his incoming emails, some of them spam from pharmaceutical and medical supply companies.

Flick's legs were shaking like leaves in the breeze as she entered his office. She looked across the room at the man who had made love to her on that fateful night and she knew immediately that there was no regret in her heart. No anger. And definitely no blame, as she had willingly invited him into her bed.

'Flick.' He was stunned and his voice didn't mask his surprise at seeing her in his office. She looked even more beautiful. She had a glow, he thought as she stood before him in her shapeless hospital scrubs. He knew underneath she had the most gorgeous body but her beauty went so much deeper than that. She had a wonderful, warm spirit and the fact they couldn't be together ate him up inside.

It took less than a minute, with Flick standing so close, to realise that his feelings for her were real and that made it so much harder to keep his distance. It tore at him that he couldn't act on his feelings, to cross the room and kiss away the last three months. As much as he wanted to, he couldn't let it happen. He needed to stay in control. She deserved so much better than the problems he could bring into her life.

Resolutely he knew he must deal professionally with whatever hospital matter she had come to discuss and then pretend she had never been within his arms' reach.

Flick breathed deeply and hoped she could say what needed to be said without emotion.

'Tristan, there's something I need to tell you.'

'About Mrs Roberts?' His tone was austere, just as he knew it needed to be.

Flick looked at him blankly before she realised he thought she was there about a hospital matter. His voice was cold, and he had no idea there could be anything more between them than a patient's welfare. That saddened her. She wasn't sure why she cared but she did.

'No, it's not about Jane Roberts. It's about me.'

Tristan got to his feet, suddenly hoping there was nothing wrong. He was fighting the urge inside him that that was building with every minute to reach out, pull her to him and hold her. And, in a perfect world, never let her go.

'I'm pregnant, Tristan.' she managed to mouth without a single tear. 'We're going to have a baby.'

CHAPTER TWO

TRISTAN SLUMPED BACK down on his chair. He was looking at Flick but he didn't really see her for the longest time. The news she'd delivered brought images rushing back at him. His head was filled with memories of hospitals and surgical wards and cardiologist waiting rooms and sitting on the sidelines of football games he never played but wished he could.

He saw his own childhood playing out before him and then those images were joined by vivid ones of the surgeries he performed daily on tiny babies in the hope they would live. It was his worst nightmare. She was having his baby and she had no idea there was nothing about that news he would ever celebrate. It brought him no joy. Only an instant mountain of worry.

Would his unborn child have inherited the congenital heart defect that had made his childhood a nightmare? He couldn't answer that question. It would be too early to know and it was a high-stakes gamble that Tristan had planned on never taking. Would their child need open heart surgery to live or in utero surgery to survive the pregnancy? He had no answers and it scared him more than he'd thought possible.

He was speechless. There was no need to ask if the child was his. Although he didn't know Flick as well as he would like to, he knew her well enough that if she told him that he was the father of her baby, then he was without doubt. She was a woman of integrity and in his heart he knew she was too decent to lie about it. The child's paternity was never going to be in question. It was his child. Although he wished for everyone's sake it wasn't.

He did the maths quickly and realised that she would be twelve weeks pregnant.

It would not be too late to end the pregnancy if she chose to do so and he wouldn't judge her if that was her decision.

But even with the risks, he would not want to force her hand or even suggest it. It was not his choice.

There were so many things he wanted to say but he had no idea where to start. He wanted to know if she was feeling okay; if she had great antenatal care organised, which he realised immediately was stupid since she was a midwife; if she had enough money for everything she might need, but none of it would come from his mouth. The ability to verbalise anything had vanished with the sudden announcement and the sinking feeling that had come with it.

Being a father hadn't in his plans. Not now, not ever. He was frozen to the spot with a million questions slamming around inside his head. But he needed to put them in some sort of logical order.

Suddenly he wondered why she had not told him

before. Why now? Had she hesitated because she didn't want him in the baby's life? Or was it because she hadn't decided whether she wanted to keep the baby?

Was this her worst nightmare for very different reasons?

If she was continuing with the pregnancy, was she keeping the baby or considering adoption? He knew how important it was to not blurt out everything he was thinking. He had to appear calm and in control. That was the way he behaved. He was always able to keep his emotions in check but he needed a few minutes to put his thoughts in some order. He needed to be proactive, not reactive, in this situation but he didn't know how.

Flick looked at Tristan sitting behind his desk in silence. There was nothing coming from him. No statements, no acknowledgement, no questions. She was suddenly very embarrassed that she had even come to his office to tell him. She felt like a fool.

She took a few steps backwards.

'Flick, I….I don't know what to say…'

'I understand,' Flick said, but she really didn't understand at all. 'I won't be bothering you again. There's no need for anyone at the hospital to know you're the father and I can manage everything on my own. I don't need anything from you, Tristan. It was a courtesy call, nothing more.' Pride had added the last line of her conversation. She wasn't about to appear needy or desperate for him. Needy and desperate was how her mother always behaved. Begging a man to stay and sacrificing her children along the way.

Not Flick. She would stand on her own two feet and hold her child's hand. She had wanted her child's life to be different from her own and for a father to be a part of it, but that would be Tristan's choice. He could do as he pleased and it seemed obvious to her from his reaction that it was going to amount to nothing.

Without saying another word or waiting for Tristan to respond, Flick spun on her heel and left his office, with tears streaming down her face. Her heart was breaking but at least he hadn't seen her crying, she reminded herself as she rushed into the first bathroom she could find. Morning sickness came any time between waking and lunchtime, and it was now twelve o'clock. So now she had two reasons to heave.

Tristan raced after her. They needed to sit and talk calmly. Even if she saw it as just a courtesy call, he didn't. He wanted to offer more. Exactly what that looked like, he didn't know. But they would work it out. They were two intelligent people who needed to plan their child's future. Although he had no idea what that future would be and if it would mimic his own, dotted with specialists and hospital stays, corrective open heart surgery or a possible heart transplant, he intended to be there for all of it. The good and the bad.

But the possible congenital problems didn't need to be talked about yet. He didn't want to stress Flick unnecessarily. There were risks in her knowing too. Even though they were slight, there were still risks that anxiety over health issues that might not exist could cause her to lose a potentially healthy baby.

He needed time to work out the best way forward for

all of them. But he also knew that Flick had to be upset at his lack of response. He had to tell her it would be all right. They would work it out.

Blindly rushing around the first corner near his office in pursuit of Flick, Tristan almost slammed straight into Oliver Evans. He stopped and looked down the length of the empty corridor. She was gone.

Tristan's chin dropped. There was no sign of her. Perhaps it was better that way, he mused. It would give him time to work out what to do and cement in his mind if there was any need for Flick to know about his condition. And if there was, then when the appropriate time to tell her would be.

He wanted to do the right thing. Let her know without hesitation that he was there for her and the baby. There was no way that he wanted to freeze again and have her run away. They had so much to sort out. Emotions aside, they also needed to be practical about what lay ahead for all three of them.

'Are you needed somewhere or do you have a minute to come down and speak with one of my patients?' Oliver asked. 'I have a twenty-week gestational diagnosis of hypoplastic left heart syndrome. I'd naturally prefer to operate in utero but the parents want to hear about possible postnatal surgical options.'

Tristan drew in a deep breath before he spoke. 'Sure, I can see them now.'

Flick had run off with good reason, but now was not the time to try to reason with her. They needed to sit down somewhere private and talk everything through without an audience.

He turned back and walked towards to his office with Oliver just as Flick exited the bathroom.

Oliver was aware that something wasn't as it should be with his normally composed friend and stopped. 'I can come back if there's something important that you need to see to now.'

'No, let's see your patient. I can deal with my other issue later,' Flick heard Tristan say, before they headed off down the corridor.

Flick froze. She felt physically ill hearing their baby referred to as *his other issue*.

Her doctor had not referred to her child as an issue when, in a compassionate but matter-of-fact tone, he had delivered the news to her just two weeks before. Tiredness and nausea had sent Flick to the GP for some routine blood tests and the results confirmed that she was pregnant. She had not thought about that possibility, which she realised in hindsight was ridiculous for a midwife. It should have been obvious. But they had used precautions and perhaps trying to block out Tristan for all those months she had blocked out the possibility of anything tying them together.

The doctor had referred to her baby as the bundle of joy that would be arriving in six months' time. The news had been a shock to Flick but even in her shocked state she'd never thought of her pregnancy as *an issue*.

She'd expected so much more from Tristan. Not for herself but for their baby.

When she'd decided to tell Tristan, it was to be with no blame, no demands, no tears, just the words he needed to hear. He was going to be a father and although she'd known it would come as a shock, he had a right to know. She'd prayed she would tell Tristan as calmly as her doctor had told her.

And she had.

But Tristan's reaction was nothing close to how she had pictured it. Although the pregnancy was the result of one night of passion and Tristan had not spoken a single word to her since, she'd hoped he would show an interest. But he hadn't and she realised she was nothing to him, neither was the child she was carrying.

She'd never thought for a moment that when she'd woken in Tristan's arms that she'd already been pregnant with his child. Barrier contraception had failed that night three months ago, it was that simple. Tristan needed to know but he didn't need to act. And it appeared he wasn't about to do that. Fortunately, Flick wasn't depending on him or building her world around any particular reaction from him. She felt that he had the right to know she was carrying his child and what he did with that information was up to him, but she had expected something more than silence.

She had agonised over the decision for two weeks, losing sleep most nights as she'd thought about what was best for both of them. She didn't want Tristan to feel obligated. Or to make some grandiose gesture that was coming from a place of duty, not that she'd imagined he would. But she'd known she couldn't keep the knowledge that she was carrying his child from him. A child he might want in his life or not want to ever meet. Whatever his reaction, it wouldn't change her decision. She was having her baby.

And clearly his lack of interest in her since that night they'd spent together went a long way in showing her what the night had meant to him—nothing more than casual sex. A nice way to end the evening but not the beginning of anything. And, despite her disappointment, she didn't blame him. He hadn't coerced her into sleeping with him. She'd willingly invited him into her bed and now she would pay the price.

But her child never would. It wasn't great timing and it would be difficult at times, but she would love her baby, she knew that already.

Aware every minute of every day that a new life was growing inside her, Flick's fear was hushed by the love surging through her as she rested her hands protectively across the tiny bump of her stomach. She didn't try to hide from herself the hope that Tristan kept their time together close to his heart, just as she did. They were two people who vaguely knew each other, but when the stars had aligned it had felt right to spend the night in each other's arms. And that was what they'd done. And the child inside her was the result.

As she made her way to the lift, Tristan's face, as he'd moved slowly to kiss her the very first time, came rushing into her memory. His freshly shaven jaw a few hours later had had a dark shadow of stubble as he'd lain holding her next to him. Her heart ached with the knowledge it had all been so insincere. She had read too much into it. Whenever they'd seen each other in the hospital corridor since, Tristan had been so distant and cold, as if he didn't want to remind himself of what they'd shared that night. Pretending it had never happened. Flick had been crushed but she didn't want to admit it to anyone, least of all to herself. She was just another one-night stand.

She hadn't shared the ending to that night with anyone. Sophia hadn't pried. And Megan had no clue. Both of them had assumed it had ended at the door after an innocent drive home. Flick hadn't lied to either of them, she'd just chosen not to elaborate. Their night of lovemaking she'd planned on being her secret for ever. A secret she shared with only Tristan. But now that would be impossible. She would have to let them both know soon. Megan was her sister and about to become an aunty. And Sophia, she hoped, would be her midwife so she had to know.

She was a big girl and she'd known what to expect when she'd taken him home that night, she reminded herself. He'd made no promises and she told herself that she was liberated enough to accept a one-night stand had happened, albeit her first and quite definitely her last. Although she didn't regret it happening, she wished she didn't still remember how wonderful it had been. She wished that there wasn't a tug at her heart every time she heard his name paged or saw him fleetingly in the corridor. She wished she could numb her emotions but, try as she may, she hadn't up until now. But his reaction had changed that. He was once again back to his preoccupied professional self. Nothing like the man who'd swept her around the dance floor and spent one night in her bed.

That man had only apparently existed for one night. Dropping her gaze to her stomach, she vowed that she would give her baby a happy life. Without Dr Tristan Hamilton.

* * *

With the shock announcement of Flick's pregnancy still taking front row in his mind after Oliver left his office, Tristan needed to push through and focus on his patients and then sort out his personal life.

He wished he could feel elated by the news. If he had been looking for a mother for his child, Flick would no doubt have been a wonderful choice. More time getting to know each other before embarking on parenthood would have been preferable but he'd never planned on children so her suitability as a mother hadn't been an issue.

The question hanging over him had nothing to with Flick. It was about his suitability to be a father.

When he arrived in NCIU and saw Mr and Mrs Roberts, with worry visibly and naturally consuming their every moment as they sat beside their newborn son's incubator, Tristan couldn't feel anything but anxious. It suddenly became personal and hit home for him. He knew full well that he and Flick could be in that same situation in six months. They could be facing the news that their baby had a potentially life-threatening condition. And just like Tristan had throughout his early life, the child could face years of corrective surgery and uncertainty. And if early surgical interventions were not successful then he or she too would need a heart transplant.

Tristan couldn't change what had happened. Flick was pregnant. They'd slept together three months ago and obviously the precautions had failed. This wasn't just a scare. Flick would know it to be a fact, he knew she would never have come to him if she didn't know it was accurate. And there was no point in wishing things to be different or looking back. He couldn't undo the night they'd shared any more than he could predict the health of his child's heart. And despite the potentially tragic outcome, Tristan wouldn't take back that night. Just the result.

The night would be etched in his heart for ever.

Although he knew his own feelings about what they'd shared, he had no idea about Flick's feelings at that moment. Had she informed him of the baby out of a sense of duty? Or was there more?

There were so many questions and doubts and unknowns. Their child's entire future was unknown. But he was determined not to burden Flick with the worst-case scenario right now. He'd seen how it had scarred his parents and he never wanted to see Flick suffer the way they had if it wasn't necessary. Carrying the baby for weeks, not knowing if the child was afflicted, was unnecessary and cruel and a direction that Tristan was determined to avoid until he saw the scans. If the baby had the issue they would deal with it then; if not, he would be the only one to have carried that worry.

If he sat and thought it through he could send himself mad. He wished with every fibre of his being that their child was healthy and had a normal childhood, nothing like the one he'd spent wrapped in cotton wool and fearing boredom would send him crazy. He'd just wanted to kick a goal, fall down on a wet, muddy football field or crash a go-kart, but he'd had to spend his time reading, watching movies, and the only racing he did was slot cars on a circuit set up on his bedroom floor.

Tristan pulled himself back to the present. He had to focus on what he could do, and his next step would be to find a legitimate reason to visit MMU later in the day and ask if Flick would be willing to talk things through privately.

'Good afternoon, Mr and Mrs Roberts, I'm Dr Hamilton, a neonatal cardiothoracic surgeon here at the Victoria, and with me today is Jon Clarke, a third-year medical student with an interest in neonatal cardiology.'

His greeting was polite but brief as he immediately turned his attention to his tiny patient, now covered in small sticky pads and cuffs attached to a sea of cords leading to monitors recording his heart and respiratory rate, blood pressure and temperature. He was fast asleep on a blue and yellow spotted sheet, completely unaware of what would be happening in the next few days. Noting the child's name, Callum, which hadn't been decided at the time of the procedure, Tristan checked the medical records, and was happy with the observations that had been recorded since the procedure.

'As you know, I performed a non-surgical procedure on Callum earlier today. The paediatric resident explained the procedure before you signed the consent, Mr Roberts, but you both still may not have a complete understanding of the reason behind the urgency of this morning's procedure, so I'm happy to answer any questions you may have in a few minutes. It's important that you're both informed about everything regarding your son's treatment.'

'Thank you, Dr Hamilton. We really appreciate you taking the time.'

Tristan continued checking Callum's vital signs and spoke briefly with the NICU nurse. Within a few minutes he felt satisfied the procedure had been successful and directed the parents to a small private sitting room about twenty feet away. Callum's mother was only a few hours post-partum, dressed in a hospital gown and confined to the wheelchair her husband pushed into the small room. Tristan asked Jon to close the door behind them before he sat down with his hands clasped in his lap.

'As you are aware, Mr and Mrs Roberts, Callum's condition at birth was potentially life-threatening due to low oxygen levels throughout his body. The procedure I performed allows more of the oxygen-rich blood to circulate. The procedure is, however, only a temporary measure meant to help Callum survive until further corrective surgery can be done. Everything went as well as can be expected.'

Both parents nodded in silence, allowing Tristan to continue.

'Dr Hopkins explained to you that Callum has transposition of the great arteries. You will hear the term TGA used by the medical team and myself. Quite simply, it means that the arteries to the lungs and the body come off of the wrong part of the heart.'

'Can you operate here or do we have to travel to Sydney for the specialist there to do it?' David Roberts finally asked, his voice pitchy with emotion as he wrapped his arm around his wife's shoulder and held her tightly.

'I can definitely operate on Callum. There's no need to travel to Sydney, neither would I advise it. I've been in contact with Dr Hopkins and he is more than happy for us to take over Callum's care in the immediate future. We will be following the same treatment plan Dr Hopkins discussed with you after the twenty-week scan identified your son's condition. In the next two days I propose an arterial switch operation that would reverse the condition and send the blue blood to the lungs and the red blood out to the body, as it would in a normal heart.'

'I don't recall everything he discussed with us. It was such a shock. A lot of it's a blur,' David offered as a response. 'Is it a simple operation?'

'The arterial switch is not in itself complex,' Tristan began tentatively as he reached for a notepad and, pulling the pen from his shirt pocket, began drawing a diagram of the heart. 'It's a relatively straightforward procedure but what is more technically challenging is that we also have to move the coronial arteries at the same time.' He pointed to the narrow arteries on the drawing. 'These tiny arteries are about two millimetres in diameter and they supply the blood to the heart. They need to be removed, rotated and reattached during the operation.'

Callum's mother had held her emotions in check but with this news she broke down and wept in her husband's arms.

'I realise this is stressful for you both and the rest of your family, but I also want to add that Callum is an otherwise healthy baby boy, a good weight and, while the risk is not negligible with an operation of this nature, survival rates have improved dramatically.'

'I…just want to hold my little boy.' Jane Roberts stumbled a little over her words as she mopped her tears with a tissue.

Tristan reached for her hand. 'And you will. Although this is overwhelming for you both, it is routine for my surgical team. Callum is in good hands.'

'When will you operate?' David asked.

'I checked the Theatre schedule prior to meeting with you, as the arterial switch is around a five-hour operation, but it's urgent and takes priority,' he told them, still maintaining eye contact and a reassuring tone. 'So I've scheduled Callum's operation for the day after tomorrow.'

They looked at each other for a moment, relieved that it would all be over so quickly but nervous that they had so little time to prepare emotionally. Their little boy would be having open heart surgery in forty-eight hours' time.

'Will I take him home with me when I leave?'

'No,' Tristan began, shaking his head. 'Even though you had a Caesarean delivery and will be staying in the ward for a few days, Callum will be in hospital for at least two weeks. You can visit any time. There's no restriction on parents visiting. Right now, though, I would advise you to get some rest, Mrs Roberts. You have undergone major surgery yourself and you need to recover. Callum will be monitored around the clock and you can come back down with one of the nurses as soon as you feel up to it.'

* * *

Tristan noticed a nurse at the door of the consulting room with a clipboard in hand. He told Callum's parents he would be in touch regarding the exact time of surgery and not to hesitate to call him with any questions. Then he left them alone in the room.

'This was left for you at Reception about ten minutes ago,' the nurse said, giving him an envelope with his name handwritten across it.

Tristan thanked her and walked away and opened it in private.

Inside he found a copy of the appointment card for Flick's twelve-week scan in two days' time. There was a note attached telling him that she had intended to give it to him in his office and that there was no obligation to attend. Again it was just a courtesy to let him know she was proceeding with the pregnancy in case there was any doubt in his mind.

Tristan folded up the note, strangely pleased with the knowledge that she was proceeding. There was an almighty weight on his chest and adrenalin coursing through his veins but he was glad of her decision. He knew that it would not be easy but he didn't want his child's life to end without a fight. Even if it was a fight that Flick knew nothing about.

He checked the time of the scan and knew that he now had Callum Roberts's surgery scheduled that day. He wasn't sure he could make both or if Flick really even wanted him at the appointment. Perhaps it was a statement rather than an invitation, he mused as he tucked the note and card back into the envelope and slipped it into the pocket of his white consulting coat.

But if he could, he would be there, despite the fact the scan might confirm his greatest fear. Just being the father may have already sealed the fate of their unborn child.

CHAPTER THREE

FLICK TRIED TO mask from Sophia that she had been cry-ing when she returned from her break. She was well aware that her moods were a little erratic and tears often seemed close to the surface but she hoped somehow that Sophia hadn't noticed. Although she'd sensed Sophia had been able to tell there had been a lot on her mind when they'd been assisting Jane Roberts to prepare for her emergency delivery earlier in the day.

Flick was always focused and attentive but that morn-ing she had been neither and she felt certain Sophia had noticed. Nerves knotted in her stomach when Sophia called her over.

'Flick, can I see you for a moment?'

She knew that her sadness must show on her face. How could it not? Telling Tristan had been worse than she'd imagined. But she had to keep her emotions in check, make plans and think about the baby's needs now. And make sure her situation didn't affect her clin-ical placement. She loved working with Sophia and all of the other midwives and would do her best to ensure nothing upset that. 'Sure,' she replied, following her line manager into a small office in MMU.

Sophia closed the door and took a seat, asking Flick to do the same.

'Flick, you know I think you are a wonderful midwife and your clinical placement has been beyond reproach, but lately I've noticed you seem distracted or worried. Is something wrong? Are you having second thoughts about being here or is there a problem at home?'

'No, I love my work,' Flick replied. 'I've just had a personal issue on my mind, and I apologise if I've been distracted, but I'll be fine. I've sorted it out in my mind so I can focus again on what's important, I promise.'

Sophia looked at Flick and what she was saying did not match the obvious distress she was attempting to mask.

'I don't think you're fine at all. It isn't just today, Flick. You've been distracted for about two weeks now and I know you thought you had a tummy bug that was making you feel lethargic but you haven't been right for a while now, and I'm worried.'

'Honestly, I'm fine, and I promise things will get better.'

Sophia was far from convinced. 'I want you to see a doctor. You need to run some bloods and get to the bottom of it. Flick…' Sophia hesitated before continuing. 'I don't want to put my foot in it a second time, but if I didn't know better I'd think you were pregnant.'

Flick suddenly choked on the tears that she'd thought she had under control. Just hearing the words from

Sophia's mouth made it seem real again. She was pregnant. And now she knew she would be facing it alone.

Sophia's expression fell. Her eyes met the look of fear in Flick's face.

'Oh, my God, that's it.'

Flick nodded, too upset to say anything.

'Oh, Flick, I should have known,' she said. 'You've had all the tell-tale signs, and I noticed that you were drinking water instead of your usual white wine socially. I was so embarrassed that I'd mentioned pregnancy before but assumed you probably did just have a bug.'

'I'd only just found out,' she managed to say between tears. 'I'm sorry, I wasn't up to talking about it.'

'There's nothing to be sorry about, but I want you to know, Flick, I'm here for you. As a friend and mentor, you can trust and confide in me, particularly with something like this.'

'I…I was confused and shocked and I…didn't know what to do.' Flick dropped her head in her hands as she sobbed. She cried for allowing it to have happened in the first place, for the way Tristan had reacted, for stupidly thinking he might care, and for the uncertain future she faced. It all rushed at her and she couldn't suppress it any longer.

Sophia moved closer and wrapped her arm around Flick's shoulder and didn't try to stop her tears. 'Let it out, you've been bottling this up inside and it's bad for you and your baby,' she told her, as she brought the tissue box closer too. 'I'm in no hurry. When you're ready, we can talk about everything.'

* * *

Sophia left the room for a moment to fetch a glass of water. After a little while, Flick finally felt ready to talk. The words were interspersed with tears but they were coherent as she told Sophia that the blood tests with her GP had confirmed she was pregnant and according to her calculations she was already twelve weeks along.

'You didn't suspect earlier than now? Didn't you worry when your period was late?'

Flick shook her head. 'No, I've always been irregular so it was nothing out of the ordinary. Sometimes when I get stressed, like close to exams, I know my period will be late or I'll just skip one completely. I was tested three years ago for polycystic ovary syndrome but it was negative. I didn't have any cysts interfering with regular ovulation and they looked at my thyroid but that was fine too. Sometimes I will be like clockwork and then for no known reason I will be all over the place and miss one or more periods.'

'It's not surprising that you had no idea you were pregnant.'

'Finding out was a huge shock,' Flick returned with a desolate expression.

'And the father, does he know? Is he being supportive?'

Flick felt herself stiffen on hearing the question. She was angry and hurt and disappointed. She couldn't believe that a man who had built his career around saving newborn babies' lives wasn't interested in his own child. It didn't make sense to her.

'He's aware but I don't think he wants to have a place

in my baby's life. I have informed him but from his re-action I don't think he wants anything to do with me or the baby.'

'That's sad, for him and your baby,' Sophia said as she handed another tissue to Flick. The tears had subsided slightly but her eyes were still watery. 'Maybe he'll change his mind in time. It's a huge shock for both of you and he might just need time to adjust. Let's hope so and if not, your baby will have such an amazing mother and an army of midwife aunties that it won't matter.'

Flick shrugged. 'I'm not giving him too much thought or planning on him changing his mind now. I guess it wasn't meant to be.'

'Flick, you can tell me to stay out of it but…he's not married, is he?'

'Not to a woman,' Flick began. 'To his work apparently.'

Sophia shook her head. 'That is one of the worst excuses from a man trying to avoid responsibility. And I've heard it before. No doubt it's designed to let him walk away as if he had something to blame his lack of commitment on other than his own selfishness. He's too busy saving the world in a convenient self-serving manner. I dislike the man immensely without knowing him and you don't need someone like that in your life.'

The two women stayed in the privacy of the small office until Sophia was convinced that Flick was up to heading out on a home visit. Sophia had tried to convince Flick to go home but she'd refused.

'I've thrown up *and* cried in the last hour,' she told

her. 'So I should be good for a while.' Flick was trying to be brave. She didn't see any other choice.

Sophia's mouth curved to a half-smile with Flick's attempt at humour.

'I have three prenatal home visits scheduled if you're sure that you're up to it.'

Flick smiled. 'I'd really like to accompany you. I need to. It will do me good to get out and stop thinking about my own problems. Some things in life can't be changed and this is one of them.'

Sophia nodded and, sensing the inner strength of Flick, continued. 'It does seem as if death, taxes and dating the wrong men just can't be avoided.'

They both nodded and rolled their eyes as they headed out into the bustle of MMU.

'I'm the primary midwife for a home birth due any day now,' Sophia added, as she picked up the keys to her car. 'But I checked in yesterday and my mother-to-be, Sandy, is fine and showing no signs of having an early delivery. Due date's next Wednesday.'

Flick's face lit up a little. 'I hope she delivers on one of my shifts.'

'How many births have you attended now?'

'Forty, and I've caught eleven babies,' Flick told her with pride.

'It might be forty-one by this time next week,' Sophia said as they made their way outside and off to the first home visit. They chatted on the way about how Flick was feeling and her antenatal care, and then about other things. Sophia did not bring up the father of the child again and Flick was grateful. In her mind that was a closed book. She needed to keep her focus broader to get through what lay ahead.

The appointment was straightforward. The young woman, Giselle, was thirty-two weeks pregnant, low risk and it was her second child. Sophia went through the standard but thorough health assessment procedure, and after she and Flick had taken the mother's observations and checked the baby was progressing well, they sat and answered a few questions the mother-to-be had about the impending birth. Sophia's approach, like that of all the midwives of MMU, was holistic and ensured that the emotional as well as physical needs of the mother were met, and Flick was learning a lot from her.

It was just as they left that the call came through. The home-birth mother, Sandy, had gone into labour a few days early. Flick was going to raise her count to forty-one births in a few hours' time.

Sandy had already been in labour for five hours when Sophia and Flick arrived at her home. It was her second child so she was relaxed and hadn't rushed to call them. Instead, she had rugged up and gone for a walk to the local park with her husband and their three-year-old son, enjoying the last of the sun before winter set in. She'd returned when her contractions had grown closer.

'Sandy, Jerry, this is Flick.' Sophia began the introductions. 'She's a final-year midwife student on clinical placement. Flick's been present at forty natural births and she will be assisting us to deliver your beautiful baby daughter.'

Sandy and her husband greeted Flick just as a contraction arrived. It was a short, breathless greeting from Sandy. Flick smiled and let Sandy concentrate on the waves of the contraction, which passed quickly. She smiled a silent acknowledgement to Jerry.

'You've been the epitome of good health throughout your pregnancy, so the birth should be straightforward,' Sophia told her. Then she looked at Sandy's son, who was sitting on the floor, playing happily with building blocks with one hand while eating a sandwich with the other. She continued, 'Is someone able to supervise your little one towards the end? It can be overwhelming for a child and you'll need your husband's complete support.'

'My mother's on her way. She's taking him out for the afternoon and will bring him home after our daughter is born,' Sandy replied. 'She knows I'm committed to having my second baby at home and she supports me in it. She had all four of us in a hospital but that was the done thing back then. And if she'd tried to have a home birth, my father would have thought she was crazy.'

Sophia smiled, knowing that Sandy was in her early thirties, and agreed that home births had not been generally accepted when Sandy and her siblings had been born. 'You managed very well with your first natural birth in MMU. No epidural, episiotomy, or any of the other interventions that are routinely applied in hospitals.'

'I know, and I loved having the baby at the Melbourne Maternity Unit, but I really feel comfortable at home and it will be wonderful to know that our baby was born here. We can tell her when she grows up that she came into the world right here.'

Sophia nodded. 'I'm just going to perform an internal check to see how baby is progressing.' Sandy's cervix had dilated to three and a half inches so Flick knew that the birth was close. Suddenly Sandy's waters broke and while they all assumed that the baby would arrive quickly, it didn't happen. Her labour did a backslide and the baby moved back up the birth canal and her cervix retracted.

'Your cervix dilatation has unfortunately returned to just under three inches,' Sophia informed her. 'It's not unusual, it just means we'll be waiting a little while longer for the baby.'

Flick could see that Sandy was growing in discomfort and without prompting, began to massage her back, just as Sandy's mother turned up and took her grandson to her house for the afternoon. She wasn't far away and told the midwives that they would both be back when it was appropriate.

Sandy then suggested to Jerry that they could walk around their garden. They all agreed the park wasn't a good idea at this stage as labour could progress quickly without warning. They hoped that gravity and movement from walking would help the baby get back into position. Flick accompanied them while Sophia prepared the inflatable birth tub that the couple had purchased. They asked for it to be set up in the lounge room, which Sophia did, filling it with warm water to ease the pain of strong contractions. When the mother-to-be returned from her short walk she undressed and climbed into the tub and crouched on her hands and knees. Her husband, now stripped down to his swimsuit, climbed in with her and began massaging her back.

'I'll pour this warm water over your back as well, Sandy. It should give you comfort during the contractions.' Flick knelt beside the pool and gently poured bowl after bowl of warm water over Sandy's tense body as Sophia's gloved hand attempted to rotate the baby's head and initiate movement down the birth canal.

'It didn't hurt this much last time,' Sandy complained between clearly painful contractions.

'Labour is a little different this time,' Sophia replied. 'But hopefully it won't be much longer. I can give you something for the pain if you'd like.'

'I'll try and hold out a little longer.'

Sophia listened to the baby's heartbeat with a handheld monitor. 'One hundred and twenty beats per minute. You daughter is doing well.'

Flick continued to pour the soothing water as her husband massaged her back but Sandy's discomfort was growing and Sophia suggested moving to the bed, which had been covered in clean sheeting. While it was cold outside, the home was heated by ducted air-conditioning and it allowed them to move easily from one room to the other as needed.

'It will be easier if you are on your hands and knees,' Sophia instructed her. 'Flick, I'd like you to manipulate Sandy's cervix to encourage the baby into the birth canal.'

Flick slipped on a latex glove and gently moved the

baby as Sandy pushed, but the baby seemed determined to stay tucked inside her mother's uterus.

The midwives were aware the labour was slow and were becoming concerned that the baby could be in a posterior presentation with her head resting against Sandy's spine, which would explain the extreme pain she was experiencing, or too large to deliver naturally. It had been almost two hours of pushing and Sandy was tired.

'We can move you to MMU, if you would like,' Sophia offered.

'No, I want to have my baby here,' Sandy argued, as she caught her breath between contractions.

'I understand, and you know I support your wishes, but I'm a little concerned the slow labour may be because the baby is too large for your pelvis. That's not a good situation and we may be looking at C-section.'

'Let's leave it a little longer.'

Sophia nodded. 'I will leave it another twenty minutes and then I'll need to call and have you transferred. I'm not taking that risk.'

'What about a walk again, or I could take a shower? Maybe the hot water and the standing will move things along.'

'Warm water,' Sophia instructed. 'Hot water can speed up your baby's heart rate and I don't want that to happen.'

'I'll run the shower and check the temperature,' Flick said, as she opened the en suite bathroom door and turned on the light.

'I'd like something to take the pain away, before I get in the shower.'

Sophia prepared the narcotic shot as Flick put a non-slip mat in the shower alcove.

'Should we just go to MMU now and not risk anything going wrong?' her husband asked, as he grimaced at the sound of her cry from another painful contraction.

'No,' Sandy spat back. 'I've come this far and the pain relief should kick in soon. I'm having this baby at home.'

He bit his lip and continued massaging in silence. He knew better than to argue with a woman in labour.

'The shower is ready when you are,' Flick called to them from the bathroom.

Sandy sensed she had reacted badly and reached for her husband's hand affectionately. 'Let's see if this shower can start it all again. If not, then call the ambulance and I will have the baby in hospital, I promise. Just give me ten more minutes.'

Jerry supported Sandy under the shower, where they both stood in the running tepid water for fifteen minutes. Finally they emerged and Flick patted Sandy dry as she walked to the bed. Sophia checked her cervix again and it was finally fully dilated.

She smiled at the mother-to-be. 'Looks as if you were right. You're having your baby at home. It's time to really push.'

Suddenly Flick could see a glimpse of the baby's head. 'Your little girl is arriving and she has a mop of dark hair!'

'Just like her daddy,' Sandy muttered, before she put her effort back into pushing.

To prevent any tearing of Sandy's perineum, Sophia applied warm compresses and swabs of olive oil. Finally, after more than twelve hours of labour, Sandy pushed her baby daughter into Flick's hands. Overcome with the joy, Flick's face lit up as she gently transferred the baby girl to her mother's bare stomach. 'She's beautiful.'

'Her name is Alida—it means the little winged one,' Sandy said as she looked lovingly at her newborn.

Sophia clamped the umbilical cord and handed Jerry a sterile surgical knife.

'Would you like to cut Alida's cord?'

Jerry nervously cut the cord and then leant over and kissed his wife and new baby daughter.

'Is there anything in the world more special than this?' Flick asked of no one in particular, and everyone in the room smiled in agreement.

Sophia delivered the afterbirth and ensured that Sandy was fine before she undertook a standard neonatal baby exam, just as if Alida had been born in MMU. She measured her head and chest, took her temperature and pulse, listened to her heart and lungs, then checked her genitalia and examined her mouth for a cleft palate. Alida scored nine out of ten on the Apgar rating.

Mother and baby were doing very well. And father was relieved. And she and Flick would be back the next day to check on all of them.

'That went well, all things considered,' Sophia told Flick as they climbed into the car to go home. It had been a long day and it was now after eight at night. 'I must admit, if Alida had not arrived when she did I was going to insist on transferring Sandy to MMU. I won't take unnecessary risks.'

'I think she would have fought you on that,' Flick replied as she buckled her seat belt, acutely aware that she was safely strapping in two lives as she did it.

'You'll learn, Flick, that while the mother's voice is important and we support their decisions, it can only be up to a point. If the life of the mother or baby is at risk in any way, we will insist on a hospital birth. And you need to always remember, no matter what the mother's or father's wishes, home births cannot be considered for multiple births, premmies or breech deliveries.'

'That makes perfect sense,' Flick agreed, pulling herself back to the conversation. She was determined to stay focused, despite the weight of her personal issues. 'No one wants to risk either the mother's or baby's survival. I learnt the cardinal rule of a midwife early in my studies. Always have a back-up plan.'

Sophia smiled at Flick. 'You did a wonderful job in there, assisting Sandy, despite what a terrible few weeks you've had.'

'I can't fall in a heap. I almost did, and I'm sorry that I let you down.'

'You didn't let me down, but I worried that you were letting yourself down. You will be such a wonderful midwife but you need to qualify and it's so close, Flick.'

'I appreciate your belief in me.' She paused and looked out of the window into the cold evening sky. 'I will do it, even though it will be a close call.'

'And after you graduate, there's some additional training I would like you to consider.'

'What training's that?'

'The Advanced Life Support in Obstetrics course,'

Sophia replied. 'It's helpful in cases like Sandy's and if you ever work in more isolated units, such as stand-alone maternity services or public home-birth services. There's a lot of theory along with the practical but it will help you to better understand and manage emergencies that might arise in maternity care. It's another string to your bow and will place you in high regard as a midwife.'

Flick was pleased that Sophia thought she would be capable of taking on additional study and responsibility. She admired Sophia and looked up to her as a role model. Despite the hurdles she would face, being a single mother, she was determined not to let Sophia down. Neither would she let herself down and walk away before she completed her studies.

'Let me know if there's anything I can do to help.'

'Give me a miraculous cure for morning or, in my case, all-day sickness.'

Sophia pulled up at the traffic lights. 'It should ease off soon. Second trimester is the *golden period*. You'll feel full of energy and ready to take on the world. You've just had a pretty horrid first trimester…but having said that I'm surprised when the sickness hit you weren't a little suspicious that you were pregnant.'

'I know. I guess I should have realised but it was only this bad for the two weeks before I saw my GP and he suggested including a pregnancy test in the blood tests. I thought it was the gastro bug that's been doing the rounds. So it's only been a month of feeling this awful.'

Sophia pulled into the hospital car park and found a parking space.

'Have you decided on a home birth or hospital delivery yet? I know there's still a little while to decide.'

Flick didn't answer for a moment. She was already thinking about how she would be delivering the baby without a husband or partner to help her through. There would be a midwife but she felt a tug at her heart knowing her baby wouldn't be lovingly kissed on the head by the father, the way Alida had been.

'I'm still undecided but I was hoping...' she paused for a moment '...that you would be able to be my primary care midwife.'

'I'd love to,' Sophia told her.

'Thank you so much. It really does mean a lot to me and I feel so comfortable around you.'

'That's what it's all about. Who's your obstetrician?'

'Darcie Green. I saw her last week and she assured me that she wouldn't tell anyone about my pregnancy until I was ready to announce it. She's scheduled the NT scan for tomorrow.'

'Darcie's lovely. I also loved working with Isabel before she left for her secondment to London. That all happened quite quickly but I must say they are both great obstetricians. Who did you want as midwife back-up care?'

'I really don't mind. Everyone's great so whoever can fit me into their caseload, but regarding the birth, I'm not sure I could fit a birthing pool in my apartment...'

She suddenly stopped speaking and froze. Tristan was crossing the dimly lit lot to his car. The same car in which he'd driven her home that night. She remembered resting back into the seat with her bare shoulders touching the cool leather. She closed her eyes and thought back to everything that had happened and felt a knot build in her stomach.

This time the nausea wasn't caused by morning sickness, it was from regret that she'd opened her heart to a man who didn't have one.

CHAPTER FOUR

TRISTAN NEVER SAW Flick that night in the car park or at the hospital for the next two days. She did her utmost to avoid him. It was too painful for her to know how he felt about her and their baby.

He simply didn't care.

She doubted he would bother attending the twelve-week scan. She was preparing herself so that she wasn't disappointed. She also had to learn not to care about him.

Tristan woke on the day of baby Callum's surgery and Flick's scan to thoughts about the woman who was carrying his baby. Thinking about Flick was the way he woke every day. Filled with regret but trying to find hope. Hope that the baby would be healthy or, if not, hope that Flick would cope with the news when he thought the time was right to tell her.

There was a fine line he was walking and he wasn't sure it was even the right one to be walking. There were many things to consider and one was definitely not burdening Flick unnecessarily. There was the slight risk early into the pregnancy that she could lose the baby if she were to react badly to the potentially dire prognosis. He wouldn't forgive himself if that was to happen. His medical ethics told him that she had every right to know; and then his feelings for her, feelings he was fighting, made him want to protect her from something that she might never need to know. He was being torn in so many directions. There was no right or wrong answer.

He decided that two out of three lines of thought were erring on the side of keeping it quiet for the time being so he kept on that path, and headed to the hospital and his first patient for the day.

'Today's procedure is critical to Callum living a healthy life but I'm not about to tell you there won't be potential issues as he grows older, neither can I say the surgery is risk-free. But there's nothing to weigh up. It's not optional, the surgery is necessary to keep your baby alive.'

David Roberts took his wife's hand. 'What risks are we looking at in the future?'

'With all surgery there is the risk of complications,' Tristan told them honestly. 'The complications of Callum's surgery that may or may not occur later in life include narrowing of the arteries that supply blood to the heart, heart muscle weakness and occasionally problems with heart valves.'

They looked at each other with expressions that did not hide the overwhelming fear that threatened to engulf them. Jane Roberts was also dealing with her rollercoaster of emotions post-partum and this additional stress had her teetering on the edge of emotional collapse.

Tristan was well aware of her shaky disposition but

he could not disregard or omit any of the risks. There was no absolute guarantee that their child would live a long life but neither was his fate sealed.

'Until about twenty-five years ago, newborns with this condition were managed by alternative surgical procedures to what Callum will be undergoing today. Those procedures were called the Senning or Mustard operations. As a result, surgeons don't yet know the truly long-term effects of the arterial switch operation we now undertake beyond young adulthood as it's a relatively new procedure and the patients are all only teenagers or in their early twenties.

'After corrective surgery, and your return to Sydney, your baby will need lifelong follow-up care with a heart doctor, like Dr Hopkins, who specialises in congenital heart disease to monitor his heart health. Dr Hopkins may recommend that Callum avoid certain activities that raise blood pressure and may stress the heart. But he will talk to you over the coming years about what type of physical activities your son can do, and how much or how often.'

'So after today,' David began, 'Callum will have check-ups but he's guaranteed to never need further surgery on his heart?'

'I wish it was that straightforward and finite, but unfortunately it isn't. As I said, for the majority of patients who have corrected transposition and no other associated abnormalities, no future treatment may be required and their life expectancy has been reported to be near normal. At this stage I can't predict if Callum will be one of those patients but for your child's sake you should both remain positive.'

Jane rested her head on her husband's shoulder as tears trickled down her cheek. 'This is my fault. I shouldn't have suggested the trip down here to Melbourne.'

'Mrs Roberts, your trip to Melbourne had nothing to do with what Callum is facing. Nothing, at all,' he reassured her. 'It just means that he's having the surgery in Melbourne rather than Sydney and you have a different surgeon. But I can assure you the surgical procedure is identical. I've been in constant contact with Dr Hopkins and he will continue to be made be aware of each step of Callum's progress until he returns to his care in a few weeks. And I will come and see you in the ward as soon as the surgery is completed.'

Callum's parents drew in deep breaths at the same time, leaning into each other for support. Their closeness did not go unnoticed by Tristan. He hoped that he and Flick would have that same united front if, or when, they needed to face a similar uncertainty in their child's future. It was something he had never considered would be a part of his future but now it could be. While he dealt with the natural anxiety of parents almost every day, it wasn't something he'd ever thought he could be facing. He wondered how he would react when face with his own child's mortality.

After scrubbing in, Tristan approached the operating table, where Jon stood eagerly waiting to observe.

'Good morning, team.'

They all nodded and continued with the Theatre

preparation of the newborn who was now sedated on the small surgical table.

'Ready,' the anaesthesiologist said, signalling the surgery would now begin.

'We will perform an arterial switch operation over the next few hours, moving the pulmonary artery and the aorta to their normal positions. The pulmonary artery will be connected to the right ventricle, and the aorta connected to the left ventricle. The coronary arteries will also be reattached to the aorta,' Tristan told them, as he began the first incision along the baby's tiny chest.

The operation took just under six hours. There were no additional complications but the tiny coronary arteries required additional time to reattach. Jon was exhausted from just observing and his admiration and respect for Tristan's skill was evident during and after the procedure.

'Today was a pivotal moment for me,' he announced as he left the Theatre with Tristan. 'I'm definitely specialising in neonatal cardiothoracic surgery. I'm in awe of what you did in there.'

'Great,' Tristan replied. 'You came prepared, you understood the condition and while you had limited Theatre experience your understanding of the theory was excellent. You're welcome to scrub in with me again.'

Tristan was aware that he didn't have a lot of time to talk about the procedure. He needed to visit with Callum's parents and then get to Flick's scan. The operation had run over and he would be cutting it fine, but he would still do his best.

On the way to MMU, he stopped in Jane Roberts's ward and told them that Callum was a strong little boy and he had pulled through and would be in ICU for a few days.

'What about medicine?' David Roberts asked. 'Will Callum be taking drugs for ever?'

'No, ongoing medication use is uncommon,' he informed them, and that news appeared to make them very happy as he bade them farewell and told them he would see them in the morning.

Now he just had to make it in time for Flick's twelve-week scan. MMU was on the other side of the hospital. He knew it would take a good ten minutes, if he didn't get held up in the elevators.

He looked at his watch as he pulled the appointment card from his coat pocket. He was already ten minutes late. Would they have gone ahead without him? More than likely, Flick didn't want him there. She'd made it clear that the appointment card was nothing more than notification she was proceeding with the pregnancy, not an invitation to be a part of it.

But she didn't have the complete picture, he reminded himself.

Even if she didn't want him present, he wanted to be there for her and their baby. He would convince her in time that no matter what the future held he would be right beside her. There was no time to waste.

So he took the stairs.

Flick sat in the waiting room of the diagnostic sonography unit, wondering if Tristan would show up. It was five o'clock and she had finished for the day. She knew from the way they had left off that the chance of him turning up was somewhere between slim and none. And the brief conversation she had accidentally overheard between Tristan and Oliver Evans resonated in her head. There was no mistaking his attitude towards her and the baby. *He would deal with the issue later.*

Flick was more disappointed than she'd thought possible. The father of her baby didn't think she or the baby were important enough to cut short a conversation to find her. She questioned her reasons for letting him know about the antenatal scan but decided that at least he would be aware she intended to keep her baby. His lack of interest wasn't about to sway her decision. She was more than capable of raising a child and he could stay quiet about his involvement in the conception if he wanted to.

She didn't want or need his money. Supporting both her sister and herself through their studies had more than proved to her that she could support a child on her own. There was no need for paternity to be anyone's business but hers and one day in the future an important talk she would have with her child.

'Just checking, Flick, did you have a full bottle of water as instructed?' Amanda, the student sonographer, asked Flick and brought her thoughts back to the task at hand. Amanda and Flick had begun their placement at the same time in MMU.

'Yes, I finished one about an hour ago. Sophia told me the images are clearer with a full bladder. Although I'm not sure how long I can hold in that much water.'

'Hopefully not too long,' the young woman answered with a knowing smile. 'We've got two consulting rooms for first-trimester scans both booked out back to back for the entire week. Must have been a lot of romance in the air in February.'

Flick wondered if the ball had been the reason for more than just her baby. Perhaps the stars had aligned and there were other women who had been swept off their feet and also found themselves waking up with a handsome almost stranger in their bed.

'Did I mention you're Prue's last patient for the day and we're running about ten minutes late? Prue and Ginny are both working flat out.'

Flick stepped back from her reverie. Ten minutes would give Tristan even more time to make his way there. *If he had any intention of showing in the first place*, she reminded herself. She sighed and looked around the room. She had visited there during orientation but never imagined herself sitting there as a patient.

'So after this NT there won't be another until the twenty-week mark?'

'That's right,' Amanda replied. 'Some women are offered another first-trimester scan, which is done vaginally, between six and ten weeks of pregnancy. But according to your notes you're definitely twelve weeks into your pregnancy so that won't be needed. Sometimes they call the early scan a dating or viability scan.'

'Dating scan?' she muttered under her breath. 'It wasn't a date, we just slept together.'

'I missed that. Did you say something, Flick?'

'No, nothing, honestly.'

'Anyway, it can be used for a lot of reasons but one is for women who aren't certain about when they may have conceived.'

'That won't be necessary,' Flick said quietly as Amanda turned away for a second. 'I know exactly when this baby was conceived.'

A young couple arrived together, holding hands, and it reminded Flick that she was alone. Flick had no one beside her to hold her hand and reassure her. And it made her sad for both her and her baby.

'I'm Mrs Barrows, I'm here for my twelve-week scan.'

Amanda smiled. 'Please take a seat, Mr and Mrs Barrows. We're running about ten minutes late, I'm afraid.'

The woman smiled at Flick and she sat down, looking around the room a little like first day at school.

'I'm so nervous,' she said suddenly, directing the words at Flick.

Flick felt her midwife persona kick in instinctively. 'Don't be. This is the easy part. Six months down the track will be the challenging time for both of us.'

'You're pregnant too?'

'Yes, twelve weeks, like you.'

'I didn't realise. I saw you sitting in your scrubs, so I thought you were here with a patient. I didn't know you were expecting too.'

Flick wasn't sure what made her want to validate herself and explain her lack of partner to a complete stranger, however nice she seemed. But something was suddenly triggered inside her and she didn't want pity or judgement. She didn't want them to know she was facing impending motherhood alone. She had almost convinced herself she would be fine but at that moment she realised she didn't want to be facing anything alone. She wanted Tristan to be beside her.

'My partner couldn't make it today. He was caught up at work.'

Amanda looked sideways at Flick but said nothing. She was fairly sure that Flick wasn't dating anyone. MMU wasn't that big a unit and both gossip and news travelled fast, and there had been nothing about her seeing someone, particularly not for that long or that seriously. She had just assumed it was a fling.

'Hopefully he can make the next one but at least you can show him the photos.'

Flick smiled but she was caving inside. Her dream to have him beside her was just that. A dream, wishful thinking that would not come to fruition. She doubted Tristan would be interested in seeing the images of his child. It probably didn't rate that highly for him on a scale of importance.

Just then a couple exited one of the rooms, and Flick was ushered in.

It was dimly lit and the diagnostic sonographer was replacing the bed coverings.

'Hi, Flick. I didn't think you'd mind me doing the housekeeping in front of you so I called you in early. Won't be a minute,' she said, as she placed the last of the disposable blue sheets over the narrow examination bed and then washed her hands in the small handbasin. 'How are you feeling?'

'Not great. The morning sickness has been terrible,

I've been ill at least once a day but the last few days it's been first thing and then again around lunchtime. I'm hoping it will subside soon.'

'That's the worst,' Prue replied. 'I've had four children. The last pregnancy was twins, and I was so ill through each and every one of them. It's a wonder that I had a second after the first one. My husband was fortunate that I suffered amnesia when it came to pregnancy and I completely forgot the bad when he talked me into increasing our brood. When I discovered I was having twins, I told him that was it. I was finished. He had the snip when I was twenty weeks pregnant with my boys. He knew he had no choice or he'd have to find a new place to sleep because I wasn't sharing a bed with a fertile rooster!'

Flick tried to smile but it didn't come easily. Her stomach was still churning, her bladder threatening to burst, and she was a melting pot of emotions. She was excited about seeing her baby's image for the first time but sad that Tristan wouldn't share the experience. No matter what she thought of him, he was the father and she wanted him to have the same level of involvement, but unfortunately he didn't feel the same way.

'Please, hop up on the table and lift the top of your scrubs.'

Flick followed Prue's instructions. The sonographer then tucked a disposable sheet into the elastic band at the top of her scrub pants and rolled them down to expose her slightly rounded stomach.

'It just looks like you've eaten a large meal, you're so tiny still,' Prue said, as she applied the conducting gel and, moving her eyes from Flick's stomach to the monitor and back again, began the examination.

'There's no risk to the baby with the scan is there?'

'The low as reasonably achievable principle has been advocated for an ultrasound examination, which means keeping the scanning time and power settings as low as possible but consistent with diagnostic imaging, so any risk is minimal and outweighed by the advantages of having the scan,' Prue explained, then continued, aware of Flick's role as a student midwife, 'Do you understand why you have the NT scan, Flick?'

'Well, the main reason is to work out if my baby has any chromosomal abnormality, such as Down's syndrome, isn't it?'

'That's definitely one reason,' Prue replied, as she moved the hand-held device over her stomach and adjusted the image on the monitor. 'Another is to see if you're expecting twins or even triplets. It's crucial to know about twins early on, as it's easier to see whether or not they share a placenta. Finding out about having twins early in pregnancy also gives you more time to prepare for the birth and for your doctor or midwife to plan your care.'

Flick didn't want to think about having twins. One baby was going to be a challenge on her own but two was more than she could contemplate.

'I'm quite sure it's only one,' Flick said, hoping to somehow influence the result with her nervous prognosis.

Prue didn't answer as she hadn't completed the

examination and wasn't yet ready to rule out a multiple-birth scenario.

'This scan is the most accurate for the head to bottom measurement of your baby. This measurement is called the crown rump length and after thirteen weeks the baby can curl up and stretch out, so measuring the length becomes less accurate. That's when we measure the width of the head and the length of the thigh bone to gauge size.'

Flick needed to know if she was expecting twins and she couldn't be patient any longer. The thought hadn't even crossed her mind until now. Finding out she was pregnant had been sufficiently stressful, without looking for additional worries.

'Is there more than one?'

Prue hesitated for a moment then turned to Flick. 'I can definitely tell you that you have only one baby, Flick.'

Flick felt her breathing become easier.

'I'm just going to check your baby's heartbeat and other developmental markers such as—'

Suddenly the door was pushed open and both women looked up in surprise.

'Did I make it in time?' Tristan asked, as he rushed into the room, slightly breathless from the dash through the hospital corridors and the stairwells.

Flick couldn't hide her shock at seeing him standing there beside her in his scrubs. Seeing his state of dress, she realised he must have come straight from surgery to be there with her. Happiness stirred inside her when she realised perhaps she had misjudged him and he did care about her and his baby. Suddenly doubt was replaced with the feeling that everything might just be perfect after all.

'Tristan, I didn't know if you could make it.' He voice was soft, not hiding the happiness she felt.

'I got your note but I didn't know how long the surgical list would take today. I didn't want to make a promise and not be able to keep it.'

Prue looked over at Amanda, who was still holding open the door. It was obvious now to both who the father was but neither made comment before Amanda closed the door and went back to Reception and the other six-o'clock patient.

'I heard you mention the heart,' he began. 'How is that looking?'

'Good so far. Obviously, the twenty-week scan will be more accurate but Flick's baby looks healthy.' Prue continued the examination, stopping now and then to take screen shots of the foetus.

Tristan moved away from Flick and closer to the monitor. His eyes roamed the screen, scrutinising the black and white images.

'So no visible abnormalities?'

'None that I can detect. Obviously, as I said before, the twenty-week scan will give us a better picture—'

'Stop,' he cut in, pointing to the screen. 'Can you go back so that I can see the heart chambers?'

'Sure, but it's very small. I think all we can be guided by at the moment is the presence of a strong heartbeat.'

Tristan stared at the monitor, not noticing Flick's concern at his behaviour growing by the minute. Her mood suddenly took a turn and she wondered if his interest was purely medical. He was cross-examining the sonographer like a medical student researching a paper.

'The placenta is functioning well and the baby's size is appropriate for gestational age?'

'Yes, everything is within normal limits and looks perfectly healthy.'

Flick felt herself become agitated with the intensity of his questions. It was far from what she imagined the usual reaction of a father-to-be was.

'So you're happy that the foetus has no obvious health issues?'

'Tristan, I'll print the films and you can have a closer look. The digital files will be available for you as well. If you'll excuse me, I'll leave you while I collect the films and I'll send you the report in a day or so. When you're ready, Flick, please pop out and see Amanda.'

'Thanks, Prue,' Flick said, as she pulled her top down and her pants up as the woman left the tiny room. She stared at Tristan with frown lines dressing her forehead. She was very confused by his behaviour.

'What on earth was with the twenty *negative* questions?' she demanded, sitting upright and staring at Tristan in indignation. She had been excited to see him but his interrogation had seen her joy morph into irritation.

'I just want to know that everything is fine, that there are no medical conditions that we need to take into consideration. I think that's quite normal.'

'There's nothing normal about the Spanish inquisition of a sonographer. Why *would* there be any medical conditions?' she demanded in a lowered voice. 'I'm only twenty-five years of age, I exercise regularly, walk almost every day, eat a healthy diet, and my last glass of wine was at the ball…before I became pregnant.' She rolled her eyes when she thought about that night. She wished she could blame their night together on the wine but one glass could not be held accountable for them falling into bed together. One glass had not swayed her judgement. She'd been very aware of what she'd been doing when Tristan had carried her into the bedroom.

'I'm a cardiothoracic surgeon, of course I'm going to be interested in all aspects of our child's health.'

'There's no history of any congenital problems so your questions are uncalled for. I am not one of your patient's mothers or some medical case study.'

'I just want to be thorough.' His jaw tensed as he spoke. He didn't want to divulge any more to Flick. The child had an equal chance of being healthy. There were two parents and no guarantee that his genetic condition had been passed on.

'I didn't sense thoroughness a minute ago, Tristan. I would call your line of questioning a little obsessive and unnecessarily worrying to me, to be honest. I know this was far from a planned baby but I would like to find some joy along the way. I want to leave practicality at the door, and if there's anything to deal with I will, but I'm not going to watch the sky nervously just in case it falls in.'

'I just want to have a general overview.'

'It was far from a general overview, Tristan. Your questions were very specific. I get that you specialise in cardiology and you're surgically correcting congenital heart defects all day, but there is no reason to think our child will have cardiac problems so just stop looking for a drama.' She was tired and, she knew, a little short-tempered. 'Look, I'm struggling a little with the pregnancy and I don't need added or unnecessary stress.'

'What's wrong?' Tristan asked, his concern almost palpable. 'Can I help you?'

Flick knew he couldn't make anything better. He could just stop making it worse. He wasn't there for her, and she wasn't convinced about his feelings for the baby now. Was he attending the scan from a medical specialist standpoint or as a concerned father of her baby? She sadly suspected it was the former, so she turned her response to one of a patient. Because clearly that was all she was to him.

'I still have dreadful morning sickness, it's dragging on longer than I thought it would and I'm so tired still. I'm not sleeping that well and I wake exhausted every day,' she told him, climbing down from the examination table. 'Sophia reassured me the second trimester should be much easier. Apparently in the next two weeks or so the *golden period* of my pregnancy will kick in and the nausea will decrease, sleep patterns will be better and I should feel increased energy levels. I just want to stop throwing up soon. So unless you have a magic obstetric wand, there's nothing you can do except to stop creating problems and concerns where there are none.'

After hearing about her struggles with the pregnancy, Tristan knew he had made the right decision not to raise the possibility of a serious problem. He didn't want to add to her woes.

'What if I support you financially so that you can give up work and focus on the baby?'

Flick felt her blood pressure sky-rocket and her heart sink. She hadn't thought he could make it worse but he had. He hadn't mentioned anything more than a financial arrangement. No emotional commitment, instead a way for her to step away from the workforce and tend to the baby with no effort from him other than opening his wallet. He'd just projected her back fifty years. She was incensed at his suggestion.

'Give up work? So close to completing? Have you gone completely mad? I'm the one with raging hormones who is supposed to be irrational and you come up with that completely illogical suggestion.'

'I didn't think it was that bad,' he said, taken aback by her reaction. 'It's a simple way to reduce your stress. If you don't have to get up every day and go to work, you can slow down and the symptoms may not seem so severe.'

'But then I won't be qualified. How am I supposed to support myself and my child without a qualification? And I don't want to be kept by you when I am perfectly capable of earning my own way, doing what I love.'

'It's *our* child, not just your child, and I intend to support the baby too. You might be a single mother but you are not a sole parent. There's a difference.'

Flick was surprised by his serious tone.

'Our baby will never go without,' he told her sombrely. 'I intend to be there every step of the way and if there are medical issues we will deal with them, not just you—*we* will deal with them.'

'Why do you keep going back there, Tristan? You are like the doom-and-gloom father-to-be. If you can't help yourself, please don't come to any more appointments. Honestly, I would rather attend all the antenatal visits alone than have you looking for problems that don't exist and then on top of that telling me to throw in my career.'

Tristan was beyond frustrated. He was trying to protect and take care of her as best he could under the circumstances. He was well aware that pregnancy brought about a wave of emotions but he was surprised that a woman who had been clearly in control of her emotions three months previously was suddenly so emotional now. And defensive along with it.

'Not throw in your career, maybe delay it a little while until you feel better or until after the baby is born.'

Tristan hoped that that the baby would be healthy and Flick could pick up her studies again. Devoting every waking moment to looking after a sick child was not the way he wanted her future to play out. His medical condition had been all-consuming for his parents and the reason they'd never had a second child. And, he suspected, the reason why they'd finally separated when he'd been eighteen. It had been years of stress and it had finally taken its toll on their relationship.

They had parted as friends because friendship was all that there had been after eighteen years of worry and focus on their son. The romance and passion had no doubt dissipated in sterile waiting rooms and ICU wards over the years. Tristan was sad that his relationship with

Flick hadn't even made it that far, but it had been a joint decision in his mind. Even though it had ended after one night, his responsibility would last the child's lifetime, whether or not the child suffered his genetic condition.

'Flick, I'm in this with you.'

'I understand that you want to be responsible. That's great, Tristan, but I'm perfectly capable of getting through this without you.'

'I'm not walking away from you.'

'I think you mean you're not walking away from our baby, Tristan. We never had anything more than one night, so you can't walk away from me—you were never with me.'

Tristan was dealing with the news of the pregnancy, the problems that might ensue, and promising more to Flick at that moment wasn't possible. He didn't know if perhaps she was drawn to him because he was the father of the baby. She hadn't reached out during those three months any more than he had. If the baby hadn't brought them together, he wondered if she would have visited his office at all. He still had feelings for Flick, they had not disappeared since the morning they woken together, but how she truly felt about him wasn't so clear. But his devotion to the baby she was carrying was very clear in his mind and in his heart.

'Don't push me away now, Flick. I meant when I said. I am here for you, whatever you need.'

'Fate has given us this baby, but we don't have to pretend that there's anything else between us,' she told him, not wanting the words to be true but knowing in his heart they were. 'Let's not try to fool ourselves. This is not a relationship you wanted. Let's not pretend that there's anything between us.'

'I think we both made a decision not to pursue a relationship. I'm not into long-term relationships. You could say that I'm married to my career. It wasn't anything personal.'

'Great to know that when you made love to me it wasn't personal.' She stormed over to the door. 'Be careful, Tristan. You're making it worse than it was. And it wasn't good when you left my bed that morning without so much as a goodbye.'

'Flick, let's not go there. I'm not the only one who felt it was best that I left. It was obvious that you wanted me gone. Staying that long in the bathroom was clearly my cue to leave.'

Flick stood staring at him, dumbfounded by his statement.

'Your cue? I've never done anything close to that before. I was feeling overwhelmed, I needed a moment to myself. But you left without a word. Clearly I was nothing more than one night. Don't try to change that now. It's too late,' she said, as she closed the door on Tristan and his hold on her heart.

CHAPTER FIVE

IT WAS ALMOST two weeks since the scan and their confrontation. Flick had continued to avoid Tristan, which wasn't hard since she was out on community antenatal visits and still completing her external study load.

Her morning sickness was still dragging on. Although it wasn't as severe, it was showing no sign of leaving. Most nights she tossed and turned, thinking about Tristan and what they had shared. For him, she reasoned it had stopped at just one night but, despite what she'd said, for her it had been so much more. A baby was for ever and she knew the memories of the night they'd spent in each other's arms would last in her heart for the same time. She couldn't stop her feelings for him. She wanted them to go way. To disappear overnight so that she woke to feel nothing for him at all.

She hated that she woke thinking about him.

The man who had not even tried to contact her seemed at odds with the man who spent those hours sitting talking on her tiny balcony in the sun, and the man who had made her feel as light as air on the dance floor at the ball and the man who had carried her to bed and made love to her all night long. He had slipped away in the morning light. She wondered if he was just like all the other men her mother had brought home.

She wasn't sure how she could have been so wrong about him.

But she was finished with him. She had to be for her sanity and what was left of her heart.

Tristan had requested the digital images from the twelve-week scans to be sent to him electronically so he could take additional time to examine them. Every day he would scrutinise them, looking for something he knew wouldn't be visible that early into the pregnancy, but he did it anyway. He was searching for confirmation one way or the other. Not knowing was driving him to distraction. Not being able to protect Flick and his child was breaking him.

But also the knowledge that she hadn't wanted him to leave that morning made it harder to fight his feelings and made him want to be with her even more. He now knew it hadn't been just a one-night stand. And perhaps there was more than the baby bringing them together. But logic reminded him that, no matter how she'd felt about him the morning they'd woken together and perhaps even did still feel, it might change when she had all the information.

He would stay late at the hospital, poring over reports and updates about the latest medical breakthroughs in neonatal and in vitro surgical corrections of the defect. The need to immerse himself in work and research potential surgical interventions for their child drove him. He was desperate to be able to tell Flick there was hope when or if the genetic diagnosis was given to them. Until then, he had nothing of value he could say to her. He couldn't provide comfort and he worried that his anxiety, however he attempted to mask it, would seep through his bravado and make her suspicious.

Distance was everyone's best friend at that time, he decided, and, in the meantime, focusing on medical advances was preferable to allowing his mind to wander to what he wished his life could look like. For his child and for Flick.

It was pointless to try to ignore what he knew both of them could face. A life not dissimilar to his childhood. There had obviously been advancements made in medical technology and procedures but it didn't change the harsh reality that their child would not have a normal childhood. Neither would they have a normal entry into the life of parents. But he was not about to burden Flick with that now. Dealing with a difficult pregnancy was already challenging her and he wasn't going to add to that.

The scrutiny of the scan by Tristan was ridiculous in Flick's mind but she didn't want to argue with him any more. She lay awake some nights wondering if the wives of all surgeons and doctors had to listen to over-zealous husbands interrogate obstetric sonographers about the babies they were carrying. Or if she'd just managed to get pregnant by the only specialist in the world who imagined the worst.

She surmised that perhaps years of seeing children suffer might have affected him and it wasn't perhaps his fault entirely. She also knew that distance was, against her will, making her heart grow fonder. Her mind kept wandering back to the feeling of contentment when she'd lain in his arms. She would look down at her baby and think that, no matter how confused and disappointed she was, she couldn't hate the father of the baby she already loved so much. It wasn't possible.

That reminded her, she needed to find the strength to tell her sister that she would be an aunty before year-end and then attend her first appointment with her obstetrician, Darcie Green. First she would make the call that she was dreading.

'You're what?'

'I'm having a baby.'

'Oh, my God, I can't believe I'm hearing this from you,' Megan replied incredulously. 'I didn't know you were even seeing anyone, let alone seriously enough to want a child. How could you not tell me you had a boyfriend and all the plans you two were making?'

Flick stalled the conversation with a silent pause. Her sister's voice was a mix of surprise and excitement and she wasn't sure how to break the news that she was wrong on both counts about the boyfriend and the planned pregnancy.

'The baby wasn't planned, was it?'

'No, a complete surprise, actually.'

'And is there a boyfriend?'

Flick shook her head at the phone. 'No to that one as well.'

'So the creep did a runner when he found out?'

Megan sounded furious that a man could win over her sister and then disappear when the news broke. 'I'll kill him, Flick.'

'It's not exactly the way it happened. He didn't run away when I told him, he actually left the morning after we, well, you know… And I hadn't spoken to him for three months. Then four weeks ago I found out I was pregnant.'

'And he's back now?'

'Well, he knows about the baby. The news landed like a lead balloon and I haven't spoken to him in nearly two weeks. Although he did come to the scan—'

'How good of him,' Megan interjected sarcastically. 'He got you pregnant, did a walk of shame in the morning and didn't contact you for three months? He's a jerk, plain and simple. How did you get in touch with him to even tell him about the baby?'

'We work in the same hospital, so I see him now and then but, to be honest, I'm avoiding him. I've come to the conclusion that it's easier on my own. His attitude is so strange, I'm not sure if it's from years of being around sick children, but it's like he's looking for a problem with my baby before it's born.'

'Is he a medico or midwife?'

'A neonatal surgeon.'

'So he's shown no interest in helping out?'

'He's offered financial help, but to be honest I'd rather do it alone. I'm not sure he'd really be helping me long term. I think he might actually make things more difficult.' Flick was still terribly confused by his attitude.

'You have to do what's right for you and the baby. But don't let him shirk his responsibility either.'

'He didn't want more than the one night all those months ago, so I think we should leave it at that. I'm not chasing him to be involved in my life or the baby's.'

'I still can't believe any man would walk away from you and his baby. He's clearly insane and you don't need him!' her sister wailed, and Flick could picture her pacing the hallway in her house over five hundred miles away. 'You know the problem here? You're too sweet for your own good.'

'Clearly not sweet. I got pregnant on a one-night stand!'

'That has nothing to do with being less sweet, it means you were played. That creep took advantage of you.'

Flick knew it wasn't true. She had willingly gone to bed with Tristan with no promise of what would happen in the future. He hadn't told her something to make her believe he would be there for ever.

'No, Megan, he didn't take advantage of me. I wanted to spend the night with him. And I did. I just didn't think for a moment that I'd get pregnant. We were careful.'

'I don't doubt it, Flick, but nothing's foolproof,' Megan replied. 'Are you really going to be okay?' Her tone was warm and comforting.

'I'll be fine, or, should I say, *we'll* be fine.'

'I know I don't need to ask if you are keeping the baby, that goes without saying.'

'Yes, I'm keeping the baby and we'll get by. I've got some savings and the rent on my place is next to nothing. I'll be qualified before I have the baby and I can return to work after a few months.'

'Oh, Flick.' Megan paused before continuing. 'For all you've done for me over the years, don't hesitate to let me know if you need any money. I owe you more than you know. I have a career because of you.'

'No, you have a career because you studied.'

'And because you paid for it, and I'll never forget that.' Megan sounded choked up. 'No matter what, I'll be there for the birth. I'm the aunty and I wouldn't be anywhere else.'

'I know you'll be an amazing aunty, and I'd love you to help me through the birth if you can get away from the practice.'

Megan sighed. 'Of course I can, but I'm still angry, it's just unfair. You shouldn't be dealing with this alone.'

'I'm not alone. I have you and I have my baby.'

Flick was the obstetrician's last patient before lunch and she sat, reading, in the waiting room. The receptionist was running an errand and Darcie was taking a phone call so Flick picked up a parenthood magazine and started flicking through the pages, looking at the pages of nursery images and articles on every aspect of raising a child, including a few that she hadn't even considered.

Every day she learnt something new about the role of a mother.

And about herself.

And the feelings she had for Tristan that just wouldn't go away. He wanted nothing to do with her and it hurt. She knew she had pushed him away but he certainly hadn't fought to come back. The pain was there every day and she just wanted it to stop. She wanted to stop caring about a man who didn't care about her. It had been two weeks and he hadn't reached out. She tried to keep busy but her mind would return to him at random times during the day and it didn't help that his name would be brought up by nurses and doctors around the hospital.

Unsettled by her thoughts again, Flick dropped the magazine onto the table and walked into the adjacent waiting room to get some spring water from the cooler. The light was switched off as the room was only used for overflow patients when both obstetricians were consulting.

The door suddenly opened and she turned to see another of the hospital obstetricians, Sean Anderson, walk past the darkened room in the direction of Darcie's office. She heard him knock on Darcie's door but he was clearly on a mission and didn't wait to be invited to enter. From the look on his face, he was clearly distracted by something. Flick stepped back to her seat just as he disappeared inside Darcie's office and, without closing the door behind him, began talking.

Flick didn't know him very well. But she did know that he had arrived at the Victoria at the end of her third-year clinical placement to take up the role of locum obstetrician so he had been on staff for about six months. He seemed nice enough, very handsome, almost as tall as Tristan, and everyone seemed to like him.

'Darcie, I can't get any answers from Isla and none of it makes sense. Isabel just up and leaves after I've been here for barely two months. It was too convenient and I want to know what's really behind it.'

His voice was loud enough for Flick to hear every word but there was nowhere she could go so she began reading and tried in vain to block out the conversation.

'Sean, I honestly can't help you,' Flick could hear Darcie reply. Her voice was lower and she wasn't sure if it was because Darcie knew there was a witness to the conversation. 'You know as much as I do. I was offered the secondment and I took it. Isabel is over at the Cambridge Royal, acting in my role, and I'm here. I don't think there's anything sinister or mysterious about it. It was a career development opportunity we both wanted.'

'You live with Isla, you must know more than that.'

'I do live with Isla, but I don't make a habit of eavesdropping so, no, Sean, I don't know any more than you and I really don't think there's any more to know! I think you're over-thinking the situation and I have no idea why.'

'I intend to get to the bottom of it, with or without your assistance. I know there's something going on. Isla and Isabel are hiding something. I just don't know what it is.'

Flick kept her eyes on the magazine. The conversation ended abruptly and she knew Sean would be leaving Darcie's office. She didn't want to acknowledge him or that she had heard anything. She wasn't interested in hospital gossip so she didn't make eye contact and continued reading as he rushed back past her.

A few moments later Darcie appeared at the door to her office.

'Flick, please come in.'

Flick lifted her head to see Darcie smiling, and she wondered if it was half from embarrassment from Sean's whirlwind visit and abrupt departure.

Flick had no idea what Sean's problem was and had no desire to find out. She had quite enough of her own problems. She also thought that other people's affairs should be just that. Clearly relieved that Flick didn't ask about the conversation she had overheard, Darcie ushered her in and closed the door as a deterrent to further unannounced visitors.

'I've had a look at the scans you had two weeks ago, Flick, and everything was within normal parameters for the twelve-week mark of your pregnancy. You seemed quite sure of the conception date, but due to your irregular cycle the first day of your last normal menstrual period was not clear. Your baby's due date is a little clearer after the scan and should be in early November, somewhere between the seventh and the tenth, which is around the time you estimated. Tell me, how are you feeling?'

'The morning sickness is less intense,' Flick told her, as her lips curled into a half-smile with the news of the baby's birth date. It made it even more real and gave her something to feel happy about. 'I've had three days in a row that I haven't actually thrown up. I'm crossing my fingers it might be the end of it.'

'That's good news and you could be right,' Darcie commented and made note of that in Flick's records. 'I've made a bit more time for your visit today, Flick, because you did seem a little overwhelmed with everything on your first visit and I wanted to make sure you understood everything. Being a midwife gives you an advantage over other mothers-to-be but it's still daunting with your first baby.'

Flick nodded. It was overwhelming for many reasons. And one of them was Tristan.

'Although the birth is quite a few months away, and your background gives you a solid knowledge of what to expect, I thought we could talk about your needs during the pregnancy and the birth, along with the type of birth you'd like. I'm not sure if you've decided on delivering your baby at home or here in MMU. Also, I wanted to raise interventions such as an episiotomy, the use of pain relief and how you would like to approach the day and what you see as important.'

Flick had given thought to all of Darcie's questions and answered her honestly and also told her about wanting Sophia as the primary care midwife. Darcie listened to Flick's plans then took her blood pressure and asked her to step on the scales and noted both.

'Blood pressure's good, and now your morning sickness is lessening you'll start to have a slow and healthy weight gain. I'm pleased that you've made informed decisions about how you want this baby brought into the world. Assisting at so many births has certainly allowed you to choose the right delivery for yourself. Sophia is a great midwife.'

'She's wonderful and after shadowing her for the last few months I couldn't think of anyone else I would want with me.'

'What about the baby's father?'

Flick took a deep breath and looked down at where her baby was resting safely inside her. 'I don't think he'll be a part of the birth, but I'll have Sophia and my sister. That's more than enough.'

Darcie patted her arm gently. 'You're in good hands with Sophia and there's nothing like having sisterly support too.' Then she continued with the examination. 'If you could climb up on the exam table, I'd like to check your baby now.'

Flick loosened her scrubs and lay down.

Darcie began the examination, gently pushing her fingers into the softness of Flick's stomach to measure the height of the uterus before she listened to the heartbeat. Happy with the baby's progress, she turned her attention to Flick and listened to her heart and lungs, then felt her breasts for any lumps, before checking her throat to ensure her thyroid wasn't enlarged. Finally she asked Flick if she'd noticed any varicose veins, before directing her down off the table.

'Not yet, and I'm hoping to avoid them. I elevate my legs at night,' Flick replied as she tucked in the T-shirt she wore under her scrubs and sat back down on the chair.

'That's a sensible idea with the standing you do all day. I'm sure that you don't need any dietary advice but if you do I can refer you to one of the hospital dieticians, and yoga can help with any back pain over the coming months.'

'So you're happy with the baby and my health?'

'Very. You're extremely healthy and everything seems fine.'

'Then I'll just make another appointment in four weeks to see you again?'

Darcie paused. She wasn't finished with Flick. There was something that she needed to ask but she had decided to complete the physical examination before she raised it.

'There was another reason why I requested this longer appointment. There's something I need to ask you.'

Flick was taken aback. She had no idea what Darcie would need to know that she hadn't already covered.

'I was checking the records and I noticed that your scans were released to our cardiothoracic surgeon, Dr Hamilton, with your approval.' Darcie's pretty face became drawn with concern and she maintained eye contact with Flick. 'Is there a reason why you're concerned about the baby's heart? I've read your medical history and there appears to be nothing that would lead me to believe that there's any risk but obviously seeking Dr Hamilton's expert opinion is not something you would do lightly.'

Flick's pulse suddenly quickened and her eyes darted around nervously. She had momentarily forgotten about Tristan's behaviour at the scan and how the sonographer had offered to send him a copy of the images and report and that she had agreed.

She wasn't about to lie to her obstetrician but the idea of telling her the truth made her stomach knot. It had already been established that the father of the child would have little or no hands-on involvement in the pregnancy but now she'd have to divulge his identity.

'If there's a need for genetic testing we can arrange

that to be done,' Darcie continued, sensing there was something on Flick's mind that was causing discomfort. 'And if there is an issue we have the best surgeons and counsellors to help you through the process. I know you are going through this without a partner, but I'm hoping you have a good support network. Family or friends?'

'There's no genetic issues that I'm aware of, none at all. But…for some reason the father of my baby wants to be doubly sure the baby is healthy. He's going completely overboard but I guess that may have something to do with his line of work.'

'So the father of your baby requested Dr Hamilton look at the films.'

'No, no one called Dr Hamilton. He requested them himself.'

'I see,' Darcie replied, as she drew a deep breath. 'So Dr Hamilton has more than a professional interest in this baby?'

CHAPTER SIX

TRISTAN WAS ON rounds in MMU when he came upon Flick. She looked tired and a little pale and he surmised morning sickness had taken its toll. He didn't want to keep his distance any longer. He wanted to be there for her.

Looking at her struggle made him ache inside. The time apart had made him miss her in a way he hadn't expected. She was carrying a part of him and that made the feelings he had for her so much harder to ignore. But he couldn't shake the feeling that it was something so much more than the baby drawing him to her. She hadn't been far from his mind before he'd found out she was carrying his child and now she never left it at all.

'Flick,' he called, as he saw her disappearing with Sophia and a very pregnant woman in the direction of an empty consulting room. 'We need to talk,' he said as he drew closer.

Flick noticed Sophia's ears prick up when he called her name. The tone was almost endearing and when he dropped his gaze to her tiny bump she knew there was the chance Sophia would put two and two together.

'I'll begin the antenatal with Julia and you deal with the *medical enquiry* with Dr Hamilton,' Sophia told her with a knowing look as she led the pregnant woman inside and closed the door. From Sophia's expression and remark, Flick realised her secret was out but she was relieved to see that it hadn't been a look of disapproval or any form of judgement.

Despite how he was making her feel, she had to stand strong and keep him at bay.

His behaviour was absurd and she was resolute in her decision that he would not attend any further scans. She wanted to look over at the tiny black and white image of the baby growing inside her and think about the future. About everything her child might achieve and how wonderful everything would be when she welcomed her baby into the world. She felt nervous and excited. And she had no time to dwell on doubts and unfounded fears. And she wanted to keep working and complete her qualification. Having Tristan around was going to affect her ability to do both.

But there was the reality of how unsettled she felt around Tristan. He still affected her physically. Despite her anger, she still felt drawn to him. She tried to reason it was because she was carrying his child. It was some strange fact of nature, she assumed, making the mother want to be close to the father for protection. She didn't want it to be anything more. She was angry with him and with herself.

'What do you want, Tristan?'

He couldn't help but notice her reply was curt and it let him know immediately where he stood. He was out in the cold. And deservedly so, he reminded himself as he thought about how she would be viewing the situation.

'I just wanted to check up on you.' He hated that she was struggling with the pregnancy and wouldn't accept his help.

'I'm good,' she told him. Her voice was flat, masking all signs of emotion. 'Nothing else to report.'

'What about the morning sickness? Has it passed?'

'No, it's still happening but it's not as bad.'

Tristan didn't miss the defiant angle of her jaw, along with her brief answers and her eagerness to leave.

'You know I didn't mean this to happen...'

'Clearly, neither of us did,' she retorted. 'But it did happen and I'm dealing with it. You don't need to check up on me. I'll let you know after the baby is born and you can decide if you want to be in the child's life.'

She turned to walk away. Just being close was tearing at her heart. She didn't want to admit how much she wanted him when he didn't want her. His concern was born of guilt and she wanted more. For her and the baby.

Tristan stepped forward. Finally she had opened up with more than a brief response but her words had been cold. She was pushing him away and he was not about to let that happen. 'Don't go. I want to ask you something.'

She turned back to him. 'What else do you wanted to know, Tristan? I'm busy, I don't have time to go over everything that I'm feeling or the progress of my pregnancy. But you're welcome to go and see Darcie Green. She's my obstetrician and she knows about us. Your need to have the scans and report sent to you made it impossible to hide but she will be discreet and has no intention of sharing the father's identity. Ask her the million and one questions. Honestly, be my guest. I'll let her know you'll be calling.'

'That's not what I want to ask you. I have a proposal…' Tristan began, then hesitated when he saw the disturbed expression on Flick's face. Not wanting to appear foolish, he quickly added, 'No, not that sort of proposal. God, no… I know that's not what either of us is looking for.'

Flick's heart fell. It wasn't that she was *expecting* a proposal of marriage after all that time but the way he dismissed it so quickly was cold. As if marrying her was the furthest thing from his mind. An almost unthinkable act. It certainly cemented where she stood. And her roller-coaster ride of emotions just took another dive.

'I meant that I'm proposing you move into my place. Yours is great, don't get me wrong, it's got a great view and loads of character.' He tempered the line of his conversation. 'It's just that you're not feeling well and I can take care of you on the bad days. I also having a cleaning service so no mopping, or bending.'

She shook her head, betraying no emotion. 'I'm fine. It's passing so there's no need for me to move anywhere.' Least of all closer to you, she thought.

Folding his arms across his chest, he shook his head in frustration and pressed on, not wanting to accept her answer. 'You have two flights of stairs and no elevator. As you get closer to your due date that will be awkward, and once the baby arrives a pusher would never make it up there. You can hardly carry a fully loaded pram and baby up two flights. Even a six-foot marine would struggle with that job.'

His reasons for wanting Flick near him were not all about being practical. Her apartment wasn't suitable, it was small, impossible to navigate with a pusher, and the tiny balcony was a risk as the balustrade was constructed from thin iron bars that a little head might get stuck between one day in the future. There was also the harsh reality of the heart defect and if that were to happen then Tristan wanted to be close to monitor the baby's progress so together they could make informed decisions about the treatment. But there was a third reason that he struggled with every day. A part of him wanted to see if there was more than one night of chemistry between them.

'So you've moved past the need for me to quit work and be confined to home duties for six months?'

'I never meant you to give up and stay home indefinitely, I was just trying to help you through the worst of it.' Even as the words passed his lips he wasn't sure if morning sickness would be the worst of it.

'Well, I'm over the worst so let's leave it at that,' she said defiantly. 'I can deal with everything else you've raised as it becomes a problem.'

'So you'll stick your head in the sand until then?'

All Tristan wanted was to wrap his arms around her protectively and demand that she stop being stubborn and just let him take care of her, but he couldn't. Not yet anyway. He had to either find out that the baby was fine or tell her everything and then see how she felt about him.

'I'm sticking my head in the sand?' she spat angrily. 'I'm carrying this baby and I'm well aware of what lies ahead. I've been sick and I'm still working, all the while making plans for the future which includes finishing my studies, and you dare to tell me that I'm in denial. Where the hell have you been for the past two weeks? Hiding in your office or the operating Theatre and hoping that it's all a bad dream that will just go away if you don't see me?'

'I haven't been hiding from anything. I gave you the space I thought you wanted. I'm trying to do whatever I can to make it easier but you just don't get it. You're so determined to be independent and stand alone when you don't have to. Not now and not ever. I want to help in any way I can. Don't push me away and punish me for a mistake we both made that night.'

Flick knew that Tristan's words did hold an element of truth. She was pushing him away and punishing him. Her dream of the perfect life with a husband and child was disappearing before her eyes and it was overwhelmingly sad. Her life, as she had imagined it might be, would never happen. And he was making her face the fact that it wasn't his fault any more than hers. And it definitely wasn't her baby's. Robbing the baby of time with Tristan would be spiteful and wrong. Her mother's behaviour had stolen that from her and she couldn't do the same. She had to put the baby first and deal with her feelings separately.

'Where exactly is your place?' she demanded, showing no interest or excitement in her tone. She had to treat it as a business proposal. That was the way he was promoting it and the best way for both of them. A practical solution to her impending housing problem.

'Toorak, so it's reasonably close to the city centre and the hospital, and not too far from your favourite beach either. So you can continue to walk along the beach every day during the pregnancy.'

'Do you live in an apartment or a house?'

'A house, six bedrooms with a pool, but don't worry it's fenced off so no risk to our baby,' he told her, nervous that might give her a reason to refuse his offer. 'You sound like a realtor assessing the place.'

Flick's mood shifted slightly when she heard him say *our* baby. They were two adults about to have a baby and they barely knew each other. Finding out she was pregnant had been a shock to both of them. Perhaps his reaction was normal. She had no idea, she had never delivered that news to a man before. And to think he would propose anything more than a convenient living arrangement was a dream ending that she knew would never happen. Her life would not be a picture-perfect love story.

'Do you live alone?'

'I do.'

'Then why do you need six bedrooms?'

'The house was a good price and I saw it as an investment,' he replied. 'You drive a hard bargain.'

'I'll think it over and get back to you tomorrow,' she told him eventually.

'You and the baby will be safe and you can stay there as long as you like.'

Flick wasn't sure how to take his sudden desire to have her and the baby close.

'I have a home visit this afternoon,' she told him, 'so as I said, I'll get back to you tomorrow with my decision.' She gave him no clue as to how she was thinking or what her decision might be. Partly because she wasn't entirely sure herself.

Tristan took solace in the fact she hadn't refused point blank to move in with him. Perhaps she didn't hate him. She was fiercely independent and he knew she could more than take care of herself, but he wanted to help. And if the worst-case scenario was realised then it would change everything. It would be his problem too and he wasn't walking away from Flick or his child.

Flick headed back to Sophia, who was waiting to take her to see Phoebe, one of their home-visit mothers. She was confused and although she knew what she should do, what the right thing would be, she still wasn't sure she could see it through. Living under the same roof with a man who stirred feelings she didn't want to have was a recipe for heartbreak, and she didn't want to go there again.

Sophia updated Flick on the short trip about the young war widow, who was six months pregnant and dealing with both grief and pregnancy at the same time.

'I feel so stupid for being melodramatic about my troubles,' Flick said. 'She has so much more to deal with than me.'

Sophia was not so quick to judge. 'I don't think you

should compare yourself with Phoebe or diminish how you're feeling. She's going through a grieving process but, from what I gather, her husband Joshua was on active duty for most of their eight-year marriage and she really didn't see him very often or for very long. They had a relationship that was intense but then she would have long periods on her own so they lived quite separate lives. Losing her husband is tragic and, of course, the child growing up without knowing his or her father will be very hard, but Phoebe will pull through because, like all war widows, this was a possibility she lived with for many years.'

'But I wasn't dating, let alone married to Tristan, so I can't comprehend what she must be feeling every day,' Flick said, as they pulled up to the modest home in the outer suburbs of Melbourne. It was well kept, with the lawns freshly mown, pristine flowerbeds and neat hedges framing the pathway to the door. 'Does she have family to help with the household maintenance? I shouldn't imagine she'd be up to doing all of this.'

'Not family. Unfortunately they've all passed away,' explained Sophia, as they walked up the pathway. 'Her only living relative is her brother and he's in England. So I'd imagine the garden is her landlord's doing. She told me that she's renting this home.'

'Oh, my goodness, it gets a little sadder every minute. Having no family to provide support during her grief would make it so much harder.'

'It's very sad. Phoebe's been through a lot,' Sophia agreed, knocking on the door. 'But she's a resilient woman and very sweet. She's a primary-school teacher apparently, but not working at the moment. I assume she's receiving some sort of military pension.'

Just then the door opened and a young woman, with a mass of light red hair hanging in long curls around her pretty face and shoulders, invited them inside. She was wearing an oversized charcoal jumper with black tights and flat shoes.

'Hi, Phoebe, this is Flick, a student midwife. Are you okay for her to be present during my visit?'

'Sure. Pleased to meet you, Flick,' she replied. 'Come into the sitting room and take a seat. I've put the kettle on and we can warm up with a tea or coffee. Instant, I'm afraid, as I don't have a coffee machine or plunger.'

'Nothing for me,' Sophia said. 'I've already had one coffee today and that's about my limit.'

'I'm okay too,' Flick said.

'If you're sure, I suppose we can begin the check-up and see if you feel like one afterwards,' Phoebe replied, sitting on a chair near a small wooden dining table.

The house was clean and tidy inside, just like the garden, but it felt strangely empty to Flick. Not of furniture but of emotion and warmth. She noticed there were no photographs to be seen. It made her feel so sorry for the young woman. Having no family around, then to lose her husband and have her only brother on the other side of the world was a burden for anyone, let alone a pregnant woman.

Flick felt her problems dwarfed by what she knew Phoebe was dealing with at that time. It also made her decide that she had no right to put additional barriers between Tristan and the baby. Life was so tenuous and she would never want her child to be alone in the world, like Phoebe. Her baby needed as much family as she could provide in case something happened to her one day. Despite how hard it might be, Tristan was part of that family.

'How are you going with it all?' Sophia asked.

'Not bad, a little tired and some days are harder than others,' Phoebe admitted. 'But I'll get through. I told you on your last visit, Joshua and I loved each other but just as we started to reconnect when he was on leave it was time for him to return. It was hard on both of us, he needed to readjust to being home and away from the conflict over there, and I had to open my heart and my life again to him.'

'I think serving in the military is admirable and so brave but a lot of people don't understand how hard it is for those left home, waiting,' Sophia added.

Phoebe nodded. 'And for me it got harder, not easier, so even though I still cry a little every day, I knew over the last few years that every time he left me could be the last. The odds were beginning to be stacked against us. I didn't really know what I was getting into when he proposed. I was crazy in love and only nineteen. I thought it was romantic and it would be like the movies every time he returned to me. But it wasn't. It was awkward sometimes and like starting over, but each time we were reunited it was a little more distant. So in many ways I felt closer to a widow than a wife before he died.'

Flick felt her heart breaking for Phoebe. It was such a lot for someone to go through at such a young age and now she was facing motherhood alone.

'I think your baby will have a very strong role model,' Flick said softly. 'He or she will be very lucky to have you as their mother in a few months' time.'

Phoebe smiled. 'Thank you, Flick. That's very kind.'

'Speaking of a few months' time,' Sophia added. 'Have you thought about the birth, Phoebe? Home or hospital?'

'I think I'd prefer to have the baby in MMU. There's not any point in staying at home, it's not as if it's our family home and will have meaning as my baby grows up. Who knows how long I'll be living here.'

'That's probably a good decision. You're a low-risk birth but if you feel more comfortable in hospital and don't have support at home for the first twenty-four hours, having your baby in MMU is a sensible choice.'

Sophia and Flick completed the antenatal check as they chatted to Phoebe. They were concerned about the lack of support she would have postnatal and Sophia made a note to have additional visits scheduled for the first six weeks. A first baby with no respite was going to be difficult.

'I have a question,' Phoebe began tentatively. 'I'm not sure if you can help me.'

'I'll certainly try,' Sophia answered as she packed away her stethoscope.

'Joshua had a good friend who, I discovered, has moved to Melbourne. His name is Ryan, and they served together in Iraq. Ryan was a military medic and Joshua wanted me to reach out to him. I'm a bit nervous about it. I didn't know if you might know him.'

Sophia frowned slightly. 'I'm not sure how I can help you.'

'He just started work in MMU as a midwife. He's American...'

'Oh, you mean Ryan Matthews,' Sophia cut in. 'He's a lovely man. American accent, very nice looking. He doesn't talk about his time in Iraq and none of us are surprised. We can only imagine what he saw over there. He keeps to himself but he's one of the finest midwives I've ever worked with.'

'That's nice to know.'

'I can ask him to call you if you'd like.'

'Please, don't. I would rather meet him in person than try to talk over the phone. It would be another awkward moment and I've had enough of them. I'd rather just see him face to face but I wanted to know what he was like. Joshua said Ryan was his best mate over there but you know what men are like, and I just wondered what he's like from a woman's perspective. I have his address so I might pop over one day soon.'

'I'm sure you two would have lots to talk about. It might be good for both of you.'

Sophia and Flick said goodbye to Phoebe after making an appointment for the next visit in four weeks. They were both satisfied that she was in good physical health and managing her grief very well, and agreed that giving birth in hospital was a sensible decision.

'I hope that Ryan can help Phoebe, particularly if he was close to her husband. Something positive could come of it for both of them,' commented Sophia as they got into the car. 'They could probably both do with a friend at this time. It's hard to be alone in this world. Ryan's a lovely man. Who knows, he might even help to fill a void in the baby's life left by Joshua.'

Flick agreed as they headed off to the next home visit. 'I have some news about my baby's father.'

Sophia looked at Flick from the corner of her eye. 'What sort of news?'

'He's asked me to move in with him, for the sake of the baby. Nothing romantic,' Flick said, to temper the reaction she thought Sophia might have to her announcement. 'I was hesitating up until today and visiting Phoebe. But now I'm convinced that I should make the move. I don't want to rob my baby of being with Tristan. It's not about me any more. Phoebe's baby will never have the opportunity to meet his or her father and that is a tragedy caused by the war. I don't want to be a barrier to my child experiencing the love of a father. I never knew my father and it hurt as I grew up, not knowing what it felt like to have a family with a mother and father. There was always something missing. I won't let my child feel that way.'

'I can see where you're coming from but if you move in with him then you better watch out the sparks don't start flying again,' Sophia said, as she glanced from the road to Flick.

'It's not the way it looks. We're having a baby, he wants to help out. I can continue working and qualify on time. Besides, my place is too small and the stairs would be impossible as I get closer to my due date, and how would I get a pram up there?'

'It sounds as if he already convinced you.'

'No, this visit did. He just planted the seed. We can live together in a purely platonic sense. I'm not about to go looking for anything more. I don't want to get hurt again, so I will be setting some boundaries.'

'I think we need to talk this through. You're swimming in a dangerous pool right now and I don't want to see you heartbroken if it doesn't work out. You have to think about what is best for you too,' she said, pulling up out the front of a little café in Brunswick. 'Let's talk over something to eat. We're early for the next antenatal visit so perhaps we could stop for twenty minutes.'

'With my appetite, you don't need to ask twice.'

The two made their way inside and found an empty table. They ordered and sat back sipping the complementary water the waiter had given them.

'I can see the prospect of being there makes you happy,' Sophia said with a smile. 'As long as you can keep it in perspective and keep him at arm's length.'

'I'm not sure happy is the word. It's just the right thing to do for the baby and for Tristan...'

'What about you? Is it the right thing for you?'

'Yes, it is. It shows that he wants to be in the baby's life, even at the birth, and that's all I can ask of him. To be in our child's life is more than I had thought would happen a few weeks ago.'

Sophia looked over the menu and ordered a chicken wrap and sparkling water and Flick ordered the same. The waiter took the menus with him as he left to drop the order into the kitchen.

'It will be good to have Tristan, Megan and you there to coach me through the birth.'

'About that,' Sophia started, and unfolded her napkin and placed it on her lap in anticipation of her meal arriving. 'I didn't want to say anything to upset you but now you seem settled and you're over the angst with Tristan for the moment so I need to tell you that I'll only be able to be your primary care midwife for about another six weeks.'

Flick looked at her with a puzzled expression. 'I'm not following you. What's happening?'

'I have something wonderful to tell you, but I didn't feel right with what was happening in your life,' Sophia began, with her voice lowered.

Flick was intrigued by the sudden soft announcement and dropped her voice to a similar soft level. 'What is it? I'm excited for you already.' Flick was suddenly seeing life through a different lens. Meeting Phoebe made her want to cast her disappointment from the window and appreciate what she did have. It wouldn't be the diamond ring, the church or the picket fence, but it was something that resembled a family unit for her child.

'That's so sweet of you. With everything you're going through, you're excited for me.'

'My life isn't so bad. I have a baby on the way, and the father is now committed to the child and us all living together. It's not the way I saw it all happening but at least the child will grow up having a loving father. So I'm okay. Now, tell me what's your exciting news?'

'Aiden asked me to marry him.'

'Oh, my God,' Flick squealed, and attracted the attention of the patrons at the next table.

Sophia looked a little embarrassed.

'I'm sorry,' Flick answered in not much more than a whisper as she smiled meekly at their neighbours. 'I'm just so thrilled for you. Aiden is the most wonderful man, and I've seen the way he looks at you. He adores you.'

'And I adore him.'

Flick was so happy for her friend. 'Of course he would want to marry you. He's lucky to have you as his wife and you two will have a wonderful life together.'

'I know we will,' Sophia answered, knowing she was to marry a man she loved more than life itself. 'Now we just have to find you a new community midwife because I'll be going on honeymoon.'

'That makes me so happy. And one fairy-tale ending out of two is still great. Besides, at least being friends with Tristan is a vast improvement on a few weeks ago.'

'I'm not saying anything but I'm worried it won't stay that way. There's way too much chemistry between you two. However much self-control he professes, I don't think he'll be able to keep his distance for too long. And there's every chance he won't get a say in it.'

'What do you mean?'

'Your second-trimester sex drive surge.'

Flick seriously doubted what Sophia was telling her. 'I'm only just starting to feel human now. I can't imagine wanting to suddenly jump into bed with Tristan just because we're sharing a house. I haven't tried to seduce him over the last three months, he's been safe to wander the corridors of the Victoria. It doesn't sound even close to reasonable. He hasn't hinted at wanting to repeat that night and I am not about to force the man to make love to me. In fact, I've told him the opposite. My ground rules are not negotiable. I'm there for the baby not for a romantic relationship.'

'Reasoning won't come into it. The hormone increase of the first trimester left you tired and even if you'd had a partner back then, you'd probably be disinterested in sex. But the second-trimester hormones will make you more affectionate and increase your need for intimacy and you will have your old energy level back. You and Tristan under one roof with your raging hormones and, more importantly, the feelings you are both trying to suppress, I'm just telling you, it's a dangerous combination, Flick.'

CHAPTER SEVEN

As Flick packed the last of her belongings, Sophia's prediction of her one-night romance with Tristan being reignited was making her worry. She didn't want to be hurt or bring the child into a situation that was unstable. If they kept to the rules, and played it out as friends, they would be providing a solid home. Not strictly conventional but loving in its own way. She wanted the arrangement to last for their baby's sake, even though she doubted she was being practical.

A removalist had collected the large household items an hour earlier and taken them to a storage facility just out of town. Her clothes and personal things were in two suitcases and half a dozen small boxes. Not knowing exactly how she was feeling, she looked around her sunny apartment and thought how one night had changed her life for ever.

Then, looking back down at her tiny bump, she smiled to herself. 'We're in this together, you and I… and no matter what the future holds, you will be loved every day of your life.'

There was a knock at the door and Flick could see

Tristan's broad outline through the glass pane. Her heart began to race and her stomach turned a few somersaults as she made her way to him with a suitcase in her hand to open the door.

This was the beginning of a new life. And she was more scared than she had ever been before.

'Hello, Tristan.'

'Hi, Flick,' he replied, and then quickly reached and took the bag from her. 'Let me get that. It's too heavy and you're not climbing downstairs carrying anything heavier than your handbag.'

'I'm pregnant, not an invalid.'

He lifted his very dark eyes to meet hers. They were twinkling in the sun. 'It's my protective side, you'll have to pull me up now and then but only after the baby's born.'

'I will, you can count on that,' she said, trying to reclaim the bag.

He refused to release it to her as he held it tightly. 'I said you can pull me up after the baby arrives, so you can forget putting yourself or our child at risk by trying to climb down a few hundred steps while dragging a suitcase behind you. Not happening on my watch.'

Flick gave up. 'It's not even forty steps, but I'm not going to argue with you. But before we go, we need to talk.'

'What is it?'

Sophia's words were ringing in Flick's head. Not a delicate ring, it was more deafening alarm bells. 'I need you to know that what happened to us in *this* house won't be happening in yours. My agreeing to be there is strictly about the baby.'

A frown formed on his brow and his long fingers rubbed his chin thoughtfully. 'I told you that I wanted you there to take care of you. I'm not just looking for a living arrangement with benefits, if that's what you're thinking. I respect you, Flick, and you're going to be the mother of my child because of what happened here that night, but that's not why I want you with me. I just want to make sure you and the baby are well taken care of.' As he spoke he had doubts. Not of his promise to take care of Flick and the baby but his reassurance to her that there were no residual feelings. He knew that he wanted more but only time would tell if she would want the same.

'Great, that's sorted.'

She bit her lip and berated herself silently for being suspicious. Perhaps it wasn't him she worried about. Maybe it was her emotions and needs that had to stay in check. She didn't want to fall for him or become overly dependent.

And if she heard him walking around the house while she was lying in her bed in her room, feeling lonely, she would have to pull up the warm covers and block out the sounds. They weren't playing house, just housemates. Flick would never risk her child witnessing heartbreak and the demise of an adult relationship, the way she and Megan had time and time again.

'I'll see you downstairs,' she told him, her chin raised as she walked away. She was practising her friendly but cool demeanour.

'Watch your step, I'll be right behind you.'

He was being gallant and chivalrous and it was nice. The last thing she wanted to do was topple over on the uneven, white-painted steps or fall in love with Tristan so she would definitely be *watching her step*.

'I need to drop the keys back to Mr Papadothomakos. He's on the ground floor so I'll wait down there by his door for you,' she told him, but then, spying her stack of belongings, she felt a pang of guilt for turning Tristan into a removalist. 'There's quite a few boxes and both suitcases. I really am happy to help.'

'I don't doubt that you are but I've got it. Go and say your goodbyes while I handle this.'

Flick shrugged and left him to it. She found that her landlord was out so she waited for Tristan to load the car and lock her apartment before she dropped her key in his letterbox. Her emotions were mixed. The second-floor apartment had been home for three years and her land-lords were like family to her. And she was now moving in with the father of her child, and with the arrival of her baby they would become her family. Perhaps not in the way she would have liked but, nonetheless, a real family.

The drive to her new home took less than twenty minutes. They chatted about the hospital and her studies and Flick became anxious about how easy it was, being with him. As much as it was fun and relaxing, it also worried her as she thought how easy it would be to fall in love with him. Despite what they had been through, the unexpected pregnancy and his intense scrutiny of all things medical, she couldn't ignore the chemistry.

He was everything she was looking for and more. He was caring and chivalrous, intelligent and fun, and he made her skin tingle and her stomach jump in a good way whenever he came close.

But she knew better than to think he felt the same way. He was being kind and almost eighteenth-century noble by asking her to move in so he could take care of her. She wanted more. She needed more and she told herself that she would stay until the baby was born and then she would work out what was best for all of them. Whether she would stay indefinitely was undecided and a long way off. She wasn't looking for anyone else, and a part of her knew after being with Tristan for only one night that she would probably never find a man who came close to him. She was angry that she had allowed him to sweep her off her feet, to take a piece of her heart and ruin her for anyone else. She doubted that even if one day she met a man who wanted to return the love she was capable of giving he would be enough for her.

Tristan pulled the car into the driveway of the elegant two-storey home in a picturesque tree-lined street in Toorak. It was designed with simple understated elegance, Flick thought as she stepped from the car and looked up at the mansion that her baby would call home. Tristan unlocked the front door and she stepped into a huge white marble entrance. She looked up and saw the ceiling was two stories above them, with a large winding staircase with an intricate black iron balustrade leading to the upper-floor landing. It was breath-taking.

'Your room is on the ground floor,' he said, pointing down a hallway 'First door on the left. I'll get your things.'

Flick walked down the long hallway, admiring the stunning artwork on the walls, until she found her room. It was gorgeous. And huge compared to her tiny apartment. A four-poster queen-sized bed was almost lost in the spacious room, which had a bay window looking out across the picturesque garden. The windows were open enough that the scent of jasmine had subtly filled the room. Each side were drapes made of the softest mint-coloured heavy silk. There were two large dark wooden doors to the right and, driven by curiosity, she soon found that one opened to an en suite bathroom with an ivory and jade colour scheme. There was a luxurious bath, double shower and vanity and a vertical wooden rack filled with plush white towels. It was like her very own personal day spa.

Wondering what was behind the other door, she stepped from the marble tiles back into her cream-carpeted bedroom and opened the second door. A light automatically turned on, illuminating what she quickly ascertained was the world's largest walk-in wardrobe. There was enough room for dozens of shoes. Hanging space that would rival a department store, and drawers that she couldn't hope to fill in two lifetimes.

'The previous owner was a buyer for a national department store chain, or so I was told.'

Flick turned to find Tristan standing in the doorway, carrying her two small suitcases.

She looked at the size of the bags in his hands and back at the space around her.

'It shows. I think they could fit an entire season for

a store in here,' she replied. 'I think my belongings will fill less than two per cent of this space.'

'I've got a similar walk-in wardrobe in my room,' he told her. 'My things looked a little lost when I first moved in but I think we become a little like goldfish and our belongings grow to fit the space. Large storage space breeds hoarders because you don't have to throw anything away.'

Flick closed the door, thinking about Tristan's theory, but wondered if she would be there long enough to accumulate more clothes. Only time would tell if the arrangement would work. He was being gracious and she wanted Tristan to be in their child's life for ever. However, living together might be good on paper but in practice much more difficult. She was terrified she might fall in love. And if she fell in love with the father of her child, she was setting herself up for heartbreak. He had already told her that he wasn't the marrying kind. Not even the dating kind. It was left to be seen if he was father material but he was at least trying.

'What if I leave your bags over there and make us some lunch?' he asked, and Flick swallowed hard as he approached her and carefully dropped her bags by her feet. The scent of his cologne suddenly made her feel light-headed and sparked a torrent of memories. She remembered the same scent so close to her when he'd taken her to bed and made love to her all night long. And how it had lingered on her skin when she'd woken.

But she couldn't let those memories consume her. She had to pack them away neatly where they belonged and build on the very sensible, friendly arrangement they were creating for the sake of their child.

Passion was not the foundation of a practical relationship.

She needed to remain level-headed.

'That would be lovely,' she muttered, feeling very self-conscious. 'I just need to freshen up and I can find the kitchen in a few minutes and help you.' She wanted him to leave.

'No need to hurry,' he said, with his face only inches from hers. 'I'm a damn fine sandwich maker. So settle in, take your time and head out when you're ready.'

Flick did just that. She went into her luxurious en suite bathroom and splashed cold water on her face. She shook her head as she looked at her reflection in the mirror. Then she looked down at her ample cleavage. It wasn't fair. All her life she had been an A-cup and now it was as if her tummy and breasts were in competition. And her breasts were winning. They were huge by her standards and that was making her feel sexy and desirable. And being in his house wasn't making it any easier. Everything was conspiring to turn her into an emotional mess. She wondered if Tristan had any idea that a pregnant woman who didn't want to be in the same room with him only a week ago was now fighting her desire to sleep with him. And she couldn't blame it on pregnancy hormones alone. Unfortunately for Flick, there was more to it than that.

She had moved into his spare room so there was little space between them. Between the new living arrangements, feelings she had for him that had never gone away and her fluctuating hormones, her life had become very complicated.

'There's salmon and lettuce, egg and mayo or cold cut meat and mustard.'

Flick was hungry and the sandwich choices Tristan was listing sounded lovely. Anything to pull her back down to earth.

'Lunch looks amazing. Thank you so much for going to the trouble.'

'It's the least I can do for you. You've been through a tough few weeks of morning sickness. And our miscommunication added to your stress. I'm just glad it's over and you can start to feel back to normal and prepare for the birth.'

Flick smiled but she felt anything but normal. Tristan was being gallant and hospitable and she wanted so much more. It was only day one and she was struggling to keep to the rules that she had written. He had delivered suitcases to her room and offered to make lunch. If his home was a hotel, her thoughts were tantamount to wanting the ridiculously handsome concierge and the equally attractive chef. She had to snap out of it for everyone's sake.

She hadn't realised how hungry she was until she sat at the table and finished two sandwich halves without taking breath. It also helped to distract her from him being so close.

'Delicious,' she remarked, sitting back in her chair and feeling a little guilty for barely acknowledging

Tristan between bites. She also realised it was almost a week without morning sickness.

'Don't stop,' he told her, with a smile dressing his chiselled face. 'I made enough so you can graze during the afternoon.'

Tentatively she reached for another egg and mayo half. 'If you ever grow tired of surgery, you could definitely open a sandwich bar.'

He grinned. 'I'll keep it in mind.'

They enjoyed each other's company through lunch and then, after cleaning up and putting the leftovers in the refrigerator for Flick to nibble on later, Tristan excused himself as he had an afternoon of consultations back at the hospital.

'Please, make yourself at home,' he said, as they made their way to the spacious living room. 'Because this is your home, for as long as you and the baby would like to be here with me.'

Felicity felt her pulse quicken with his words. She knew that for Tristan it was the baby bringing them together and she didn't try to fool herself into believing he saw more than that. It felt nice but it wasn't real. He was charming and funny and she enjoyed being with him but she had to remind herself it wouldn't lead anywhere. They had fun and she knew living together would not be difficult as long as she kept her feelings under control. Tristan obviously had no residual emotions from their night together and she had to get to the point that she could say the same. She hoped in time her romantic daydreams would be a distant memory.

'I might stay in and watch a movie or read since I have the next two days off.'

'My movie library is sadly lacking in chick flicks but I have cable so you should find something to keep you amused until I get home, and then I can bore you with my day. That will send you running to the hills in no time.'

Flick laughed as he collected his belongings and made his way to the door. So quickly she felt like part of an old married couple the way he spoke and the plans he made for coming home to her. It tugged at her heart that they were just playing house and there was nothing deeper or more lasting than that.

'Have a restful afternoon and I'll see you tonight,' he said, and winked just before he closed the front door, leaving Flick lying on the sofa inside. It felt strange but good to hear Tristan bid her farewell and know he would be back with her in a few hours. She stopped herself for wishing for more. It wasn't about to happen, he was just trying to make the best of an awkward situation. And for that she was grateful. For all three of them.

She looked down at her stomach and smiled. 'Your daddy is a good man, my love.'

CHAPTER EIGHT

THE DAY HAD caught up with Flick and she hadn't even switched on the television before her head rested against the oversized cushions and sleep forced her eyes to close. The room was warm. Tristan had stoked the fire before he'd left and the logs were burning slowly and keeping the air toasty.

When she finally woke almost two hours later, she ventured back into the kitchen and took another sandwich from the refrigerator. The baby was indeed hungry, she told herself. It definitely wasn't for her. She could never normally eat the amount she was consuming now. She wondered if the baby would grow into a weightlifter with the amount of food she was needing to satisfy her appetite.

Once she had finished what she reminded herself firmly was the last sandwich for the day, she began wandering around the living area. It was beautifully furnished. Elegant and timeless and not overly masculine, which surprised her. She had assumed that it would be decorated more in line with bachelor appeal. Instead, she found it had a lovely family ambience. The rain began to fall and she could hear it on the iron roof. Looking around the house from her vantage point, she thought the only thing missing was a cat by the fireplace.

As if on cue, she saw a large ginger cat rush to the white French doors in the kitchen and rub its body the length of the glass as it stared at her. She'd had no idea that Tristan had a cat but didn't want the poor creature to get wet and cold so she crossed to the door and unlocked it. The moment the door was opened, the large Persian rushed past Flick without showing even a hint of gratitude and made a beeline for the rug in front of the fire.

'You're welcome,' Flick said as she closed the door against the bitterly cold breeze and made her own way back to the living room. The cat was busy grooming the water from her fur in the glow of the fire. She knew her way around and this confirmed Flick's assumption that the cat belonged to Tristan, or, probably more accurately, Tristan belonged to the cat.

Not knowing its temperament past selfish, Flick decided to let it settle in and went to her room and unpacked and put away her few belongings. Her few clothes looked a little silly hanging in the concert-hall-sized wardrobe, she thought as she closed the door and began to decorate the room with her framed photos and scented candles. Her household belongings were boxed up and placed in storage and the herb garden had been a parting gift to Mr Papadothomakos a few days before she left. He loved basil and oregano so he was thrilled and thanked her for being such a sweet tenant.

'Not too many good girls like you around any more,' he told her. 'If I had a son, I would marry you two off.

Too many young women nowadays, they bring different boys home every night but not you. You're like my Effie. A good woman and you'll make a good wife, Flick.'

He didn't know about the one *boy* she had brought home and the unexpected outcome of that. She had told him she was moving in with a work colleague closer to the hospital and he had no reason to doubt her. They left on good terms as she had been an exemplary tenant, paying her rent on time, never making a noise and, of course, *not bringing boys home*.

Flick smiled as she wandered around, looking at the house that was now her home. The cat was sound asleep with its fur nicely dry and the fire crackling gently.

Three silver-framed photos on the mantelpiece caught her eye. Mindful that she did not disturb the cat, she crossed to look at them. There were two boys and a girl. They all looked about nine or ten years of age. One boy appeared to be Indian in heritage, with big brown eyes and a gorgeous toothy grin; the other boy, who she assumed to be Vietnamese, looked a little more serious with very neat straight black hair and his striped shirt done up at the collar; and finally she picked up the framed photograph of the little girl with exotic looks. Her wavy dark hair was softly pulled back from her face and she wore stunning hand-made jewellery around her neck and adorning her ears. Her simple white cotton dress looked as if she was going to church or a wedding. All of the children looked very happy and sweet.

There were no other photos in the house but these obviously held pride of place. She reasoned they must be important to him, perhaps children of friends or children who had been his patients. She thought she would ask him when he returned from work but that was a few hours away so she decided to call Megan and give her an update. So much had changed in a week.

'You're living with him? In *his* house?' Megan asked in disbelief at what Flick was telling her. 'I thought you never wanted to see him again. I'm sure you used the word creep to describe him.'

'No, that's the word you used actually.'

'It doesn't matter who said it, it was said because it was the truth,' Megan argued. 'What's happened to make you want to move in with him?'

'We talked. He's not cold-hearted, it's just that he isn't the marrying kind. We had one night together and neither of us expected me to fall pregnant but he wants to do the right thing by me, and the baby. I can't ask for more than that…'

'Yes, you can,' Megan cut in. 'You, my amazing sister, can ask for the world from any man and he should be willing to give it to you. I don't understand the whole *not the marrying kind.* He'd be lucky to have you in his life. Don't settle and don't waste your time.'

'I'm not wasting my time, I'm doing what's right for all of us.'

'I'm not sure if you're setting yourself up for heart-break,'

'I'm hoping not, at least for our baby's sake.'

'So you're sacrificing your happiness for your baby?'

Flick closed her eyes for a moment. 'Nothing I did

would ever be a sacrifice, it would be what my baby deserves and nothing less.'

'Wish our mother had thought that way for just one day when we were growing up,' Megan said sadly. 'Speaking of our mother, are you planning on telling her about the baby?'

'Only when I have to,' Flick admitted. 'It will hurt too much to hear her tell me that I'm repeating her mistake.'

'And how the child will ruin your life, just like we ruined hers?'

Both sisters were silent for a moment. They each tried to be flippant but the pain of rejection when they'd been young was still raw.

'I got a postcard from her,' Megan finally managed.

'Where is she?' Flick asked, not overly upset she hadn't received one.

'Yours is probably on its way to your former apartment. It looks like she's getting married tomorrow on the beach in Bali. Thanks for the invitation, Mum.'

'But she met him less than two months ago.'

'I know, and this would make it husband number four. I've lost count of the boyfriend tally,' Megan said, her voice flat and drained of emotion and signs of caring. 'The good thing is that no matter what happens with this doomed relationship we can't be blamed or made to pay the price when it all comes unravelled. And we both know it will.'

Flick sighed. 'That's the good side of getting older, we can see that all her failed relationships weren't about children getting in the way, it was about her rushing in and choosing the wrong men.' Flick stopped in mid-sentence. That was just what she had done. She had rushed into sleeping with Tristan. And now she was living with him. She suddenly felt a knot in her chest and an emptiness in her stomach with the thought she was her mother's daughter.

'I guess the apple didn't fall too far from the tree…'

'Don't go there, you're nothing like our mother!' Megan cut in.

'I got pregnant from a one-night stand…and now we're shacked up. It sounds a lot like our mother.'

'You would never dream of letting your child feel anything less than the most special little person in the world. I know you, and you're the most loving, giving woman who would lay down her life without question for her child. Our mother wasn't, and still isn't, capable of that level of love and loyalty. It isn't in her and you have it in spades. What you sacrificed for me over the years is ridiculous and I would need two lifetimes to repay you. And from what I'm hearing, you've put your needs aside so that your child will have both parents around. That's not chasing a man, it's being a wonderful mother.'

'I'm not so sure.'

Megan spent the best part of ten minutes convincing Flick that she should never again compare herself to their mother. She appreciated the way her sister defended her but while she wasn't convinced that she hadn't repeated her mother's behaviour in rushing in, she vowed she would stop any similarity there. The child she was carrying would be cherished and adored for life.

* * *

'So the fur beast from next door conned its way inside, I see,' Tristan said with a smirk as he looked at the cat sleeping by the fire when he arrived home, a little damp himself from the rain that was still falling.

'Next door? I thought it belonged to you and it was pouring down outside.'

'No, she wants to belong to me, and knowing the houseful of noisy children who live next door I don't blame her. I provide a refuge or respite when it all gets too much but fur beast is trying to move in permanently, so I will only open the door for short visits.'

Flick smiled but his words, however unintentional, hit a deeper chord in her. Allowing the cat to stay over was a kind gesture and she wondered if the same applied to her. Was he offering her refuge from the storm? Just a short stay for her too, so she shouldn't get too comfortable?

It was subtle analogy, and perhaps not intended, but it had been effective in unsettling her just a little. Perhaps she needed that, she thought. She didn't want to get too settled as he might ask her to make her own way once the baby was born. She really couldn't see past the next few months. She wished with all her heart that they would bring up their baby together in a loving home long term, but the reality for them was not that clear.

'What gorgeous children you have in the frames on your mantel,' she commented, passing over the mine-strone soup she had cooked slowly on the stovetop during the afternoon. 'Are they your friends' children?'

'That's Aditya, Danh and Lucia,' he told her as he

reached for a piece of crusty bread. 'They're not children of my friends. They're mine.'

Flick nearly choked on her spoonful of soup. 'Yours?' she managed through the spluttering sounds. 'I thought you spent your life avoiding commitment and more particularly children. Now you're telling me you have three children. I'm just a little confused right now.'

'Sponsor children,' he said with one eyebrow raised. 'It would have required affairs on three different continents to have fathered those children. I was a little busy with studying and my surgical internship ten years ago to have done that too.'

Tristan had never imagined being a father in the true sense of the word but he loved children so this was his chance to watch and support these amazing little people grow into adults with his financial assistance. He felt they filled a void in his world and he hoped that he gave them something they all needed. One day he hoped to guide them into careers that would make a difference to them, their families and their communities. He had a sense of pride about their achievements and it was a feeling he cherished.

Flick laughed nervously. 'They're truly gorgeous children.'

'Inside and out, they're wonderful children and a credit to their families. I've visited with all of them and they're amazing, intelligent individuals. Lucia is almost ten and her family lives in Casa Grande in Peru, Aditya is twelve and his home is in Bombay with his grandmother and Danh is also twelve and he's from Saigon, where he and his eight siblings live with their mother and elderly aunty. My sponsorship assists the families with day-to-day expenses and education. I live in a lovely home and have a great, albeit busy life, and I want to pay it forward. I've been sponsoring all three since they were only a few months old.'

Flick smiled warmly at the man sitting opposite her. There was so much she didn't know about him and so much she wanted to know. There was a genuine humanitarian side to him and there was fun and humour and so many wonderful qualities that she was discovering as they spent more time together. He was chivalrous and old-fashioned but she had also experienced a level of passion with him that she'd never dreamed possible.

But he was also off limits. Not the marrying kind, she needed to remind herself as she looked into the warmth of his smiling eyes. Taking a little breath to steady her fluttering heart, she wondered what made him avoid commitment. What had happened in his past that prevented him from wanting to enjoy a long-term relationship? What allowed work to replace love of the lasting kind?

She doubted she would ever know, so she accepted they would share a child and only memories of one night together. And she was trying her best to be okay with that. A happy life with a picket fence, husband and children was a dream she had held since she was a little girl. She had never been a part of something that perfect but it was what she had always wanted and now she knew it would never be hers.

Being friends with the father of her child and a

man she respected and cared about was better than the choices her mother had made.

'Let's head in and get comfortable in the living room,' he suggested, as he stood and pulled out her chair.

He made her feel special with little effort.

'What about the dishes?'

'They're not going anywhere, but I suspect you might get tired so I can do them after you fall asleep. Until then I want to spend some quiet time with you.'

He led her into the spacious room that was dimly lit by the crackling fire and a lamp by the window. They sat in big armchairs opposite each other. Flick needed to keep some distance between them as she was scared at how quickly her walls were crumbling.

'So now you know about my children, Flick, tell me about yourself. I need to be able to tell our baby about his or her mother in some depth. We have about five months for you to tell me all about your family and where you grew up.'

Flick curled her socked feet up into the softness of the oversized chair. She was feeling a little vulnerable and the thought of talking about less pleasant times didn't sit well with her.

'Honestly, Tristan, there's not much to tell,' she said evasively, and reached over for a book sitting on the coffee table nearby. After reading the dust jacket, she began flicking through the pages. 'This looks interesting. If it's okay with you, I might head to bed and read.'

Tristan got up and gently took the book from her hands and put it back down on the small carved table. 'You can read the book later,' he said, not taking his eyes from hers. 'But I want to know more about the mother of my child. In years to come, our child will ask me questions about you. I'm not planning on saying that we only spent one night together and I don't know anything about you.'

'But it *was* just one night,' she reminded him with no bitterness intended.

'Yes, it was, but now we have the chance to make it more and we both owe that to our baby. I want to be able to talk about you to our child the way parents should, telling stories about each other. I know so little, just that you're a midwife...student midwife, you love cooking with basil and you grew oregano just to give it away to your Greek landlord.'

Flick was so happy to hear Tristan say that he wanted the chance to make it more. Whatever that meant. He wanted their child to feel special and that meant the world to her. To know that he wanted to make an effort for the sake of the baby made everything feel right and good. Suddenly she felt safe.

'I have a sister, Megan, who lives in Sydney. She's a speech pathologist and she volunteers at an animal shelter every second weekend.'

'Married, single?'

'She's single by choice,' Flick replied. 'I don't think she's fallen in love yet.'

Tristan wasn't sure if Flick had fallen in love yet either. Before he'd met her, Tristan knew he hadn't but now he wasn't so sure. He thought it felt a lot like love whenever she was near.

'Father, mother, other sister, brothers?'

'Never met my father, but did hear about him numerous times and nothing of my mother's portrayal of him is even close to flattering. Then there's my mother, who is apparently getting married tomorrow on a beach in Bali, and I don't have any other siblings.'

Tristan could hear the change in Flick's voice from describing her sister with pride and then her mother and non-existent father with clear disdain. 'You didn't want to go to her wedding?'

'I wasn't invited. My sister only told me today. My invitation, if there is one, will be at my old place. But don't worry, I'd prefer to not go. I don't like getting attached to my mother's boyfriends or husbands as they are all transient. I gave up at fourteen trying to find a father figure in the turnstile of my mother's flings.'

'I'm sorry to hear that.'

'Don't be,' she said, trying to stay positive and not look back over the emptiness that was her family life. 'I had my sister, she's amazing and we both learnt to deal with our mother's desire to be fancy-free, translation, single without children, when the need arose.'

'That's surprising,' he said bluntly.

'Why do you say that? You've never met her.'

'I know you think I don't really know you, but I feel I do have some insight and I can't imagine you thinking that way, particularly where a child is concerned. It sounds nothing like you.'

Flick was grateful to hear she was worlds away from her mother, even if it was from a man who had never met the woman. It was still a powerful and reassuring message.

Suddenly she felt a tumbling motion inside. She wasn't sure but it felt like it was the baby moving. She gasped as she felt it move again.

'Is everything okay?' Tristan asked, when he saw her expression suddenly change. 'This isn't about your mother, is it? I promise our baby will never hear those stories. They're safe with me.'

'No, it's not about her.' She paused and then her eyes met his. 'I think the baby just moved.'

'That early?' he said. 'You're barely fifteen weeks now.'

'Oh,' she gasped again. 'No, our baby is definitely doing a little dance.' She stood up and walked to his chair. She sat on the armrest and instinctively placed his hand on her stomach. 'See if you can feel it too?'

She could feel the warmth and tenderness of his hand through her thin shirt as it rested gently on her stomach. He sat still, waiting for something, but not entirely sure what he would actually feel so early into the pregnancy. Without warning he too felt some movement. At only fifteen weeks he wasn't sure what he had felt, he knew that it was around twenty weeks that movement could be felt externally but he loved that she wanted him to be a part of it. His face lit up with unexpected pride.

'And it can feel the warmth of your hand, I'm sure of it,' Flick told him.

Tristan looked lovingly at the mother of his child. She was a beautiful woman and a gentle soul and if only things were different he would pull her into his arms, tell her just that and then kiss her.

She was within his reach, physically and emotionally, but he couldn't let it happen. He didn't want to rush their relationship. They had to take things slowly. Let it unfold the way it should have all those months ago, and when the time was right, he would sit her down and explain the potential risk to their child.

He fell silent, wondering if he should tell her. Was that night the right time? Would it be for the best for her to know? Something inside begged him for more time. He had promised his offer of a home to Flick and the baby and he needed to prove to her that she could feel safe with him around. He didn't want to bring up the issue so early. It could wait as it wasn't going to change the course of her pregnancy until at least twenty weeks.

Sitting bolt upright, his stature became quite rigid as he removed his hand from the softness of her stomach and handed her the book. 'Perhaps you should get some rest. You can read in here or in your room while I do the dishes. I think I'll turn in early too. I have a full Theatre schedule tomorrow.' Quickly he rushed from the warmth of the room and the pull of the woman who was very close to having his heart.

Without showing any hint of the disappointment welling inside, Flick took the book, dropped her head onto her chest a little and went to her room.

The night was over. And she thought she knew why. She wondered if perhaps she wasn't the only one with feelings. But she wasn't about to admit to hers either.

CHAPTER NINE

'I MIGHT HEAD out and pick up a few things for the nursery,' Flick announced over their shared breakfast. It had become a ritual that they'd settled into quickly during their first week of living together. Both had made a silent pact without the other one knowing to keep things simple for the sake of the baby.

Their feelings still simmered close to the surface, though both had decided not to act on them. Each left the room when they felt they were losing the battle with their feelings. It was working. For the time being at least.

Flick cooked the oatmeal while Tristan squeezed the fresh juice and then they sat and ate at the large kitchen table. Some days they read the paper; some days they talked. But always they enjoyed each other's company. And since it was Saturday and neither had to rush off to work, they were both still in their winter pyjamas and robes. Tristan's feet were bare, Flick's were bundled into thick bedsocks and fluffy slippers.

Tristan lifted his head from the sports section. He still loved to follow the football scores and upcoming matches. Even though he had never been well enough to play, it hadn't stopped his love of the game. His local football team was aware of his medical condition and had allowed him to attend their private practice sessions, even giving him a jersey in their red, blue and green colours.

'What do you need?' he asked, thinking how cute she looked with her long blonde hair in messy plaits and her face scrubbed free of make-up. Cute and sexy. And it grew more difficult with each day not to give in to to his desire to have her. And his abrupt exits to have a cold shower were increasing, not subsiding.

'Honestly, I have no real concept of what I'll need but I don't have anything so I guess I should start looking. The time will fly by, what with my studies and last few months of clinical placement. I'll blink and find myself in the labour ward, with nothing prepared. You'll be running around trying to buy nappies and a bassinette.'

Tristan sensed Flick felt both overwhelmed and excited and he wanted to help her to feel less overwhelmed so that she could actually enjoy the feeling of excitement.

'Do you feel like company on your shopping trip?'

Flick was surprised that he wanted to accompany her and guessed that he didn't know exactly what it entailed. She doubted that a pregnant woman's indecision in a store filled with baby supplies would be his idea of a fun Saturday afternoon.

'You might not be able to deal with it,' she warned him light-heartedly.

'I've heard that nursery shopping is quite a battlefield,' he cut in wryly. 'But I'm sure I'll survive.'

* * *

An hour later, Tristan was driving Flick in the direction of the largest baby supply store in Victoria. They'd made a list of what they thought they would need as they'd finished breakfast. They laughed at how two neonate medical professionals were borderline clueless on where to start with their own baby's needs.

'That's why they have experienced salespeople,' Tristan said, as they pulled into the half-full parking lot. The day was cold, but it wasn't raining and they were both in jeans, long-sleeved T-shirts and warm jackets. Flick's jeans had a stretchy panel that allowed her tummy to expand and she had donned a scarf and gloves that she removed when she entered the air-conditioned store.

'I'll grab a trolley and follow you,' he told her as he unzipped his jacket. He was pushing away thoughts of what might lie ahead and concentrating on letting Flick enjoy selecting everything she needed for their baby. There was time to be practical and there was also time to just enjoy being parents-to-be like other customers.

He walked beside her as she lightly fingered the soft woollen blankets, and patchwork comforter sets.

'And since you have to carry our baby, and let's not forget give birth at the end, I'm paying for whatever he or she will need. There's no point arguing because I won't back down.'

'But that's not fair to you…'

'If any sane person was to compare handing over a credit card to nine months of pregnancy, they would say I got the easy way out,' he said, as he tossed a satin-

edged baby blanket into their trolley. He had seen her
hesitate and look back at it twice and had assumed it
was one she liked. He wanted her to have everything
and it wasn't guilt that was making him feel that way.
Every moment he spent with her made him realise that
his feelings were growing.

'I suppose we should look at prams and bassinettes
too…and then I'll need a baby bath and a change table.
It's too much, really it is. I can pay half.'

Tristan shook his head. 'Your money is no good in
this store. Accept what I'm telling you and move on.'

Hours passed as they roamed the huge store, selecting
all the necessities and then some not-quite-so-essential
baby needs. The trolley was laden with romper suits,
bath toys, a nightlight that projected stars onto the ceiling, and more. There was a small coffee shop inside the
store so they parked the trolley and sat and ate a piece
of banana bread each, along with a cup of tea. Before
long, they were up and in search of some baby socks
and bath products.

'I'm liking the four-poster cot,' he remarked as he
steered their purchases in the direction of the mahog-
any-stained bed fit for a prince or princess. 'What do
you think?'

'It's stunning but a little extravagant.' Then she came
back to reality and her body became a little tense. The
man who was showering their baby with presents hadn't
spoken of anything past the birth of the child. She had no
idea where she would be in a year's time. There might
not be a long-term living arrangement. She wondered if
she was like fur beast with a slightly longer lease. 'Let's

not rush into the big pieces of furniture. Who knows where we might be then?'

Tristan came down to earth with a thud. He felt a vein rise in his forehead. Flick was right. Their reality was not the baby store. That was a bubble for one day. Her future might not include him and it might not even include a baby if the prognosis was not good. Suddenly the thought of walking past an empty nursery if Flick and the baby left or if the baby did not survive cut deeply. He had not expected to feel that way. Being so close made it all so real and the risk weigh so heavily.

He knew that he had to tell her sooner rather than later but he wanted her to have a few more days of enjoying her pregnancy.

The rest of the day was spent unpacking the purchases and setting up the nursery. It would be next to Flick's room. The walls were already a soft yellow and both agreed that, no matter if they had a boy or girl, it would be perfect. Tristan moved the heavy things around to suit Flick. The room already had a bed and tallboy, along with built-in wardrobes to house the blankets and quilt. The change-table, pram and bassinette all found pride of place in the room that very quickly became a very pretty nursery.

Tristan knew it wouldn't be his decision but he hoped that after she knew the facts she would feel closer to him and together they would get through whatever lay ahead. He decided that he would tell her everything soon. He had hoped to leave it until after the twenty-week scan, when he would know for sure if there was a problem, but now he felt that would be wrong. She had every right to know, he just needed to find the right way to tell her.

Tristan and Flick both left home at the same time the next day. She felt less like fur beast by the day. She also found it amusing that said cat had spent most of Sunday stretched out in front of the fire with a satisfied look on her face.

It was as if she had moved in too.

Tristan really wasn't the loner he made himself out to be. Far from it, in fact, and as she drove into the city and the Victoria Hospital, with Tristan's car in her rear-view mirror, Flick felt the happiest she had been in a very long time. It felt right and although it was complicated and might never be more than it was at that time, she felt content. And if this was all he could offer, she decided she would be okay with it. At least for the time being.

Tristan followed behind her, hoping that by the end of the week there would be no secrets between them. Everything would be out in the open and he hoped Flick would understand why he'd kept his condition from her.

His early morning rounds included Callum, who was now progressing very well. Jane Roberts was no longer a patient at the hospital and she and her husband spent every waking moment by their tiny son's side.

'Will we be able to take him home today, as planned?' Jane asked, as Tristan checked the nurses' notes.

'I've been speaking with Dr Hopkins and we are both happy for Callum to travel back to Sydney with you tomorrow. He's progressing well so I'm happy to sign the discharge papers today.'

He added that their cardiologist would ask for heart

tests over the coming months, including ECGs, echo-cardiograms and cardiac MRIs, and not to be alarmed as they were routine.

Callum's father hugged his wife tightly then he out-stretched his hand to Tristan. 'Thank you, Dr Hamilton. We owe you our son's life.'

Tristan met his handshake and smiled. It was a good outcome and that always made him feel happy.

The morning was filled with post-surgical consults and the afternoon was Theatre. It was just before five when he headed down to see if Flick had returned to MMU. There was something he wanted to ask her.

'So what about you and I go out tonight?'

Flick turned to find Tristan dressed in scrubs. It was almost five o'clock and she had only just returned from a home birth with Sophia where they had assisted the mother for nearly six hours. She was tired and couldn't wait to get off her feet. And now, after his invitation, she suddenly felt tired and confused.

'Pardon me?'

'You heard me, Flick,' he said, pulling the surgical cap from his head. 'I think going out on a date is the least we can do for our child.'

Flick dropped her voice to not much more than a whisper. 'A date?'

'Yes, a date. How can a child grow up thinking that his parents lived together before he or she even arrived in the world but they'd never been on a date?'

'But our child won't know whether we dated or not.'

'I would,' he countered. 'And it's not good enough

for my child's mother to not have been taken somewhere special before she gave birth.'

Tristan knew his feelings were taking over his logical nature by the minute. Hearing Flick rattling cutlery in the kitchen when he'd woken that morning was a sound he didn't want to live without. And a sound he would never take for granted. It was strange how knowing she was in the house made him feel whole and he didn't want to lose that. He wanted to begin again and do it properly this time and honestly.

He also knew he needed and wanted to tell her that night about his heart transplant, the condition that had led to it and what might lay ahead for their child.

'But I'm only four months pregnant, there's plenty of time.' Flick wasn't sure why she was trying to talk her way out of a date. Once she would have jumped at the opportunity to date Tristan but now everything was settled and she didn't want to see that change. She didn't want to open her heart and find he was still off limits. And she was exhausted from a very long day and she was finding it difficult to think properly.

'No time like the present,' he told her, before he headed back to his afternoon consults. 'Why don't you head home and have a nap, see how you feel when I get home at seven?'

Flick did just that. But when she woke and while she showered and dressed, butterflies filled her stomach. Morning sickness had well and truly abated but it had been replaced by uneasiness of another kind.

The idea of a date was unsettling. Her feelings for Tristan were as strong as ever but she was unsure how he felt. They were living together but she knew the baby had made that happen. Without the pregnancy, she wondered if they would be even talking, let alone going on a date. So much time had passed after their one-night stand without so much as a word from Tristan, and as much as she wanted to think he did have feelings for her, she suspected their living together was more from a sense of duty and doing the right thing for the child.

For that reason, Flick decided to keep her heart tucked away. She didn't want to fall further in love with the father of her child. Falling in love had already happened, almost four months ago. Now she was trying to fall out of love, and that was so much harder.

'Are you ready, Flick?'

She ran the brush through her hair once again before she looked down at her slightly rounded tummy inside her knee-length black dress.

'Looks like Mummy and Daddy are going on a date,' she muttered under her breath, as she grabbed a warm coat and left the safety of her room.

The drive to the restaurant took fifteen minutes and Tristan filled it with questions about Flick's day and about how the home birth had gone that morning with Sophia.

'It was intense,' she told him. 'I've been at home births quite a few times now but this one had an audience of millions.'

'Must have been a big house.'

Flick smiled at the absurdity of her statement. He was making her relax and she loved being in his company.

'Well, perhaps I was exaggerating a little. Maybe close to thirty.'

'That's still a huge number,' he replied, as he pulled into the street near their destination. 'Big family?'

'Quite a few family members but I think most were from the yoga class the woman teaches.'

'Now, that's taking the lesson to the extreme.'

Flick had thought the same when she'd arrived with Sophia to find the house bursting at the seams with people.

'I must say, during the labour they were all so lovely and supportive and not one tried to interfere or cause any issues. They were celebrating from the moment we arrived until the birth. They'd set up a small birthing pool in the family room and the helpers kept bringing warm water and generally offering assistance without distracting from the mother's needs.'

Tristan pulled up in the restaurant car park and turned to Flick, grinning. 'You're not thinking you'd like to do the same in a few months, are you?'

'Well, actually…' she paused for a moment with a slightly mischievous smile curving her lips '…I thought that we could invite the entire medical staff from the Victoria who aren't on duty at that time. Maybe set up the birthing pool in the cafeteria.'

'I'm not sure if it would positively or negatively affect the lunch trade.' He laughed. 'But if that's what you want then I'll pick up the birthing pool next weekend. I can have it on standby in my office.'

Hearing Flick giggle made him feel very at ease and comfortable. It was the way she'd made him feel on the beach that fateful morning. She was so natural and sweet. But she was far from naïve and he knew she would challenge him and make him a better man. He already felt like a better man, just being near her. He was confronting his worst fear and yet with her beside him it didn't appear overwhelming any more.

Dinner was lovely and they both agreed that the baby would have to love Italian cuisine as they couldn't get enough of the delicious pasta and garlic bread.

'I should slow down,' she said, after finishing her second piece of the herb and butter-coated bread. 'I've had enough carbs for an army.'

'You are eating for two,' he reminded her.

'Two, not twenty.'

Tristan smiled but it was bitter-sweet, thinking about the child. He hoped after that night he wouldn't have to hide his feelings about Flick. He just didn't know how she would feel about him when she learnt about the risk to their child.

'Is everything okay?' she asked, her curiosity piqued by the way he suddenly seemed lost in thought. 'You seem a little preoccupied.'

Tristan decided that when they got home he would sit her down and, like two intelligent people with medical backgrounds, they would discuss the options and accept the challenges ahead.

'I'm good,' he told her, confident that he would be once he had explained what might lie ahead for them. And how they would get through everything together from now on. 'Let's order dessert.'

'At this rate, I'll roll into the hospital cafeteria to give birth.'

Tristan shook his head. 'Neither will happen, believe me.'

As they walked to their car in a side street not far from the restaurant ominous-looking clouds suddenly opened. There was no shelter other than a few overhanging branches from the large trees that had lost most of their leaves in preparation for the winter months.

'We can run for it,' Flick said, as the rain pelted down, soaking her hair and her clothes.

Tristan pulled his jacket off and wrapped it tightly around her. 'We're not running anywhere in this. The pavement's slippery and I'm not taking that chance.'

'But now you're getting drenched, and it's freezing.'

'Don't worry about me. I'm just fine.' His white shirt quickly became wet through and clung to his body, but he didn't care. His sole focus was in his arms and, secure in the knowledge that Flick was safe and warm, he walked her slowly to the car as the rain kept pouring down. At that moment he realised he had everything he wanted and would not let it slip from his fingers. He was chilled to the bone and he had never been happier in his life.

'You're absolutely soaking,' she told him, when he finally climbed into the driver's seat. He had already tucked her into the car. 'Take your shirt off and put your jacket back on. At least then you might not get pneumonia.'

She wiped the rain from his face with her fingers and instinctively tried to brush the water from his hair.

'I'll be all right once we get home,' he said, unbuttoning his shirt and discarding it on the back seat before he slipped his jacket over his bare chest. 'We can sit by the fire and warm up. Let's just get you home, you're the important one here.'

'You're very sweet, and you'll be a wonderful caring father, Tristan.'

Without thinking, she suddenly leant over and kissed his cheek.

The feeling of her lips on his skin unleashed a passion that he had been fighting for too long. He was powerless to contain it any longer. Cupping her face in his hands, Tristan turned her gently towards him. Looking into the beautiful blue eyes that were staring back at him in anticipation, he said nothing. Instead, he took her mouth with his and wouldn't let her go. Tenderness turned to desire as he explored the softness of her lips and the warmth of her mouth with his tongue.

Flick wasn't sure what was happening but it felt so natural to be in his arms. Her head was spinning and her heart was beating very fast as he kissed her with the same passion she so vividly remembered.

Suddenly he pulled away and sat back in his seat, staring straight ahead. 'Should I apologise?' Tristan asked, his voice low and breathless.

'I don't know, should you?'

'I would apologise if it was something you didn't want me to do,' he said, turning to look at her.

Flick had been hiding her feelings for too long. She had imagined it was only her who wanted more than a sensible arrangement for the sake of the child, but his kiss proved there was so much more than duty on his side.

She leant over to him and let her lips find his again. 'Sorry won't be needed tonight.'

Tristan pulled her back into his arms and felt the curves of her body as his hands explored every inch that the confines of the car would allow. He continued kissing her the way he had wanted to every day since he'd left the crumpled warmth of her bed.

'Let's go home.'

CHAPTER TEN

Flick's heart skipped a beat when Tristan's hand reached
for hers as they walked to the front door. The rain had
stopped but he still held her hand tightly. His grip was
strong and she felt secure. She had a feeling that they
might just have their fairy-tale ending after all. He was
perfect and everything she could want in a man.

For the first time in her life she felt safe letting herself lean on someone else. She didn't have to stand on
her own any more and be strong. A smile spread across
her face as she thought about the three of them in a few
months. The baby's arrival was early in the relationship
but the way he'd kissed her and the way he was holding
her hand told her that he wasn't going anywhere. Everything she could ever want was right beside her.

Tristan unlocked the front door and switched on the
soft hall light so Flick could get out of the cold quickly.

'Why don't you take off your coat and boots and I'll
get the fire going.'

Flick smiled as she watched his broad silhouette lean
over the dark fireplace and load wood into the hearth.
His chest was bare under the heavy jacket and she felt

her heart race as she pictured him holding her into the night. He lit a match on some rolled up newspaper that he wedged between the logs and she could see the glow of the flames.

She felt like the luckiest woman in the world as she walked to her room to drop off her coat and boots and slip off her damp stockings, wondering if she would wake in his bed or he would wake in hers. Wherever they woke, it would be the three of them. Tristan, Flick and their baby.

A few minutes later she returned to find Tristan missing but the fire burning nicely.

'Make yourself comfortable, there's a towel for your hair,' he called out from the kitchen. 'I'm making something to warm us up.'

Flick rubbed her hair dry by the warmth of the fire then curled her legs up onto the sofa and drew the mohair blanket up across her feet. The prickly fibres tickled her bare skin. The room was warming quickly and she knew that once Tristan moved close to her, there would be even more heat.

Tristan returned with two mugs of piping-hot chocolate, put them on the low coffee table then sat down next to her. The room was still lit by just the glow of the fire now taking hold and enveloping the room with gentle warmth.

He looked at Flick, curled up beside him, and realised that the moment had come to tell her everything before they took their relationship back to the bedroom. He wouldn't do that for a second time without her knowing everything. Reaching for her hands, he took them in his. There would be no secrets between them any more.

'There's something I want to tell you.'

Flick drew in a deep breath and closed her eyes for a moment. Her heart raced. She prayed that she would like what he wanted to tell her and that it had something to do with committing to her and to their baby.

'After that wonderful night we shared I wanted to call you,' he began, with his warm hands holding hers and melting away the every last remnant of her resistance. 'But I couldn't.'

Flick didn't say anything. The room was quiet, save for the crackling fire and Tristan's voice, and she wanted to hear every word of the man who had captured her heart so totally.

'It wasn't that I didn't want to ask you out, Flick. Believe me, whether we slept together or not, I thought you were amazing and if things were different I would have asked you out immediately. I would have pursued you to the end of the earth but I had to think about you and what you needed long term. And in my mind it wasn't me.'

'I'm not sure why you would think that.' Lovingly, she searched his eyes for an answer. 'Was it because you're a workaholic? I hope not, because I'm more than okay with you being dedicated to your career. I admire you more than you probably know for how hard you work and how much you give to those babies and their parents.'

Tristan didn't doubt anything that Flick was telling him. Her support was something he wouldn't question.

She was equally dedicated. It was something he knew they shared.

'My marriage to my work and avoiding commitment aren't the issues, Flick, they are the results of something else. They've been shields for me to hide behind. Ways to avoid relationships and block out what I went through as a child.' His hands gripped a little tighter around hers.

'What you went through?'

'I had a heart transplant when I was sixteen.'

'Oh, my God, Tristan. I didn't know,' Flick said, not masking her surprise at what he was telling her. 'Please, believe me, that doesn't change how I feel about you. If there are problems in the future, we can get through that together. I don't want you to live in fear.'

'I don't fear for me,' he said in a serious voice. 'I gave up being scared about my mortality years ago.'

'The scar down your chest, that was from the open heart surgery.' It was a statement, not a question, as she remembered the scar from the beach.

'Yes, over twenty years ago. I was sixteen when I received another man's heart. I guess it made me determined to live two lives out of appreciation for what I'd been given. His life had been cut short and mine had been saved. I thought I owed him something for it.'

'So you became a workaholic out of respect for the donor?'

'In a way,' he started. 'I decided to study cardiology and then specialise as a neonatal cardiothoracic surgeon in the hope of helping children with similar cardiac defects.'

Flick remembered thinking the scar was faded and

the way he didn't hide it had led her to believe he had come to terms with whatever had happened. His line of thinking had been so mature at such a young age when he'd decided on medicine as a career but clearly he wasn't at peace with what had happened. He had residual issues that were driving him to stay alone. It didn't make sense. He was through the worst of it and still lived in fear of something.

'If you're not fearful of dying, and clearly you shouldn't be, then what are you scared about?'

Tristan swallowed and paused. He knew what he was about to tell Flick was no longer about him. It was about the baby she was carrying, and while she could be strong for him he wasn't sure how she would react to the same news about her child.

'I was diagnosed at birth with HLHS, which is hypoplastic left heart syndrome. It's congenital and hereditary.'

'Hereditary?'

'Yes, it's genetic.'

'So you can pass this on to any children that you father?' she asked, realising that the heart condition was something very different from what she had imagined. Wrestling her hands free from his, she rested them on her stomach protectively.

'Yes, although now it can be operated on in utero,' he replied, to calm the concern he saw on her face. 'And it's not definite that our child will automatically inherit the condition.'

'But it's very serious,' she said, biting the inside of her cheek nervously. 'Our baby might die?'

'Flick, I didn't plan on having children for good reason…'

'You didn't answer my question. Could our baby die from this condition?'

'Yes…but I will do everything in my power to make sure our baby lives.'

Tears welled in Flick's eyes and trickled down her cheeks. Defiantly she wiped them with the back of her hand as she struggled to fill her lungs with air.

'A heart transplant is not always necessary now. Surgical intervention has come so far since I was a child.'

'Why didn't you let me know sooner? When I told you about the pregnancy or any of the days since then? I took a chance on you that night. I opened my heart to you and you've kept something this important from me for the last four weeks.'

'We used protection so I never thought for a moment you would fall pregnant. And it's why I walked away the next morning. I knew you loved children, you're a midwife. I thought that if we were to take our one night and turn it into something more, I would one day have to tell you that I didn't want to have a family and maybe you wouldn't want to build a life with me. To me there was no point in pursuing you and getting in too deep and then having you leave me when I couldn't give you what you needed. I suppose I was being selfish. I didn't want to have my heart broken when you walked away, which was inevitable, but neither would I agree to have children and risk them going through what I went through as a child.'

'And that's why you were asking all the questions at the scan.'

'Yes. I just wanted to know what we might be dealing with, but, having said that, there may be no problem with our child.'

'And you planned on telling me all of this tonight after dinner?'

'Yes, I just wanted to find the right time to tell you,' he told her honestly.

'So the kiss was just a way to soften the blow?' she asked, unable to bring herself to look at him. Then suddenly thinking about how ready she'd been to invite him into her bed, she felt ill. 'If we hadn't been drenched in the rain and needed to dry out, would you have told me this after we'd made love? Would you have used sex to cushion the delivery?'

'No,' he argued. 'The kiss happened because I have feelings for you and I wanted to tell you before we made love.'

'Of course you would have,' she spat angrily. 'I'm supposed to believe that even though you haven't kissed me in almost four months, you've suddenly developed feelings and had the need to kiss me, and it just so happens to coincide with the same day that you let me know our baby may need a heart transplant. How convenient.'

Flick felt so angry and hurt and humiliated that she had believed the kiss to be real when his mouth had met hers. She'd mistakenly thought that Tristan had feelings for her when he had just been trying to prepare her for the devastating news. News that he'd had no right to ever hide from her.

'My feelings for you have been real since that night we spent together, only I buried them, but since you've moved in it's been getting harder each day to ignore how I feel.'

'And I'm supposed to just blindly accept this double confession? You tell me that you care for me and our baby might die in the same breath. I don't know what to say…or to feel.'

'I know my timing isn't great.'

'Your timing is appalling.' Without saying another word, she threw the blanket to the floor, climbed to her feet and walked into her room. She stood by the window, looking out into the darkness with her head and heart spinning at lightning speed and threatening her sanity. The rain had subsided, and the sky was lit softly by the cloud covered moon, but she saw none of it.

'We need to talk,' he said as he followed her to the doorway. 'My feelings for you are real and we can work through this.'

She turned and crossed back to where he was standing, with a calmness that belied the turmoil inside her. 'We have nothing to discuss. The risk hovering over our child, a risk I knew nothing about until now, is why you asked me to live here, and your kiss was some sort of buffer to what your conscience forced you to divulge tonight. If it wasn't for the possible medical problems with my baby, who knows where I'd be living? You never thought of me as anything more than the accidental mother of your child and guilt made you bring me here. So if the baby's healthy you can walk away then.

Is that how this will pan out? This isn't something long term or real.'

Tristan stood firm in the doorway. 'Our baby is real and the night we spent together was real—'

'The baby is real and that's where it ends,' she cut in angrily, as she slammed her door shut.

CHAPTER ELEVEN

TRISTAN DIDN'T HEAR Flick pack her belongings or make her way to the front door but he heard the car leave his driveway at six in the morning. He'd stayed up until the early hours of the night, trying to make sense of what had gone wrong and he'd fallen asleep sitting upright on the sofa just before five o'clock. He knew that waiting to tell Flick had been a risk and he had played it badly.

She would send for the rest of her belongings later, Flick told herself as she headed down the still-dark street, not sure where she would go but sure she had to get away from Tristan and his deception. Her heart was breaking, and tears were trickling down her face as she realised she had trusted too soon. She felt so foolish and little better than her mother. She didn't want to call Megan. Broken relationship news was something Flick and her sister had been given by their mother at all hours of the day and night throughout their lives and she wasn't about to repeat that selfish behaviour and drag Megan into her drama.

They hadn't had a chance to celebrate the news of her pregnancy, which in itself had been a bombshell.

Flick had hoped to fly to Sydney and share every detail in person and have a huge sisterly hug. After the news Tristan had dropped, it would be commiserations and a time filled with anxiety about her baby's future, so she needed time to put the pieces together in her mind and sort through what she intended to do before she burdened Megan.

Now, she just needed a place to stay. Mr Papadothomakos had already let her apartment so she couldn't go back there. Her phone rang so she checked her rear-view mirror and carefully pulled over to the side of the road under a streetlamp. She was in no rush since she had no idea where she was going. Pulling the telephone from her bag, she saw the caller ID. It was Sophia.

'Hello, Sophia. Is everything okay?'

'You tell me, Flick. What happened between you and Tristan?'

Flick was stunned that her friend was privy to the argument. 'How did you find out so quickly? Did he call and tell you what happened?'

'He apparently heard your car take off a few minutes ago and called me. He said that he screwed up badly and that you left his place and he thought you might have come to me. He didn't want to ring you and have you any more upset if you were driving. What on earth happened between you, Flick? Is there something more to this than a convenient relationship for the sake of your baby? By the tone of his voice, it sounded to me like something far more serious. He sounds desperate to make it up to you. I did worry that you two living under one roof might spell disaster.'

Flick sighed as she collapsed back into the car seat. 'I thought yesterday there was something between us but not any more. I can't live with him and raise this baby together. He's not the man I thought he was. He hid something from me that I deserved to know and now I do there's no chance we can work it out. I just need to find a place to stay for a while till I can find an apartment to rent.'

'Come here,' Sophia implored. 'You know where I live. I'll put the kettle on and you can tell me all about it when you get here. There's a guest bedroom with no expiry date so you can stay until you have found the perfect place. Besides, I'm your midwife so I can keep an eye on you. Arguments and stress like this are not good for you or the baby.'

'But what about Aiden? You're planning a wedding and a honeymoon in little more than a month's time. There's so much happening in your lives, I don't want to intrude.'

'Aiden won't mind. He's only met you a few times but he thinks you're a sweetheart, which I happen to agree is true, so he'll be happy for you to stay as long as you like,' Sophia said. 'And he left about an hour ago for the early shift so you can pour your heart out without him hearing a word. I've got a few hours till I have to leave for work so get your tush over here now. It's freezing out there, the ducted heating's on already and I've got porridge and toast on offer.'

Flick saw Sophia's porch light on when she approached the house twenty minutes later. She felt blessed to have such a good friend who would open her home so readily in a time of need. There was no way she would stay more than a day or so. There had to be a place to rent that would be suitable for her and the baby and which she could move into immediately. She had no intention of being a burden on her friend and dampening her joyful wedding plans.

'Get inside before you get frostbite, we can get your other things from the car later,' Sophia ordered, as she opened the front door to her old home. She had heard Flick's car pull into the gravel driveway and ushered her in quickly. She could see Flick had been crying and the tears were recent. From the dark circles under her eyes, it looked like their predecessors had kept her awake all night.

'Winter's going to be hideous this year,' Sophia commented, to avoid the subject of her friend's distraught appearance as she closed the door. Then, putting her arm around Flick's shoulder, she walked her into the country-style kitchen. Flick could smell the percolating coffee and raisin toast that had just popped up from the toaster. It was comforting to her rumbling stomach.

Sophia took Flick's oversized handbag and put it on the arm of the chair that she had pulled out for her friend.

'Sit down and I will feed you and bubs while you tell me what the hell has happened between you and Dr Tristan Hamilton. What could he possibly say to get you into this state, Flick?'

Flick didn't know where to begin as she sat in the comfort of the warm room. Sophia was still dressed in her pyjamas and fluffy slippers, with her deep red wavy hair piled high on her head in an a-hoc ponytail arrangement, and was busy buttering the warm toast.

'It's complicated.'

'If it involves a man, it usually is complicated,' Sophia said, as she put a large mug of coffee in front of Flick with a plate of toast and pulled a chair out for herself. She reached across the large wooden kitchen table and patted Flick's still-cold fingers. 'Now, tell me between mouthfuls. I can deal with bad table manners. If you tell me everything, I'm sure we can find a solution. If two intelligent women put their heads together, they can generally solve any mess a man has made!'

'I'm not so sure.'

Flick wanted to unpack her thoughts slowly and not blurt them all out to Sophia. She ate her breakfast, saying little. She was grateful that Sophia didn't push her for details and she promised that she would explain everything that evening but wanted to have a shower and then start on her search for a place to live. She was not going to stay with Sophia and Aiden.

Alone in the house, she wandered around, thinking about everything that had happened since the fateful day on the beach when she'd opened her heart to a man she hadn't known. Her life had looked so different in her daydreams. She'd pictured it with a man who loved her and would never walk away. A man who cherished her and their children. A man who equally trusted and confided in her and one who would make her childhood longing for stability disappear.

She tugged at the sleeves of her top as a chill ran over

her. Life wasn't going to be anything close to what she had imagined only a few hours ago. He had kept something very serious from her and he'd had no right. On the drive home, she'd thought her world was safe and then after the kiss her heart had raced away and let her think life was wonderful and perfect and storybook. Her cold fingers touched her warm lips and she hated that she could still taste his kiss. She had fallen in love with a fraud. A man who couldn't commit, who didn't want to commit, and who had been driven by guilt to invite her into his home. There was nothing else. Nothing deep, nothing solid or permanent. She was pregnant with a child who might carry a gene bringing insurmountable challenges.

With tears spilling from her eyes, she sat down, her head drooping into her hands. She loved her baby but she wished she had never gone walking on the beach that morning, and wished even more that she had never invited Tristan into her bed. He was a selfish man who thought of no one but himself. And he would never change.

Her phone rang and she stirred from where she had fallen asleep in the living room. The night with little sleep had forced her tired eyes closed and she had dozed for an hour. She pulled it from her bag as she slumped into a chair by the window.

'Hello.'

'Miss Lawrence?'

'Yes, who is this?'

'It's Thomas Daniels from Barrett and Associates, family practice attorneys.'

Flick was still only half-awake. 'I don't need a lawyer. Why are you calling me?'

'Yes, I'm afraid that Dr Hamilton omitted a few details in the paperwork and I need to confirm them with you.'

'Dr Hamilton? What sort of paperwork?'

'His will.'

'His will,' she repeated incredulously. 'Why on earth are you calling me? You should be calling him. Goodbye.'

'Don't hang up. Please, this is about you, not him.'

Flick sat up and rubbed her eyes with her free hand. 'Truly I have no idea what this is about.'

'Miss Lawrence, you and your child have been made sole beneficiaries of his will.'

'What are you talking about?'

'Three and a half weeks ago Dr Hamilton came to see me and drew up a new will,' the attorney replied. 'He wanted to ensure that you and his child were well taken care of should anything happen to him. Understandably, he has no life insurance as that is not possible for a heart-transplant patient. However, Dr Hamilton has substantial stocks and bonds and a real-estate portfolio valued at over three million dollars, and he wants that to go to his new family, you and the baby. There are also his three sponsor children and he appointed you to oversee the financial affairs of Aditya, Danh and Lucia if he was not around to do so. For that reason, he has put you down as power of attorney.'

Flick was stunned. Tristan had done all this when they hadn't even been talking. When she had told him to stay away he had still thought of her and his baby as his family. He'd never said a thing. He hadn't tried to sway her feelings by telling her about his plans. He'd just silently ensured she and the baby would be safe if he wasn't there.

Tristan wasn't moving on or taking their relationship lightly.

'There's no need to provide proof of paternity, Miss Lawrence. Dr Hamilton assures me the child is his so I just need your date of birth. You obviously have a very strong relationship built on trust for him to make all these decisions.'

In a daze, Flick provided the details before she dropped the phone. Her head was spinning.

The man she had walked out on had never doubted her. Not for a moment, and long before the kiss or the promise of another night together he had chosen to take care of her and the baby for ever. And trusted her to oversee the futures of Aditya, Danh and Lucia.

Before that moment, she hadn't thought about Tristan's belief in her. It had been all about her doubt of him. He had accepted her word from the day she'd arrived unannounced in his office and told him she was pregnant. He'd never asked for any proof or questioned that he was the baby's father. He'd stepped up and accepted responsibility because he believed in her. She hadn't appreciated the trust he had shown.

Perhaps he'd had his own reasons for not telling her about his medical history. She suddenly realised that she had never given him the chance to explain. She'd been up on her high horse, ready to be Miss Independent and think the worst about him, when he had never done the same to her. She had been waiting for him to disappoint her. Like all the men who had disappointed her mother. But he wasn't like them. He was nothing like any of them.

Tristan had never swayed in his belief in her, despite her lack of faith in him.

She grabbed her bag and her keys. She needed to see him and talk to him properly and without blame. It wasn't about the money, she would have been just as impressed if he'd had a hundred dollars to his name. It was everything about him that was wonderful and that she had overlooked. It was as if secretly she had been waiting to be let down. To have him walk away, and when he hadn't, she had pushed him. She was shaking with disappointment in herself.

Suddenly she heard a car pull into the driveway and she could see through the window it was Tristan. She ran to the door, opening it wide to see him standing on the porch. His eyes were red and Flick suspected she wasn't the only one who had shed tears overnight.

'I'm so sorry, Flick,' he began. 'I was wrong not to be completely honest with you from the very beginning. Please, believe me when I tell you I didn't want the shock and the worry to cause you to lose the baby or make your pregnancy harder on you than it already was. That's the truth. It's that simple and that stupid. I should have trusted you would be strong enough to deal with what lay ahead but I didn't... I know now that I should have told you sooner but I thought I was doing the right thing for you…and for our child.'

'No, it's me who should be apologising,' she cut in. 'I should have trusted you enough to know there was a reason for what you did.'

'No, you shouldn't. I was a fool to think I could walk away from you after our night together. I don't want to lose you, or our baby. I can't live without you.'

Flick wrapped her arms around his neck and silenced him with a kiss. 'We're not going anywhere. No matter what the future holds, we'll be together.'

'Then there's only one thing to do.' Carefully, Tristan pulled a pale blue box tied with a white bow from his jacket.

Flick's hand covered her mouth instinctively. She had never dared to dream that after their crazy impulsive meeting four months before they would have a fairy-tale ending.

'I've had this on my bedside cabinet for a week. I wanted to give it to you in bed last night but we didn't get there…'

'That was my fault.'

'No, it wasn't. It was my mistake, thinking that I needed to hide something we need to face together. And thinking it was the right thing to do when what I really needed to do was be honest with you and let you make the decision. I know now that I have to stop making decisions that aren't mine to make. You're a strong woman, Flick, and you don't need me, but I hope you want me.'

'I do want you.'

'Then, knowing all the facts, Flick Lawrence, will you marry me and make me the happiest man alive?'

'I will,' Flick said without an ounce of hesitation.

His mouth met hers passionately. She had no more questions about his feelings. His kiss told her everything she would ever need to know.

* * * * *

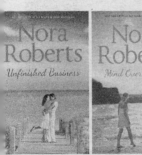
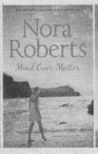
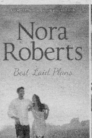
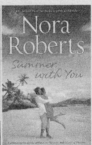

MILLS & BOON®

It's Got to be Perfect

* cover in development

When Ellie Rigby throws her three-carat engagement ring into the gutter, she is certain of only one thing. She has yet to know true love!

Fed up with disastrous internet dates and conflicting advice from her friends, Ellie decides to take matters into her own hands. Starting a dating agency, Ellie becomes an expert in love. Well, that is until a match with one of her clients, charming, infuriating Nick, has her questioning everything she's ever thought about love…

Order yours today at
www.millsandboon.co.uk

MILLS & BOON®

The Thirty List

* cover in development

At thirty, Rachel has slid down every ladder she has ever climbed. Jobless, broke and ditched by her husband, she has to move in with grumpy Patrick and his four-year-old son.

Patrick is also getting divorced, so to cheer themselves up the two decide to draw up bucket lists. Soon they are learning to tango, abseiling, trying stand-up comedy and more. But, as she gets closer to Patrick, Rachel wonders if their relationship is too good to be true…

Order yours today at
www.millsandboon.co.uk/Thethirtylist

MILLS & BOON®

MEDICAL ROMANCE

THE ULTIMATE IN ROMANTIC MEDICAL DRAMA

0515/03